Mary Eyre

A Lady's Walks in the South of France in 1863

Edition 2

Mary Eyre

A Lady's Walks in the South of France in 1863
Edition 2

ISBN/EAN: 9783337002671

Printed in Europe, USA, Canada, Australia, Japan

Cover: Foto ©Andreas Hilbeck / pixelio.de

More available books at **www.hansebooks.com**

A LADY'S WALKS

IN

THE SOUTH OF FRANCE

IN 1863.

By MARY EYRE,

AUTHOR OF 'THE QUEEN'S PARDON,' ETC.

SECOND EDITION.

LONDON:

RICHARD BENTLEY, NEW BURLINGTON STREET,

Publisher in Ordinary to Her Majesty.

1865.

ARGELÈS.

DEDICATION.

To one who permits me to style him, what he has indeed ever proved, 'My Friend, and the Friend of my Family,' — whom this age honours, and posterity will reverence as one of those God-sent men who act as pioneers in the march of Human progress and educate nations,

To the Lord Brougham and Vaux,

This book is inscribed with the deepest feelings of gratitude and veneration by the Author,

MARY EYRE.

December, 1864.

PREFACE TO SECOND EDITION.

I WISH to write a few brief words by way of Preface to the Second Edition of 'A Lady's Walks in the South of France.' They are very pleasant words to write.

I have to thank my publisher, Mr. Bentley, whose enterprise and energy in bringing out the book has helped materially to make it a success: and to thank the many friends who have zealously interested themselves about it, and the public at large, whose cordial reception has rendered a Second Edition so soon necessary.

Further, I have to acknowledge gratefully the generous and frank recognition of my book's merits, by many of the leading journals who influence public opinion, and whose praise is to a work what the die of the Governor and Company of the Bank of England is to the piles of square, cut, white paper—conferring on them an intrinsic value which turns them into gold.

To my unfriendly critics—to those who write spitefully, simply because it is *easier* to abuse than to praise, and less trouble to attack an author personally than to *read* her book—I have also a word to say.

It is this. Whatever these would-be critics may say, I do not blush for honourable poverty. I esteem it a duty to live within my income, to economize 'half-francs,' or quarter-francs if necessary; so that I may pay everybody their just due, and have a little to give away to those still poorer than myself; and that, to my mind, there is true nobility in a well-born and delicately brought-up woman's struggling, single-handed, with *undeserved misfortune*, and winning her way back to ease and affluence by honourable exertion.

Lastly, I benefited so much personally in health and spirits by my free mountain life, and living almost perpetually in the open air; I found so much more amusement and gained so much more real information as to the customs and character of the Pyreneans, the nature and produce of the country; I saw so many more picturesque glens, and lovely shady little nooks, carpeted with wild flowers, in the lonely recesses of the hills, than I should have done had I been rolling luxuriously through the country in a carriage, and merely seeing, as such travellers do, the regular stock-sights of every place I came to—*and I have travelled formerly in that way too*—that if anybody (and I wish somebody may be so charmed with my books as to do it) would leave me three thousand a-year, I should prefer when I travelled to go precisely as I went to the Pyrenees, unencumbered by heavy trunks, and untroubled by packing, rambling from village to village with my dog and my knapsack.

The encouragement my first Walk has met from the public, has induced my publisher to propose to me a second tour through the Eastern Pyrenees to Spain, which I hope to present to my readers in the autumn.

MARY EYRE.

March 10, 1865.

PREFACE.

In offering this book to the public, I have a few brief words to say. Though many other works have been published on the South of France, none of their writers travelled under the same circumstances, or probably searched for the same kind of information as myself. I bring, therefore, a collection of nearly entirely new facts to my readers.

My extremely slender means compelled me to travel humbly, and to mix a good deal with the people; I saw, therefore, much more of actual French life among the middle and laborious classes, than most travellers do. I flatter myself that though English, I am unprejudiced; and that in comparing the customs of the two countries, and the manners of their people, the balance has been fairly struck. It was not always on the side of my own country-folks.

The great mistake that most English wanderers make is to look at everything in the countries through which they travel from an English point of view. It is the same with some of our newspaper correspondents. They abuse the French Government for not allowing the same free comments on its acts in the public press that are allowed in England; not recognizing, or not choosing to recognize, the very different characters of the nations; and that, while the phlegmatic Englishman will content himself with a mere grumble over an unpopular edict, or revenge himself by a satirical caricature in 'Punch,' the more inflammable Frenchman will try to excite an *émeute.* The first Revolution has ·left deep traces on the mind of the people; they have not forgotten how humble peasants and petty shopkeepers rose to power, to wealth, and even to thrones; as in the cases of Murat and Bernadotte. Every fiery, idle, and ambitious young man is ready to believe, that, if the present Government — no matter whether that of a King, or a Republic, or an Emperor— no matter how wise and beneficent that rule may be— were overthrown, he, that now insignificant individual, might quit his stool in the counting-house or office, and rise—who knows how high?

It behoves him who rules to have, as he has, a strong, brave heart, a quick, far-seeing eye, and a tight rein on these fiery, impatient spirits, or they would soon kick over the traces and upset the state carriage.

By the elderly, the more reflecting, and prudent Frenchmen, and, above all, by the Pyrenean peasantry, who love the present Emperor with absolute passion, 'because,' say they, '*he has done us good like his uncle:*' all this is acknowledged and felt.

In the above lines, I have not so much expressed my own opinion (though fully subscribing to it) as that of the most enlightened and unselfish Frenchmen with whom I conversed. In every country it is the idle, the dissipated, and the worthless, who are most eager for change, simply because they may possibly gain somewhat, and they have nothing to lose.

With regard to the multifarious contents of my book,

it may be truly said that probably no English traveller has ever before condensed so much information regarding the quaint manners, peculiar customs, language, ancient legends, songs and music, and botany of the Pyrenees, into any work. So far as I know, few of the legends, and none of the beautiful airs and poetry of the country, have ever found their way into English print; and yet the Pyreneans have their poet, who is as much a true poet, and as popular among them as Burns with us, but Despourrins is scarcely known in England by name. Had time served, and if it would not have occupied too great a share of my work, other equally beautiful and little-known gems of music and song might have been given. The difficulty was where so much was beautiful to select.

If, therefore, I have failed in making a novel and interesting book, the fault is mine. The quarries of rich marbles were there: if the edifice be neither striking nor interesting, the builder is to blame.

There is one subject which my readers may perhaps wonder has not been touched on—the nature and uses of the Thermal Springs. I left them unnoticed on purpose. I am neither a chemist nor medical man. And Murray's Guide-book tells all that need be known on these subjects.

Lastly, my grateful thanks are justly due to the many kind friends, both French and English, who aided me in various ways in my task, especially to the Countess of Carnwath and Miss Le Grice, for copying me some of the Pyrenean airs ; M. Frossard, the French Protestant pastor of Bagnères, and well-known writer on various subjects ;

and Mr. Lyte, the celebrated photographer, who borrowed
for my use various rare and valuable works, now out of
print; M. de Soubise, and others, who so kindly lent
them,* and Mrs. Teulon, who kindly aided me in correcting the proofs of the music.

I am deeply indebted to M. Philippe, the well-known
botanist and naturalist of Bagnères, for aiding me to class
the various plants found in my rambles, which classifi-
cation I have verified by reference to the botanical works
in the British Museum.

And last—not least—my thanks are due to my old
schoolfellow and kind friend, Mrs. Headlam, for the
beautiful sketch illustrative of Pyrenean scenery which
forms the frontispiece to my work.

Surely, a book to which so many have contributed,
ought to have some merit.

MARY EYRE.

* Most of the legendary tales are translated from Eugène Cordier, Karl
des Monts, whose works are out of print, or from Baron Taylor. The
singular customs of Béarn and Bigorre are chiefly extracted from the Introduction to Rivarès' ' Airs et Chansons de Béarn,' and from Tain, Nicolle,
and a host of other French writers.

December, 1864.

CONTENTS.

A LADY'S WALKS

IN

THE SOUTH OF FRANCE.

CHAPTER I.

ENGLAND TO EAUX-BONNES.

I LEFT England in the autumn of 1862, intending to try
whether the south of France was really, as I had been
told, a cheaper place of abode than England. I travelled
(for a lady) in rather a peculiar fashion, for I took with
me only one small waterproof stuff bag, which I could
carry in my hand, containing a spare dress, a thin shawl,
two changes of every kind of under clothing, two pairs of
shoes, pens, pencils, paper, the inevitable 'Murray,' and a
prayer-book, so that I had no trouble or expense about
luggage. My plan was to locate myself by the week, in
any town or village that took my fancy, and ramble about
on foot to botanize, and see all that was worth seeing in
the environs ; and as I was 'a lone woman,' I took for my
companion a mischievous but faithful and affectionate
rough Scotch terrier, to be my guard and companion in
my long solitary walks.

I resolved also to mix as much as possible with *the
people.*

I crossed from Newhaven to Dieppe, a far pleasanter
passage than *viâ* Boulogne, and Dieppe is a far prettier

B

and more interesting town. Thence I went to Saumur,
Tours, Bordeaux, and Pau, staying awhile at each place.
I omit all mention of them, partly because this is to be a
one volume book; and to describe all my wanderings
would augment it to two.

I left Pau for Eaux-Bonnes, on the 11th September,
taking the early morning coach, which starts from the Rue
Serviez at 6 A.M., that I might arrive at my destination
earlier, and have time to look for lodgings. I fancied
myself again in Germany, when inquiring for my bag, I
was told it was *dahin—dahin*, by the hostler, *i.e. inside*, or
'there.' Then just after I had taken my place, up rushed
a little fat man, quite out of breath, who bawled out franti-
cally, '*Plazas*' (so I understood him) '*por tres personas.*'
The idiom here—seems to me to be a compound of Béarnais, Spanish, Latin, Italian, German, and French, and I
know not how many other tongues. Half of it, to my un-
trained ear, sounds rather like a prolongation of vowels
like a-a-i—a-o-u than actual syllables; but when spoken
by educated people it is very soft and sweet.

Las tres personas arrived: a mother and two daughters,
bound for Eaux-Chaudes. We four got in, 'Keeper' on my
knee, and the omnibus started, taking up a passenger here
and there, as we bowled through the wet, plashy streets.
It seemed full already, when it stopped once more, and a
French gentleman and his wife, and *their dog*, got in, which
affronted Keeper very much, and for some time the two
canine travellers snarled at each other from their respective mistresses' laps, but finally yielded to representations
of the impropriety of quarrelling under present circumstances, and lay still. The day was hot and close, the
rain poured down in torrents, hiding the country we were
travelling through, in a manner that was most disappointing,
and the omnibus was so closely crammed, we could not
move; but French fellow-travellers are usually polite and

good-humoured. The ladies crushed those abominable *crinolines* into the smallest possible compass, and the gentlemen wedged themselves into such narrow spaces, that it was marvellous to behold. I began verily to think those square-built men were compressible, like india-rubber cushions, and inflated themselves for appearance sake. Everybody began to converse, and we got on well enough. By-and-by a postman got on to the step of the omnibus, and went a few miles with us. Most of the gentlemen spoke *patois*, and began to talk to him. Badly as our English postmen are paid, I learned that the French have still lower salaries, and this one had a long weary mountain road to traverse twice a-day, in all weathers. Poor fellow! He was very thankful for a bit of a lift upon the step.

Soon after he left us, a neatly-dressed woman sprang into the vacated place, and, clinging to the door, rode in that way, in despite of the pouring rain, till we reached a spot where two roads met, and where the diligence of Eaux-Chaudes relieved us of most of our passengers. The little boy in the corner was hers, he had been staying at Bordeaux with his grand-parents, and was now going with them to Eaux-Chaudes, and this wet ride was nothing to her, so she caught a sight of her child's face, and those of her parents. Having embraced them, and seen them into the Eaux-Chaudes omnibus, into which almost all my late fellow-travellers also mounted, she went and washed her gown, which had got splashed nearly up to her knees with mud, while she rode on the step, and her neat *lady's kid boots*, in the brook that ran by the road-side, and then took her seat with me for Eaux-Bonnes. One of my fellow-travellers had told me I should find cheap accommodation at an hotel I will not name. I went there, and had scarcely entered, when the rain fell again in torrents, and I had no choice but to engage a room, for I knew what mountain storms are, and there was every appearance of this lasting all day. I had left my two bags at the omnibus office, and so could neither get out a book to read, nor eat the provisions I had brought with me therein, though I was desperately hungry. There was no *table d'hôte* before 5 o'clock, and anything ordered expressly for myself would cost a good deal, while I had provisions in my sac. Moreover everything around looked so filthily dirty, I could not make up my mind to eat in the house, and felt an unspeakable horror at the thought of passing a night there. The landlady came into the room to take the sheets, that had been slept in the night before, off the bed, and in so doing she found two half loaves of bread, the long *pains* used here, in lieu of our square loaf, which is not made in France, secreted there by the servant girl for her own use, which did not add to my desire to eat in that house, as I felt very sure those loaves would not be thrown away, because they had been put between soiled sheets. For two hours I alternately watched the rain falling in torrents; and the proceedings of my opposite neighbours, whose wide open windows gave me as clear a view of their doings, as if I had been their inmate, and patted Keeper, who yawned, stood on his hind-feet, and looked inquiringly and beseechingly into my face, as much as to say, 'Why don't we go away from this horrid place?' There was not even a strip of carpet by the bedside; and that to Keeper's mind, who is a dog accustomed to civilized society and carpets, betokened that it was not 'a hole fit for a dog to live in.' Neither of us felt very comfortable, and we consoled one another, as friends should do under misfortunes. The opposite view was not very entertaining. I saw the *bonne* make the beds in two of the rooms, and then the occupants, father and son, weary like me, apparently of the wet weather, sit down to cards; and the *blanchisseuse* folding and ironing her linen in a third ; and then Keeper and I adventured to the other side of the house to see what could be seen there.

On this side, each floor had a long wooden gallery, running the whole length of the house, and it fronted a green sloping hill dotted with trees, at whose base foaming and roaring, and covering the huge boulders that obstructed its path with wreaths of snowy foam, dashed a mountain torrent. Every now and then, when a gleam of sunshine broke out, and the misty veil parted a little, I caught sight, far beyond, of an emerald valley, shut in by hills robed in grey mist, which ever and anon, as the sun struggled more and more with the roke and partially dispersed it, revealed a grand and lofty mountain, one of the long chain of the Pyrenees. From these galleries I watched the glorious view, glorious in spite of storm and mist, and perhaps even more glorious for them, as long as the horrible smells would permit me to remain. If the bedrooms and sitting-rooms had all opened on to these galleries, and creepers and flowers been twined around them instead of their being devoted to unseemly purposes, and the inn itself had been comfortable and clean, travellers need not have wearied here, even in wet weather. A mountain view never wearies anyone who has a heart or soul for the beautiful. You may look at it for ever. It is never twice the same.

I like to gaze upon mist-covered mountains, and to see the clouds that veil them suddenly unroll and display all their grandeur, while here and there the sunlight lies lovingly on little patches of emerald sward, which gleam out in transparent tender greenness, and contrast so beau-tifully with the sombre and darker lines around, and little rills of water trickle down the steep mountain sides, looking like white threads, or wavering like a ribbon of satin among the grey crags, stopped here and there in their course by some huge fragment of rock, and anon catching the sunlight, dazzle one's eyes by their diamond-like radiance, and then flow down again a long snowy wreathe to form the torrent that foams in the ravine below. I leant over the balcony and looked into the dark depths of the chasm beneath, upon huge stones that had been hurried downwards from the mountain top by the force of the water, perhaps ages ago when the world was young, and that were now covered many inches thick with green and black-looking moss, the growth of centuries, over which the white foam whirled; while from the abrupt and broken sides of the fissure, young trees and brushwood sprouted, and white con-volvulus, and sweet-scented clematis, and other plants stretched in long fantastic wreaths. It was a scene worthy of an artist or a poet; and the *propriétaire* of the hotel and his tenant, the landlord, preferred an interior view of the apartments of a *cordonnier* and a *blanchisseuse!* At last the rain ceased a little, and Keeper and I sallied forth to see if we could better ourselves.

We had not far to go. Eaux-Bonnes is literally built in a *cul-de-sac;* there is one long principal street, on one side of which is a narrow green, shaded by a few trees with benches underneath them, called the English garden. The houses on each side of this street are built so im-mediately under the hills, that they look as if they would some day be buried beneath their *débris;* and it slopes upwards till it ends in the rock, part of which has been blasted away to make room for a row of houses. In one of these, La Maison Courtade, a large house with a flight of stone steps leading to it, and hidden from the street by the Hôtel de la Paix, of which M. Courtade is the pro-prietor, but not the landlord, and to which it is a *Maison succursale*, I engaged a small room. Then I went back to the dirty inn, and gladly paid a franc *not* to sleep there, and selected my bags from the omnibus office, and after refreshing myself and Keeper from their contents, sat down to write my journal. My new apartment is at the back of the house, and looks into a little garden of three terraces, one above the other, cut out of the overhanging rock, and which are reached by little white wooden bridges, springing from the gallery in front of my room, across the deep area between the house and the rock.

Madame Courtade is very civil, and my wee room is very clean, free from *b* flats and *f* sharps. At dinner-time I sent Luisa, the *bonne*, to the Hôtel de la Paix, for a *portion* of fowl and a *potage*, for each of which I paid a very moderate price, namely, ten sous, and dined without incurring what I cannot, alas, afford, the expense of a *table-d'hôte*. I say alas! not altogether for the sake of the dinner, for I am not *gourmande*, and can dine well content for weeks on fruit and bread. *Nay, I rather prefer it*, but because even in France, where money is not quite so much thought of as in England, because the people in general are not so wealthy, and property is, *as it ought to be*, more generally and evenly divided owing to the French law of inheritance, *a poor gentlewoman* has much to contend with. *It is not what one goes without oneself, it is the way one is looked down upon for going without; it is the being thought mean when one is generous.* The being *forced* to economize sous and half francs, and *the bitter knowledge that one is disdained for doing so, when one can only pay one's way by the closest, sternest self-denial of the common daily comforts of life, that is hard.*

Why, then, go to the expense of travelling? says my reader. Dear reader, I live upon so little, that I do not spend much more than I should in cheap lodgings at home in England, and I hope that this book may win me some fame and some profit, while away a few sad moments from other sad hearts, and show other poor gentlewomen brought up like myself to no occupation, that they may do better than stay lamenting over their past prosperity in gloom and isolation and discomfort at home. There is something enlivening in the very change of country. Every thing and every person one sees has something quaint, peculiar, and picturesque about them unlike what one has ever seen before, that turns the mind from disagreeable prospects, and enlivens one in spite of oneself. To travel about with what ladies generally consider *the necessaries of life*, namely, two or three heavy trunks filled with shawls, dresses, &c., would be impossible for women of very limited means, for the expense of all luggage beyond the very small weight allowed to each person by continental railways and *diligences*, would cost half as much as the actual journey ; but a woman who is content to rough it a little, may go far and see much for a small sum. There are disadvantages, however, in this gipsy style of travelling which I did not foresee when I set out.

It is impossible to get one's linen home from the laundress before the week's end, and sometimes they keep it eight or even ten days; though, as a rule, the linen sent on Monday is brought back the following Saturday. They wash everything *au ruisseau*, in the cold water of the brook, using wood ashes instead of soap. The articles are all put to soak on the Monday night in a strong ley, previous to their being taken the next day to the stream ; and if you send clothes in the middle of the week, *they will be kept for the following week's wash*. In many places they are neither starched nor ironed, but simply sent home rough dry, though an Englishwoman will be charged the same prices as if they were properly got up, until she has learnt the real prices of the country. Everywhere, and in everything, an English person must expect to be charged twice as much as a Frenchwoman. The French ladies usually have their clothes washed by a *blanchisseuse*, and starched and ironed at home by a *repasseuse* or ironer, who goes out by the day. If, therefore, like me, the traveller have but three of each article, *she must wash them herself and wear them rough dry.*

It requires, too, a good deal of philosophy to bear the contemptuous looks of *Misses*, who seem to think that if * '*worth* makes the man,' *dress* makes the woman; and the supercilious sneers of those *demi-demoiselles*, yclept swells or dandies, as they gaze on the plain, dark water-proof cloak, rain-cottered, rumpled gown, pilgrim hat, and stained gloves, that *must* be the result of travelling through wet and storm, climbing hills, and gathering wild flowers.

Continental nations think even more of costume than English misses and dandies. They never travel themselves, except *aux eaux*, or to a *bain-mer*, rather to show off themselves and their habiliments, than for any real love most of them have for picturesque scenery. There is to me something excessively ludicrous—were they not so fearfully dangerous—in seeing a lady tourist in one of those wide *crinolines*, so ill adapted for getting into, or out of, railway carriages and steamboats, or for scrambling among rocks. In descending, they are always catching on some point or corner, and jeopardizing your life twenty times in a walk; and in ascending, one is for ever hitching one's feet in them, and running the risk of falling under a railway train, down a ravine, or into the sea, as the case may be.

When will good taste and simplicity again regulate women's dress? Not in my time, I fear. Show and parade seem the order of the day. The *costume de rigueur*, at *les bains* this year, seems a black chip hat, almost like a

---

* ' Worth makes the man, and want of it the fellow,
    The rest is nought but leather and prunella.'

man's, with two long ends of velvet and lace hanging down behind from the band of the same encircling the crown, and a bouquet of poppies, roses, or some gay-coloured flower in front, often placed in a *nœud* of black ribbon, lace, or velvet, a *very wide skirted* dress, with a long jacket of the same material, and irreproachable gloves, fitting the hand like a skin. How those gloves are ever got on is a mystery to me. The colours most in vogue are some shade of grey, stone, or buff, and both dress and jacket are trimmed with black velvet, or richly braided with narrow black braid. The gown is looped up to show the ornamental coloured skirt underneath, which is sometimes black, with a broad band of dark blue, bright crimson, or scarlet at the bottom. The prettiest—too pretty indeed for *jupons*—are of a narrow black and white stripe, trimmed with several rows of black velvet, or one narrow flounce of the same material as the petticoat itself, edged with black velvet. The *brodequins*, collars, cuffs, parasol, &c., are irreproachable as the gloves, all better fitted for the Champs Elysées or the boulevards of Paris, than for donkey riding, climbing mountains, or walking along muddy, boggy paths, through wet copses, to views and waterfalls. There is a want of true taste in all this. The full dress of a court, or a race ground, is ill adapted to the country, and therefore in bad taste.

I think it was last year that some English gentleman was kind enough to write repeated letters to ' The Times,' complaining that his patriotic feelings were cruelly wounded by the appearance his countrywomen made on the Continent, where ' they walked about foreign watering-places and gay cities in battered crinolines, rumpled skirts, and hats and cloaks that bore evident traces of repeated wettings.' ' I was ashamed of them,' these are his words, ' when I contrasted them with the elegantly-dressed ladies of other nations.' The writer of this letter forgot that foreign ladies, in general, are neither sketchers, botanists, nor hearty lovers of beautiful scenery —they are simply *dressers*. Dress is the thought and passion of their lives; and it is a known fact that many a French husband has been *ruined* and forced to sell his property by his wife's inordinate passion for dress.*

The English woman travels through a wide expanse of country, perhaps through two or three empires, to improve her mind, and store her heart with images of beauty. The Continental woman goes to some *one bad*, or *bain, for the season*, to show off her finery. It is impossible for a *crinoline* that has been squeezed up, day after day, in diligence or omnibus, or worse still, broken and bent by riding on a donkey, to be otherwise than 'battered' by such cruel usage. Our wiser grandmothers only wore their hoops in full dress. We, and our servants, wear them at the washing tub and the kitchen fire; our mill girls wear them in the manufactories, and sad and horrible have been the many accidents of all kinds this hideous, inartistic, ungraceful fashion has caused! I should like to have the statistics of *crinoline*, and to know how many unfortunate women and girls have died a dreadful death from wearing crinoline.

I spent my first evening at Eaux-Bonnes shut up in my little bedroom, writing my journal. The next morning, between the storms, I got out, and went the whole length of the beautiful walk called La Promenade Horizontale, which was begun and completed during the season, in forty days. It is really a wonderful work—and so are the two smooth roads or terraces, as, in fact, they are, that wind below it—all blasted out of the solid rock, or cut through the rough copse and brushwood, or raised above

---

* I heard from Lady ——, who had lived in Brussels, that many a man had to sell his estate because his wife would have a ball-dress of Brussels lace. In Paris, years ago, I heard from French people that many a family was ruined by the wife's love of dress.

the hollows and bogs on solid masonry.   The promenade is so even and flat, that invalids can be drawn along it in a Bath chair, or cripples walk fearlessly over its smooth surface.   To the left, winding walks are cut through the woods above it for the younger and more adventurous pedestrians; to the right, this terraced walk looks down on the beautiful valleys of Aas and Ossau, sprinkled here and there with villages built of greystone, and small white churches, resembling those in Wales, or at the English lakes, girdled in by mountains, while below them the Gave brawls, and foams, and leaps in his rocky bed, adding the exquisite music of its dash and murmur to the charm of the scenery.   There, on that round hill, is the little hamlet of Aas; a few houses clustered round a small white church. Yet Aas deserves mention, for there lives Pierre Gaston Sacaze, one of those self-made men, of whom France has so much right to be proud, and of whom every Pyrenean town or valley seems to have one or more.   He has been a mountain guide, but being now too old for such toil, has returned to the employment of a shepherd, exposed in advancing years to all the inclemencies of the weather.   It seems to me, that it would be worthy of a great nation like France to grant small pensions to Sacaze, and men like him, who confer an inestimable benefit on science by collecting and preserving materials for the natural and geological history of the country.   Gaston Sacaze is a good poet, a painter, a geologist, and one of the best botanists in France, although entirely self-taught, except that an elder brother, who is a priest, instructed him in the elements of Latin.   He is said to be as humble-minded and modest as he is full of genius and information.

'You must go and see Sacaze,' said one of my pleasant companions in the omnibus, the husband of the lady with the little dog, to me; 'everybody knows Sacaze.   He is the best botanist we have.'

I hoped to know him too, and to see the beautiful collection he has made of Alpine plants ; and if he were disposed, and equal to the exertion, to have him as my guide on a botanical excursion—but man proposes, and God disposes. Aas was only three short miles from Eaux-Bonnes, but the incessant rain never suffered me to go even that small distance.

Farther on, as the path curves gently round the bold brow of the hill, the scenery grows grander. The view opens into a gorge or defile between lofty mountains, all varying from one another in colouring, form, and outline, and all grand and august. I supposed this to be the valley of Ossau, but I had no one to tell me. Green fields divided by the rough walls of unhewn stone, common in Lancashire and Cumberland, trees, and boxwood, clothe some of these mountains to the very summit. One stands prominently forth, rugged and bare of trees ; round its head, which towers higher than the others, rest grey clouds ; patches of green sward and lichens give it a solemn beauty of its own. It is not so sternly grand as the barren rocky escarped Pic de Ger, on whose peaks no mosses or verdure grow ; but it is a glorious mountain, magnificent in form, tinted with every shade of blue-grey, with spaces of the most vivid brilliant green scattered here and there among the darker shadows that painters love.

Below it to the right winds the green valley leading to Pau, with the small town of small greystone houses through which we passed in coming here—seeing nothing of all this loveliness for rain and mist. As I slowly walked along the terrace, I felt this was one of the golden hours of life. I was scarcely conscious of the want of a companion—my heart was too full for speech—rapture has no words. Never since I left my dear cousin Cassandra's house at Coniston, have I seen anything so gloriously beautiful as these green valleys shut in by the sublime range of the Pyrenees. The hill above me was richly fringed with wood, through which I saw winding paths, and under their shade grew beautiful wild flowers, gentianellas, and saxifrages, and the pale heath, which to my fancy is not so pretty as the purple, and silver clear water trickled in little drops down its sides, through the overhanging roots of the beech trees, from which the earth had crumbled away since the road was made, or from the green mosses and flowers that overhung its ledge; and one rill, larger than the others, rushed foaming down a small ravine.

On the wet swampy ground, and on the damp rocks, the white grass of Parnassus grew more thickly than I had ever seen it grow before, and the small delicate pale yellow-green leaves of a plant whose flower was over—but which I am sure was Pinguicula*—clung like lichen to the damp rocks in little green stars. I thought I saw a primula on one cliff, and with some difficulty, and even danger, on account of my lameness, I scrambled after it over the loose boggy ground, expecting every moment to be knocked down by Keeper, who insisted on following me, and seeing, I suppose, an anxious expression in my face, tried to encourage me by frisking in front of me, and endeavouring to jump upon me, which I parry by threatening him with my umbrella, on which he darts off, but returns two minutes after, just as I have got one foot on a loose stone and the other in the bog, and

---

* It was the Pinguicula. I afterwards saw plenty at Bagnères de Bigorre. Its lateral leaves clasp the damp ledges of rocks, like a lichen, and from their centre rises a little rosette of green leaves of the most exquisite tender hue,

am feeling my way with my umbrella. At last I reach the point, in spite of Keeper; but it is not the Alpine primula, it is only the common bugle—but such a bugle!— This plant sometimes produces larger, handsomer, deeper, blue flowers in the autumn, than in spring, in England; but the labiated petals of this are as long as those of a salvia, and its bright purple colour is enhanced by the rich dark velvety Vandyke-brown of its calyxes. It is a floral gem, and might furnish a beautiful design for a jeweller with its central whorl or wheel of deepest, loveliest brown, from which radiate the long purple flowers. I could not believe it was a common bugle, till I found it growing on the same root with the smaller flowers. I gathered a nosegay of these rich hued blossoms, which contrasted well with the pale yellow leaves of a plant I did not know, but suspected to be the winter cherry * (farther on, I found it still green and in blossom), and the autumnal tints of the box, which assumes every shade of vermilion and orange, the delicate grass of Parnassus, and the dear blue English harebell, than which no lovelier flower grows.

I returned home with quite a *gerbe* in my hand, and the fine people who had meanwhile come out like flies in the sun, looked at my *bouquet* as I passed, and seemed to wonder at my gathering such trash, but added to one another, ' *Mais c'est beau.*' *It was beautiful*, and I had it on my table all the five dreary days I spent at Eaux-Bonnes to cheer and delight me, and left it still beautiful on my mantelpiece when I departed. I can see it now. 'A thing of beauty is a joy for ever.' I am often told 'field flowers do not live in water.' It is because people do not take the trouble to make them live. When I get home after a walk, I always put the stalks of my flowers in water,

---

* It proved to be the Winter Cherry.

in my washhand-basin, taking care the flowers do not crush one another, and that the air can circulate freely between the leaves and stalks, and then, with a delicate hand, sprinkle a few drops of water over them. When they are quite revived, I take them out, pull off all the lower leaves, that they may not putrify, cut the ends of the stalks afresh, and put them into vases. Thus treated, most wild flowers will live for a week, if the water be daily changed.

CHAPTER II.

SATURDAY proved a beautiful morning. The sun shining
in at my window awakened me betimes. I jumped out of
bed, ran to the casement, and looked out; the misty veil
which had covered the face of all things was withdrawn,
and I determined, if possible, to walk to Eaux-Chaudes.
I could not judge much of the weather from my bedroom,
for the space the Maison Courtade stands upon has
evidently been blasted away from the rock behind, which,
like a great wall, covered with bushes and creepers, rises
up beyond the three narrow little terrace gardens, to the
very sky; and effectually intercepts all view. I dressed
and breakfasted, called Keeper, and set off. One great
advantage of a mountainous country is the rapidity with
which the roads dry even after heavy and continuous rain.
When I walked up *the* street yesterday evening, it was
slippery with mud and rain, this morning the water had all
run off, and except here and there in a deep rut the road
was firm, smooth, and dry. The meadows looked green
and beautiful in the sunshine, the Gave seemed to sing
a song of gladness, and every hill and mountain rose clear,
defined, and distinct, in the ambient air. I asked the
way to Eaux-Chaudes, and was directed to take the lower
of the two roads I had seen from the *Promenade Horizontale.*

As I went down the hill, a woman with a basket offered
me some grapes at a moderate price, and I was glad to
purchase about a pound for *douze sous.* Fruit is dear at

Eaux-Bonnes, for it has to be brought all the way from Pau. In England, if fruit were cheap and plentiful in a district less than thirty miles off, it would be brought in quantities to watering-places so much frequented as Eaux-Bonnes and Eaux-Chaudes. I cannot help thinking the *octroi*, or duty paid upon every article of food or commerce going into a town, from fruit to wood, is a great hindrance to the comfort and prosperity of both France and Germany. I know that no government can go on without means, and that taxes are necessary to raise those means, but the *octroi* seems to me a bad way of raising them. It prevents a free exchange of the surplus productions of one town or province, against the different surplus productions of other places. Each town and village contents itself with its own produce, as far as it is possible, and articles that are plentiful in one department are wholly unknown in another.

A lady I knew lived at Bieberich on the Rhine. Bieberich is a miserable place, not deserving the name of a town, and it was very difficult to get anything for dinner. If one butcher had veal, the other butcher had veal, *and nothing else*. There was no regular market, and no poulterers' shops. Just across the river was Mayence, where there was plenty of fruit, poultry, game, &c., but she could not buy a fowl or a goose, or even a basket of cakes or fruit in Mayence, without having to pay the *octroi*. It is a worrying inquisitional kind of system—that peeping into carts and carriages and baskets—that impossibility to shop at the nearest town, and to get the best goods at the most moderate price, and must be a great bar to the prosperity and progress of the country. So here, though the markets at Bordeaux and Pau and Tarbes were *over*-supplied with fruit, butter, poultry, and eggs, all these things, and indeed *everything* from a bottle of ink to a muslin dress, were bad and dear at Eaux-Bonnes

and Eaux-Chaudes, or not to be had at all. I had gone
without fruit since I came, and this hot sunny day my six-
pennyworth of grapes was a great luxury.

When I had descended the long, steep hill below Eaux-
Bonnes, I came to a place where three roads met, and felt
quite uncertain which of the two before me I ought to
take. While I was considering, a peasant woman came
up, and I asked my way. '*Je ne comprends pas le français,*' was her answer. 'Eaux-Chaudes,' I said. '*Je ne
comprends pas le français.*' I held out both my hands,
pointing to the roads—'Eaux-Chaudes?' interrogatively.
'*Je ne comprends pas le français.*' Now as the names of
places do not alter in *patois*, I thought she might have
guessed from my pantomime that I wanted to go to Eaux-
Chaudes; but the peasants have no quickness about them.
They seem to go on in one jog-trot way, and not to have
a thought beyond it. Even when they do speak French,
they take no interest in anything that does not immediately concern themselves. If one sees a ruined castle,
they can tell you nothing of its history—there are no local
traditions: 'It belonged to *un monsieur*, or *un comte*, long
ago'—'*C'était brûlé*, a long time ago;' that is all you can
ever obtain. Madame Reybaud mentions in her interesting tale of '*Mademoiselle de Malepierre*,' that thirty years
after the Revolution, all memory of the family that had
been seigneurs of Malepierre was forgotten.

I hoped, in my wanderings in France, to learn many
interesting traditions, such as attach to old castles in
Ireland and Scotland. I have not been able to obtain
one. Fortunately, some haymakers—they seem always
making hay in the Pyrenees, where they have two or
three crops a year—came up, and one of the men could
speak French. He was going the same way as I was, for
some time, and he would tell me where I must turn off
for Eaux-Chaudes. So he accompanied me, and the rest

of his party struck off the nearer way, across the meadows
to a little village—it looked a very pretty walk, and I
longed to leave the high road, and go with them ; but
then I might not have another fine day to visit Eaux-
Chaudes, so I went on.   My companion told me the children were all obliged to learn French at school ; but as
they grew up, they usually forgot it, more especially the
women.   They learnt to write in French, as well as to
read it ; but as *patois* was the habitual dialect of the
country, they did not keep up their knowledge after they
left school, unless they went into service.   I observed, the
country was very beautiful.   ' Yes, in summer ; but it was
a *triste pays* in winter.'   So I should think it was.   One
misses in France the gentlemen's parks and houses, which
enliven an English landscape.   One misses them more as
centres of civilization.

I never knew the infinite use our country squires and
clergymen, and their families, were of, in keeping up
habits of cleanliness, order, and decency, till I came to
France—and especially to the Pyrenees.   Here, wretched
as they look, almost every peasant one meets is a landed
proprietor.   I think it is Henri Taine, one of their own
writers, who expresses his amazement at learning during
an excursion in some of these mountains, that a farmhouse and farm he saw at a distance belonged to the bare-
legged girl who had waited upon him at the small inn
where he had passed the night ; and, again, that he was
just about to bestow a franc or two on an old shepherd to
whom he had been talking, and who was a mere bundle of
rags, when the man prevented him, by saying he had been
very unfortunate the preceding year — the roof of his
stable having fallen in, and killed two thousand francs'
worth of sheep—*i.e.* a hundred pounds' worth.

There is no progressiveness in the Pyrenees, and little
in the heart of France, in the habits or dwellings of the

peasantry, however well off they may be. I should imagine that if one could resuscitate one of Henri Quatre's old soldiers, or even an ancient Celt, he would find himself very much at home in most French cottages of the present day. He would probably be disgusted by the change of costume; but I do not fancy he would feel any annoyance from the increase of refinement. And, to judge by their clumsy appearance, I should imagine the carts, ploughs, harrows, and other implements of husbandry, were just what he had been used to. It is impossible to describe the total want of all the commonest and most necessary decencies of civilized life, even among those whose amount of property would render them in England well-to-do farmers. What can these people do in sickness? However, they are always kind and civil to the wayfarer.

I feel no fear in walking alone among their mountains and valleys, with no other guard but Keeper. So far, thank God! I have met nothing but courtesy! The peasant went with me till we came nearly to the new road leading to Eaux-Chaudes, and then, pointing out to me that I must go by *that*, and not by the old road, he left me. I followed his directions, and soon came to it.

What a road it was! It was as smooth, wide and even, as that of Mary-le-bone Road, but blasted with great labour and ingenuity out of the living rock which towered above it, making one feel as if at any moment one of those impending crags might topple over and crush one. Some carriages came behind me just as I reached the bridge, and I instinctively squeezed myself as close as I could to the parapet while they passed; but there was no danger, there was plenty of room for them to pass each other without endangering the foot passenger.

Water trickled down from the rough cliffs on my left hand, and formed a little brooklet along their base; and in the clefts and fissures of the rock grew the bright green stars of the pinguicula leaves, and quantities of the grass of Parnassus, the beautiful pale lilac-fringed pink, and the pink centaury, as well as the blue centaury. By the way, why have botanists agreed to give the same name to two flowers belonging to two perfectly different classes? —the one a cruciform, the other a compound flower, and having no similarity of structure in stem, leaf, or root.

Just opposite the ruined bridge, belonging to the disused old road, I stopped to have a talk with the *cantonnier.* Each *cantonnier* has a certain distance of road allotted to him, and within that distance he is expected to be found every day at work. Meanwhile the dog had spied a young goat browsing on the banks of the Gave and immediately gave chase, frightening the poor thing so, I was afraid it would leap into the torrent in its fear. I bawled, and the *cantonnier* bawled, and two boys who were herding the goat bawled, but that villain Keeper regarded none of us. At last, when he had had his fun, he came up panting and breathless; I caught him by the scuff of the neck, the *cantonnier* pulled out a cord from his pocket for which I gave him ten sous, and the sinner was made fast, and condemned to be led the rest of the way to Eaux-Chaudes, but bound as he was, he forthwith commenced a fight with the *cantonnier's* dog; and I was obliged to drag him away, and leave *cantonnier statistics* for a future time.

And now the road grew wilder, and grander, huge mountains hemmed me in on each side, like a wall, reaching from earth to heaven. Not a human creature was in sight, not a bird winged its way across the clear deep-blue sky. There was no sound save the continuous incessant chirping of the grasshoppers, and the roar of the Gave dashing ceaselessly among its huge boulders. I never saw any scenery before so wild and so magnificent as that mountain defile. As the road wound round the

brow of the hill, I turned to look behind me at the ground
I had traversed; an apparently impassable barrier of huge,
rugged, majestic mountains, barred all exit. Their heads
touched heaven, their bases seemed to meet; all trace of
the way by which I had come was lost. On each side
rose the rocky walls upon which the blue sky seemed to
rest; while before me, still loftier mountains appeared
to hem me in. The whole scene was inexpressibly awful
and solemn; it seemed a temple to the Divinity built by
his own hands in the wilderness, its roof the sky, its
choir the murmuring Gave. I never before so completely
realized the majesty of God. I could hardly breathe, I
was oppressed even to tears, and I felt thankful that I was
alone. One cannot amidst the noise and laughter of a
party of friends *feel* the full grandeur of the mountains
as one does alone. I seemed lifted above earth, and
nearer to God. I forgot all my bitter troubles and trials,
and had no feelings left, but those of silent adoration.

So I walked on; every turn in the road, every clump of
pines upon the heights, every fresh view of the foaming
Gave, adding new beauty or sublimity to the scenery, till
I entered the valley of Eaux-Chaudes, and advancing up
it saw a wooded height on my right hand above the
torrent; on my left, high broken ground backed by lofty
mountains, before me a narrow rocky valley with a few
white-washed and stone houses, rising amid trees; this was
Eaux-Chaudes. There is nothing in it to describe. There
are two apparently good inns, and two narrow streets,
consisting mostly of lodging-houses. I had the curiosity
to enter one or two, and was asked twice as much for very
inferior lodgings, as I was paying at Eaux-Bonnes, though
here, as there, the season was over. Here too, as in most
French towns, the lodging-house keepers objected to letting
by the week and wanted to pin one down to stay a month.
I thought I should very much like to spend a week here,

but a month alone, in comfortless lodgings, would be too much, and, besides, prevent my seeing Bagnères, and other places I wish to visit. I felt hungry and went into a baker's shop, where I bought a large flat cake of bread; I suppose it was maize, for it was dark-coloured, sweet and . sticky. It tasted very much like bread made of sprouted corn. Keeper despised it, for he will only eat the best white bread, and tossed the bits I threw him disdainfully into the air, and played at ball with them as he always does with food he disapproves; but I thought it very eatable, and sat down upon a bench under the trees of the little *Place*, to eat it, and quenched my thirst with some water trickling from a rock into a natural basin a little farther on.

My repast finished, I followed the road, which I was told led to Gabas. Here I met *las tres personas*, with whom I had travelled from Pau. They asked me what I paid at Madame Courtade's, and told me they paid six francs a day for the rooms they occupied, exclusive of food, and that that was considered wonderfully cheap. One of the daughters had a bad hand, and they had come to Eaux-Chaudes on her account. I wondered they had not rather gone to Eaux-Bonnes, where the water is considered so healing that, according to Murray, 'the wounded soldiers of Henri d'Albret, after the battle of Pavia, resorted to it for the cure of their injuries, and first gave it its name of Eau d'Arquebusade.' I remember, in reading old magazines and receipts, being sorely puzzled as to what the same Eau d'Arquebusade could be; I believe, nay, I am sure, I once went the length of inquiring concerning it of a druggist, who was as ignorant as myself; little did I dream it was a mineral water of the Pyrenees.

I followed the road across a bridge, and after crossing it, the Gave, which for some time had flowed at my right hand, now flowed at my left, until I came to the second of two saw-mills its waters turn. I should have liked to walk on to Gabas, but I considered I had to get home that night, and unwillingly left the blue mountain ravine, which seemed to stretch forth so invitingly before me to return. The whole of this walk is beautiful. On one side a steep shingly hill, on the other the Gave, wider and more like a river than before reaching Eaux-Chaudes, with a lofty hill clothed with pine and beech trees rising abruptly beyond it, and in front a mountain defile that promised to be yet wilder and grander than any I had passed through. Some carts and horses were standing near the second saw-mill, the horses seeming very restless and unquiet, stamping their feet and tossing their heads and manes, every move-ment producing a wild musical clang which yet did not sound like bells. No one was near them, and I really thought they were all about to set off at full speed by themselves; I went cautiously near to them, to ascer-tain what caused the sounds, and found their bridle reins passed through coloured glass rings, and was wondering whether these glass rings would bear the strain of a hard pull, in going down a steep mountain road, and trying to discover whether there were not also iron ones, though my short sight did not enable me to see any, when I found out the cause of the poor brutes' restlessness, and was my-self attacked by the hornets which were tormenting them. One hornet was most pertinacious. It buzzed menacingly about me, round my gown, under my umbrella, which I was holding up for a shade, and under my hat. In vain I walked away, it followed me, so I determined to attack it. I furled my umbrella and tried to hit it, and at last it flew away, and I escaped unstung.

On my way back, I met two women and a girl walking from Eaux-Chaudes, and with the familiarity common among the working classes in France, they turned and joined me. They were at Eaux-Chaudes for their health. One of them came from Oleron, which town she told me was situated in a very pretty country. All three were knitting busily. Indeed the women one meets are always twirling the spindle or knitting. This sounds as if they were very industrious, whereas the fact is they are very idle. They walk about, or gossip together at their doors, or congregate in the public walks, knitting in hand, just as the Bedfordshire girls and women do with their straw plaiting; and the consequences in both cases are untidy, dirty, slovenly, neglected homes, though the Bedfordshire cottages are neat, compared with those of the Pyrenees. I was desperately hungry when I again reached Eaux-Chaudes, so I went into one of the hotels and ordered a mutton-chop and some wine, and while I sat at my repast in the *salle à manger*, in came another of my fellow-travellers—the mistress of the little dog of whom Keeper had been so jealous in the omnibus. She had a present for *le chien*, she said bashfully. She and her husband lived at the *table d'hôte*, and she had a hamper with fowls, &c., in it, and, in short, they could not get through their provisions, and when she saw Keeper at the door of the *hôtel* she knew I must be there too, and had come into the *salon* to look for me. She hoped I would not feel offended by such an offer, but she wished to give *le chien* a chicken. I knew quite well this was a pretty way of giving *me* a cold roast fowl, but I like to take things exactly as they are meant. I had been very much pleased with both this lady and her husband, who was an *ancien militaire*, and come to the baths in hopes of their removing his lameness; so I followed her to her room, and had a quarter of an hour's pleasant chat with her and Monsieur, and they promised to return my visit at Eaux-Bonnes on Sunday; and then they wrapped the cold fowl in paper and gave it me *for Keeper*, and I set off homewards, with many injunctions from Monsieur to be sure and visit Sacaze the botanist.

When I got to the place where Keeper had chased the goat, I saw, to my amaze, that a couple of yards of the low stone wall which protected the road from the Gave had given way since I passed it. So I went up to my friend the *cantonnier*, who was still sitting on his stool, breaking stones close to the bridge, and asked what had happened. Five minutes after Madame had passed, there had been an *éclat de rocher*; a large piece of rock sapped by the continuous rains of the preceding week, had been loosened from its bed of earth and fallen right across the road, carrying part of the wall with it into the Gave, 'but, as God willed,' nobody had been hurt, though it fell precisely between two carts; the first one full of young girls, who were terribly frightened, the other, which a man was leading, laden with wood. *Five minutes after I had passed!* There had therefore been *but five minutes* between me and a dreadful death! For the *éclat* had fallen on the very spot where I had been botanizing as I passed on my way to Eaux-Chaudes. Surely, a special Providence guided the fall of that huge fragment of rock, so timing it that no one was hurt, though so many people passed just before or at the time of its fall.

The neighbourhood of Eaux-Bonnes and Eaux-Chaudes seems particularly liable to such *éclats de rocher*, as they are called; and I would advise no one to ramble far among the hills without a guide who knows the nature of the ground. There is one terrible and melancholy history of such an accident attached to Eaux-Bonnes. Madame la Marquise de Thuisy, a young, beautiful, and accomplished woman, was at Eaux-Bonnes for her health, which had been seriously affected in 1835, and, to the great joy of her friends, was fast recovering. She was walking on the mountains with her husband and her mother, the Countess de Béarn, when she was carried away by the fall of a rock before their eyes. The shock was so violent, and the dis-

appearance so prompt, that at first they did not know
where to seek for her.   It was only some hours afterwards
that her bruised and broken body was found on the other
side of the Gave.   I thanked God for my escape when I
heard the *cantonnier's* story, and walked on subdued and
thoughtful.   How continually death is close to us, and we
know it not !

The grey shadows of evening began to close in long
before I came to the bottom of the steep hill there is to
climb, before reaching Eaux-Bonnes.   First one mountain,
and then another, seemed to fade out of sight, and only
the abrupt, peaked, barren Pic de Gers, whose yellowish-
white rocks showed clear in the twilight, was visible.   I
began to feel I had delayed my return too long, and that
I ought not to be out so late.   I met several men returning from their work, who asked me where I was going,
and if I was not afraid to be out alone at that hour.   I
answered, boldly, 'No; I was going to the Maison Courtade,
where I was expected;' but my heart beat violently, and
I breathed a silent prayer to God, who had protected me
from the falling rock, that he would protect me from all
danger now, and bring me safely home; and just then
three women came up, and they also asked if Madame
was not afraid to be out so late at night alone, and I joined
them and walked in their company to the bottom of the
ravine, in which Eaux-Bonnes is built: there they left me.
The lamps were lit as I walked up its one street.   I
reached Madame Courtade's weary and thankful.   My first
act was to kneel down and thank God for keeping me safe
throughout the day.   Then I had some food and went to
bed.

CHAPTER III.

To-DAY is Sunday; the rain pours down incessantly. No getting out to church or chapel, as I had intended. I could do nothing but read my own prayer-book at home, and write. Whether my long walk yesterday, or the shock of seeing the danger I had so narrowly escaped, or the proximity of my bedroom to the rock, and the torrent that dashes down it, or the incessant damp from the rain, has affected me, I know not, but I am very unwell, and suffering from slight cholera.

Monday.—Wet weather again, and again I am very unwell; yet I was so tired of being shut up in my little bedroom, with nothing to look at but a rock covered with shrubs and creepers, all dripping with the rain, that I availed myself of an hour's cessation in the afternoon, and went again to the Promenade Horizontale. I do think mountain scenery is even more beautiful in wet weather than in fine. I never see the clouds veiling a mountain summit without thinking of Horeb, and how the Almighty spoke to Moses out of the cloud. There is something so grand in these processions of grey clouds sweeping across the mountains; and when every now and then they part for a moment, and one sees between them a lovely emerald valley, glittering in the momentary gleam, it seems like a glance into Paradise. Just as I got to the end of the Promenade Horizontale, it began to rain again, the fine, small rain, like mist, that wets one more thoroughly than a driving shower, and it did not cease till I reached the

village. In front of Madame Courtade's, a Capuchin
monk—the first I had seen—was walking up and down,
talking to two priests, who were staying in the same house
as myself. He was a very tall, handsome man, and his
picturesque costume, brown-hooded cloak, and sandalled
feet became him greatly. The people of the house told
me he came from a neighbouring valley, was a celebrated
preacher, and had delivered a most beautiful discourse the
preceding day. A Russian family of distinction has been
two or three months in the Maison Courtade, and as I
passed through the hall, some of their goods and chattels
were packing up. On the floor stood an immense heavy
urn, about twice as big and twice as high as an English
urn, which I was informed by the *fille*, was '*pour faire le
thé.*' It had a little grate under it for charcoal, and I
suppose both heated the water requisite and served also as
a teapot, but it seems a huge cumbrous machine to carry
about into foreign lands. I have read in a French translation of a Russian novel, that the Russians—even officers
—never travel without their tea *équipage*.

Tuesday.—Wet again, and I am still ill. The only
incident of to-day was that horrid Keeper running after
one of Madame Courtade's fowls, and nearly killing it. I
told Pierre, the man servant, that I would give *him* a franc
if he would give Master Keeper a good flogging the next
time he ran after the fowls, as I cannot beat him severely.
Accordingly in the afternoon, I heard three very slender
squeaks, just loud enough to let me know he had been
struck, but not by any means the howl of a well-thrashed
dog. The villain makes friends with everybody, notwithstanding his naughtiness, and I can't get anybody to give
him a good thrashing even by paying for it. A while
after, I met one of the priests in the corridor. 'Ah,
madame!' said he, 'I heard your *petit chien* cry; it gave
me pain. I also had a dog, and whom I loved greatly;

but he, too, would run after fowls, and sheep, and
everything, and I thought there was no curing him, and
when I heard your dog cry, it made me quite sad. I
shall always regret my own, and I blame myself now for
having had him .killed, he was such a beautiful dog, and
he loved me!' The old man was ready to cry. 'It was
a pity,' said I, sympathizingly. 'I hope to cure mine in
time; but you must get another dog.' 'No—I can never
have another dog; he would always bring back the first
to my mind. I loved him so much, and was so grieved to
have him killed; and when I see yours, I think of him.'
I understand from Pierre, that Keeper has found out that
the old priest is a lover of dogs, and visits him every
day at dinner time. There seems to be a great number of
priests and nuns at the different watering-places in France.
Go where I will, I am sure to travel part of the way with
one or the other, or both. There are four nuns now in the
Maison Courtade, and how many priests I do not know.
Two nuns are located opposite my bedroom, and two of a
different order are lodging in the front of the house.
They seem to live very well, to judge from all the plates
and dishes I see outside their bedroom door; and one day
I was in the corridor when the dinner was carrying in to
the two occupying the front room. There were six dishes
in the box which the *bonne* of the Hôtel de la Paix had
just brought in, including one of fruit and a salad, and
they all looked very good and tempting.

Wednesday.—Still unwell, and forced to take brandy
continually; yet I managed between the showers to go to
the new walks now making, which are to be called
Promenade de l'Impératrice, in honour of the empress,
who was here for a day or two last year. They are formed
in a little ravine, which branches out sideways behind the
hill forming one side of the *cul-de-sac*, in which Eaux-
Bonnes is situated; and are really very pretty, with lovely

views from them, here and there. This is a most enchanting country, if it did not always rain, and if my dresses, by being always damp, did not give me cholera. I told Madame Courtade to-night, that I felt so unwell, I thought I must return to Pau, and that I fancied my room was cold and damp from its vicinity to the rock which kept out all sunshine, and down which a stream poured into a ravine below. She very courteously offered me my choice of any room vacant at the same price, and I looked at several, and had half made up my mind to stay. I want so much to see Lacaze, and the walks round Eaux-Bonnes are so exquisitely beautiful, if the weather would but clear up; but towards evening I grew so much worse, I dared not remain. A serious illness in a strange country, where I have neither friend nor maid with me, and by which my slender resources would soon be exhausted, would be a terrible thing. So I put on my hat, went down to the coach-office, and bespoke a place in the diligence, that starts for Pau to-morrow morning. By the way, there are *two prices*, even at the coach-offices, one for the English, the other for the French. I was let into the secret by one of the office-keepers here, who thought it his duty to protect the English, because 'his daughter was an English-woman,' that is,' said he, 'she married the son of Sir Humphrey Davy.'

'But,' said I, 'Sir Humphrey Davy had no son. I read his life lately, and it expressly stated that he had no child.'

'Ah! *bah!*' said he, 'then it was his nephew, it is all the same; look here, this was my dead son-in-law's;' and he showed me a telescope, with 'William Davy' engraved upon it.

Thanks to the Davy connection, I paid only the French price at the other office from which the morning diligence started, though perhaps it was rather a spirit of rivalry with the other office, that my friend had betrayed the secret to me. Before I conclude this chapter, I must describe the picturesque costume of these valleys, which I here saw for the first time. One of our pretty maids comes from the valley of Ossau, and wears a scarlet *capulet* or hood, and a broad band of black velvet, fastened by a golden heart round her neck. There is nothing peculiar in the rest of her dress. The *capulet* is a sort of cloak, resembling a sack split up one end, and one side, and falls, in heavy graceful folds, a little below the shoulders. It is never laid aside, even when she is making the beds, or hanging out linen; but sometimes she folds it into a sort of square, which lies on the top of her head, to be more out of the way. I asked her if she did not find it very hot, and very inconvenient, but she replied, she was used to it. This costume is very becoming, and gives an air of grace to all her movements.

I watched her one day aiding Luisa to take down the linen that was drying in the small garden before my window. They doubled all the sheets and towels into squares, and piled them on Marie's head. Luisa was called away, and Marie went on folding and piling linen on her head, till she had a pile more than half a yard high upon it; and it was astonishing how easily and grace-fully she did it, though her *capulet* was hanging down to her waist, and, I should have thought, would have impeded the free motion of her arms. Madame Courtade also wears the *capulet*, but as hers is black as well as the rest of her dress, I took her for a widow, till one day, when I had occasion to go into her domains in the lower part of the house, and she was speaking of the great charge such an establishment was—'especially,' said I, 'for a widow.' I heard a hearty laugh from a tall, red-faced, jovial kind of farmer-looking man, who was going up the passage; and who came into the room where we were, as if to show

M. Courtade was yet in the land of the living. *C'est mon mari*,' said Madame. How oddly people are mated, not matched in this world. Madame has a low soft voice, a nun-like meekness, and even grace of manner; who could have supposed that red-faced man was *her* husband!

I feel quite sorry to leave Eaux-Bonnes, the house is so clean, so free from insect plagues, and the mistress so civil and even kind. If it were not for the rain and the cholera, I should like well enough to winter here; but I have made inquiries, and am told there is a great deal of wet weather here in winter. So to-morrow I shall go back to Pau, and thence to Bagnères de Bigorre, which the all-knowing 'Murray' affirms to be a very pretty, pleasant place, and 'a good deal resorted to by English families, to whom cheap lodgings are an object, as apartments are very reasonable, when the season is over.' If I find this account correct, I shall winter there.

CHAPTER IV.

IT rained heavily as I walked down the hill in the grey
of the early morning to the diligence.   It rained all the
way down the beautiful hills and valleys through which
we passed, so that we could see none of their beauties,
and we were obliged to amuse ourselves by talking. French
fellow-travellers are much more conversable than English
ones.   They are not so dreadfully afraid of making a low
acquaintance.

One of my companions was an engineer; he had set off
to walk to Eaux-Chaudes the same day I did, and coming
a little later, witnessed the fall of the rock.   There was a
wonderful contrast, he said, between the calm demeanour
of the man leading the cart laden with wood—who was in
much more danger than the other cart full of women,
which was a good way in advance of the spot where it
fell—and the screams of the girls in it, who were in no
real danger at all.   He was very severe upon their want of
self-command, which, he said, was '*just like women.*'   I
asked him what he thought of Eaux-Chaudes.

' I did not see it,' said he.

' I thought you were on the road when the *éclat* occurred ? '

' Yes; I set off, meaning to go there; but I was so
shocked by the *éclat*, that it made me quite ill.   I felt it
quite impossible to continue my walk; and I returned to
Eaux-Bonnes.   In fact, I was ill the whole day in consequence of the shock to my nerves.'

'Here is a pretty hero, to find fault with the cowardice of a set of young girls,' thought I; but I did not say so. The engineer is not the first person I have known who can be virtuous and valiant for others, and show great moral qualities by finding fault with their conduct, but who, when put to the test, fails still more pitifully.

As we left the mountains, the sun broke out, and the mist gradually dispersed. When we got into the level plain in which Pau stands, it was quite fair. A good big boy came to the door of the diligence in a village where we stopped for a moment, and begged for a *sou*. No one was inclined to encourage him, and, barefoot as he was, he ran nearly a mile after us, crying out—'*Un sou, s'il vous plaît? Seulement un sou pour du tabac—un sou pour du tabac.*' At last a lady relented, and gave the desired *sou*, more, I believe, to be rid of his noise and importunity than anything else. Tobacco, *i.e. snuff*, seems a necessary of life to the Pyrenean peasants, and indeed to most French people of the middling and poorer classes. Men, women, and boys of sixteen, all *prisent*; and the consequence of this disgusting, filthy habit is, that when they grow old, they have generally a black drop hanging at the end of their nostrils. I have no objection to men's smoking in moderation; and I know by experience that, shocking as it may sound, a cigar is the only thing that relieves intense toothache or tic-douloureux in the face. Thank God! it is two years since I had any necessity for smoking one; but, at a time when continual money losses, and the being obliged in consequence to break up my home had fearfully shattered my nerves, nothing relieved the intense and excruciating pain I suffered in the face, but smoking for a quarter of an hour, and then laying the hot cigar on the outside of the cheek over the part affected (taking care not to burn the skin), till it drew the inflammation outwards. It often puffed the cheek up to a level with my

nose in about twenty minutes, and then the pain immediately ceased. But there seems no earthly benefit to be
derived from a custom so contrary to instinct and nature,
as choking the nostrils and brain up with a pungent dust.
I firmly believe this beastly habit brings on disease in the
brain, and the more, because I knew one great snuff-taker
whose voice was entirely spoiled by it, and who died of
apoplexy when quite a young man.

When we reached Pau, behold it was a brilliantly fine
day. The streets were as dry as a bone, and not a drop
of rain had fallen for at least twenty-four hours. I had
just time, as I passed through the streets, to buy two
yellow peaches to quench my thirst, before setting off for
Bagnères. I felt quite a new creature the moment I got
out of the damp atmosphere of Eaux-Bonnes into the
blessed sunshine. All faintness and inclination to cholera
vanished, as if by magic. I took my place in the diligence in connection with the *Paris Messageries*, and had
to pay two or three francs more for it than all my late
fellow-travellers had done, which I thought was hard, as I
had no luggage, save a little plaid bag; but it was the
only one which started in the middle of the day for Tarbes,
so I could not help myself.* The sole other occupant was
an elderly gentleman, who had travelled a great deal in
Switzerland, Germany, England, and elsewhere, and who
was not therefore so prejudiced as untravelled Frenchmen
usually are, and was very well-informed and agreeable.
He had been to Bagnères de Luchon, and left it because
of the rain, and was now going like myself to try if
Bagnères de Bigorre had a better climate. We passed
through a very pleasant country, and had a splendid view
before us of the distant mountains we were going to visit;

---

* Another instance that my friend the office-keeper at Eaux-Bonnes was
right when he said there were always two charges made at the diligence-
offices, one for English travellers, a lower one for the French.

but, alas! as we drew nearer to them, we got into the region of clouds and mist; the ground was wet, the hedges were wet, the ends of the tree-boughs hung down loaded with moisture, and the rain-drops trickled from their leaves just as at Eaux-Bonnes.

'*Je suis venu de Paris pour mon plaisir*,' said the Frenchman, grimly, grinding his teeth fiercely, and shrugging his shoulders, as he pronounced the word *plaisir*. '*J'ai quitté Luchon parcequ'il pleuvait toujours, et voilà qu'il va pleuvoir à Bagnères de Bigorre. S'il fait mauvais temps, je m'en vais demain matin.*'

When we reached Tarbes, it rained heavily. Tarbes is a dreary, dirty, dull-looking little town, with narrow streets; and when I got out of the diligence, the coach-man and the office-keeper made me pay four francs for Keeper's journey, which, as I was entitled to a certain amount of luggage, and had literally nothing but a few things tied up in a small, thin, plaid bag which I had made myself, and could carry in my hand, I thought very unfair. I had never been charged anything for him either in going to or coming from Eaux-Bonnes; they had considered him as my baggage. This charge, with the three francs I had paid above the prices, my fellow-travellers had told me, I ought to pay for my fare from Pau to Tarbes, made an unexpected extra expense of seven francs; and this, and the rain, did not incline me favourably to Tarbes. My elderly companion and myself paid our fares, and hastened to mount into another diligence, which was crammed full of people. One of the passengers was a nun. The nuns seem to be always gadding.* The

* There is a cause for this. Rising early in the morning, watching and praying in the church at night, and severe manual labour in washing the clothes of the sick and tending upon them, or the exhausting labour of teaching poor children in small ill-ventilated rooms, soon enfeeble the constitution of the uncloistered and most useful nuns. 'Few sisters,' said a French lady to me, 'can teach more than a year without their health giving way.'

old gentleman glanced out of the window at the dense mist and falling rain—view there was none—shrugged his shoulders, and ground his teeth in despair.

'*C'en est fait*,' said he to me ; '*je m'en vais demain matin. Il pleut toujours dans ce pays-ci*.'

Rain, rain, rain. The old gentleman was cross because it rained. I was cross because I had spent seven francs more than I ought to have done, and seven francs would nearly have kept me in food seven days. The other people were cross because it rained, and because we were all so jammed together we could not move. We were not uncivil to one another, but we were all clearly in low spirits and unsociable, and thankful when at last we reached Bigorre.

' Do you know of a reasonable inn ? ' said I to the cross old gentleman, as we all got out.

'*Je m'en vais à l'Hôtel de Paris*' ' I am told it is a good hotel, and it is but for one night,' answered he, grimly.

' Where is it ? ' said I, desperately following him ; for it was dark, wet, slippery, and I was impatient to be housed, as it was 9 o'clock in the evening. *He did not seem much gratified by my company*, but as we entered the hotel he relented.

'*C'est une dame qui est venu avec moi de Pau*,' said he, presenting me to the hostess. ' She wants a room.'

Then he asked if some ladies he expected to meet were there, and was answered in the affirmative. This smoothed his temper. I went up to my room, and when I entered the *salle à manger* to have a chop and some wine, for I had had nothing but two yellow peaches, a bit of bread, and a little brandy all day—he was radiant.

' I found my family here,' said he to me. ' *Mais je m'en vais demain*.'

I could not eat my chop after all. Bed was what I wanted. I commended Keeper to the care of the stable-boy, saw him fed, and went to my room ; it was clean and comfortable, and I slept well. In the morning the first thing I did was to look out of the window. Rain, rain, rain. I had some *French* tea, cold, weak, and insipid, for breakfast, and then I went to the post-office to look for letters which were awaiting me. I returned and read them, hoping the day might clear. But still the rain fell. It was clear this large hotel, and a *table d'hôte* dinner, of three or four francs, would not suit my purse; there was no use in waiting for fine weather to go lodging-hunt-ing. I had brought an introduction to M. Frossard, the French Protestant Minister, from Madame Lauga. Lord Brougham's kind introductory letter had served me well in my distress at Pau, and was now to serve me here. M. Frossard was not at home, but his sister who lives with him, gave me the address, 'Maison Jalon.' In an hour's time I was located there. I had told Madame Llias, the mistress of the Hôtel de Paris, I was not rich, and I had had little. My bill there was, therefore, moderate, yet it came to about nine francs for those few hours. I paid it, took Keeper and my bag, and departed.

No untravelled English reader could imagine what strange places these French or rather Pyrenean houses are. How am I ever to describe Mademoiselle Jalon's, which by the way is greatly resorted to by the English families who come here, as it is large and well furnished, and the apartments are *regularly waxed*, so that there are no fleas? A very necessary thing at Bagnères, which swarms with them as much as Dieppe, but sadly neglected by most of the lodging-house keepers here, who content themselves with making their rooms clean, but make no attempt *to keep them so after they are let,* for cleanliness and house-wifely activity are not indigenous among these mountains. I thought, as I entered Maison Jalon, I had never seen so strange a house; I have seen many like it since. It is entered by an immensely wide passage, up which a carriage could have been driven with ease, though it must have backed out again. At the end of this passage were low white *gates*, about a yard high, dividing it from the rest of the passage leading to Dr. Subervier's consultation rooms, and to the kitchens which faced the front entrance, but were masked, as it were, by a door which always stood open, and a huge glass window, *or rather wall*, which gave the first kitchen a borrowed light—the only one it had. Behind this wall was a small flagged court, always damp and open above to the sky, upon which the two kitchens opened. Beside the window of the first, some old Roman pilasters were incrusted into the wall. On the wall opposite the front door, over what was termed *la fontaine*, but which was no fountain at all, but merely a tap whence water was drawn, was a full-sized female figure in white plaster. Entering the gate, but leaving the kitchens on one's right, one ascended a wide, handsome staircase, which led to the first floor, where there are good large salons and bedrooms. On the landing-place, at the foot of the stairs, is a glass door, which leads to a gallery running round the four sides of a square, open at top to the sky, and overlooking the court in front of the kitchens; some of the rooms whose windows open upon it, occupied by Dr. Subervier, have, of course, only a borrowed light. These rooms are one story high, and the roof comes down to the top of their walls, just as if they were outside a house, not within it. Re-entering the glass door, one ascends another wide staircase over the first; then comes a long corridor, with rooms on each side, like the first floor—it opens by a glass door on to a wooden gallery running the whole length of the house, and commanding a pleasant view of the Thermes or Baths, and Mont Olivet. I have two little rooms at the end of this corridor, opening on to the gallery, and find them very pleasant; but they would not do for me in winter, as there are no fire-places in them. After having settled myself, I went out in despite of the rain to look about me.

Bagnères seemed to me rather prettily situated on the slope of a green hill. I met my fellow-traveller from Pau, buttoned up to the throat, and grimmer than ever.

'You are walking in this *charming weather*,' he began. 'I have been walking, too. There is really a pretty walk over that hill (Mont Olivet), *if one could see it*. I recommend you to go there *when you can*. As to me, *je pars demain matin*. I cannot live in a place where it does nothing but rain. It rained at Luchon. I left it; it rains here. To-morrow I am going to Vichy; if it rains there, I shall go back to Paris. I hate rain. Humph!'

The little man looked so stern and grim as he said this, as if he meant *to punish* the weather by departing, that it was impossible to forbear laughing.

'*Ah! ah! vous riez, vous? Moi, je ne ris pas. Je m'en vais.*'

I suppose he went, for I saw him no more. If he had only had twenty-four hours' patience! The next day it was beautifully fine, and I saw that Bagnères de Bigorre was not merely situated at the foot of a hill, but surrounded by mountains. I took the walk the little man and Murray both recommended, along a sort of terrace cut through a hanging wood above the Thermes, named Mont Olivet, and which is a continuation of the small mountain directly above the town, known as the Bédat. The whole of this wood and the base of the Bédat are intersected by winding walks, but I followed the straight one, leading towards La Bassère. There is a beautiful view from it in all directions.

Below in the green valley, watered by the clear, ever-murmuring Adour, lies the small white town of Bagnères, with its strange ugly cathedral, with *one* little pepper-box stuck on one side of its gable end, as if it had never been finished, and the graceful octagonal tower of the Église des Jacobins, which was pulled down in the mad, blind fury of the Revolution, and nothing left of it but the tower, the new Église des Carmes, the small chapel belonging to the Carmelite nuns, and the Carmelite monastery and nunnery. Two or three villages lie beyond Bagnères. One of them, Pouzac, has a very pretty square-towered church, with a wooden gallery running all round it, and above that a small spire. There were not so many flowers on Mont Olivet as on the Promenade Horizontale at Eaux-Bonnes, nor were the bugles so intense in colour. They were more of a deep lilac, but still very pretty.

I found no gentianellas, but the meadow saffron grew under some of the trees, and the delicate little parasite dodder, and the graceful and delicate pale-blue ivy-leaved campanula. I have no work on botany with me, now that I am constantly wandering about. When I get settled I shall buy Philippe's 'Flore des Pyrénées,' and then I shall be able to give the proper Latin botanical names of the plants I find. I hate those Latin names, and though Shakespeare does say that 'the rose by any other name would smell as sweet,' the common names of plants are much more poetical and descriptive than the Latin ones. The word snowdrop awakens a thousand associations, but what poet could write about the 'Galanthus nivalis?' Dr. Walter Johnson, of Malvern, once told me that he was walking one day with the Laureate, when they found a flower the latter was unacquainted with, he inquired its name. Dr. Walter proceeded to give him a learned botanical name. 'I don't want that,' said the poet, '*what I want is the common name the ploughmen and milkmaids give it.*'

I returned from Mont Olivet with a lovely bouquet, arranged it, and put it in water, rested awhile, and then went through the town of Bagnères. There is not much

to see in it. The Thermes is a handsome square building
of grey marble, as Murray informed me. But for the red
book, I should, with my bad sight, have taken it for greystone, as it is simply hewn, and not polished marble. In
like manner, I should never, but for Murray, have discovered that all the door-posts, lintels, and window-sills
of the houses in Bagnères are of the same marble of the
country. But I should have found out for myself, that a
little brook of running water runs down each side of the
street and keeps the houses cool and the streets clean,
while some of the bath-houses are surrounded on two
sides, at least, by broad streams looking like canals. A
very small boat might certainly row along them. There
is a good deal to say for and against these street rivulets.
They are very convenient for the dogs, and they wash
away all refuse ; but I should not like, were I living at
No. 20, to have my wine decanters, and my saucepans,
and my vegetables washed as I see these things continually done, in the stream at which the dog of No. 19 had
just been drinking, the shopman of No. 14 rinsing his
hands, and the mistress of No. 17 washing some exceedingly dirty linen. To do the Bigorrais justice, they do
not usually fill their drinking vessels from *le ruisseau*,
the women fetch the water from the fountains, of which
there are several in the town. But, with all this abundance of water, the Bagnérais are not a clean race. It is
not the custom to wash the floor of the rooms, or the
passages, or the shop floors, or the counters, or tables, or
anything that is commonly washed *every day* in England.
The peasants are consequently walking *ménageries* of *f*
sharps, not to say of other things which I have heard a
Bagnéraise lady declare were to be caught on the benches
of the public walks. The peasant women lounge all day,
with their knitting, on the seats in the Place des Coustos,
where the stalls of knitted work are spread out under the

trees, and on those in the walks of Mont Olivet, and sometimes leave testimonies of their having done so, not over-pleasant to ladies and gentlemen.

The peasants' dress is much more respectable-looking and whole than that of our working people. The men wear round jackets, waistcoats, and trousers of brown un-dyed home-spun wool, and blue or brown flat caps, called *berets*, resembling the Scotch bonnet, only larger, on their heads. In bad weather, they wear a huge brown cloak of very thick felt-like cloth, with a peaked hood to it, which they draw over the head like a Capuchin friar. It seems very droll to see a man digging in this costume, when an Englishman would be working in his shirt sleeves; but I suspect it is the wiser plan to protect themselves from the weather. Anyhow, they look very picturesque. Some-times the men wear a brown or blue woollen nightcap with the end hanging down instead of the *beret*. The women's dress is not becoming; they wear a handkerchief twisted round the head, a pretty enough head-dress for a young woman when the colours are well selected and it is coquet-ishly put on, but the elder women always choose shades of yellow and maize and *feuille morte* intermingled, which does not set off a wrinkled, yellow skin; over this they lay another folded in half, the corners hanging down be-hind, and the two ends, which are rarely tied, floating on the shoulders like the Bordelaises; I always wonder they don't blow off into the *ruisseau*. Their gown is usually of dark-coloured linsey-woolsey or merino, and over this is a handkerchief, very untidily pinned across the bosom; knitted stockings, and generally *sabots* or wooden shoes usually complete their attire, but many go barefoot. The *capulet* is rarely red here, and is generally made of white flannel, the grey selvage forming a stripe down the back. In bad weather they wear a dingy, dark-coloured cloth cloak, of the same sack-like shape, that reaches nearly to the ankles. The *bourgeoise* wears a cap in fine weather; in wet, a sort of cloak of black merino, generally lined with purple silk, and shaped something like a Talma cloak, but with a small semicircle cut in the middle for the face, and it is held together under the chin by one hand. Bonnets are not in vogue, except for ladies, and hats still less so; but even the peasants, at least the smart ones, wear crinoline.

I think the cleanest creatures in Bagnères are the pigs, which are regularly driven into the water every day; they seem to enjoy it amazingly, and to be far more sensible of the benefits of ablution than the dirty men and women who drive them to the streams. The pigs, indeed, and all the animals, seem highly civilized here; I suppose, because they are kindly treated and frequently spoken to. They come when called; and when, in walking among the mountains, I hear the shepherds calling to their flocks, and see the docile sheep going the way they are directed, I am often forcibly reminded of our Saviour's words, '*My sheep know me, and hear my voice.*' The horses are also often washed, but not the poor cattle that draw the teams and plough the fields, who need it more, and whose buttocks are often covered with dry clotted cow-dung, that must make their skin very sore and painful.

The female sex have not a good time of it in the Pyrenees. One sees the women and girls working bare-legged in the fields, following the plough, and spreading manure with their hands, and sometimes ploughing, while their husbands and brothers have good warm stockings, as well as *sabots* or shoes : and the ploughs and carts are more frequently drawn by *cows* than by oxen. These cattle are something like the Breton cows, but rather larger, pretty, gentle, fawn-coloured creatures, with beautiful soft large eyes. Juno never could have been the vixen she was, if she had really been ox-eyed.

There are large fields of maize about Bagnères; they tell me it is planted as a second crop after the corn has been reaped. Here too, they seem to be always hay-making. The fields are nearly all water meadows, and in all are dams and sluices, by means of which irrigation is carried on. The land seems wonderfully fertile if it were well farmed, but everything here is done in a slovenly sort of manner, and the farm implements are of the rudest, clumsiest make.

There is a pretty walk to the left of Mont Olivet, past the French Protestant church, called Salut,*from a mineral spring which rises there in the fields; the path lies through emerald meadows, and the stream runs part of the way close beside it, and farther on, murmurs under the trees at the verge of the meadow. White cottages dot the hills here and there, each under its own chestnut trees, and all around rise the mountains, no two resembling each other in form and outline, but all beautiful. This walk leads through a plantation to *Les Bains de Salut*, and if you please to vary your walk, you may return home by the shady road.

A French lady joined me one day as I was walking up towards some chestnut trees on the base of the Bédat, and proposed we should ascend it together. So we got a little shepherdess from a neighbouring *métairie*† to guide us, and went to the summit, from whence there is a very beautiful view on all sides. On one side, the wide fertile plain dotted with villages and chestnut trees, and ending in a blue haze, that made one almost sure one saw the sea beyond; on the other, mountain after mountain rising like huge waves that have suddenly been stiffened into rock. It is impossible to look at the Pyrenees when thus seen from a mountain height, without thinking that they must once have been fluid.

* *Salut* signifying *health.*   † A dairy farm.

From the Bédat one sees most of the principal mountains of this range. The Monné, the Pic du Midi de Bigorre, the highest of all, and rarely, except in the height of summer, free from snow (now in September it was quite white, forming a beautiful contrast with the green Bédat, and the brown fern-covered Monné); Lheris with its pine wood, and many others. As we came down, I gathered quite a large bouquet of the beautiful fringed pink, which scented my room with its sweet perfume for many days after. Mademoiselle D'Orville was at the baths with an invalid mother, and had no walking companion, so we agreed, as I too was alone, to make some excursions together. She spoke English well, and was a pleasant, well-informed person. One day we hired donkeys, and rode to the valley of Campan, whence the white, and green, and flesh-coloured marbles are quarried. On our way, in passing through the dirty little village of Baudéan, we saw a slab in the wall of a house commemorating the birth there of Baron Larrey, the friend and physician of Buonaparte; and his erection of the village schools. There is nothing to see at Campan, except the pretty green valley up which one rides, hemmed in by mountains. The Adour murmurs through it all the way, and not only sings, but *works*, for it turns several marble works and saw-mills. In one respect Campan is better off than Bagnères, for it has a covered market-place. There is also a pretty stone fountain in the centre of the village.

Another day we hired a carriage, and set off at 8 o'clock A.M., to the Col d'Aspin. It was a gloriously beautiful morning, and the meadows and mountain peaks seemed to exult in the sunshine and put on new beauty. One never tires of mountain scenery, for every day varies its aspect, by some enchantment of light or shade. Thus Campan to-day looked brighter and greener than Campan the other day. We passed several other villages beyond, gradually ascending the mountain, until we came to an inn belonging to three different parishes, where we stopped to bait our horses, and while they were feeding, we walked to a pine-wood across the meadow. Mademoiselle D'Orville had a fancy for entering it; I thought we might lose our way, and proposed following the beaten track which led up a pretty little valley watered by a murmuring stream. Here we lingered and botanized, but found nothing rare, and then Mademoiselle would go into the pine-wood, where we got bogged. Some of the pine-trees were very large and old, and from their branches hung a curious brown moss, like coarse human hair, some of which, as also a young *sapin*, I gathered and preserved in 'Murray.' When we got back, our guide was very angry. He declared we might have met with wolves, which are very common in the higher mountains, and we should reach the Col after the sun had set, too late for the view; but nevertheless, he dawdled another half-hour, during which time we sat down on the hay in the meadow, and ate the cold fowl and grapes we had brought with us, and went into the house and got some execrable sour wine to drink after it. The house was full of flies. I never saw such a quantity, except once at a house on the Niederwald, also on high ground. I suppose they like mountain regions.

At last the carriage was pronounced ready, we took our seats and ascended the mountain. Such a glorious view it was all the way! The road wound up the side of the Col, from which we saw all the neighbouring mountains; in many places there was nothing, not even brushwood, at its edge. It was a relief to my mind when the trees of a *sapin* wood *seemed* to break the sheer descent, though I knew if we had been upset, they would not have afforded any safety. Happily, God watched over us, and we had good horses, and a careful though bold driver. The higher we advanced up this terraced road, which had

E

evidently been blasted out of the solid rock, the wilder
and the grander grew the scene. Mountain after mountain appeared in the blue distance. At last we reached
the Col, and got out to walk to the point whence we
could best see the view. The whole chain of the Pyrenees
lay spread out like a map before us, but as the guide had
predicted, we were half-an-hour too late to see the more
distant ones distinctly. Nevertheless it was the grandest
sight I ever saw. Far grander than the defile between
Eaux-Bonnes and Eaux-Chaudes. A very old white-haired
shepherd came to us and told us the names of the principal mountains. We could even see some that rose in
Spain. Mademoiselle D'Orville could not forgive herself
for having dawdled so long in the pine-wood and lost the
sunset glow, and the distant view. The old shepherd told
us there had been a most magnificent sunset half-an-hour
ago. What a place to see it from! He pointed out the
Maledetta, and the Pic du Midi, and Mont Perdu, and
the Vignemale, and we ought to have seen la Brêche de
Roland, had we but been in time. There was another
party just before us. They also had come too late. Our
guide summoned us to return; very unwillingly we turned
away from the magnificent view, over which the shadows
of evening were now rapidly darkening. And this is the
road to 'Luchon par la Montagne.' When I read those
words on Ribette's coach-office, at Bagnères, how little I
realized what a road it was. Oh! I hope next year I
shall go to Luchon par la Montagne, and see that magnificent chain of mountains again.

I wanted to see Cauterets and Argelés. The diligences
had ceased to run, for the Bagnères season was over. But
Monsieur Gazave, of whom I bought some boots, told me
I could go for two or three francs with Madame Armiral,
the dyer, who went every market day to Argelés. To
Madame Armiral, therefore, I went. She told me she

started at half-past 5 A.M., and waited for no one; so if
I wished to go with her, I had better sleep at her house.
She could give me a clean bedroom, and it would only cost
me a franc, to which I agreed. Then I made arrangements for returning to lodge at Bagnères in a fortnight,
but not with Mademoiselle Jalon. Her servants do not
cook for people, and it would cost me three francs a day to
have a dinner sent in from an hotel. Hitherto I have
lived on bread and yellow peaches and grapes; but in the
winter I shall need meat.

CHAPTER V.

I BADE adieu to Mademoiselle Jalon about 8 o'clock in the evening, and went to sleep at Madame Armiral's. The room was clean and even handsomely furnished, and the bedding good, as is usual with France; but alas! for the *f* sharps! Small rest did I get that night. It is no use complaining of fleas to a Pyrenean. '*Il y en a partout*,' is the invariable answer. If one suggests that the curse—for to people with sensitive cuticles it is as a curse—might be obviated by washing the floors regularly, they reply, '*On ne lave jamais le plancher ici, ça gâte le bois*,' seeming to consider that argument irrefragable; but if with insular pertinacity you continue to urge the multiform advantages of cleanliness, and gently intimate that it rather on the contrary benefits the wood, and that in the houses of respectable people in England, where it is not so necessary, as the climate is not so hot, and insects are fewer, the floors of uncarpeted rooms are regularly washed, they clinch the argument by adding, '*Personne ne lave les planchers ici, même dans les bonnes maisons. Vous irez partout—où vous voudrez—on ne laverait pas les planchers non plus. Ce n'est rien, les puces!*' I comforted myself with the thought it was only for one night. Glad was I when, at 5 o'clock, one of Madame Armiral's granddaughters came to call me. I was already up and dressed, thanks to the fleas.

It was a raw, bleak morning that 30th of September, when, by the dim light of a lantern on one side held by the hostler, and a guttering tallow candle that flared in the wind held by the maid, I and Keeper ascended into the front seat of the little double phaëton, in which we were to travel to Argelés, while Madame Armiral got up behind, and packed herself tightly in with bundles of wool, cloth, and flannel. We could scarcely see the dim outline of the houses as we drove out of the town. I could not recognize the road we were taking. By-and-by the black of night yielded to grey, which became every moment lighter, and by the time we reached a village I was informed was called Pouzac, day had dawned. The whole country round Bagnères is pretty throughout the long, flat, fertile valley in which it stands, with sloping hills and woods bounding the distance in most parts; while the range of lofty mountains, at whose feet it lies, closes in the view. I lost, of course, the most beautiful prospect, as the mountains were all behind me, except the wooded slopes of Mont Olivet and the Camp de César, which last is directly above Pouzac. We passed through two or three other villages, but saw nothing particularly interesting till we turned off towards Lourdes, when the road grew more beautiful every moment. The scenery is much wilder and more romantic there than at Bagnères, but it is not a place to live in. On each side of the road were steep, rocky, blue-grey mountains, down whose ravines rushed mountain torrents, foaming and splashing over the stones. Every now and then we crossed small stone bridges over narrow, clear, winding streams, getting, as it seemed, more and more into the fastnesses of the mountains, till we turned the shoulder of a hill, and saw the gloomy-looking, strongly-fortified Castle of Lourdes,* standing on the summit of a steep, abrupt rock dominating the plain before us, and a few seconds afterwards, the town below it came into sight.

* Lourdes is a kind of border fortress between France and Spain.

Lourdes, as we drove through it, seemed rather more of
a town than Bagnères.   It was clean and dull-looking.   It
is a garrison town, but it was too early for any of the
military to enliven its streets by gay uniforms.   Few of the
windows were yet unclosed.   We stopped more than twenty
minutes in front of one of the inns, not to rest or feed
our poor weary steed, who, small as he looked, and heavily
as he was laden, had done his journey wonderfully well,
but that our driver might go to a barber,—'*pour faire sa
barbe*,' as Madame Armiral informed me.   Out he came at
last, quite a new man, well shaved, his hair curled, and a
smart Magenta tie replacing the old woollen comforter
round his neck.   '*Les jeunes gens aiment à se faire beau
pour le marché*,' said Madame Armiral, approvingly, in my
ear.   Meanwhile, I had been regaling myself and Keeper,
who had been allowed to run most of the way, and was
highly indignant at being put back into the carriage, with
a roll I had taken with me.   Madame Armiral called a
gamin out of the street, and proffered him a *sou* if he
would go and buy her a new roll.   He returned with an
old, dry one.   '*Je ne puis pas le manger*,' said she, 'with
my old teeth ; I am seventy-seven, and can't do with such
hard crusts.'   Of course I offered her part of mine, which
she declined, saying we should soon reach Argelès.

'You surely are not seventy-seven?' said I, looking at
her.

'*Soixante-dix-sept ans bien sonnés.*'

'And do you often go this long journey, and so thinly
clad ? ' said I, looking at the hardy old woman in amaze,
for she had nothing but *one* cotton handkerchief tied
round her head '*à la mode du pays*,' and a thin shawl over
her gown.

'*Toujours*,' she answered ; '*toutes les semaines, l'été et
l'hiver.   Même quand la route est tout couverte de neige.*'

Think of an old lady of seventy-seven getting up once

a week out of her warm bed, before 5 o'clock in the
morning, and driving, without her breakfast, across the
mountains, for hours. Her husband, she told me, had
been dead thirty years; but one son and his family lived
with her; the other was cook to a regimental mess, and had
been in England seventeen years. He talked of coming
to see them this year, but he had talked of it every year.
She thought it would end in talk. She was a fine, stout,
stalwart old lady, clearly quite accustomed to hold the
reins, and to see everyone bend to her will; but the tone
of command in which she addressed everybody—even me,
whom she told what I ought to do and to leave undone,
and how I ought to manage my journeys—had a touch
of motherly kindness and warm-heartedness in it which
made her obvious love of governing very different from
the dictatorial manner of a hard, cold, bitter, domineering
old maid, who expects human hearts and feelings to go
like machinery, and never get out of order; and, having
suffered herself, finds a certain grim consolation in seeing
others suffer. I cannot help it. I am a maiden aunt
myself; but I do think maiden aunts (when they take
to managing, or rather *mis*-managing, their nephews and
nieces) are the pest of creation, and worse in their cold,
deliberate murder of human hopes, hearts, and affections,
than any murderer of the body that ever was gibbeted.
But the *mother who has loved, and been beloved*, usually
retains some sympathy for the young and their trials.
She loves to order as much as a single lady, but, then,
one sees and feels that it arises from the habit she
has acquired of having a set of young people to think
for, and provide for. By dint of continual clucking, and
spreading her wings to shelter her own chickens, she ends
by considering all who are a little younger than herself
as a part of her brood. She tells you home truths in the
roundest manner, and settles all your affairs for you just

as if you were a baby ; but, somehow, it is all done in such a kind, hearty manner, and is so entirely for your good, and she generally (unlike the strong-minded spinster) takes so sound, and practical, and genial a view of every-thing, that you resign yourself meekly to her guidance with a mental smile, and—'I do believe she thinks I'm an infant still '—and do just as you are bid.

'*Nous arriverons à Argelés à midi,*' said Madame Armiral to me; '*aussitôt que j'ai ouvert ma boutique, je dîne. On m'apporte une soupe et un plat et tout ce qui me faut de l'hôtel. Une soupe vous fera du bien : vous dînerez avec moi, et puis vous irez vous promener pour voir le pays.*'

Our driver whipped the horse. Away we clattered over the stony road of the stony, rocky, bare valley—'the unpromising vestibule,' as Murray calls it, 'which leads into what has been called the paradise of Argelés.' I did not think it unpromising. To me there is something grand and sublime in rocks piled upon rocks—grey, bare, and stern, almost to the sky, with water-courses rushing and tumbling down their ravines, whose white foam relieves, and gives life and light to the dark, sombre, blue-grey and brown hues of the crags, while their glad, fresh murmur breaks a silence that might otherwise soon become oppres-sive. We rounded a hill, and then the scene widened into a plain, above which, on the left hand, was a small monticule, partly fringed with wood, and surmounted by a ruined tower, grey, bare, naked, and desolate, that com-manded the whole valley below. This tower was Vidalos. The valley of Argelés is a long, low, oval basin, richly cropped, especially with maize, and surrounded on all sides by hills or mountains. Through it flows the Gave, the same river that runs by Pau ; but it is not a distin-guishing or beautiful feature in the landscape, being divided by shallows and sandbanks into innumerable small

streams, and lost, as it were, in an ocean of sand. I was
disappointed in Argelés. It is, no doubt, beautiful, but it
is a tame kind of beauty. It is not half so beautiful as
the vale of Abergavenny, with its old grey castle, from
whence one looks on rich green meadows, golden with
buttercups; the broad Gavenny and its double-arched
bridge—that for passengers and carriages, and the one for
tram-carts above—giving it the appearance of a Roman
aqueduct; the beautiful hanging wood near Llan-Ellen,
the broad-shouldered Blorenge, and the blue, abrupt
Skyrid beyond.

To the right of Argelés, just a little before you enter it,
is a modern castle or château, belonging to Madame de
Sales, the widow of a former *juge de paix* there. She is
an Englishwoman, and, as Madame Armiral informed me,
takes boarders. The town of Argelés is about as dirty and
uninteresting a place as ever I saw. My intentions of
wintering there vanished at once. '*Ma chère, c'est un
pays de loup,*' had been the remark of a French lady to
me, to whom I confided my doubt as to whether Argelés
or Bagnères would be the more desirable winter abode—
'*Ici vous pourrez vivre, mais là vous mourirez d'ennui.*'
Yet there was an English family obliged to leave Pau in
consequence of reduced means, who lived and died here.
Madame Armiral pointed out the house where they had
lodged, at the corner of the market-place, opposite her
own shop, as we drove past. What a dreary existence
theirs must have been in this town of peasants, without
books, without society, without comfort of all kinds! The
carriage stopped, and out we got. Madame Armiral
fetched the key of her shop from a neighbour's, and proceeded to open it, lifting heavy packages out of the
phaëton and into the shop, and arranging them more like
a strong man than an old lady of seventy-seven. When
all was laid in order to her satisfaction, she went to the

hotel, next door, to order our dinners. I had said I would have no soup.

'*Je vous ai commandé une soupe, c'est bon pour l'estomac,*' said she, on her return.

I saw I was doomed to soup, and did not argue the point; and she cleared her shop-counter, dragged two old chairs out of a corner, one for herself within the counter, and one for me without it, and I sat down, waiting till the dinner should come, and looking on the market-place of Argelès, all full of life and bustle, with groups of *paysans* in their blue *beret* caps, and suits of brown homespun wool; jacket, vest, and trousers usually alike; a smart silk necktie, as fashionably narrow as those in London or Paris; a snowy shirt, and sometimes the end of the scarlet or green woollen sash just peeping from under the vest, being the only approach to a *costume* among the men; while the *paysannes* wore dark-coloured gowns, often of woollen, sometimes a jacket, and sometimes a cotton handkerchief pinned over the bosom, and the handkerchief twisted round the head,—those who came from a distance frequently wearing, also, the white or red *capulet;* but there was none of the gay colouring I had expected to see in a foreign market-place. Costumes are fast dying out everywhere. The more the pity, for they are replaced by ugliness and dirt. The sombre, dirt-hiding hues of a Pyrenean peasant woman's dress is certainly far better than the tawdry finery of women of the same rank in an English town, but there is nothing gay or picturesque about it.

The girl now brought our dinner from the inn, and after spreading a snowy table-cloth on the counter, placed before each of us a large piece of bread and a clean napkin and a pint bason of soup (nobody ever dines without a napkin and a *potage* in France). The *potage* was full of bread, and unlike any I had ever tasted before, but it was good, and I ate it all, to Madame Armiral's great content.

'*Ça vous fera du bien!*' she exclaimed, for the sixth time.

Then we had some veal *aux tomates*, good also, and half a bottle of *vin ordinaire*, between the two, of which we took what we thought fit; *chasse café* accompanied by a small glass of *eau de vie*, and a little saucer of six or seven lumps of sugar, was set before each of us. I had refused *café* and brandy altogether at first, but I was not well. I had not eaten the meat, not because it was not good, but because I felt sick and squeamish, and I thought with Madame Armiral, some strong coffee and brandy would do me good, and took it. After dinner she brought out some grapes, and seemed quite hurt when I refused them.

'*Tiens,*' said she, 'I bought them on purpose for you, when I went to order dinner.'

When the *fille* came to clear away and be paid the bill, our dinner had cost us *douze sous*, sixpence, and the *chasse café, six sous*.

'And now,' said Madame Armiral, 'I have my shop to look after, there is not much room in it, and all the peasants will be coming to fetch the things they have had dyed, so you had better go and look about you. If you go down straight through the market, past the Hôtel de France, you will have a pretty view of the country.'

So I and Keeper, who had dined well on the veal I could not eat, and the soup-meat, set off together. We went down the hill towards Pierrefitte. The view on all sides was lovely, and the road was bordered nearly to the bridge with beautiful green tree-shaded meadows, and watered by silver runnels cut across them in all parts, and reflecting the clear blue sky. I took Keeper into them, and after much difficulty succeeded in capturing him (for he makes a point of never coming within my grasp out walking, though he will play with me for hours in the house), and put him into the brooklet and gave him a thorough wash, after which I threw sticks for him to catch, and he ran after them, played at ball with them, rolled on the grass, and threw them up into the air and caught them, and when I drew near, bounded off with them again, as if defying me to catch him. Then I continued my walk. I passed a very pretty house on the right-hand side standing back from the road, in front of which were a pair of tall iron gates, leading up to an avenue of monthly roses in full flower, shaded by a second avenue of that favourite French tree the poplar. This pretty château is let in apartments during the summer months to visitors, and the inside is as clean and tempting, as the delicious view from the windows, and the shady garden around it, is alluring. I longed to lodge there.

Farther on still was a dirty little village, whose name I forget. I went into the church, but there was nothing worth seeing there. I asked a peasant woman I saw at one of the best houses to let me go into her house, and she took me up stairs into her bedroom. It was a good large room with two windows, both, as was that on the staircase landing, as large as bedroom windows usually are in a gentleman's house in England, and both wide open. Fortunately, the French peasants are particular in ventilating their houses, doors and windows generally stand wide open all day, or the consequences of their filthy habits would be terrible. The room was as dirty as I expected to see it, and strewn with cobs of the maize drying, but the beds were good, and the coarse homespun sheets, for the beds were still unmade, perfectly clean. On the mantel-shelf was a statuette of the Virgin, with a few cheap artificial flowers round it, and a crucifix with two cheap coloured prints of saints hung over it. I saw most of the house, and sat some half-hour to rest myself, and have a gossip with the mistress, whose heart I won by admiring a fat chubby bright-eyed baby, who lay wide awake in his cradle, the

only thing there was to admire in the whole establishment,
and as I talked I looked about me. The floor was several
inches thick with dust, and made of a sort of composition
that looks like stone, with which I have seen cottages
floored in England. In one corner lay fagots of wood—
not for immediate use, but at least a week's provision. A
pot was boiling over a smoky fire, and a very dirty barefooted old woman was raking the embers together and
blowing them by her breath into a dull flame.

'*C'est ma mère,*' said my hostess, whose tanned skin and
filthy dress were worthy of such a mother.

' And does she always go barefoot?' I asked.

'No, not in winter, but it is hot weather now.'

N.B. All the peasant women think it necessary for their
health to go bare foot part of the year, though the men
are almost invariably well shod with shoes, boots, or *sabots.*

' Is this farm-house your own, madame?'

'Oh yes, it is our own, and we have several fields also.
We are *propriétaires.*' Landowners.

So I understand are the greater part of the miserable-
looking men and women I meet, and I suppose five hundred
years hence their descendants will look equally dirty and
miserable. It seems necessary for man to have something
to look up to; some higher standard of refinement and
intelligence than his own, or that of his own immediate
circle. I never knew *the infinite value, the moral use,* of
our English nobility and gentry in setting an example of
order, cleanliness, and intelligent management of their
lands and households, till I saw the Pyrenean peasants.

Argelés is an Arcadia of beauty and fertility, but alas for
the Arcadians! When one sees the girls haggard and
wrinkled for want of bonnets or hats to shade their eyes
from the sun, exposure to which makes them contract a
perpetual frown before they are women; the women tanned
till their skins resemble York-tan leather, and *old* at thirty;

the number of females one meets who are blear-eyed or suffering from goitre, or worn out before their time—the *crétins*, the many maimed and deformed children from bad nursing, or accidents, arising from having been left alone while their parents were at work in the fields, and the filthy homes, where dogs and pigs and fowls run about as they like over the *never-washed* floors; the miserable dwellings, some of which have no windows, but merely shutters, while others are almost dark, having little light but what comes through the open door, and contrasts these filthy homes and people with the tidy home and clean bright-faced wife and rosy children of the Yorkshire labourer, one cannot but feel these people would have far more real comfort if the land belonged to intelligent, kind landlords,* able to cultivate it properly, and who would take care that the cottages on their estates were well built, well ventilated, well drained, and fit abodes for human beings, instead of tumble-down pigsties, and whose example would civilize and stimulate the people to attain habits of cleanliness and decency. There is another cause for the coarse, hard look of the women. It is the demoralization consequent upon the custom of girls working in the fields with men. Their roughened voices, their coarse language and behaviour, all bear witness to its frightful effects on their cha-

---

* Such landlords as our Yorkshire ones—men who take a pride in having the labouring classes in the villages belonging to them well and comfortably housed, not herding together like pigs, or forced to walk two or three, or even *six* miles, to their work in all weathers, and the same distance back again when they are worn out with fatigue for want of proper house accommodation near their employment, as seems to be the case in too many of the southern and midland counties.

It is a *disgrace* to any man to draw a large annual income from the soil, and not to build proper cottages near the scene of their work for the labourers who are to cultivate it. *It was the utter neglect by the rich of the miseries and necessities of the industrious classes that led to the French Revolution*, and the fearful war now raging in America is undoubtedly God's judgment upon the Americans for years of cold non-intervention on the one hand, and holding their fellow men as slaves on the other. *Neither nations nor individuals can afford to neglect a plain duty. If they do, the consequences always recoil upon their own head.*

racter. The Pyrenean men make wretched husbands—drink and abuse their wives. The women also drink as their own songs avouch, and young women invite the young men to drink, *and pay for them.* The blessedness of home is unknown. The tired peasant returns to a filthy house, where smoulders a piece of charcoal covered by ashes. No pleasant, cheerful meal awaits him. His children have cried themselves to sleep in a corner, or perhaps one of them has burnt his arms off. How can it be otherwise? The wife and the eldest girls have followed his plough all day. The weary, footsore, hard-worked set get a little bread and curdled milk (a chief article of diet in peasant life), and some fruit or chestnuts, and retire to rest unwashed, in company with their dirty animals.

As I went back to Argelés I passed *one clean cottage,* the only one I have seen in this part of France, yet the owner had more to struggle against than most of those around. She had only been confined three weeks ago and was in bad health. She was standing at the door as I passed, and on my asking a question she invited me to go in, and I sat down and had a chat with her. She was not a native of Argelés, and seemed as much horrified at the dirt around her as myself. When I got back to Madame Armiral's shop, she thus addressed me:—

'*J'ai tout arrangé.* You said you meant to stay a week at Argelés and a week at Cauterets. Cauterets is colder than Argelés, you had better go there first. I have arranged with Canon to take you back in his *voiture; c'est un bon enfant,* his wife and daughters will take care of you, and will cook for you if you wish it, and next market-day he will bring you back to Argelés. You can stay a week here, and return this day fortnight with me to Bagnères.'

I thought the arrangenent good and agreed to it, and Madame sent her man to conduct me and my bag (which

I carried in my hand) to Canon's carriage, but scarcely had we reached the middle of the market-place, before a man came up and took it from me, crying ' *La voiture vous attend—Venez.*' My guide turned round and left me, so I thought it was all right.

' Are you Canon ? ' said I.

' No, not Canon, but I will take you to his carriage—it is there, *en face* of the Hôtel de France.'

' I knew that before,' said I, rather glumpily.

When we got to the hotel, Canon was not there, he had *not* sent my self-elected guide, and the *voiture* was not ready. I took my bag and the man wanted a *franc*. A franc for carrying a light bag (not a carpet bag, but one I had made myself) about thirty yards! I retained possession, telling him I wanted no porter, and should never have let him take it, if he had not said Canon had sent him for me. He threatened me with a *procès* and made a terrible noise, and the French gentlemen standing round the many *voitures* seemed to think it was very disreputable, and that as a lady I ought to pay the franc. I would not, on principle— I hate to be cheated, and the Hôtel de France could be seen from Madame Armiral's shop, just a few yards beyond the market-place, while he had only carried the bag *half* that small distance and that *unasked.* I offered him *six sous*, which he refused with disdain, saying majestically, ' *Je vous fais cadeau de mes services.*'

' Oh! very well,' said I, quietly putting them back into my purse, and taking my seat on a low walk by Canon's *voiture.* He waited, but seeing no signs of a franc or even half a franc, burst forth furiously :

' *Je vous ferai un procès—Je vous citerai devant le maire,*' &c., &c. ; ' *vous refusez de me payer après m'avoir employé,*' &c.

' I did *not* employ you,' said I. ' You took my bag out of my hand, saying Canon had sent you. I offered you *six sous*, more than enough for carrying a light bag across half the market-place, and you said, rather than take so little, you made me a present of your services.'

' Well, give me the six *sous* then.'

I gave them, glad to be rid of him, and he went off grumbling as if he was ill-used. Travellers should *never* let people seize their luggage in this way—that is, *if they can hinder them.* Canon came up at last, helped me and Keeper and the bag into a carriage belonging to him, and full of people returning from the market, and which one of his men was to drive, he himself *conducting* the other, as they have it in French, and we set off. It was a glorious evening, the light lay lovingly upon the blue mountains at the foot of the valley of Argelés, and touched the fading chestnut groves on the slopes at our right with gold.

We passed the church and village of St. Savin, perched upon a high cliff, from whence my companions told me there was a magnificent view, and that of Ste. Marie, a little farther on. Then a large handsome-looking house, whose high terrace overhung a wooded slope, formerly the property of a Marquis. A peasant had bought it, and eighty *journaux* of land for about eighteen hundred pounds; and now he and his family, though rich (he was stated to have above a thousand a year English money), lived like other peasants in the kitchen, and made the beautiful upper rooms into corn lofts and hay chambers. Even my French fellow-travellers agreed that ' *c'était bien dommage, car c'était une belle maison.*'

We passed through Pierrefitte, a cleaner-looking village than Argelés, from whence one road branches off to Luz and St. Sauveur. We took the other to the right, and began a steep ascent up a road such as I never saw. It was as smooth and level as any street in London, but blasted out of the lofty rock that towered, wall-like, above it, or built on solid masonry flanked by strong buttresses

F

that protected it from the incursions of the Gave in the ravine below. Onward we drove. A wall of grey precipitous rocks sometimes clothed with foliage, with here and there small cascades dashing like long white ribbons down their sides, and lovely little green fields, shaded by rees—fields one longed to walk in and to sit in—perched on the top of the crags, or lying between the rocks or at the base of the mountains on each side of us, and I gazed and gazed, and drank in large draughts of beauty and grandeur, until the shadows of evening deepened over the grey rocks—the green fields became no longer distinguishable, and the woods looked a sombre black, for there was no moon. There was something awful in that evening drive, when one could only just dimly see the white curves of the road, and the huge masses of mountain on either side, while the torrent roared hoarsely and wildly in the deep ravine below.

We had nearly reached the Col du Limaçon, when our driver lashed the spirited horses, and checked them at the same time; they swerved suddenly, and wheeled half round, the back of the carriage actually *touched* the low parapet wall that protected us from the precipice; there was but that low wall of some four feet between us, and a fearful death. I prayed mentally to God to bring us safe to our journey's end, and my gentlemen fellow-travellers coolly remarked—'Our driver has had a cup too much.' He still flogged and curbed the horses, and they grew momentarily more unmanageable.

'We shall be thrown down the precipice,' said I.

'Not so, I hope,' said a French priest; 'but if Mademoiselle is afraid, she had better get out and walk up the Col—there is a footpath which is shorter than the road.'

I gladly assented, got out, and walked up it. At the top of the Col they took me into the carriage again, but my heart beat all the rest of the way. I expected our tipsy driver would upset us. We stopped at last at a house on the slope of the steep hill, the driver got out to ' get a light,' he said; he did not return directly, and the horses set off. Now it was the gentlemen's turn to be alarmed— they vociferated and scolded—the priest quietly got out of the carriage, seized the reins which had fallen with a firm hand, and stopped the horses.

' Thank God,' said I.

' *Que diable faites-vous ici?* ' said a hearty voice, as another carriage came up behind us.

' The driver is drunk,' said the gentlemen.

' We shall certainly be upset,' cried I.

' *Oh! que non,*' said Canon, cheerfully. ' *Nous sommes à Cauterets.*'

We dismounted—each went their way, and Canon escorted Keeper and I *up* a short steep street ending in a long flight of steps, at the top of which a woman with a candle in her hand met us, and lighted us the rest of the way to the house. It was Madame Canon. A few minutes afterwards I was in possession of a large room with two beds in it. Sheets were put on one of them—towels and water placed on a table—Keeper laid down in a corner quite tired out with his journey, and I, equally tired, after having thanked God for preserving us from all accidents, undressed and went to bed.

CHAPTER VI.

Of course, the first thing I did on arising, was to look out of my window. The view was rather cheerless, for the day was foggy; Canon's house was in a very narrow street, with a row of poor-looking dwellings on the opposite side the way, and beyond I caught sight of a high mountain. I dressed, had some *café au lait*, and sallied out. Cauterets is built on the side of a mountain, which rises so suddenly and precipitously, as it were overhanging a part of the town, that one cannot help feeling rather nervously afraid lest it should fall down, and crush one to death. I passed through the small town. What a contrast to dirty Argelés, are those lofty white stuccoed handsome houses with their gilt and bronzed balconies! Many of their doors and balconies are painted a kind of bronzed pale-green, which I never saw used in house decorations before, but which has a very good effect. It is a gay, clean-looking, pleasant little town, whose houses, with their wide open lofty windows, spotless muslin curtains, and ever-open doors, seem to say to the passing traveller, 'Come and lodge here. You will find yourself comfortable.' Even the back streets, like that in which Canon's house stands, have a more respectable appearance than the market-place of Argelés.

I found the steps I had gone up the night before led to the principal bath-house, which is large and handsome, and contains comfortable bathing-rooms. But there are many different springs at Cauterets, some in the town, some nearly two miles beyond it, as La Raillière and the Petit St. Sauveur. The waters of Cauterets are very powerful, and should not be taken without good advice. Every year some one or other hastens their death by incautiously using them. Just before I went there a young man who was consumptive took them ; they brought on spitting of blood, and he died within a fortnight ; yet they are said to be good for consumption, and the doctors frequently order them for that complaint.

It was not fine enough for climbing mountains. Madame Canon advised a walk to La Raillière, and directed me thither. Passing from the flight of steps before the Thermes, what is grandiloquently called the market-place, but is merely a little space of ground, rather wider than usual there, between two rows of houses, one turns to the left, up what I consider the main street, for the best houses are there, and follows the road till it reaches the bridge. No fear of losing your way. On either side rise steep, black, sombre-looking mountains, whose sides are covered with loose rough stones of all forms and dimensions. Stones, stones, nothing but stones, their hues varied by lichens, meet the eye in walking up the narrow valley by the side of the Gave, which chafes as if it were angry at being unable to force a passage through the huge massy rocks that confine it as in a prison. Yet desolate, bare, and treeless as the view is, it had a wild picturesque grandeur of its own, that pleased me. I thought as I sat and rested on one of the large boulders, that were I an artist, I could make a grand picture of this gloomy valley. When, for instance, those sharp peaks are lit up by the glow of sunset, and the rocky, stony valley is flooded with the purple shades of approaching night, or seen as now in a grey October morning, with masses of dense vapour curling upwards, and veiling parts of the hills, while the white foam of the river gives the necessary contrast and relief to the sombre granite rocks.

La Raillière seems the favourite bath, for the few people still left at Cauterets were all going there, or returning homewards, or drinking the waters. I peeped into the baths, which seemed just like all other foreign baths in their arrangements. I never taste mineral waters, and cannot imagine why travellers seem to think it their bounden duty to taste every nasty spring they come to, any more than they would taste every bitter drug in every apothecary's shop they went into. *Life has bitters enough.* I like something sweet. I pursued my walk by the side of the torrent, curious to see if my ignorance could discover 'where the granite and the slate formation met,' as 'there,' a geologist told me, 'the thermal springs always rise.' At the end, as it were, of the valley, a white stream foams down from the mountain on the left, crosses it, and falls into the Gave on the other side. These waters are so strongly impregnated with sulphur, that the very air is, as it were, tainted. I turned quite sick from the mere smell, and continued so most of the day; and the same effect was produced, but in a less degree, every time I walked to La Raillière. Two priests were walking up the ravine between the hills at the end of the valley, and I longed to walk up that steep path beside the roaring, tumbling, foaming water, too, especially as the disagreeable odour from the water ceased after one had passed the Bains du Petit St. Sauveur, but alas, the ancle I had sprained at Bordeaux, gave me notice that climbing up rocks whose sides were strewn with steep stones did not suit it, and I returned home.

I had learned a lesson by living at Bordeaux with Pauline, and I inquired whether I could not have a *potage* and a small *plat* or dish of meat fetched from a decent-looking second-rate hotel near Canon's. The master of it

agreed to supply me with a *soupe* and a *plat* for fifteen
sous, about eightpence a day, if Canon's daughter would
fetch them and take back the empty plates, and I found
it far more economical and better than attempting to cater
for myself. They sent me daily a large basin of soup and
a *plat* or dish of good wholesome well-dressed meat, quite
enough both for Keeper and myself. The *plat* was evidently
the remains of the *table d'hôte;* once, for instance, I had the
leg of a duck, two necks and part of the wing and breast
of a fowl. What did that signify? it was not off people's
plates, and it was far more comfortable than eating day
after day the same dry, disgusting piece of meat; ill-cooked
on Monday to begin with, cold on Tuesday, warmed up
Wednesday and Thursday, till in utter despair at seeing
the dried-up, greasy, tasteless food, will last yet another
day, I give it to Keeper. What kind of a dinner can
a single woman who is poor have cooked for herself?
Steaks and chops are far dearer than a joint, and one gets
tired to death of them. The French who are *en garni*
always dine at a *table d'hôte*, or have their dinner from an
hotel, but the masters of hotels do not like the English
to know the prices at which they serve their French
customers.

Mademoiselle D'Orville advised me to have my dinner
sent to me while I was at Bagnères, as the servants of the
house I lodged in would not cook for anyone, and recommended the Hôtel du Soleil, from whence she and her
mother had theirs. But the Sun would not help to vivify
me. They would not serve me under three francs a day,
more than I could afford to spend for dinner and lodgings
too. Wherever the English congregate, everything grows
dear *to them.* Those who have money at command are
always comparing French prices, and English prices, *and
will overpay.* They do not consider the serious injury they
are doing their poorer countryfolks who emigrate for

cheapness, and who will ever after be charged at the same rate their richer countryman or woman has *voluntarily paid*. In the prices of apartments, the hire of carriages, horses, and guides, and even of the very fruit in the market, there are two prices, one *pour les Anglais*, another for the natives. This foolish ostentation of the rich English sadly cramps and mars the comforts and enjoyments of the poor, and it is money thrown away, for it wins them no gratitude; their generosity is all set down to the English whim of appearing *plus grand que les autres*, or to their being so rich, that they really do not know what to do with their money.

I went one day to the Grange de la Reine Hortense, from whence there is a beautiful view down the valley. A boy there and his mother were preparing to carry two loads of fagots on their backs down the steep hill, very hard work, for which they are very badly paid, a large load of wood carried from the mountain to a house in the town costing only thirty sous, wood included. I offered the lad ten sous, the French equivalent for sixpence, to show me the way to the top of the hill, mountain it could hardly be called. An English boy would have accepted it gleefully, not so the French one. My request had immediately elevated him in his mother's eyes and his own to the rank of a guide.

'*Dix sous pour aller au sommet de la montagne !*' exclaimed both, in a tone of injury; '*ça ne vaut pas la peine pour si peu.*'

'*C'est un travail moins fatigant que de porter cela à la ville, et peut-être sans le vendre ;*' said I, '*mais ce m'est bien égal, je connais la route.*'

It was even so, Canon had told me I might safely walk to the top; so I set off alone. The path was clearly marked; and when I reached a *sapin* wood, I found a whole party of men busily engaged cutting through rocks, levelling hollows, and cutting down trees, to make as they told me a bridle-road to the summit against next season.

'Are you not afraid to go about alone?' said they.

'Afraid—what in France! I have travelled all through the middle of France, and walked about everywhere with no companion but a dog, and I never yet found a Frenchman uncivil to me. They have always been courteous and kind.'

'But you had better have a guide; you may lose your way, else.'

'I will guide you,' said a bright-eyed lad of sixteen.

'I am afraid you would ask too much. I can only afford to give ten sous.'

'*Trois francs, j'irai avec vous pour trois francs,*' said he, insinuatingly.

'Ten *sous,*' said I, in the most uncompromising manner. 'I know the road already. Canon has told it me. You know Canon? I live at his house.' (I thought Canon's well-known name might be a protection to me.) 'I am not rich, and I cannot afford more.'

'Not rich!' said the boy, unbelievingly. 'You are English, you are *dame, et vous portez chapeau!*'

'It is my *costume,*' said I; 'everybody in England, even the beggars, wear *chapeaux.* So they do in Switzerland, and even in many parts of France; a *chapeau* is no sign of wealth.'

'*C'est vrai,*' said one of the men, '*les pauvres les portent à Paris; j'y ai été.*'

'*Vous m'excuserez, mademoiselle,*' said the youth, with the courtesy of a gentleman. '*C'était mon ignorance. Je n'ai jamais quitté ce pays-ci.*'

I went on alone, and the workmen said nothing uncivil to me, though they were clearly annoyed at not getting three francs out of *l'Anglaise.* When I was about half-way up the mountain, a mist came on. It rose from below, and as the height seemed clear, I thought it best to go on; but it increased rapidly in density, the grey vapour shut out not only the valley, but the sapin wood I had just passed, like a wall. I dared not turn back, and I could only dimly see for about a yard before me. I just managed to keep the track, and that was all. Now I began to feel seriously alarmed. I felt glad the peasant boy from the Grange de la Reine Hortense had not accompanied me— glad that I had left my little dog at home, lest he should run the sheep. I recalled all the stories I had ever heard or read of people lost in the mist, and I felt glad that if such was to be my fate, I should die alone. I knelt down on the grey rock, and besought the Almighty to preserve me. A feeling that I was as safe there, under His protection, as anywhere else, came over me, and rising, I walked steadily on. I saw a little wild pink among the grass at my feet, it looked like an eye watching over me. I gathered it, and have it now. Every now and then the dense mass of mist moved a little, and seemed lighter, and then grew darker than ever, and again and again my heart failed, and I said to myself, ' I shall die here;' and each time I felt this terrible dread, I came upon some solitary flower—another pink, or a meadow crocus—and absurd as it may sound, they seemed to me like living eyes, looking upon me to cheer me, and assure me that the God who preserved them from the browsing sheep and the devastations of insects, and blight and storm, to blossom there so far apart on the solitary mountain, would protect and watch over me ; and no words can tell the sustaining power their beauty shed upon my heart. At last I could go no farther. The mist was so dense I could only dimly see my own hand. It closed me in on every side like a wall, and I sat down fearing I might unknowingly walk to the edge of some precipice and tumble down. I sat there about ten minutes, not daring to move, and praying the Almighty to preserve me. Then the heavy mass of vapour began to move. It grew a little lighter for a brief moment or two, the mist cleared a little above and below me, and I saw above me something like four white pillars, which I concluded was the Chalet I knew to be on the top of the mountain; below me was a sheer descent. I was sitting upon the very edge of the precipice.

'Thank God for the light!' said I, with a full heart; and then I turned carefully round, and *crawled* on hands and knees up to the top of the little cone above the ledge on which I was sitting. I got to the white pillars—they were the legs of a rough deal table, before the front of the Chalet. First I thanked God for having brought me safe through the fog; and then finding the Chalet door locked, and the ground wet and cold, I lay down on the table to rest, and again the dark, grey mist closed in, so that I could not even see the door of the Chalet, though it was not more than a yard from me; then even the dim outlines of the Chalet itself faded. I could see nothing but the thick, grey vapour which invested me like a shroud. I should think I lay there twenty minutes; but I had no watch, and could not have seen the time had I possessed one, and then the darkness grew lighter. I could see the outline of the Chalet, then I saw it distinctly, then all the platform on which it stood, and a rock behind, and I got up and looked about me. The door of the stable that adjoined the Chatlet was unfastened, and I opened it and went in. The clay floor was a mass of wet mud from the trampling of sheep, and there was not even a truss of hay, or an empty bucket that I could turn down to sit upon. The prospect of passing the night there was not pleasant. There was a wheelbarrow wedged into an empty pig-sty, and I began seriously to consider the feasibility of getting it out, that I might have something better than wet mud to sit upon if I had to stay up there all night. But the mist suddenly rolled off for a moment, and I went to the edge of the platform and looked down. I could see trees and fields, and silver streams glistening in the green valley below, and then it rolled together again an opaque grey wall.

It was rather tantalizing, for Canon had told me I should have a magnificent view into the valley below, from the Col; but I was too thankful to God for having preserved me from falling down the steep, rocky precipice, and being dashed to pieces, to be inclined to grumble; and when at intervals the dense grey vapours rolled off for a minute, there was something singularly beautiful in the gleams of light upon the green hill sides and meadows. It was like a glimpse into Eden, and then the clouds came together again, and veiled it with a vapoury curtain from my sight. I could only see for a yard or two around me, and durst not yet attempt to descend. I amused myself by botanizing on the rock behind the Chalet. I was surprised to find meadow saffron growing so high. A little lady's bedstraw, thyme, and the small, yellow creeping potentilla, were the only other plants I found besides grass. The mist did not grow denser, but if anything, a little lighter; but I could still only see about a yard around me. So I knelt down again, committed myself to the care of God, and then set off to try and find my way down to Cauterets. It was a curious feeling I had as I walked slowly on; it seemed as if *I myself* had been a living lantern, for I could only see about a yard, or two yards at most, all round myself; but beyond that circle, all was grey mist. When I had gone a few yards—perhaps thirty—I turned to look at the little platform and the Chalet upon it; neither was visible, nor could I see anything of the hill side before me, or the mountains that I knew rose beyond the valley of Cauterets. I felt as if my guardian angel hovered above my head, and shed a radiance upon me, and perhaps he did. For a small circle—of perhaps, at most, four yards in diameter, but I should say three, everything was faintly but plainly visible in a kind of moonlight—I could see the blades of grass, the tiniest moss at my feet, and notice every shrub and plant I passed; beyond that circle all was like a dense grey smoke.

I noticed in descending—and gathered—seeds of the *Rose des Alpes*, the first time I had ever seen the rhododendron growing in its native wildness. When I got nearly half way down, the mists began to look thinner and fleecier; I could see the tall dark *sapins* directly through them, and by the time I reached the wood, it had cleared away entirely, the fog only covering the upper part of the mountain. As I passed through the wood, the labourers, who were collecting their tools previous to leaving work, hailed me—

'*Vous avez eu du brouillard;* were you not frightened all alone up there?'

'Rather; but I trusted in God, who always protects those who trust in Him; I prayed to Him to bring me down safe, and you see He has done so.'

'*C'est vrai,*' said one of them, crossing himself devoutly. '*Il faut toujours se fier à Dieu.*'

'*Cependant,*' said another, 'you must have been frightened if the fog had not lessened? And who knew where you were?'

'Canon,' said I, stoutly, 'for it was he who told me I could go up safely alone, as there was a good path to the top, and if I had not returned by dinner-time, he would have got guides and sought me.'

I am afraid this was a stretch of my imagination. Canon had advised me to take this walk on account of the beautiful view from the Col; but did not know I had done so to-day. My interlocutor was silent a moment, and resumed—

'*Il est bon enfant, Canon.*'

'*Oui, très bon enfant,*' said I; 'but the evening falls. I shall be late for dinner, and frighten them all—*bon soir.*'

'*Bon soir, madame,*' cried he.

'*Bon soir, madame,*' cried the whole twenty heartily.

If they had been English navvies, they would probably have cheered me for finding my way so well down in the mist. There is nothing bodies of men respect so much, as a little pluck. I was once living alone, with only a maid servant, in a semi-detached house, the other half of which was unlet, the backs of both looking on open fields, while above sixty navvies were employed in constructing huge drains along the road in front of my house, for nearly five months. I always spoke in a friendly, open manner to them, as I passed out of my garden, and never showed the least fear of them. Not only they never showed me the slightest rudeness, but they were even thoughtfully courteous to me, placed planks at my gate, when their work and the rains made a large puddle there; and when I returned home one evening in the dusk, after drinking tea with a friend, stumbled over one of their heaps of earth, and fell, two or three of them ran to me, picked me up, hoped I was not hurt, and lighted me to my own gate with their lanterns, lest I should fall again. I never gave them a farthing—not because I should not have gladly done so, but because at that time I was in great pecuniary distress and had not the means. Once they asked me for some beer. I answered, 'I have not a drop of beer in the house, my men, and you are more than sixty in number, and I am very poor, how can I give drink to more than sixty men? If I were well off, I would gladly give you all a glass.'

'Thank you for that,' they replied, 'it's true, we *are a lot*; and I wish you were well off.'

So much for the good feeling and character of *the roughs.*

both in France and England.* Rough oak has often a closer, finer grain, than common wood covered with French polish.

When I reached the Grange de la Reine, the mother and son were still dawdling about the premises.

'*Bon soir*,' said I; 'I have been to the top of the Col.'*

'And you found your way alone?' answered she, discontentedly, and scowling as if she wished I had *not*.'

'Yes! I found my way alone; Canon had told it me, I got to the *chalet*, but it was locked. I sat down upon the table in front of it, and carved my name, Mary Eyre, upon it; *bon soir*.'

As I descended the hill—quite clear towards the base from all fog, I heard steps clattering behind me. It was the whole army of roughs, each with a huge load of wood upon his back, that I think none of our sturdy Yorkshire labourers could have lifted, and all running down the steep, abrupt hill in their *sabots*, as nimbly as if they had not done a hand's turn of work that day. So much for habit. Since I have been at Cauterets, and seen the enormous loads of wood, women and children carry up and down these steep slippery hill sides, I begin to believe there may be truth in the story of the Persian Sultana, who beginning by carrying a young calf up a ladder daily was found by her lord and master (who had discarded her for replying dryly, 'Practice makes perfect,' when he boasted of his skill in the chase) carrying a full-grown cow up it. 'Good-night,' said each, as he passed me swiftly.

* Since this was written one of the navvies employed in making a tunnel for the Atmospheric Parcels Delivery Company pelted me with heavy brickbats because a street urchin had mischievously set his dog to fight mine, and a battle ensued between them—his companions looking quietly on all the while. If one of these half-bricks had hit my head and killed me, I presume they would *then* have fetched a shutter to carry my dead body on to the police station. I could not help telling the man who pelted me so savagely, it was a cowardly thing to strike a woman who had not done anything to provoke him, to which he replied, 'He did not care if he killed me and my dog too.'

They were all out of sight but one when I reached a piece of wild stony ground, watered by a little stream betwixt the mountain, and that on whose base Cauterets stands.

Some women who had been standing in the brook there, washing linen as I passed in the morning, were standing there still, bare-legged and miserable-looking, washing. Theirs too, is a hard life. It seems astonishing to me, that modern conveniences should have been brought to bear so little upon the habits of the Pyreneans, and indeed of the French peasants generally; but they set themselves against any innovation, and would rather endure any amount of discomfort and fatigue, than do differently to what their grandfathers and grandmothers did; and it is my firm belief, they will never wash their kitchen floors, keep the pigs and fowls out of their houses, or wash anywhere except *au ruisseau*, as Nausicaa did, till the Millennium. It was dark when I reached Cauterets, tired and hungry.

CHAPTER VII.

JOVE sometimes nods, and Murray is not always to be relied upon. He says 'several formal avenues and alleys on the outskirts of the town, by the side of the road to Pierrefitte and the Parc, on the margin of the Gave, satisfy the wants of French visitors as promenades, but must appear wearisome to English; indeed, except in the society of friends, or with the inducement of illness to make one tarry, the attractions at Cauterets are few.' Jove was certainly not only nodding, but dreaming when he thus wrote. Where did he find those formal avenues and alleys on the road to Pierrefitte? There is but *one* road to Pierrefitte, the magnificent one by which I came, and certainly no alleys or avenues are near there. I often walked down that road to admire its grandeur, and the wild beauty of the ravine through which it passes. Once I walked as far as the Col du Limaçon. I met two girls on asses, who begged importunately, indeed, as a rule, all the children, and most of the women, in the Pyrenees beg. '*Donnez-moi un petit sou,*' is the certain salutation whenever you pass a group of people or meet a solitary wayfarer. They seem to think travellers, *les Anglais* especially, are walking money-bags come to the Pyrenees to thin themselves, and obtain beautiful figures, by scattering showers of gold, silver, and sous, on everybody they meet with. These girls were well-dressed for their rank in life, mounted on good donkeys, and yet not ashamed to beg. Next I met a poor woman holding a handful of

G

peeled osiers, got into a talk with her, and finally accompanied her to cut fresh ones. She dared not take any in the fields which belonged to private owners, but thought it no harm to take them from Government lands, on the waste grounds bordering parts of the Gave. She asked if I was married.

'No, I was not.'

'*Ah ! Madame ! vous êtes bien heureuse d'être seule.*'

I told her I did not find solitude so agreeable. We talked of the condition of women in the South of France. She said they were very miserable—worked to death in the fields—*les hommes le voulaient*, and if they did not work they were *abattus de coups de bâton*. Men never thought women worked enough. Her husband did not drink, but scolded her for ever, work as hard as she could ; and she always worked hard—so hard. Both husband and wife were basket-makers, she had taught him the trade. She earned a franc a day.

'I wish I could earn as much,' quoth I.

She stared. It is so hard to convince any of the labouring classes, that a lady can be poor as well as themselves ; and yet a poor gentlewoman is the poorest of all poor. She is fit for so few things. She cannot dig, to beg she is ashamed, and it is so difficult, not to say *impossible*, to procure remunerative employment. There is but the dreary resource of teaching—and, alas! that profession is so overstocked that few obtain more than a bare pittance, hardly enough to buy clothes—nothing out of which they can save for a rainy day. I know one case in which a countess is not ashamed to give a highly accomplished woman twenty pounds a year, less probably than her maid's gains, who has I should suppose the usual wages, which are twenty pounds a year and all her mistress's cast-off clothes, often worth from thirty to fifty pounds a year, if her lady goes much into society, and attends Court. In these days parents had better bring up their children to be cooks, than governesses.

To return to my basket-maker. The French need not, as they often do, reproach the English with beating their wives. This is the second French wife who has told me how *customary* wife-beating is in France; the basket-woman did not *say* her husband beat her, but it was clear he did. Poor woman! She looked hollow-eyed, and sad enough; I never saw anyone who seemed more utterly broken down. 'She had lived,' she said, 'twelve years as *bonne* with an English family at Pau,' and she sighed heavily, and paused as if looking back. Those were her *beaux jours*. Then she married, and *he* was ten years younger than she was.

'Ah!' said I, 'there it is. It should have been *dix ans de l'autre côté.*'

I went with her through some of the loveliest fields I ever remember to have seen. The turf was as fine as that of any gentleman's lawn, and of the most vivid emerald green. Nothing, indeed, can exceed the beauty of the pasture here. Besides the sparkling Gave, whose clear waters rippled over stones, and here and there eddied round the large boulders in jets of white foam, innumerable little runnels of clearest water ran sparkling and singing, silvery bright, through the thick grass, which was starred over with the brightest hued lilac autumnal crocuses I ever saw. Their deep vermilion tinted orange stamens were longer than I ever remember seeing them before, in the half-blown flowers, they often rose an inch above the cups, forming a rich and beautiful contrast with their deep glowing lilac hue. The flowers of foreign countries are often the same kinds that grow plentifully in England, but their hue and manner of growth are rarely the same. In Germany, I noticed that many were of a paler hue, and more straggling and luxurious growth.

Here, in France, their colours are generally more vivid and intense, and they are scarcely ever infested in either country by insects, which I attribute to the want of the high, close hedges, which in England intercept the free current of air, and I am convinced cause the plagues of insects that have of late years been so common.

'Nothing to attract anyone in Cauterets!' I shall remember that field full of graceful self-sown ash trees, mostly of three or four stems rising from one root; the fine velvety green turf studded with lilac crocuses, the silver clear streamlets that ran nearly round it, making it almost an island, the murmuring Gave flowing in its rocky bed between green meadows fringed with trees, and dotted here and there with white cottages that looked *at a distance* the perfection of rural cleanliness and felicity, the small fawn-coloured deer-like cattle on the slopes, that gazed at me with their beautiful large soft-brown eyes, the tinkle of their bells as they moved along, and the high, rugged, peaked mountains that framed in the picture, to my dying day. Well may Shelley say:—

> 'A thing of beauty is a joy for ever.'

To descend to prosaics. The female sex seems generally over-worked and ill-treated in the Pyrenees. Not only the poor women work in the fields, but the poor cows work also. Beside what we consider cows' duties in England—namely, to rear calves and give plenty of good milk—they have in France to plough all the fields, draw all the carts, and even terribly heavy loads of timber, up and down those break-neck, stony, ill-made mountain roads, for the good roads are confined to *les grandes routes*, and those leading from farm to farm are horrible. The Pyrenean peasant-farmer does not, like the Jewish ones of old, plough or draw with two yoke of oxen, but with two poor cows. They must also suffer dreadfully sometimes,

from the filthy farm-yards and stables they repose in after
their work is done. One sees them with their haunches
covered with dry cow-dung, clotting the hair together, and
of course putting them to torture at every step they take.
It is painful to contrast these poor animals, with their sore
skins, and the few better-kept ones, one now and then
meets, covered with good clothes to protect them from the
flies, a white, or gay-coloured, dyed lamb-skin under the
yoke to keep it from pressing on the flesh, and their fawn-
coloured coats all sleek, and bright, and shining. I delight in the cows of this country ; and one of my wishes
is, that I could but have a home of my own, and two or
three of these pretty, gentle, intelligent animals. At
home I am afraid of cattle, for they are often wild and
fierce. Here, they seem always tractable; and the most
they ever do, is sometimes to stand and gaze at Keeper,
pointing their long, curved horns at him, and sometimes
even threatening him with them, when his war-dance and
outrageous barking is too insulting for cow patience to
endure longer. Then the peasant brandishes his cudgel—
'Ce n'est rien, ils ne sont pas méchants—Va donc.' Some
sounds follow, which I do not understand, but the cows
evidently do; and the herd march on, calm and dignified.
There appear to be several breeds, one which seems to
have a cross of the buffalo I admire extremely. When
one does see oxen, they are commonly of this race. They
are larger, and squarer built than the pure fawn-coloured ;
locks of shaggy black or dark mouse-coloured hair fall
over their foreheads, and a stripe of dark hair goes from
the neck nearly to the haunches, and blends gradually
into the dun-grey or pale-fawn of the under parts. They
are very handsome creatures.

The milk these cattle give is deliciously rich, and throws
up quantities of yellow cream ; and the butter would be
excellent if the peasant-women understood how to strain

the milk, and make it properly, and, above all, if they
pressed out the buttermilk, instead of leaving it in to
make the butter weigh heavier in the market, and turn
sour when bought. Pyrenean butter is often cheesy and
curdy, and has a bitter, rancid flavour, like the butter
made from turnip-fed cows at home. A dairy requires
cleanliness above all things, and it is only a wonder to me
these dirty Pyrenean women ever make eatable butter at
all. Now and then one gets excellent in the market.
The new milk is brought down from the mountain farms
in bottles, each of which holds about a quart. I have
a bottle a day, for which I pay four sous, not quite twopence.

When we got to a large marshy piece of waste ground,
full of a very small-stemmed, narrow-leaved willow, not so
common as most other kinds in England—the *Salix rubra*
—I left the unfortunate basket-weaver to cut twigs, and
pursued my walk alone, botanizing as I went. The stone
walls were covered with a kind of creeping sorrel I do not
remember to have seen in England. Instead of the leaves
being lanceolate, as is usual, they were shaped rather like a
horse-shoe, and sometimes this horse-shoe extended, as it
were, into a wing at each side of the foot-stalk. Near the
Col du Limaçon I found two Antirrhinums—one small,
with a grey, rather woolly leaf, which grew plentifully also
on the old walls near Cauterets ; another very lovely one,
resembling a dwarfed plant of our common garden kind,*
but with rather smaller leaves and flowers, the latter of a
cream-coloured white, with a purple streak on the lower
lip, and the whole of the plant only half a foot high. I
gathered also the common, small, dark-blue autumnal

* *Antirrhinum semper virens.* I could not find out the name of the other,
as I had no books on botany with me nor means for drying plants.

scabious—the larger blue one, the beautiful sweet-scented, fringed pink, eye-bright, saponaria, and ling.

I took another lovely walk one morning. I passed through what is called the market-place, crossed the bridge, and walked to the Mamelon Vert, the fashionable promenade of Cauterets, I am informed. The Mamelon Vert is merely a remarkably smooth, round green hill, on which one or two *cafés* are built, with a road winding below it commanding a pretty view of the clean, white, cheerful-looking town of Cauterets, and the overhanging mountain which threatens momentarily to destroy it—the Gave flowing through green, well-wooded meadows, and the wild mountain pass beyond. As I returned, I extended my walk in the opposite direction, instead of turning down towards the bridge, and came to a very smart stable of yellow and red brick, in which some cows were peacefully breakfasting, and on the walls of which was a placard, with this announcement, '*Appartement à louer.*' I was curious to know what sort of an *appartement* was over a stable; so I boldly walked round to what seemed a cottage a little behind it. There I only found three or four small children, who did not understand what I wanted, but told me ' *Papa est là,*' pointing to a garden on the slope of the hill; upon which I opened the gate indicated, and went in. It was full of purple, and grey, and white petunias, dahlias, roses, and all sorts of flowers, as thick as they could grow; and intermixed were pots of oleanders, Cape jessamine, and orange-trees; and the whole air was so perfumed with mignonette and heliotrope that I really thought I should like to lodge over the stable for a while, if I might walk and sit at will in this pretty garden. At the farther end was a fantastic sort of cottage or *chalet*—partly built in the Swiss style, with striped projecting blinds curving like the sails of a vessel from the windows down to the ground. Walking past, I saw and hailed the gardener, who told me ' the cottage, garden, and stable belonged to a Russian princess, whose name I forget. She lived herself in the cottage, but was not there now. The rooms over the stable were, as the *affiche* set forth, to be let.'

' And the cottage ?'

' The princess did not let that, and it was not allowed to be seen.'

' Not now she was absent ? '

' No.'

This was disappointing. I should like to have known in what style Russian princesses lived, 'in cottages of gentility.' I peeped in at the window, however, under the striped awning, and saw a very pretty fanciful little drawing-room, furnished much as any English lady of fortune's drawing-room is furnished, and full of china and alabaster figures, and other artistic toys. The gardener said he would show me the lodgings—' they were very pleasant—communicated with the garden—and I might even sit in the little bit of grounds under the windows and breathe the scent of the flowers, but not walk farther, as that would annoy *Madame la princesse*.'

I went up some stairs at the back of the stable, and through three rooms, which were on a level with, and two of which opened upon, the garden. They were very plainly—almost poorly furnished, but looked clean and gay from the white and green paint which decorated them.

' My wife would wait upon Madame ; she is an excellent cook, and Madame would find herself *très bien* here, *et puis les fleurs*,' said the gardener insinuatingly.

' And the price ? '

' Oh, not much ! ' said his wife, who just then came up in answer to her husband's repeated calls.

' Not much ! ' said the gardener, with the air of a man resolved to make a sacrifice.

'But *how much?*' said I.

'Oh! very little indeed—very moderate—only eight francs a-day for the *appartement*, as Madame is *seule* — Madame *est seule?*' interrogatively.

'Yes, I am alone.'

'*Bien*, that would just do—it would not be much, as Madame sees, only eight francs a-day for three rooms—such pleasant rooms—looking into a garden full of roses and heliotropes—and the services of my wife, who is a most capital cook, and whom Madame would pay as her *bonne*; oh, Madame would be well served—she would be *contente.*'

'Eight francs a-day—that makes nearly three thousand francs a-year, without attendance or food?'

'Just so, madame.'

'One could *buy* a house for that sum in two or three years' time,' said I; 'and, moreover, the season is quite passed—I know that an *appartement* sometimes fetches eight francs a-day in the height of the season; but now people are glad to let on any terms.'

'That is the price, however; *Madame la princesse* never lets them for less.'

'It is a price that does not suit my pocket.'

'What then would Madame give?'

'The price Madame gave for her lodgings was so small compared to that they had asked for these, that it was no use thinking about them.'

'What did you come to trouble us for then, if you did not want them?' said both, aggressively.

'What business had you to give me the trouble of coming out of the garden?'

'And me, of coming running myself out of breath—up stairs?' &c., &c., &c.

To all this volley of abuse, I made no reply, but walked as quickly away as I could; but they were wrong. I did not ask to look at these lodgings from pure curiosity. Cauterets pleases me ; but though Canon's family are honest, kind, and civil, their unwashed, dirty floors annoy me, and if I could have got these rooms for the same price, I should probably have wintered here ; but my small means will not allow me to give eight francs a-day, even for rooms that look upon a garden, and for the honour of having a princess for my landlady.

As I strolled on beyond the princess's house, I thought I should like to walk through a wood I saw on the slope of the hill behind. Some peasant women who came up, told me there was a very pretty view from the top of the hill, and that the princess had had alleys cut all through the wood in various directions. I followed the path they pointed out, and came to an open bare hill side, on the edge of which a peasant boy sat watching a goat, which was feeding beside him, and a flock of sheep, that were grazing in the ravine between this mountain and the opposite one. I saw a narrow path running along its side, and he told me it led to a pretty waterfall ; I should have liked very much to follow it, but Keeper first began teasing the goat, which butted at, and rather frightened, him, and being driven off from her, next ran after the sheep in the ravine. The shepherd boy seemed to think it capital fun, and when I called him back again, encouraged the goat to butt at Keeper, and Keeper to worry the goat, in spite of all I could say ; and seeing the animal was in one of his naughty fits, I thought it best to go homewards. So I rose from the crag where I had been resting, and retraced my steps. This gorge or ravine between the hills is called the valley of Cambasque.

I went a little farther down homewards, and then again sat down to rest, and to survey the country. What a landscape for a painter ! In the foreground, a winding alley sloping gently down the richly-wooded hill, here and there

on the ground among the trees and shrubs on the left of
the path, huge, mossy boulders, placed by Nature, as if on
purpose for her visitors to sit down and rest upon them. On
the slope beyond them rise two graceful twin beech trees,
and nearer to me one or two other smaller ones tower
above the copsewood. On the right hand, the upland is
densely covered with young beech and hazel; here and
there, two or three stand out clear and distinct from the
rest, and lower down they close the wood in with a long
line of graceful fringe, their golden brown hue relieved
occasionally by a dark fir-tree. Behind rises the mountain, indigo grey, cold, bleak, and stern, that frowns above
Cauterets, patches of black *sapins* clothe its sides here and
there—a white fleecy cloud rests upon one part—the farthest mountain peak rises pyramidal and clear—and beyond all, a line of browner mountain, which I know to be
in reality the loftiest of the range, because already here
and there white with snow, close in the view.

CHAPTER VIII.

CAUTERETS TO ST. SAUVEUR.

An English party were going to the *Luz de Gaube*. Canon thought it would be possible to arrange that I should go with them, but, not unnaturally, they did not relish the idea of being joined in their excursion by an unknown stranger. I was rather disappointed. To console me, Canon said, "Mademoiselle, I am going to take my children, on Sunday, to St. Sauveur, a treat I have long promised them. It will cost you nothing but your dinner, if you will go with us." Of course, "I *accepted*," as the French say, resolving in my own mind I would repay Canon in some other way. Sunday proved fine, and we set off. Our carriage was a large coach, like the old-fashioned English family coaches which were so convenient for ladies going to balls in wide ball-dresses, but which unluckily went out of fashion before crinoline hoops so unfortunately revived. The children were two young girls about nineteen or twenty, and two young men, probably their admirers. Canon was to drive, and I requested to share the box with him, that I might see the country better, and not interfere with the enjoyment of the others.

We drove down the magnificent road by which I had come to Cauterets, turning off at the bottom of the pass, through Pierrefitte, instead of taking the road to Argelés. From this point the scenery was all new to me. I want words to describe it, for how can words paint the effects of light and shade upon the projecting or retiring crags; the wild flowers streaming fantastically out from some rocky

pinnacle in one place; the tree that sprang so boldly out
of a fissure in another; the white foaming cascades that
drooped down the granite rocks like snow-wreaths; the
various tints of the lichens in some places; the weather
stains and the deep red from the iron it contained, that
coloured other parts of the immense wall of rock that rose
almost perpendicularly to the sky, and out of which this
grand road was blasted on the left hand, while on the right
sloped emerald green fields, with grey rocks jutting up
here and there through the grass, and white cottages and
green trees peering out among and above them; the
snowy-wreathed cascades foaming down the hill sides to the
Gave, and the mountains rising so grandly beyond? By-
and-by the valley opened and widened, the Gave grew
more of a stream, and, instead of leaping, and murmuring,
and foaming through rocks that sometimes nearly touched
each other, flowed a clear, beautiful river, through rich
meadows on the *left hand*, instead of on the *right*. We
passed two or three villages, one with its grey church
perched upon a hill to the left; above the stream and
before us was a small white town, at the foot of a hill,
crested by an old grey ruined castle.

This was the town and castle of Luz; behind it rises a
lofty mountain, the *Pic de Bergous*. The flat valley
below was traversed by long alleys of poplars, and upon
another little monticule rose a pretty white modern church.
Far to the right, on a wooded hill-side, white houses were
faintly discernible among the trees, which Canon informed
me was *St. Sauveur*. We drove to a small inn, where
I desired Canon to order dinner, intimating that, as he
had franked me to Luz, I invited him and his daughters to
dine with me; I left the young men to pay for themselves.
While it was preparing, and while he went to the stable
to see that his horses really ate their provender, as a good
voiturier should, the two girls and I went sight-seeing.

We got a little boy to show us the way to the old church of the Templars, which, Murray says, 'enclosed *within a castle*, furnished with battlements and loop-holed walls, is a great curiosity.' The battlements and loop-holed walls are there, but I saw no castle. A high wall, which has clearly once been fortified, simply runs round the church. On the coping stone of each battlement a big stone boulder is placed, but whether for ornament or to keep the roofing from blowing away, I cannot say. These stones look, at a distance, like a row of human heads. I looked among the gravestones in the churchyard, at the back of the building, to see if I could find any of the Templars' graves, but in vain. Some masons, who were busy making repairs —not before they were needed—told me there were none remaining.

We entered the church through a rounded arch very much resembling one that I remember in my childhood, in the church of Stillingfleet, near York, but not nearly so richly carved. That, also, was considered very beautiful, and strangers sometimes came to examine it. The roof and sides of the porch were covered with half-obliterated grotesque paintings in fresco. Within the church itself my ignorance saw no beauty. A row of round heavy pillars, without capitals or ornament, from which sprang rounded arches, separated the aisles from the nave, and the roof appeared as if it had been painted in fresco in former times ; in one place I made out the Templars' well-known emblem of the Lamb. There were the usual tinsel-decorated altars at the upper end of the aisles and the chancel, and an '*autel particulier*,' all decorated with cuttings-out of blue and gold paper, as well as one or two side altars, and a chapel, which we reached by going up some steps, through a poking little room with an oaken *armoire* in it, which I suppose was the vestry. I am no archæologist, unfortunately. It seemed to me only a dirty, ugly village church, with a very handsome porch and a rather unusual form. The rounded chancel is common about this part of the country. St. Sauveur has a rounded chancel, so has the church of Pierrefitte, so, probably, have many others.

From the old church we walked to the monticule of St. Pierre. The ruined hermitage of which Murray speaks no longer exists. In its place stands a very pretty white modern church, and opposite it, nearly on the spot where the hermit's bones were found, a handsome pyramidical pillar with a cross on the top. The following inscription is graven on it:—'*A la Mémoire du R. P. Ambroise de Lombez, mort en odeur de sainteté, à l'Ermitage de St. Pierre, en* 1778.' On the pedestal:—'*Erigé par les ordres de sa Majesté Napoléon III.,* 1861.' From this hill there is a most beautiful view of the plain, intersected by long alleys of tall poplars, and watered by the clear crystal Gave; and the two white villages we had seen as we entered the valley—all shut in, like an amphitheatre, by lofty mountains.

We descended the side of the hill by a narrow path, and reached another running along the base of a hill on the left, scarcely high enough to be called a mountain, which we followed till we came to the magnificent bridge of one single arch, springing from rock to rock across the deep chasm in which flows the Gave. It is built of white stone, and the balustrades on each side are also painted white. Over the centre of the arch is an Imperial Crown, surmounting the letters L. N. It is indeed an Imperial work. So grand in its bold simplicity, bridging over that vast black chasm, and the surging, foaming torrent boiling up in the abyss below, so beautiful beyond description are the richly-wooded sides of the ravine beyond, and the magnificent mountains, rising peak above peak behind, that one gazes up at it breathless and awe struck.* This bridge, and the Arc de Triomphe at Paris, are the two grandest monuments erected by the hand of man that I have ever seen. *They are both actually sublime.* After gazing at it till it was photographed on my memory, we crossed over it, stopping at the entrance to admire a very handsome pillar, surmounted by the Imperial eagle, and bearing this inscription :—

'*A leurs Majestés Impériales Napoléon III. et l'Impératrice, les habitants de Luz et St-Sauveur, Reconnaissants.* —1860.'

It is only on traversing it that one becomes aware of its immense length, and one does not even then fully realize what a wonderful work it is, till one descends to the bottom of the ravine, through what is called the English garden. The steep cliff is cut into innumerable little terraces, protected by walls of turf, with shrubs or flower beds, here and there seats are placed, wherever the nature of the ground affords space for them ; and nearly at the base, there is a good-sized tree, with a circular wooden seat running round it, where travellers may rest, and admire this wonderful union of nature and art. And this descent is so artistically contrived, that the weakest head, and the most delicate person can accomplish it without either giddiness or fatigue. Still lower down, a wooden platform, protected by a rail, runs round the base of the rock, where one may stand and look down into the seething waters below, a mingled chaos of intense black, and snowy foam, and up to the wonderful arch that spans the chasm. It is a sight to make one giddy. One wonders first how one ever could have had courage to cross such a frightful ravine. It seems as if the bridge, which felt so firm to the tread, and was so broad and wide, as well as long, was

---

* There is a photograph of this view by Mr. Maxwell Lyte, of Bagnères de Bigorre, which is the finest specimen of photography I ever saw, and which conveys as clear an idea of its sublimity as human art can give.

breaking from the rock whence it sprang. Next, how mortal hands could ever build that arch across that immense width—as it were in the very air. It is worth while to come from England to the Pyrenees, only to see this wonderful work of human skill and intrepidity.

We reascended the sloping terrace, and regained the high road, which brought us to St. Sauveur, a village of very handsome lodging-houses and hotels, forming one long street, in the centre of which nearly, are the baths, which have a handsome marble façade, supported by stone pillars. Passing through this, we descended a flight of steps into a square court, ornamented with flowering shrubs, on three sides of which are baths. Just as we got out of the village, it began to rain, and it rained heavily by the time we reached Luz. We dined well— the dinner for four persons costing me sixteen francs, wine included—and then the carriage was ordered. There was no more sight-seeing that evening. The mountains were clothed with a dense vapoury robe. I was glad to resign my seat beside Canon, and to go inside the coach, especially as I had not been well all the day. Canon's daughters had lost all shyness, and chatted gaily with the two young men. While I sat quiet in my corner, one of them began to hum a tune; she had a pretty voice, and I asked her to sing. After a little hesitation, she began, and her sister joined in very sweetly. Then one of the young men sang, and then the three together; and so, singing and talking, we had a very pleasant drive home to Cauterets, notwithstanding the mist and rain had made the evening close in before the time. A talent for music is almost universal in the Pyrenees; and I have seldom heard richer or sweeter toned voices than most of these mountaineers possess. Their music is wild, plaintive, and original—very unlike French music.

H

CHAPTER IX.

WHEN the day came, I was really sorry to leave Cauterets, and to say good-by to the Canon family, who had one and all been most civil and attentive to me. If one could but infuse a little love of cleanliness into these mountaineers, if they could but be induced to wash the floors of their rooms, their corridors, and stairs, and if the holes and corners of the houses were clean as in England ; if, in short, that *false pride*, which is an effectual hindrance to all improvement, and which so strongly marks the Gael, whether French or Irish, could be got rid of, the Pyrenees would be a perfect Paradise. The people are so courteous and kind, and one cannot help liking them so much, that one feels a desire for their improvement and welfare beyond one's own mere personal interest in the matter, and wishes one could persuade them to keep all parts of their houses clean for their own sakes.

Unluckily, a Pyrenean thinks it would *degrade her* to go down upon her knees to scour a passage or a room, and more still to use her hands and a wet cloth to wipe up anything dirty. The nearest advance to cleaning she can be persuaded to make, is to brush off the dirt with a long brush, pour a little water on the soiled part, and brush that about, generally leaving all *worse* than it was before.

I pointed out to one of Canon's daughters, that part of the house was very dirty. She was a gentle, obliging girl, and did not refuse to clean it, but tears came into her eyes as she answered in the tone of a martyr about to be led to

the stake—'*il faut savoir souffrir.*' There is the fault of
the French servants generally, they do not look upon their
work *as work,* but as a *degradation,* a '*souffrance,*' and yet
you see these same girls who will not condescend to clean
a house properly, spreading dung with their hands upon
the fields, and eating their dinner by a hedge side afterwards, with those same hands *unwashed,* though a brook
runs close beside them. ,

Every market-day all the *voituriers* of Cauterets go to
Argelés. Canon always runs two or three coaches there
and back, and in one of these I took my place, selecting
that he drove himself. Before I go on to Argelés, dear
reader, let me say, that if you ever take it into your head
to visit Cauterets, you will find Canon a most excellent trust-
worthy guide—a '*guide de première classe,*' as the French
say. He has a whole pocket-book full of certificates of his
abilities and obliging character from ladies he has escorted
to mountains and waterfalls, and gentlemen with whom he
has hunted Izards.* He is a fine, genial, open-hearted
man too, whose frank, pleasant, cheerful countenance
makes you like him at once. If you go to Cauterets and
need a guide, as you must—take Canon.

The carriage I got into, was quite full within and without, and I travelled in high society, for Monsieur le Curé sat
beside me, and Monsieur le Maire opposite. Every little
village in France has its mayor. Monsieur le Curé and
Monsieur le Maire fell into talk, and I first listened and
then joined in. The Maire informed us in a grandiose,
pompous, and self-satisfied manner, that he was of a studi-
ous turn, and had nearly read through Buffon, being '*au
dixième tome.*'

'Ah!' said the Curé, 'that's all very well, but there
have been many discoveries since his time;' and he named

* The Izard and the chamois are one, but in the Pyrenees the animal
is always called by the first name.

other works on Natural History and Science, in a way which showed him to be a highly-educated and well-read man.

Monsieur le Maire looked taken rather aback at the idea that he had purchased, and been studying so hard at a learned work which later discoveries had proved to be incorrect in many of its deductions. He knew nothing of Humboldt and Cuvier, and numberless other sages quoted by the Curé.

I was glad to be accidentally thrown into the company of a well-informed Frenchman, for in my mode of travelling, *I see no one* but the people I lodge with, and the peasants I talk to in my walks, so I told him I was thinking of writing a book on the country, and asked him if he could give me any information about the peasants and their mode of life 'They seem,' added I, 'to be very wretched, their homes are so filthy and miserable, and they themselves look so poor and dirty, while at the same time they are so courteous and civil, one cannot help liking them.'

'The peasant is generally *bon enfant*' (a good sort of fellow), he replied, 'but he is not so miserable as you think. I cannot deny that the people are dirty both in their homes and in their persons, but there is no actual want in the Pyrenees. Nobody could give you better information on this subject than I can—not because I am a priest and mix with the people, but because (though it is against rule) I was (by the permission of my superiors) employed for some years by the government in furnishing the reports of the annual produce of every kind. I had three clerks under me, and I made them work. We had plenty to do. Every year a return is made to the government of the crops each district has produced, and thus the minister *de l'Intérieur* knows exactly what is wanting in each district, and supplies that deficiency at once, so that there is never any actual want of the means of life. I have given up that employment under government, but as a Curé I go much among the poor, and I do assure you they are well cared for. I have always money in my hands to relieve the necessitous; no one need starve here.'

'Yet I see most of the women looking the picture of misery; they have to work like horses in the fields, and they are generally bare-footed.'

'That is true. It is customary here for women to work in the fields, nor do I see how it can be prevented. The Pyrenean peasant likes to be always in the air, and requires it. If they are shut up in houses they die rapidly of consumption. I have seen this again and again,—*N'est-ce pas, Monsieur le Maire?*'

The Maire corroborated him, and instanced some young girl who leaving field for house work, had just died of decline. The Curé continued :—

'As to the bare feet, that also is in some sort a necessity. The people here are subject to a disease in the feet, if they wear shoes and stockings in the summer.'

I wondered in my own mind, if this disease only attacked women, since I saw most of the male peasants with good shoes and stockings, while the women went barefoot, but did not like to say so, lest he should think me pert.

'But their wretched homes,' said I; 'surely if they were not very poor, they would have more comfort in them.'

'You must not judge of the comfort from *your* point of view, madame,' he answered, 'but from *theirs*. And then you must remember also how little they are in their homes —our peasants' life is spent in the open air. They are besides very close-handed, and will not spend a penny they can avoid spending—but they are not wretched as you think. From what I have read, mademoiselle, *there is more actual distress and starvation among the poor of your own country.** As Curé, and constantly visiting them, I

* Looking at English statistics as reported in the 'The Times' for this

must know; and I do assure you that except in seasons of sickness, there is no actual want among them, and in those cases, I have always the means of giving relief through the donations of charitable persons. I have always more money in my hands than is required.'

He told me, further, what my own eyes had told me, that the country was very fertile, the rich low lands generally yielding two crops a year. It is usual to plant maize after some earlier crop has been gathered in, and the hay-making in the water meadows seems never ending. Even on the high hill-sides the springy nature of the soil enables the peasant generally to flood his fields with the fertilizing water by innumerable little trenches cut in the turf. It is to this practice, and to the innumerable mowings, that the meadows here doubtless owe their fine emerald green turf, and their lawn-like appearance. The greater part of the land round Cauterets and Argelés—and indeed all over the Pyrenees—seems to belong to peasant landowners. I never scarcely see a gentleman's house. Even the château which I was told had once belonged to Henri IV., and which even now looks an imposing structure from the road between Pierrefitte and Argelés, is owned by a peasant. He was a very strange man, I was told, and lived in the same hugger-mugger way as the other peasants, except being rather more morose and solitary, living quite alone, and having several ferocious dogs that would fly at a stranger in his courtyard. He is said, however, to pos-

current year of 1863, the number of *women* returned by the census as employed in field-labour, and the fearful report published by the commission appointed to inquire into the state of labourers' dwellings, at the repeated accounts of the extreme poverty of the agricultural labourers in the Southern and Midland districts of England, whose low wages (eight or nine shillings a-week when bread is tenpence the quartern loaf) *but barely provide them with bread and water for a meal, and nothing else,* while they have often to walk two, four, or six miles off to earn even that, returning the same distance at night when worn out by a day's hard labour,—*I fear the French priest was right, and that our English peasants are worse off than the Pyreneans.*

sess a wonderful talent for music, is the best musician in the country, and has actually published some of his compositions, which are very beautiful. His name I could not learn. It is astonishing how incurious the Pyrenean is about all that does not closely concern himself. He often does not know the name of a mountain in sight, or a village three miles distant from his home.

We reached Argelés about half-past eleven in the forenoon. I continued very unwell; in fact, I had an attack of cholerine ever since the day I had been lost in the fog. Madame Armiral's shop was not open, and I did not know what to do with myself and my bag. I had calculated upon her assistance in obtaining lodgings, as she seemed to know everything and everybody; so I wandered about the market-place, after committing my precious *sac* to a person whom I had seen with her the previous Tuesday. But a Pyrenean market is not so amusing as many other foreign ones. There are no gay costumes, only a few scarlet or white Capulets just break the monotonous tone of the universal dark-browns and blues; and there is nothing pretty or tempting at any of the stalls. There were the same second-hand gowns I had seen the previous market-day, and for two other market-days at Bagnères de Bigorre; and rags and *chiffons* of all kinds at one stall, among them cuttings of the gay-coloured materials used for covering chairs and making window curtains, which the peasant women were buying up eagerly. To amuse myself I also went and expended about nine sous in three of the prettiest pieces, intending to make therewith a bag, and a dressing-table pincushion—neither of which I have ever found time to make yet. And as I turned them over, I inquired what use they were put to, and was informed the peasants made caps for their children out of them. It may be so; but from that day to this, I have never seen a child with one of those gay roses in the crown of its cap. I see nothing but dingy black skull caps, or a few made of equally dingy brown calicoes, on every child's head that is under six years old.

Then I admired the fountain—a large, handsome stone vase, pouring out water into another larger, shallow octagonal vase below, which, rushing over its sides, flows into the *ruisseau* or stream that runs in front of the houses, on each side, of all the streets; and then I went back to the dye-shop, which was opened now, but by Monsieur Armiral, of whom I knew nothing, instead of my patronizing, hearty old friend his mother. He was far too busy to have time to talk to me, but I left my bag there while I went to get something to eat, and to look for lodgings, having agreed that he was to take me back to Bagnères that day if I could not find any, and the following market-day if I could. I was sick and faint, so I went to the inn whence Madame Armiral had ordered our dinner, and bespoke a *côtelette*. The *bonne* showed me upstairs, such *filthy* stairs, into a bedroom, with whose floor the street seemed *white* by comparison, so deeply was it ingrained with the dirt of ages. It might have been mediæval dirt—it might even have dated from the Deluge—so black it was; and this blackness was further set off, and enhanced, by two beds on either side the door, each with long snowy curtains, edged with lace, depending to the ground, and covered with splendid scarlet coverlets knitted of the fine Pyrenean wool, which I coveted as shawls for myself and a friend. The tables were nearly as dirty as the floor, and they, too, were Pyrenean, and peculiar. They were like small dressing-tables, with small, square spindle legs, the tops covered with oil cloth, painted to represent mahogany, which was fastened on by a narrow wooden beading, that ran all round the edge; the crevice between it and the table, forming, of course, a most convenient receptacle for crumbs and dust. They were all dusty, and all slopped.

But I came to study life and manners in Bœotia, and was not to be turned from my purpose by a dirty table. An English proverb says that 'Every one must eat a peck of dirt before he dies.' I made up my mind that I should eat a good part of my peck in the week I meant to stay at Argelés; so down I sat before the cleanest-looking, and resolutely ordered a *potage* and some *veau aux tomates.* The waitress quitted the room to order them, and left me to continue my 'pursuit of knowledge under difficulties.'

I had not sat there long before I heard the *clomp* of heavy shoes upon the stairs, and three or four peasants, in their holiday costume, entered. Soon the three small tables besides that at which I sat in solitary grandeur, were all filled. Taking the in-comers as to mere outward appearance, they were undoubtedly a fine, healthy, stalwart set of men. The Pyrenean peasant, as a rule, is tall, and well made; and notwithstanding the continual use of the heavy wooden shoe, or *sabot*, when at work, has none of the boorish, slouching awkwardness of our own working men. Nor is his dress a torn, worn, dirty fustian, or greasy, shabby, ragged coat and *et ceteras* of fine cloth, white at the seams, if not full of holes at the elbows, and a world too tight or too loose for him, showing clearly in all ways it was never made for the wearer.

No! the Pyrenean peasant is a SELF-RESPECTER. He is not ashamed of being what he is, and does not want to be taken for a gentleman; and therefore, so far as outward manners go, *he is one*. He speaks to others on terms of equality. To any one he very much respects, with a sort of proud humility, saying, plainer than words, that he holds, with Burns—

'A man's a man, for a' that.'

He never aims at being anything but a peasant. Perhaps he carries this a little too far, as we shall see to be the case hereafter, when I have time to enter more fully into the habits of the peasantry, and their mode of life ; *but there is something grand in this self-respect*. The block may be rudely quarried, but the marble is pure ; out of it God may one day carve noble men.

These men were dressed in neat brown jackets, vests, and trowsers of the same — the gay neck-tie, or the scarlet or green worsted sash, universally tied round the waist, sometimes just allowed to peep out, being their only finery. One man alone wore a black frock coat ; he had clearly travelled beyond the Pyrenees. As they entered the room, each saluted me by as graceful a bow as an English gentleman could have made, and a ' *Bon jour, madame,*' which I, of course, returned, and then each knot of friends and neighbours selected a table for themselves, and began to converse, till their dinner was served ; and, of course, ' their talk was of beeves.' Presently up came the waitress, and placed a bowl of steaming potage and a plate of stew before me ; then she served the other tables, and the clatter of knives and forks began. I was neither well, nor hungry, and soon laid mine down ; whereupon, the man in the frock-coat, thinking doubtless I was dull, opened a conversation with me.

' Madame is English ? '

' Yes.'

' Madame is come to see the Pyrenees ? ' interrogatively and insinuatingly.

' Yes, I am making a tour through this beautiful country.'

' Ah ! it *is* beautiful ! Madame does well to visit it—the country is worth seeing—but Madame will find many things she is unaccustomed to, especially as she is English. *This floor*, for instance,' touching it with his foot—' I have travelled—I have been in Germany and in England—one does not see such floors there.'

'No, indeed,' said I, continuing the conversation expressly for the inn-maid's benefit, who just then entered the room with a pile of plates and dishes, 'in England our smallest inns are perfectly clean—the floors are regularly washed, and as white as my hand.'

'It is not the *custom* here, you see, madame,' joined in another peasant. 'No doubt it is a good plan to have things clean, and to wash the floors; but then—you see—no one does it.'

'No,' said my first friend mournfully, as he again tapped the floor (on which one might have sown mustard-and-cress, with a fair chance of a good crop) with his boot (which, though it was a wet, dirty day) was certainly the cleaner of the two, and, perhaps, suggested a comparison to his mind: 'what Monsieur says is true; the people hereabouts do not like the trouble of cleanliness as you understand it, and as I, who have travelled in your country, understand it. What we think clean here, you will think dirty.'

And again he sighed, and turning to his three companions, resumed his conversation with them. I rather pitied him. He had, no doubt, been a courier, or something of the sort, to some English family, and now that he had returned home, found the ideas of refinement and cleanliness he had acquired in his travels very inconvenient.

I paid about a franc for my dinner, and a few sous for some brandy—rather more than I had paid when I dined with* Ma'ame Armiral in her shop, but then I was an *Anglaise*.

I had seen what I wanted to see—how the peasants dined in the peasants' inn, and partaken myself of the cheap, good, wholesome food—and the noise and heat were

---

* The common French people say 'Ma'ame' instead of 'Madame,' just as our servants say 'Missus.'

oppressive to me, so I rose to go. The men assembled, all bowing courteously to me again, and civilly wishing me good-day, as I passed out. After descending the filthy stairs, I found my way into the kitchen. It was a busy place; at the wide open chimney cooking of all sorts was going on; piles of clean plates and dishes, bottles of wine and glasses covered a table, behind which, as behind a counter, sat Madame, and from her seat as from a throne, she issued her commands, every now and then starting up and whisking off into some neglected corner to seize some forgotten thing, and demand quickly and shortly '*pourquoi*' *that* had not been carried to such a place before. Round three sides of the room peasant men and women were dining on heavy deal tables, such as one sees in old-fashioned farmhouse kitchens, but without cloths on them, and if the din and confusion had been great in the chamber where I had dined, and in the other chambers I had passed in coming down stairs—for every bedroom seemed full of diners—it was greater here. But it was a comfort to see that all the utensils used in cooking, and the table at which they were even then trussing fowls, was scrupulously clean—it generally is so in France. Dirty as they are in some things, in all that regards their cookery, in their linen, and in their personal cleanliness and neatness, the French maid-servants excel ours.

I was thankful, however, to leave the heated atmosphere and get out into the air again; and I walked up and down the town, looking for apartments. The small quantity of rain that had fallen had laid the dust, and the ground of the market-place looked *clean* in comparison to the rooms I had just quitted. Lodging-hunting is never a pleasant thing; but it is worse in France than in England, because, as the police order is, that every one who lets lodgings shall have a board signifying the same always affixed to the walls of the house, and people do not, as at home, put

cards with 'Furnished Apartments to let' in the window—
it is impossible to know, without ringing at the door and
inquiring, what lodgings are let and what are empty.
Mine was a troublesome search, and to save others the
same, I may as well state that there is but one good set of
lodgings, those over a druggist's shop in the market-place,
and two boarding-houses or *pensions* at Argelés. The first
were let. The mistress of one of the *pensions* had gone to
Pau on a visit, and in her absence her servants would not
receive me. I had, however, no cause to regret my walk
to Madame La Sales' house, a castellated building, overlooking the whole of the beautiful valley, shut in on three
sides by lofty mountains. Her servant showed me the sitting-rooms, and one or two bedrooms, which had all an air
of cleanliness and *comfort*, at which I should have wondered
had I not known previously that she was an English
woman. A French house is in all points most unlike an
English one. It is not merely in the absence of carpets
on stairs and in rooms, or the hard settees instead of soft
luxurious spring-cushioned sofas, which do not yet appear
to be commonly known in the Pyrenees, that the difference
lies—the French house, in its own style, is often quite as
prettily decorated as an English one, and, as a rule, more
taste is often displayed in the dwellings of the middle class
than you would see in our own country ; but there is an absence of *comfort*, which is, in fact, a word unknown in
France. It has no equivalent in their language, for they
do not understand the thing. The rooms in this house
looked really comfortable, and the view was lovely. Yet
Argelés, on the whole, disappointed me. From Murray's
description of it, I had pictured to myself a fertile valley
shut in by mountains, through whose green fields murmured a clear, sparkling, winding stream, like one of our
own Cumbrian or Lancastrian valleys, but with the softer
climate, for which 'the paradise of Argelés' is renowned.

All this is there, and yet it is not so beautiful as it sounds; for, except you are close upon it, the river is almost invisible. Its course is impeded by shallows and osier beds, dividing it in places into innumerable small channels, and it is nowhere of sufficient width to form a feature in the distant view. There can be no doubt, that as a whole, the Pyrenean scenery is of a grander character than that of our English lakes; but they are, I think, more beautiful, with their tranquil meres reflecting the golden sunlight, and the towering mountain crags beneath which they lie.

As I left Madame de Sales' house and walked disconsolately down the street, wondering what would become of me, my eye was caught by a bunch of *buis* or box, hung up in front of a small new-built wayside inn; I asked if I could have a bedroom there, and being answered in the affirmative, Keeper and I went back to M. Armiral's dye-shop to fetch the carpet bag, and having got it, settled ourselves for the night in our new abode.

CHAPTER X.

KEEPER may have had a pleasant night of it; he has
slept coiled up on the skin of a large handsome dog,
which serves as a bedside carpet, who, as my hostess informs me, was killed because he was savage; but I was
devoured by *f* sharps. No wonder. I hear from my
handsome host's pretty young wife, that *'they never dress
the feathers in Argelés,* but stuff them into pillows or beds
just as they come from the fowls.' *What do they do in
Argelés?* I should like to know. Certainly they do not
wash the floors; for in this new house, by far the cleanest
I have entered, except that of the *juge de paix's* widow,
the stains of the mortar and whitewash are not yet cleaned
off the floors and stairs, and I suppose never will be. In
other respects, the fittings-up are rather superior to those
of a small road-side public-house in England. Each of
the two upper front bedrooms has an open chimney-piece,
with a white painted compartment above it, meant to hold
a mirror, ornamented at the top with an angel's head, very
finely carved. In that of the room I occupy, there is a
good mirror, the other room is not yet completely furnished.
A handsome mahogany wardrobe stands in a corner; the
bed would be good if it had not *an animated featherbed,*
and its frame is of handsome beech wood; a table for
washing materials; the slender oil-cloth covered table,
with a beading round to collect all the crumbs and dirt,
which seems peculiar to Argelés; and a few rush chairs,

complete the furniture. The room itself has two large windows, and is good-sized; and on the open chimney-piece stand two large scarlet geraniums, which give it a cheerful look. It wants nothing but a clean floor, and the removal of that featherbed, to be fit for the highest person in the land to occupy temporarily, without complaint. There are, however, unmentionable objections. I would advise no lady traveller, who can help it, to quarter herself at a French way-side inn. What we consider the absolute necessaries of life is to the French mind superfluous luxury.

My landlord and landlady are just married, and a very handsome couple they are, and very good humoured and obliging, notwithstanding my English ideas are probably as strange to them as their Pyrenean ways to me. Madame has provided me with a large pitcher of water, in addition to that on my washhand table, and a pancheon, or *terrine* as it is here called, of brown ware, which I use as a bath. I called her after breakfast to-day, and told her *I positively must* have the featherbed removed, and the room scoured, both which she promised should be done while I was out walking.

Keeper and I then sallied forth. I passed the Château, as Madame La Sales' house is called, and walked along the high road leading towards Lourdes, passing one or two straggling, unimportant, dirty villages on the left-hand side. One of them contained a large handsome building above a large walled garden full of fruit-trees, which, I was told, belonged to Madame la Marquise, as did the village—the first gentleman's or gentlewoman's house, except Madame La Sales', I have met with in my rambles among the Pyrenees. I passed also a very pretty large two-story house, with green *persiennes*, sheltered by a noble chestnut wood at the back. It could not, I thought, be a gentleman's house, for the farm-yard was in front of the dwelling, and for a peasant-farmer, it looked too good. A man I met on the road solved the difficulty.

'It is a peasant's house,' said he, 'and he owns all the fields in front and close around.'

I continued my walk, rather envying, if truth must be spoken, the master of that beautiful home, and thought how *I* should like to have it—to knock down the farm buildings in front, lay out a beautiful garden instead. and to sit or lie, and read, under my own chestnut trees, watching the rays of the setting sun fade upon the distant mountains. My reverie was broken by a sharp, vicious bark from Keeper, who, with head erect, and tail curled up so high, that I think he must be a direct descendant of that celebrated dog whose tail curled so high that it took his hind legs off the ground, was standing at bay, growling and barking at a very large white sheep-dog, with a bloody head, who looked as if he had been in a battle already, and I called to a beggarly-looking man in a field of maize on the right-hand side of the road, to call off his dog, which he immediately did, very civilly. This emboldened me to go into the field to ask him the name of some pretty church spires and villages I saw peeping up among the trees at the base of the mountains opposite. He told me their names, which I forget; and then I asked him if he were the owner of the pretty house. He smiled, with a gratified air, and answered,

'Yes; and all these fields around were his too.'

His farm was very convenient, large enough to support him and his family comfortably, and not too large. It was capital soil, and he could see every field he had from his house, so that no one could rob him of an ear of maize— a very desirable thing, doubtless, as the Pyreneans themselves say, the fields are usually a good deal robbed.

I said, 'Your house must have cost a good deal building.'

I

'Not so much as to another, for I led my own materials when not·busy ; and wood and some other things I had.'

He named the sum in *francs*—it came to *nearly two thousand pounds.* His farm, he said, was worth what was equivalent to three more.

And here was this man owning a property, which in England would have made him a gentleman, in a rusty hat, patched and darned clothes, only fit for a scarecrow, bare legs, and wooden shoes. I asked him how property descended in Argelés, as I had heard the customs of Lavedan* were rather peculiar. He said the law allowed a father to select among his children the one he thought likeliest to keep the family property together, provided he portioned off the others suitably to their social position in his lifetime. He had had his property from his father, and could not think of dividing it; he should choose the one he thought least likely to waste it among his children, and marry and establish the others in his life-time. He thought it a pleasant thing for a father to see all his children settled and happy before he died, and I agreed with him. *How much better is the French law, which compels a man to provide for the children he has been the means of bringing into the world according to the property he himself possesses,* than ours, which, leaving the parent to do as he pleases, occasions many a family of girls, accustomed to every comfort during the lifetime of a selfish, luxurious father, who spends all he has, to be left at his death portionless upon the world.

I think a man ought to be obliged to provide for the children who owe their birth to him, according to the position of life in which they are born, out of his annual income, if he has no vested property, as in France.

We should not then have so many officers' daughters,

---

* *Lavedan* includes Argelés, Pierrefitte, St. Savin, and many other valleys and villages, under the generic title of the Valley of *Lavedan.*

clergymen's daughters, merchants' daughters, and even daughters of men with good estates, left late in life to struggle with bitter poverty, after having been used, during their father's lifetime, to the comforts of a home, where from eight hundred to a couple of thousand pounds were spent yearly.

How can any man, who has had a rosy, loving child seated on his knee, fondling ' dear papa,' go to his grave in peace, knowing that he has spent all he had upon himself, and that that child, now an old woman, has to live upon a beggarly pittance—the tenth share, perhaps, of some old relative's property, or worse still, is left with *nothing*. Unfitted by taste, by habit, and by an imperfect education (for the selfish parent rarely spends much on his children's education), even to earn her bread as a governess. I know of two general's nieces, and two general's daughters, four ladies brought up in luxury, who were, without misconduct on their part, solely from this cause, left to starve on the poor pittance they could earn as needlewomen in advanced old age, rendered yet more helpless by the utter bodily prostration of one of them, occasioned by years of sorrow and privation; and this when *the sacrifice of a few pounds yearly to insure the father's life, would secure independence to his daughters.*

Why don't parents, if they know they either can't or won't leave their daughters a gentlewoman's competence, *bring them up to work,* and place them out in shops, as governesses, or in other ways, as they place out younger sons ? I fear it is owing to that *false pride* which seems *so peculiarly English,* and from which all foreign nations are happily free.

But this is a digression—the reader will probably think—*I* could not help such thoughts passing rapidly through my mind, as this beggarly-looking peasant-farmer, with his clear head and sound heart, went on de-

tailing to me what he meant to do for his children *during
his life.*

'I don't wonder you wish to keep such a property
together,' said I; 'it's a beautiful home, I envy you.'

'It is a beautiful spot,' he answered, smiling proudly as
his eye rested lovingly upon his home; 'and I am a happy
man, for I am content. I can live by my work, and keep
my family, and lay by something. I am rich, for I am
content. I have the sense to know when I am well-off,
and would not change my lot with anyone. I have a good
wife, and five healthy children. Yes! I esteem myself a
happy man.'

His wife came up as he spoke; she was quite as dirty-
looking and very nearly as ragged as himself. Two of
the elder children were with her, *both barefooted;* she had
shoes and stockings. One of the children had his feet
bound up with a clean linen rag—I asked what was the
matter?

'Nothing,' was the reply. 'His foot is a little sore,
that is all—the air will do it good. Thank God my
children are all healthy.'

With the family came up the white dog, who, seeing I
was talking amicably with his master and mistress, looked
upon me as a friend, and invited master Keeper in dog-
language to a gambol, which invitation was promptly accepted. I inquired whether he had been fighting, and
was told the wound on his head, which was as large as my
hand, was caused by the flies biting him, and that he was
so every year. The flies are a sad pest to the cattle in the
Pyrenees, and the hornets are worse. I have seen the
cows dash madly through hedges and brooks, and over the
low stone fences goaded by their stings, while the herdsman raced after them with a heavy cudgel, which he flung
at them from time to time. At all other seasons the Pyrenean cows are a gentle, quiet race, whom even I, a cow-
fearer by nature, do not feel afraid of. I told the good-

natured looking dame how much I had been admiring her house, and complimented her upon its beauty and size. 'It is not too large,' said she; 'we are *quinze personas*, children and servants included.' I notice that many words are pronounced like Italian in the *patois*, and even the French spoken by the peasants of these districts is a sort of mongrel dialect between French and the *patois*, in which Italian and Spanish terminations prevail.

After this long talk, I called Keeper from his friend, and we returned home, I to dine on omelettes, Keeper to go shares with the dog of the house, an ugly black mongrel pointer puppy, who was always racing upstairs or downstairs, after or with him, and even invading my very sanctuary—my bedroom—if the door was left ajar. He used first to poke his black head in, then if unrebuked, to enter the room, still keeping close to the door, asking as it were permission to come in so clearly by his intelligent eyes, and by his tail, not wagging but moving with a quick vibratory movement, by which I observe dogs express their wish to do something; then, suddenly, he would turn round, Keeper after him, and both would dash into the next room or downstairs, upsetting chairs, tables, besoms, or anything else they found in their way. The noise they made was terrific, and would have driven any nervous, irritable person, mad. My host and hostess, and I myself, were only amused by their pranks. When Madame came to take away my empty plate, I asked why the room had not been washed according to promise, and received for answer that '*mon mari*' had been absent all day, and so she could not do it. I could not understand what '*mon mari*' had to do with scouring a room, but suppose Madame was busy attending to all the customers in his absence. However, the featherbed has been removed, and to-night I hope to sleep.

P.S.—*I didn't*. The animated featherbed had founded a new colony in the mattress!

CHAPTER XI.

I HAVE seen Vidalos. I walked that way this morning with the intent to reach it if possible, passing the peasant-farmer's pretty house and chestnut-wood on my way. The old white sheep-dog was in the lane, and recognized us, coming up wagging his tail to claim acquaintance, and have a pat from me, and a gambol with Keeper, after which he returned home; while Keeper, I am sorry to say, conducted himself in his usual puppy-fashion. What shall I do with that good-for-nothing animal? He ran after my peasant-friend's poultry, frightened them all into the wood, and nearly caught a very fine cock, and all this, after that flogging which cost me a whole franc at Eaux-Bonnes. I shall have to order him to be hung, and the little wretch is so playful, amusing, and affectionate, in short so nice a dog (though he is a mongrel), when he doesn't run after ducks and chickens, that I can't bear to think of putting an end to him. I beat him for his crimes, *when I can catch him;* but he generally makes off after a misdeed of this sort, and keeps at a respectful distance, stopping every now and then till I come nearly up, and gazing at me from a bank or a heap of stones, or the top of an old wall, with a sort of twinkle in his brown eyes as if he were laughing at me in his heart, which I believe he is; and the moment I near him he wags his tail, in the sauciest manner, turns round, and darts off again.

I passed through several insignificant villages, before I reached Vidalos. When I did, I found there was no visible way of getting to the tower. I tried a field, but found a high hedge I could not pass. A peasant-boy offered to show me the way and led me through an orchard-garden to the base of the hill, where a sort of rough pathway was rather trodden than cut, through the thorns and brambles. When he had scrambled half-way up, an old woman rushed out of a cottage near, declaring we had no business there, we ought to have gone *through her garden*, where there was a good path. It was clear she considered the boy had robbed her of her legitimate perquisite, by taking me that round-about way. However, we were half-way up now, and I was no ways disposed to come down again, so I gave the boy a few sous for his trouble, with which he ran off, carefully avoiding the virago below, who continued to scream and vituperate both him and me, and plodded up-wards alone. It is a bare, naked, single town, no more. Not half so interesting as I expected from the imposing figure it makes, seen from the road, surmounting its lofty conical mound, and looking grandly over all the valley; but the view from it is lovely.

From hence the Gave shows to advantage, even despite the shallows, forming a silver lakelet, there round that point, flowing a steady sensible river, and lower on again divided by shallows rippling off into so many innumerable streams, that one scarce knows at first which to call the Gave. It was a very windy day, the side next the river was very bare of shrubs to hold on by, and the grass very dry and slippery from the heat. Thus I had a tolerable chance of falling into the Gave if I went down that way, and if I went the other I must encounter the old witch below. Scylla and Charybdis were before me. I chose Scylla, and not daring to trust to my feet commenced a sliding descent as I sat towards the field below, where some twenty or more peasant men and women were making hay, doing a little botany on my way. I found a small pink flower, the sand-garlic, and a sort of aromatic thyme I had never seen before, together with a small kind of broom peculiar to the country; but as I had no botanical works with me, and no means of drying specimens of the plant, which was, moreover, out of bloom, I could not ascertain its name. Lower down I found common bladder campion, corn-fumitory, and the lovely-fringed mountain pink.* I returned home, well satisfied with my walk, and as we passed the green shuttered farm, that animal Keeper dashed after the poultry again, and caught a cock by the wing, while I screamed after him in vain. Happily the cock got away and flew off, but I am afraid he is hurt and that I shall have to pay for him. My conscience will not allow me to let Keeper lame fowls without paying for them, and I can't afford to spend money in that way; the silly little brute will compel me to order him for instant execution.

When I got home I found my host on his knees scrubbing the floor, not with soap and water and a brush, but *sciure de bois, i. e.* sawdust, put on with a cloth, which the Pyreneans use instead, and his pretty little wife, in her trim gown and smart, coquettishly-adjusted *mouchoir*, standing by, admiring his work and doing nothing. What a model husband! Fancy an Englishman scouring a floor while his wife stands idly by! Monsieur and Madame both immediately called upon me to admire how clean it was, declaring it had taken four hours to do, which I can readily believe, since it took at least twenty minutes to finish the little bit that remained undone when I returned. I must say the *sciure de bois* answers the purpose as effectually as

---

* M. Philippe, the botanist of Bagnères, doubts whether this lovely fringe-petaled pink is a variety of *Dianthus superbus*, or a genus of itself— *Dianthus monspessulanus*, as it varies continually in form, scent, scales, and hue. It is found throughout the chain of the Pyrenees.

soap, only that as time is money everywhere except in the Pyrenees, and it takes four hours to scour a room in this manner, which any English maid would scour in half-an-hour, I see no true economy in it. It gives the boards, moreover, a yellowish tint, instead of whitening them ; but the Pyreneans, especially the Pyrenean peasants, would do anything rather than spend a *sou* they can avoid spending. To save a *liard*,* they waste time which might earn *francs*, or let things fall to pieces for want of a few nails, a little mortar or thatch. It is a known fact, and related as such by French writers, that the cattle frequently die of infectious diseases, because their owners will not go to the expense of having their sheds cleaned out or white-washed.

Another day, I, and the sinner Keeper, who is still un-hung, though under sentence of death, rambled down the valley, across the bridge over the Gave near some saw-mills—not that on the high road to Pierrefitte—and up a winding-path among some rocks, hoping to attain one of the pretty churches whose spire I saw towering above the trees from Argelés. What a lovely walk it was; far lovelier than that to Vidalos. Yet I could direct no one to it, and I don't know that I could find it again myself; for I kept asking everyone I met the way to that tall spire —pointing to the church—and everyone I met gave me a contrary direction; and as I followed each in turn, I went zigzag, and backwards and forwards, and round and round, and never seemed to get any nearer the church I desired to reach. I was very thirsty, for it was a broiling day; and seeing a white farmhouse gleaming among fields and orchards, I made towards it, hoping to get some milk. I never saw a place that looked more peaceful or lovelier

* A liard is less than a farthing.

than it was—nestled under apple, and plum, and peach trees—with vines trailing up the stems of some of the oldest trees, and looking down on the lovely valley of Argelés and the low range of hills behind, while mountains closed in the view at either end. Outside it looked the picture of domestic cleanliness and comfort; but when I entered— The floor was earth-coloured—in fact, a tolerable coating of earth and mud had been brought and laid upon it by the united tramplings of men, women, children, dogs, cats, fowls, lambs, and, most probably, pigs also; for I heard a Pyrenean gentleman say that all these animals were usually allowed to run about the peasants' cottages. Upon this dirty floor some bonny, blue-eyed, flaxen-haired children—English in the type of their countenance—were playing; a good-natured but miserably dirty-looking dwarf, with a dirty handkerchief on her head, was rocking a dirty child lying in a cradle, whose quilt and blankets looked as if they had never been washed; and the fowls were amusing themselves where they liked. My entrance scared them.   One perched on the cradle-head, two flew on to the dresser, and some took refuge on the two beds which stood at separate corners of the room.

'Oh! look at the fowls!' exclaimed I.

'*Oh! ce n'est rien*,' was the inevitable reply.

It always is in the Pyrenees. If you complain of— well! it must out—*fleas*, '*Ce n'est rien;*' if there is anything dirty or untidy about your apartment, 'it is nothing.' I verily believe that if a cow walked into the room, it would still be '*rien.*' I told the little dwarf I was thirsty and longing for milk, and she instantly jumped up, with the ready kindness and politeness which, I must say, honourably distinguishes the Pyrenean peasant, and climbed on a chair to get me a glass from the closet. I followed to help her, seeing she was not tall enough to reach them. What glasses they were! I should not think they had

ever been washed since they were glasses. The dwarf held
out a dirty hand to take the one I had reached, and said
she would wash it in the pail of water on the sink hard by.
I asked to be allowed to wash it myself, well knowing that
I could not drink out of the glass *she* would think clean;
and I rinsed it three several times, rubbing the dirt off
with my fingers before it was usable. I trembled for the
milk. However, she led the way out of the house to a
sort of cupboard placed across a little rill of running water
that trickled from the hill-side above, and opening the
door with a key, showed me a clean—actually, *a really
clean*—pan full of milk, on which stood a thick, rich cream.
I dipped my glass in, again and again; for I meant to pay
for my milk and to have my money's worth, and I had
now been walking three hours in a broiling sun, and then
I thanked her and tendered payment; but no—she would
take nothing; I was welcome to the milk. Would I have
more? Madame was heartily welcome to it. I thanked
her, and again begged to pay, and again was refused with
a pleasant smile. Can one help liking a people like this,
with all their dirt? We went back to the house, and
again thanking her, I bade her good-by, and went on my
way refreshed.

After this, I dropped somehow into a little combe, so
small and so green, all shut in by mountains on three sides,
and with one or two white farmhouses gleaming in its green
depths, and there I sat me down to rest, with Keeper at
my feet. A lofty mountain was at my right hand, another
at my left, and through the opening between, the only one
in the wall of mountains encircling that little green valley,
itself perched half-way up a mountain, I looked down upon
the green valley of Lavedan, through which, from this
height, the Gave was seen meandering like a silver ribbon,
adding beauty, by the contrast of its pellucid waters, to
the brown, and blue, and green tints of the surrounding

scenery; and far beyond the long green valley rose the church spire and high-peaked roofs and balconies of the town of Argelés, against a long, low line of dark grey hills. Where can I find so fit a place to read the legends of the country as this? Lie still, Keeper; don't snap at the flies, lest you catch a Tartar in the shape of a wasp, as you nearly did just now; and don't run after the cock that crows from yonder homesteads and his wife Partlett, but close your eyes and sleep, while I read—

The Devil among the Peasants.

'A very long time ago there was a dairyman and his family living near the village of Pouyferré,* who called upon the devil† much oftener than upon God. So one day the devil took them at their word, and came and sat down among them by the kitchen hearth. They were horribly frightened at first, when they saw him come in all dressed in red. However, they consoled themselves after he was gone again, by thinking that once is not always, and that perhaps he would never come again, so they went to bed and slept well. But the day following, the devil came back at the same hour, and without more ado, sat down in the self-same place. The peasants were horror-struck at this second visit, and when he departed this time, prayed to God a little more fervently, and slept a little less soundly. The day following, they anxiously awaited the hour at which the devil had appeared the two preceding days. He was very punctual, came in without a word, and sat himself down in the chimney-corner. This time the peasants began to tremble a good deal, for they saw clearly that the evil one felt himself quite at home among them; and they

* Pouyferré is in Lavedan.
† 'Diable! Que diable!' &c., is constantly in the mouth of the Pyreneans, both male and female.

began to reflect and consult as to how they might get rid of him. Having come to the wise conclusion that he was to be dislodged at any rate, they next went to their priest and candidly told him of their unfortunate case. The priest represented to them that they had only themselves to thank for it, as they had, so to speak, invited the devil, by always having his name on their lips; but he added, that as they seemed repentant, he would do all he could to relieve them of a guest whose presence was so much against their chance of salvation. He kept his word as to the trouble he took about it, but it was all in vain. In spite of Paters and Aves, and holy water, and exorcisms, the devil came regularly at the same hour every day and sat down in the chimney-corner. The poor peasants lost all their health and gaiety; and sometimes wondered whether they were awake or asleep, for the red visitor seemed to weigh on their breasts like the nightmare, and they rubbed their eyes and tried to wake up and find it a dream—but no—*there he was!* At last they sent a petition to the bishop, beseeching him to help them. The bishop listened benignantly to their request, and promised to come himself to Pouyferré. He set out in great pomp attended by all his clergy, so that it was a grand sight to see the procession, and he came to the house when the scarlet guest was sitting there. He pronounced holy words and scattered holy water very plentifully, and as the devil never got up and went out, and everyone was afraid that after his usual custom, he would disappear through the roof, leaving a hole that no one could ever repair, it is said that the bishop actually put his own stole upon the devil's shoulders and dragged him to the door. When the evil one got there, he vanished, calling on the elements to avenge him, and immediately a black cloud broke into such a terrible storm of large hailstones, that there was no grain of any kind that year in the whole country.'

'About the same time that these events occurred in the plain, a strange thing happened to a peasant who lived near the Great Gave, which is still remembered in the valley of Davantaigue. This peasant was on the point of losing a valuable meadow, because the paper containing his title-deed was lost. The title had been placed in the hands of his uncle, but when the unfortunate peasant went to fetch it, he found his uncle dead, and the paper missing.

'In great sorrow of heart, he went to the meadow that was lawfully his. "Alas!" said he, "am I then to be despoiled of what is my just right? I had a title, but it is lost. Where shall I find it now? The devil only could help me, if the devil would. If he will but help me now in my extremity, I will give him my best pair of oxen."

'The devil replied, "I hold you quits as to the oxen, and I will still help you—but on condition that you let me have your wife."

'"I would with all my heart," replied the peasant, "but you see I can't,—I can't dispose of my wife. The woman does not belong to man, but to herself."

'The devil did not insist further. He transported the peasant into a magnificent hall, where individuals of all ages were seated on soft luxurious-looking arm-chairs, and his uncle was sitting among them. The devil then showed him an empty seat, saying, "I will restore your meadow to you, but you must make me a present of your person. I shall place it some day in that delightful seat, in the midst of this honourable assembly."

'The peasant made no reply; he felt doubtful as to the comfort of the place, but going up to his uncle whom he had recognized at once, he said, "You seem to be sitting very comfortably there, my dear uncle, and look as if you were quite at your ease."

'"As to that," said the uncle, "just touch my arm-chair with the end of your stick."

'The peasant touched it, and flame ran from the arm-chair to the stick and from the stick to him, and frightened him terribly. "Ah! Ah!" said he, "I comprehend now where I am, is not this hell?"

'"Certainly it is," said the uncle; "I live here now for my sins, and as you may see among a large company."

'"But," said the peasant, whose memory never lost sight of the object of his journey, "where is the title-deed of my meadow?"

'"Return to my house," said the uncle, "and at the back of the chimney behind one of the stands we place the resin* on, in the evenings, you will find it."

'The peasant asked nothing more; he was in a hurry to get out of the place, and one must admit that the devil was complaisant in conducting him out again. No sooner had he got free than profiting by the information his uncle had given him, he returned to his house to look for the title-deed; and there it was sure enough, at the back of the chimney as the uncle had said, and he got possession of his meadow. But at the precise moment he did so, he lost the use of his speech, and a year afterwards he was dead.'

The beautiful and melodious-voiced† maidens of Lavedan still believe that if they perceive a thread lying on the ground near the fountain, they must pick it up, and wind it as quickly as possible. The thread will lengthen under their fingers, and form a marvellous ball, out of which will come a fairy, who, delighted at being delivered from her inconvenient prison, will either give her libera-trix some handsome present, or lend her a fairy wand.

The belief in fairies is universal; and many are the

---

* The peasantry in the Pyrenees burn resin instead of tallow. It is twisted into long coils about the thickness of a little finger, and in this form ready for use, or in large cakes, is constantly sold in the markets.

† 'Melodious,' so in the original, and well do the sweet-voiced daughters of Lavedan merit the epithet.

legends concerning them recounted by the Pyreneans
as they sit round the winter fire. All mountaineers are
superstitious, in the popular sense of the word. They live
with Nature, and are accessible to influences to which the
worldly-minded would turn a deaf ear, a shut eye, and a
dead heart. The grand forms of the mountain, the solemn
rustle of the breeze through the pine-woods resembling the
ceaseless dash of the waves against the shore, the rushing
torrent pouring down the mountain side, whose white foam-
wreath looks spectre-like and unearthly, half seen through
the mists of night, and the exquisite beauty of their green
valleys, felt — even when they cannot express it — take
deep hold of their imagination and their feelings, and
impel them to a belief in the Unseen and the Wonderful.
They have the simple faith of a child, and probably for
that reason are more open to impressions from the Spirit-
world. Their legends and their music are alike the echo
of this close communion with Nature; both are wild,
fanciful, and tinged with a touch of sadness. Here are
two of the prettiest Fairy legends.

THE FAIRIES.

'Once upon a time, long, long ago, two shepherds were
sitting upon a green hill-side, watching their flocks feed,
when, like a dream as it seemed to them, two beautiful
damsels stood by their side. The two young men were
also very handsome, and, after having contemplated them
for a moment, the maidens said, blushingly—
' " Shepherds, will you marry us?   We will give you
much treasure, and make you happy besides, and your
children will be so beautiful that all your neighbours will
envy you."
' The two young men, though greatly surprised, were
charmed by the fairies' youthful beauty. They felt highly

flattered at being selected from their companions by
fairies, and signified their ready acquiescence. And the
fairies, seeing them disposed to do what they desired,
continued thus:—

' " Return to-morrow morning to the side of this meadow, but come back fasting, so that in marrying us you
may be able to break the charm which retains us captive.
We shall then cease to be fairies, and become your real
wives. Beware, therefore, both for your happiness and
ours, of eating anything whatsoever before we are
wedded."

' The next morning, the two young men returned full of
hope to the place where they had met the beautiful damsels, and soon espying them on the hill-side, hastened towards them. It was the time when the rye was swelling.
One of them, as he walked along, carelessly gathered an
ear, and detaching a grain broke it between his teeth, to
know if it was ripening. Immediately the fairy to whom
he was betrothed cried, trembling, " Thou hast replaced me
under the power of the charm from which I hoped to get
free. Alas! alas! thou hast made me a fairy for ever!"
And she disappeared instantly.

' But the other fairy, whose lover had been more attentive
to her advice, said to him, " Consider now, O shepherd!
that I am about to become thy wife, for thou hast destroyed the enchantment which kept me far from man-
kind. But if thou wouldest always keep me with thee,
remember never to call me fairy or fool. Above all,
trust in me, and have no fear of that which is about to
happen."

' While the beautiful fairy thus encouraged him, a
serpent rose out of the earth, and twining round the shepherd's stick, put his mouth to that of the youth—a kiss,
which was the superhuman consecration of the man's
alliance with the fairy. The shepherd received it in

K

silence, with his eyes tenderly fixed on her for whose sake
he endured such a caress.

'The fairy then took him by the hand, and conducted
him into a cavern, where there was much gold and silver;
and the husband and wife loaded two mules with treasure,
with which they afterwards bought themselves a rustic
house, and the finest land in the country.

'There they lived happily and quietly upon their farm,
and beautiful children were born to them, and the years
passed on.

'Now it happened one day, that the still young and
beautiful wife, who had retained from her state of enchantment some faculty of divination, looking at the sky—
where common eyes would only have seen present serenity
—read there the signs of a terrific hurricane, which
would burst over the country towards evening. So, like a
prudent housewife, she ordered her servants to cut down
the harvest, although it was scarcely quite ripe, and had
all the grain safely housed in her granaries. Her husband, who was absent, returned while they were about it,
and seeing the farm-labourers busy carrying off the corn
before it was thoroughly ripe, angrily demanded who had
set them to such a task? And as the trembling servants
replied that they only executed the orders of his wife, she
herself came out to meet him.

'"Oh, thou fool!" cried he, angrily; "how could such
a thought as cutting the unripe wheat ever enter thy
head?"

'At this fatal word, the poor wife, heaving a profound
sigh, disappeared from her horrified husband, and fell
suddenly once more under the power of the enchantment,
from which her marriage had freed her.

'In the evening, a frightful hurricane desolated the
valley. The waters broke their dams, inundated the
fields, and ruined the harvests. Then the sorrowful

shepherd, who saw his grain preserved by his wife's fore-
sight, rendered her tearfully a tardy justice. He called
her back to him with sobs, but it was in vain. Nevertheless, she returned with the dawn of every day to a lonely
chamber in the house, where her children, who were as
beautiful as the day, met her; and she loved to caress
them, and to comb their golden hair carefully, but she
begged them to tell no one that she thus came back in
secret, and they obeyed her. The father could not comprehend how their hair was always so beautifully smooth
and well arranged, and questioned them as to who combed
and washed them in this manner every day, but they
would say nothing. So at last he followed softly one
morning, when he saw them silently stealing up stairs,
and stood behind the door, and saw through the chink his
wife, looking younger and more beautiful than when he
married her, combing the bright hair of her youngest son
with a golden comb; but so soon as she saw her indiscreet
husband, she vanished like a dream, and the children and
their father never saw her again.'

There is a still prettier story, which is said to have
happened at Bagnères de Bigorre.

THE INNOCENT.

'There was in a mountain village, near Bagneres, a poor
family of many children, one of whom was an innocent,*
and could do nothing for himself. The father, and
brothers, and sisters troubled themselves little about the
poor creature; but his mother loved him, and cared for
him tenderly until she died. All the household grieved
for her greatly, except the poor fool, who slept in the
same room with the others. When they rose at break of

---

* *Innocent*—I retain this term which is commonly used in Yorkshire,
and is so much more touching and endearing than the word idiot.

day, they were surprised to see him sitting on a chair quite dressed, with his clothes properly put on, and his hair combed, and they asked him how it was.

'"My mother came," said he, "while you slept, and told me to get up, and she dressed me herself. Then she gave me a bowl full of milk and bread, and I ate it."

'The innocent did not know what death meant, and he saw his mother every day, and was happy. But his relations were uneasy that so strange a thing should happen in their house, and they went to the curate.

'"Good people," said he, "cause prayers to be said for the dead; and, in future, take the same care of that poor child that his mother did."

'So the peasants returned home, and fetched money to pay for the masses. But the spirit of the dead woman returned every day until the ninth mass had been said. Then her soul had peace, and her son obtained the affectionate care of his relatives.'

'There, Keeper; we have rested, reading, and moralizing long enough—get up, and let us be off, or we shall never reach that village, and never get home to-night.'

Keeper trotted on by my side, and we ascended the steep hill by a road a passing peasant pointed out to me, but it suddenly ended at a cottage farm; and while the pretty spire of the church I wanted to reach peered up among the trees provokingly close to me, I saw no way of getting to it but up a lane so horribly filthy, for there are no drains in the villages or farms, it was impossible to tread it. So I went up to the cottage, and rather by signs than words, for the old woman who came to the door spoke nothing but *patois*, made known my desire to reach the church. The magic word *sous* enlightened her a little as to my meaning. She called her little grandchild, and made me understand that for *sous* the girl would show me the way. The child came out, turned the corner of the cottage, and began ascending that horrible path. I told her it was impossible I could go up there, and if there were no other way, she might go back, as I knew of that before I came to the cottage. What it was, no pen can tell; suffice it to say that a farmer's midden is clean in comparison. The child had not gone a step beyond the cottage walls, and so I did not think it necessary to give her any *sous*; and the old mother came out and abused me roundly; and though I did not understand *patois*, I could make out plainly enough that she was telling me 'there was nothing the matter with the road. I had promised *sous*, and ought to give them.'

'So I would, and gladly,' said I, 'if the road were not so filthy, no lady could tread it; but I will not give *sous* to such dirty people.' And so saying, I turned homewards, leaving her to vociferate as much as she pleased. The last sounds that met my ears, as I descended, were '*Anglaise*' and '*sous*.' Lest you think me mean, dear reader, I beg to observe I refused the money on principle. There is nothing a peasant will not do for *sous*; and I hoped the loss of the expected guerdon might lead her *to amend her ways*. The sun was setting when Keeper and I reached Argelés.

Next day I was unwell, from the effects of my long walk; and fancying coffee disagreed with me, went out to try and get some tea. I went to three shops before I got any, and then I learnt I could procure it at a small shop in the market-place. Thither I proceeded. Had they tea? Yes, they had; and they produced perhaps a quarter of a pound *in an uncovered glass bottle*, that looked as if it had stood there for years, and was utterly scentless. However, I bought an ounce, and made tea with it that evening. I am convinced that tea had never been in China. Its colour was peculiar, inclining to a sage green, and its flavour was that of herbs. Being, however, feverish and thirsty, I drank it, and found, as I expected, that it was a tolerable *tisane*.

I was curious to know the mechanism by which the beautiful roads all round were kept up, for there never seemed to be any great repairs going on. So one day I asked the cantonnier of Argelés, whom I passed at his work, how it was managed. He showed me his *livre d'ordonnance*, containing the rules to be observed by every cantonnier.* 'The cantonniers must be at work from 5 A.M. to 7 P.M. in the summer, in winter from sunrise to sunset.' They are divided into three classes. The third and lowest receive thirty-seven francs a month; the second, thirty-nine francs; and the first, forty-two francs a month. Each has charge of a hundred *mètres* of road, within which he is bound to erect a staff, with his number on a plate at the top, so that the inspector going his rounds may see it, and to be in some part of that space. If absent, he is to be called three times, and ten minutes allowed for his appearance. If he is not forthcoming at the end of that time, he is fined two days' pay for this first dereliction of duty, six days' pay for the second, and dismissed from his employ for the third offence. Inspectors come at all hours, and especially when least expected. The plan answers, for I never saw such well-kept and magnificent roads as in the Pyrenees.

The wages are low—in England they would be frightfully low—but the necessaries of life are cheap in the Pyrenees, with the exception of bread, which cost me as much as in England. But then I am an *Anglaise;* and no French man or woman, whatever their rank or position, will tell an English person they have paid too dear for any article, so that it is difficult to ascertain the true prices. The French people hang together like a cluster of bees.

---

* *Cantonnier*—one charged with keeping the road in repair.

CHAPTER XII.

I DID not recover my long walk even by a day's thorough rest, and was too unwell to go out yesterday. My pretty little landlady came into my room to get out her Sunday handkerchief, and I had a chat with her while she did so, which ended in her showing me all her wedding handkerchiefs for the head. The peasants spend a good deal upon these articles, and their *mouchoirs* are often both very expensive and very elegant. The one Marie selected for to-day was a rich figured white silk fringed with purple. She had others still handsomer, of maize, rose colour, orange, and plaid, all of thick, rich, washing silk. When she had dressed, she came back again to show me how pretty the white *mouchoir* looked, well aware, the little coquette, that *she* looked very pretty in it—I told her so—and the compliment was evidently not unpleasant nor unexpected—she was wonderfully smart. She had on a very pretty gown, somewhat like that thin, silky stuff, which has been so much in vogue lately—a kind of woollen silk, if I may use such an expression. Round her neck she wore a collar, made of white beads, fastened by a little brooch, and she also wore lace net sleeves trimmed with lace. The edge of a white worked petticoat peeped from under the folds of her pale, lavender-coloured dress, and as she stooped to pick up something, I saw she wore neatly-tucked white drawers, and faultless stockings and *bottines.* The better class of Pyrenean women, and even the servants, are very particular about their under-garments, and would not, like too many of our dressy maids, consider themselves smart, unless they were clean, whole, and good, and of a piece with the rest of their attire.   But finery and neatness both are reserved for fair-days and Sundays.   The pretty Marie goes about in a soiled gown, uncombed hair, and a yellow handkerchief, doubled in half and loosely thrown over her head, and tied under the chin at other times, for which I sometimes reprove her, telling her that she ought always, now she is a married woman, to set herself off to the best advantage, and look well in her husband's eyes.   But handsome as he is, Marie seems rather indifferent to him.   I asked her some questions to-day about the peasant who owned the beautiful green-shuttered house with the chestnut grove behind it, on the road towards Vidalos.

'His wife, madame, was rich too,' Marie said, with a subdued sigh.

'Do you know them, Marie?'

'*Ah, oui! autrefois!* Madame had ten thousand francs when she married.   Her father was rich, and she and her sister—had—*all*'—here Marie heaved a deep sigh—'*all*—the brothers and sisters had as much—ah!—I might have been very happy!' she added, half to herself, and half to me.

'And are you not happy, Marie?   You seem to have a good, kind, handsome husband.   Are you not happy?'

'*Comme ça,*' said Marie, doubtfully—'ah! *the other*—madame's brother—*was* a handsome man—he was my first love!'

'But your husband is very handsome, Marie!'

'Yes, but not like *him!* and he was rich, he had ten thousand francs—this man has nothing.

'Then the house is yours, Marie?'

'It is my mother's, and my aunt's and mine, and my

sister's—it belongs to us all, and we all live together—and Jacques' brother lives with us too.'*

'Well, Marie, that does not seem to me to signify much. It does not matter which of you had the money, if your husband is, as he seems to be, steady and industrious—you may be very well off some day. Canon, with whom I lodged at Cauterets, was only a *voiturier* and guide, like your husband, and now he has two good houses, besides several carriages and horses of his own. What was your first lover ?'

'He tilled the earth.'

'Well, then, I think the *voiturier* is the better match— if that be all—you are not strong, Marie, and the hard life of a peasant would not have suited you—you could not have worked in the fields.'

'Perhaps I should not have needed to do so—Madame —— does not work in the fields, ever.'

'No—but then her husband has much more than ten thousand francs—in England, his estate would enable him to live like a gentleman ; but you could not have lived upon the produce of five hundred pounds.'

But Marie only shook her head, and repeated, '*L'autre était si beau !* '

'Then why did you not marry him, Marie ?'

'Oh, I was foolish ! I might have been *so happy*, and I would not. My father did not wish me to marry this one —none of my family wished it—and I would. We had had some words—the other and I—and I was foolish. Ah,

---

* The tie of blood is very strong in the Pyrenees, and all this family seemed to live very amicably together, for during the week I stayed I never heard an angry word from one to the other. And one constantly sees mothers or grandmothers living with married children, or two or three uncles living with a niece. The members of a family do not appear to separate on reaching maturity as they do in England, but rather to live together and throw their earnings into one common stock for the good of the whole.

well! it is no use thinking of that now. It is done, and I must make the best of it—and after all, this one *n'est pas méchant*,' said Marie, suddenly changing her pathetic tone to cheerfulness, and with a half smile, she scampered down stairs to go to mass.

In the evening I saw the whole family seated on chairs in front of the little shop kept by the aunt—playing at cards. The other sister, who was quite as pretty as Marie, was dressed exactly like her, except that she had a lace collar on instead of a bead one; and I could not help thinking, as I looked at them, how strange it was that two such neat, nice girls should live in a house whose floors were never washed, though I must do them the justice to say, it was well swept, and cleaner than any other house of the same class I entered in Argelés. This Sunday card-playing is almost universal in France, and I wonder that the priests, who set their face against much less objectionable things, do not put it down. When twilight made it impossible to see the marks on the cards any longer, Marie and her sister began to sing some of the old pathetic popular airs of the country. A girl on the opposite side of the street joined in the song; and I lay in my bed, and listened to their fresh, sweet, young voices till near midnight. I think I never heard any female voices so liquid, and so round. They had not a harsh or shrill note in them; and this seems to me peculiarly characteristic both of the singers and the music of the Pyrenees. This music is an inspiration. It seems an echo of the warble of the birds, the hoarse and continuous dash of the torrent, the soft trickling of the meadow-runnel through the green grass, and the murmur of the brook over the stones: and, as in the wild bird's song, one long note is often prolonged for a minute or two above the chords sung by the other voices, and yet blends with them into one harmonious whole. These lengthened sustained notes, which seem prolonged more or less according to the taste of the singer, are peculiar to the music of the Pyrenees.

To-day, Monday, October 13th, 1862, I have taken my last long walk at Argelés. I walked to the church, as directed by Marie, and then inquired my way to St. Savin. A little lane near the church soon leads one into an upper road parallel to, but above, that which leads to Pierrefitte; this led me into a noble chestnut wood, nearly three miles long, and some of the trees were really majestic, and between their large massive trunks and far-reaching branches, every here and there, were green glades and openings, whence one got a magnificent view of the mountains, and the valley of Argelés below.

The chestnut crop was already gathered, and a drove of pigs and a few merry children were contesting for the stray fallen ones hidden under the leaves. It is customary here to drive the pigs into the chestnut woods after the gathering is over, and the refuse fattens them well. I can't make out why pork is comparatively so much dearer than other meat in the Pyrenees, seeing the pigs appear to get half their keep for nothing. Every commune seems, as at the English lakes, to have a certain portion of uncultivated land on the mountain side belonging to it, whence the wood for the district is procured. The acorns are considered a crop, and the pigs from one village must not eat acorns off the lands belonging to another commune. There was a little crispness in the air to-day that was very refreshing, and it was very pleasant walking up to one's ancles in the crackling brown chestnut leaves that formed a thick, soft bed under the trees, and hearing them rustle under one's feet, the bright sunshine above playing upon them here and there in streaks of red light, or glancing through the boughs overhead, and turning the fading leaves to crimson and gold, or shedding a soft gleamy light upon the green hollows below. The flowers are nearly over. I gathered a few of the smaller scabious, the giant bindweed, a stray honeysuckle, some wild marjoram, harebells, and one or two of the beautiful fringed pinks.   That was all ; but I never had a lovelier walk.   I thought how pleasant it would have been to have sat whole days under this chestnut wood with a friend, reading Shakespeare or Shelley, the best landscape-painters I know, with a faithful dog at one's feet, one's hand lying on his smooth head, and looking down every now and then between whiles at the beautiful world below. The path through the chestnut wood conducted me nearly to St. Savin, a village whose neat outward appearance contrasted favourably with that of the dirty Argelés.   The market-place is square, and in the centre stands rather a handsome cross ; but I saw no pretty drinking-fountain like that of Argelés, as is common in villages of its calibre and importance.   The upper parts of many of the houses project, resting on wooden pillars, while the ends of the timbers, on which these upper rooms are built, jut out, and form a sort of ornamental border as it appears seen from below.

The streets were quite clean, although it has not, like Argelés, the advantage of a running stream before every door, that bears all impurities away. St. Savin, to whom the church is dedicated, is the chief saint of Lavedan. 'The valley of Lavedan includes those of Azun, Davautaigue, Batsouriguère, Estreme de Salles, and Pierrefitte, or St. Savin.' I fancy it also includes Lourdes, Argelés, and Cauterets; for they are always spoken of as in Lavedan. The saint, however, was of Spanish origin, being, it is said, the son of a Count of Barcelona, supposed to have been the brother of Hentilius, Count of Poictiers, and of the kindred of the Kings of France. He lost his father early, and was the sole hope and consolation of a tender mother, who brought him up with the most loving care, occupying herself with his education, in the hope it

might render him worthy of the lofty destiny which awaited
him.   Poor mother! she instilled into his mind an earnest
sense of duty and a deep religious feeling, which in that
age, when both men and women thought they served God
best by breaking up all family ties, and neglecting all near
duties, to throw themselves into a cloister, was to become
afterwards 'a sword to pierce through her own heart.'

Savin grew in goodness as he grew in years. He showed
himself in early youth to be worthy of the power and
wealth with which God had entrusted him, and employed
both in relieving the sufferings of the poor. He was yet
young when he felt a desire to visit his uncle Hentilius,
Count of Poictiers. His mother, knowing the great renown
of this Count, who was one of the greatest lords of that
time, thought a voyage to his country and a residence in
his court might be very useful to the heir of Barcelona,
by enabling him to study the manners and civil polity of
a great nation, and become initiated under so great a
master into the secrets of administration, which he would
himself be called on to exercise in his own county, and
therefore consented reluctantly to his departure. Savin
left his home sorrowfully and with tears; he knew well
that he was bidding his mother adieu for ever. He had
not undertaken this journey to gain instruction in the ways
of the world, or to satisfy a laudable curiosity. He avoided
all great towns on his route, preferring the solitudes
wherein the disciples of St. Benedict had founded their
monasteries, that he might learn of them the abnegation
which makes a saint. Old legends tell that he traversed
the county of Foix, passing through the little town of
Mas d'Azil, 'and so came at last to Poictiers to his uncle's
abode, where he hastened to make his obeisance to the
count, and was by him received as an angel, caressed as
one of his kin, and treated like a young prince.'

Hentilius soon appreciated the precocious merit and

intelligence of his nephew, and gave him the highest mark of his esteem by charging him, young as he was, with the education of his eldest son and heir.   But though loaded with the gifts of his uncle, and living in the midst of a luxurious court, Savin retained his simplicity of character and his charitable and devout habits.   He divided his time between his duties as a teacher, the care of the poor, and prayer to God, denying himself everything but bare necessaries, that he might give away the rest.   The son of Hentilius was a docile pupil, and Savin painted the mysterious charm of a life devoted wholly to solitude and contemplation, and the dangers and temptations of the world, in such glowing colours, as easily to persuade the youth that the cloister was the only sure refuge, and that his duty was to devote his whole life to the service of God, who gave it. The young disciple fled from his father's house, and forsook his future countship, to retire into a Benedictine monastery dedicated to St. Martin.   The Countess of Poictiers, overwhelmed with grief at her son's departure, sought out Savin, and, throwing herself at his feet, conjured him to seek the beloved son who had been confided to his care that he might become worthy of his high destiny as ruler of a people, and not that he might be thus withdrawn from his duties and his family.

Savin answered her no word, but set out at once for the monastery; not, however, to persuade his cousin to return home, but to encourage him to persevere in the course he had chosen.   He himself followed his example; and the same day saw the two cousins, both sons of counts, clothed with the coarse habit of the order of St. Benedict.   While one admires the devotion and purity of mind these two young men evinced in a licentious and dissolute age, one cannot help feeling how much more heroic their conduct would have been had they *resisted temptation*, instead of *fleeing* from it, and had they used the fine talents and wide charity with which God had endowed them, in endeavouring to ameliorate the condition of their respective subjects. It seems strange that even the most devout should so often be blind to the truth that there is no religion in neglecting a plain duty. God had called them by their birth to be princes, not monks; and had they remained manfully fighting in the posts where the General and Lord of all had placed them, they would have fulfilled a much higher duty than by leaving them to be filled up by less highly-principled men, and becoming ascetics.

The rigours of a cloistral life, however, were not sufficient for Savin. He pined for the complete seclusion of an anchorite. He confided his design to the abbot of his monastery—who neither dared blame it, lest he should hinder the work of God, nor yet encourage the departure of a monk who edified the whole convent by his exactitude in observing its rules, and his devout and virtuous life. But the perseverance of Savin overcame all obstacles, and he obtained at last the abbot's permission to depart with one companion only.

The two hermits directed their steps towards the mountains of Bigorre. As they passed through Tarbes, Savin did not omit to pay his respects to the bishop who then occupied the chair of St. Justin and St. Faustus, and to ask his blessing upon their undertaking. Thirty-six kilomètres* from that town, upon the side of a mountain overlooking the valley of Lavedan, was a Benedictine monastery, which had been founded on the ruins of an ancient castle or fort, probably Gallo-Roman, as the old name of *Palatium-Emilianum,* which it retained until after the death of St. Savin, seems to indicate.

Here the two travellers were cordially received by

* A kilomètre is a thousand mètres; 1 mètre is equal to 3 English feet, and 281 decimal parts.

Forminius, then abbot; and Savin opening his heart to him, told him of his desire to flee into the deserts of the mountains, and practise the austere life of a hermit. Forminius considering this wish as the inspiration of God, did not seek to dissuade him; and recognizing in him all the signs of a true vocation, wished, if he could not retain such a treasure in his convent, to keep him at least in the neighbourhood, and conducted him to a retired place three or four kilomètres from the monastery.

They fixed their choice upon the *plateau* called Pouey-Aspé, from whence the rich and beautiful valley is seen in all its extent. But Savin's choice of the spot was determined by the fact, that from this elevation he could see between two bare rocks which shut in a solitary valley opposite, a hermitage which had been sanctified long before by being the abode of a young Spaniard named St. Orens, who came from Huença about the beginning of the fifth century, to live as a solitary in a cave surrounded by dense forests—a daily memento, as it were, to him, not to stumble or fall away from the life of austerity he had chosen.

Savin's first care was to construct himself a rude shelter against the ferocity of wild beasts; but as it was only seven or eight feet long, and four or five wide, its construction could not have cost him much time, notwithstanding the difficulty of transporting materials up almost inaccessible mountain paths. The Abbot Forminius, who had, no doubt, aided him in this work, often went to visit him, that he might be edified by the example of such perfect holiness. Savin thinking his narrow prison too luxurious, after a time dug a grave seven feet long and five deep, thus literally 'making his bed in the tomb' during his mortal life, 'although the damp trickled down from all parts, above all in rainy weather, as a beautiful passage from the Office of the Saint informs us' (*sic*).

Forminius returning some time after, was quite astonished to see that Savin had dug this grave without previously informing him of his intention, and inquired the
reason of this exaggeration of penitence.

'*I only know the secrets of my heart,*' replied the hermit ;
'*therefore I only can measure the punishment with the extent
of my faults. Each one must do what he can. I do what I
ought.*'

Here, like Elias upon Mount Carmel, the saint gave
himself up to prayer, contemplation, and the rough practices of a mortified life. He outwatched the stars, and
his fasts were nearly perpetual. His occupation was
contemplation. Clothed in a coarse robe, which miraculously lasted thirteen years, he walked barefoot on the
pointed mountain rocks, even in the severest weather.
Alone in this savage retreat, and often iced with cold, his
frail cell shaking with the violence of the stormy winds,
and threatening to leave him without defence against the
wild beasts which abounded in the neighbouring forests,
he maintained his soul in a calm above all human fear,
entirely absorbed by the love of God, and the burning
desire to be reunited to Him whom he loved.

Being no longer able to relieve their bodily necessities
since he had renounced all wealth, Savin opened his cell
and his heart to all the poor and unhappy who came to
him for advice or consolation, endeavouring by his exhor-
tations to destroy the reign of sin in their souls, and re-
establish that of justice. Ingratitude and ill-treatment
did not wear out his inexhaustible charity. He looked
upon men as sick people, more worthy of compassion than
anger ; recommended them to the mercy of God in the
silence of his retreat, and ceased not to solicit His compassion for them. None of those who visited the hermitage
went away without having obtained by his intercession

L

either health of body, or some grace still more precious for the soul.

Many were the miracles he performed, some of them by letters, as may be read in the *Monographie de St. Savin de Lavedan, par M. Lagréze.*

'Once a priest, who was on his way to exercise some of his ministerial functions, had to traverse on horseback the swollen torrent of the Gave of Cauterets, at a point near Pierrefitte. The horse was borne down by the current, and the priest himself fell into the waters, and was momentarily threatened with a dreadful death by being either swallowed up in their deep abysses, or crushed to death between the huge rocks brought down from the mountains by the melting snows. In this extremity, he retained sufficient calmness to put all his trust in God, and to recommend himself to the prayers of the solitary of Pouey-Aspé. All at once he felt himself gently pushed towards the bank, which he regained safe and sound, finding, with surprise, his horse standing on the same bank, miraculously saved as well as himself.—A poor mother, named Gaudentia, found that she had no longer milk enough to nurse her starving child. After trying all earthly means in vain, she turned her thought solely to God; but recognizing her own unworthiness, resolved to implore the prayers of St. Savin. Accompanied by her husband, she undertook a pilgrimage to Pouey-Aspé, and with tears in her eyes, presented to him the frail and innocent creature, beseeching him to save its life. The saint, touched by compassion, prayed like a second Elisha; and forthwith God restored her milk to the mother, and the child's life was saved.

'Moreover,' says the legend, 'Savin was so inflamed by the love of God, that wishing one evening to dissipate the darkness of his cell, he had only to put a small wax candle that he held in his hand near his breast, and it flamed immediately; while, by a double miracle, this candle lighted him the whole night without being consumed.'

Although the holy saint's time was chiefly occupied by his devotions, physical needs sometimes made themselves felt; and as in the hot season the springs near his cell dried up, he had to go through a meadow belonging to a man named Chromatius, who dwelt in the little village of Uz, to fetch water. The wicked proprietor of the meadow refused him this feeble succour, unless he would pay for it, and ordered one of his servants to drive away the daring solitary who ventured to intrude upon his property. The savage order was well obeyed. The servant, after having abused the saint, struck him brutally. But God, who sometimes suffers the just to be tried by the wickedness and cruelty of the evil, and yet often vindicates the innocent when His wisdom thinks fit, avenged him. He who had thus outraged his saint became immediately possessed by the Devil, while the master lost his eyesight at the same moment. Savin, whose charity was boundless, was grieved at heart to find himself thus the cause of a double misfortune; and falling on his knees, entreated the Lord to have pity on those who had used him so unworthily. His prayer disarmed the Divine vengeance; the man-servant was at once delivered from the demon, and could not help owning that he owed his deliverance to the very man he had so cruelly beaten; but the master, Chromatius, who had ordered the outrage, remained blind.

, In consequence of these things, Savin determined to fetch water no more out of that field; and 'putting his whole faith in God, like another Moses,' so runs the tradition, 'he struck the rock with his stick, and a slender thread of pure water trickled out, and the spring remains until this day, though the supply of water be small.'

And now the hour came when St. Savin felt that he

was about to die, and he sent to tell the Abbot Forminius of his approaching end, and to desire that he would come to be with him in his last moments, and give him his benediction. The abbot, hindered, no doubt, by necessary cares, made answer that he could not come till the day following ; and the more because two of his monks, Sylvien and Flavian, had been for some days attending on the sick anchorite, and spoke of him as recovering.

Saint Savin despatched a second messenger to Forminius, adding that the day following he would have a more pressing occupation still than that which now withheld him from coming—alluding thereby to his own approaching death. But Forminius thought he might safely wait till the morrow. He was deceived.

During the thirteen years that he had passed in solitude, the saint's chief aim had been to evangelize the inhabitants of Lavedan ; to that his prayers and his lacerations alike tended ; and now he was dying, he chose himself the person who should succeed him in his hermitage, and continue his charitable endeavours : and having disposed of the few trifles he possessed, prepared for the unspeakable happiness of receiving, for the last time, the bread of angels, which was to serve him instead of the *viaticum.* Then, with his dying arms stretched out towards heaven and his eyes fixed on the image of his Saviour, he surrendered his soul to God, and fell asleep.

When the sound of the passing bell warned the inhabitants of Lavedan that their friend was dead, they all mourned greatly. The Abbot Forminius ordered that the body should be conveyed to the monastery, there to receive sepulchre, and prepared himself, with all his monks, to go and receive the holy remains with all the pomp and honours of the church. Chromatius, who had been struck blind for his cruelty to the holy man, touched by a late repentance, bewailed his fault ; and full of faith, had himself led to a spot that the procession must pass in going through Uz. He was told when the coffin passed, and going up to it with confidence, touched it, beseeching the saint to pardon his former brutal conduct and restore his sight. He recovered his sight immediately, at which all the assistants shouted for joy. The memory of this miracle, which the Roman Catholic priests affirm to be well attested, is preserved in one of the eight pictures in the *basilica* of the church of St. Savin, and there is yet to be seen on the façade of the house in Uz, before which the funeral convoy stopped, a niche, containing a statue of the saint, placed there in memory of the miracle. Later, the body of St. Savin was solemnly laid in the church, which replaced the Emilian Palace—that same beautiful church in the Roman style—which exists to this day, and which merits to be classed among the historical monuments of France.

The inhabitants of the place, full of gratitude and veneration for the memory of the holy anchorite, had a chapel constructed where his hermitage had stood, and taking from their *commune* the name of Villabencer, which it had hitherto borne, called it St. Savin, by which title it has since been known. This chapel, after the lapse of so many centuries, fell into ruins. At the desire of many pious Roman Catholics, the curé of the parish raised subscriptions for its reconstruction, and the foundations are now digging.

I have by me a flourishing description of the church of St. Savin, from which most of these details are taken. As I am no archæologist (I wish I was), I hope, dear reader, you will pardon my ignorance when I say that these grand descriptions by no means prepare one for what one actually finds—a very dilapidated, very curious, and dirty old church, supported by large, low pillars, and arches, with a round end to the chancel instead of a square one.

Round this chancel and the high altar, hang eight ver. dilapidated, curious old pictures, illustrative of the life of the saint; but they are so faded, that it is rather difficult to make out their subjects. The chief altar was built in the time of Louis XV., and is of various kinds of marble, and richly ornamented ; but it has never been completely finished, and like our own Westminster Abbey, *the whole place is lost in dirt.* The organ appears very old, and is very remarkable for its caryatides, its sculptural arabesque, and its greyish paintings of subjects from the Old Testament. The space between the groups of pipes is ornamented by open carved wood-work, forming a sort of drapery. Underneath, are three great masques, which roll their eyes, and open and shut their mouths, when certain pedals are touched, so as to mark the time of the music. Above the keyboard is this inscription :—

'*Hoc organum factum fuit ad honorem totius curiæ celestis, anno* 1557.'

The tomb of St. Savin is at the bottom of the chancel, and on each side are two rows of coarsely-sculptured walnut-wood stalls. For many centuries the tomb served—as was then customary—for the chief altar. It was built before the construction of the church, and is surmounted by a gilt pyramid of open-work of the thirteenth or fourteenth century.

The church of St. Savin, constructed on the ruins of an ancient Roman palace, enriched by Charlemagne, and afterwards burnt by the Normans, was rebuilt in the tenth century by Raymond I., Count of Bigorre, who richly endowed it and the monastery attached to it. Henry IV., King of France and Navarre, confirmed the charters given to the monks by his predecessors, the Counts of Bigorre.

The relics are of an extraordinary nature ; among them is a curious reliquary, containing some of the saints' bones, which is solemnly carried in procession on the day of his *fête,* the 11th of October. It may be seen by applying to the curate, and is said to be of very beautiful workmanship. I did not see it, because not having at that time read the life of St. Savin (which by the way is written by the present curé M. Abbadie, and sold by him for the benefit of the poor of St. Savin), I knew nothing about it, as it is not mentioned by Murray. The monks belonging to the monastery of St. Savin were very rich, and had great powers and privileges granted to them, both by the Counts of Bigorre and the Kings of France, and by the bulls of Popes Urban XI. in 1006, and Alexander III. in the year of grace 1168, and by briefs from many succeeding popes.

They were of the congregation of St. Maur and the order of St. Benedict; and in an inventory of the goods and revenues of the monastery, signed by Dom Charles Gerard, the last prior, it is stated that the convent fed 600 poor during Lent. The monastery is now the property of the State, and so modified, that nothing of its cloistral character remains, except the small chapter-house and the refectory. It is not shown to strangers, but I was told that a speculative *cook* had taken it as a season boarding-house, and, I should think, it would be a very pleasant summer *pension,* from the beauty of its site. I was told there was a handsome church about a mile off, dedicated to Ste. Marie, that is, to the Virgin, and as the day was most enchanting, and the views from this high natural terrace, lovely beyond expression, I continued my walk.

Ste. Marie is but a short distance from St. Savin. It is rather a handsome village church, but looks better from the outside than from within. The door, as is common in Catholic churches, stood wide open, and I walked in, and went round it by myself; but as I was coming out, an old woman, who sat there knitting, demanded something for showing the church—which I refused. My means are so limited, I cannot give half-francs to every one who chooses to ask for them, and the demands of the Pyrenean peasants are unceasing.   So I quietly walked off; the old woman following, scolding and screaming after me till I was quite out of hearing.   I might have descended the steep rock on which Ste. Marie stands, by a narrow winding path, and so reached the high road, and returned to Argelés; but I could not find it in my heart to turn back; I could have walked on and on for ever, as long as strength remained, on that beautiful day, and in that beautiful country.   So Keeper and I went through another long chestnut wood towards Pierrefitte, the entrance to which town we reached about five o'clock.   I thought it had been two or three— and was amazed to find it so late—when I inquired the time.   The days were shortening, and I had to hurry on, that I might get back to Argelés before dusk.   The high road was not very interesting after the beautiful natural terraces and their chestnut woods, and as I plodded on- wards, I found out—now that my mind was no longer kept in a state of excitement by the extreme beauty of the country—that I was very hungry.   I had no resource but to enter a field, where I saw some peasant women at work, and ask them to sell me a cob of Indian corn; the girls looked highly amused by my request, and picked me out a fine one, which I devoured on my way home, and thought very good.   It was past seven o'clock when I reached Ar- gelés, and Marie had been quite uneasy about me.

The next day I was to leave Argelés.   I was glad when it came, civil as Marie and Jacques had been to me.   It is a most inconvenient place of abode—there is no fruit to be got, except on the market-day—no regular butcher, except on the market-day—no butter—no eggs—no nothing—in short, not even vegetables, except on the market-day; few articles of any sort in the dirty little shops, and those abominably dear, and bad.   I loathed even the very bread

I ate, after I had once, in walking through the town, seen the hot loaves, fresh from the oven, placed on the filthy floor to cool. Going one day to buy some bread, I found the bakeress's family refreshing themselves with a joint of meat that stood on the table; there were no plates, but each person had a slice of meat, or a bone, in his or her hand. Upon my asking for bread, the bakeress put down the huge piece she was devouring, and was about to hand a loaf to me with her greasy fingers, when I forestalled her, and begging leave to help myself, suited the action to the word—

'You don't like the meat—*cependant c'est bon*,' said a young man.

'*I don't like my bread greased*, certainly,' replied I.

'Ah! I knew that was it; I have travelled, and I know the ways of other places are different to those of Argelés. Tell me, now, what you think of the place and the people.'

'Perhaps you will be affronted.'

'O no.'

'Well, then! I think the place a paradise for beauty and climate; the inhabitants most civil, and even kind; but I would not live among them for the world—their ways are so dirty—the unwashed floors are enough to sicken one, and yesterday I saw your neighbour, the other baker, cooling his loaves on that filthy floor. I cannot conceive, when water is so plentiful in Argelés, why people do not scour down their tables, shop counters, dressers, and floors, as we do in England.'

'No one scours floors here. The floors are not washed once in twenty years in Argelés,' said a very pretty, smartly-dressed girl, who was on a visit to the family, in rather a contemptuous tone, as if she felt herself very superior to, and much above, my vulgar insular prejudices.

'It is true,' said the travelled peasant, 'no one does it.'

'I suppose they do in respectable houses—I mean among the gentry of the place,' quoth I.

'*They don't,*' he returned; 'if the great people had their houses scoured, the little people would follow their example. But when you leave Argelés, you will find that in the Pyrenees no one has their houses scoured.'

Les convenances are not much attended to by the bakers. I generally bought my own bread; and the first time I went for some, I was startled by seeing as I entered the shop two men naked to the waist, beating up the dough in a large tub, and between every thump giving a deep guttural kind of groan, as sailors sing out 'Yo-ho!' when they heave an anchor, and looking exactly like the engraving of 'Egyptian bakers at work,' in Wilkinson's 'Egyptian Antiquities.' I drew back in dismay, and ever after bought my bread at the bakeress's next door.

On Tuesday, Marie and her sister came out as smart as on Sunday—they were each going to keep a cake-stall in the market-place of Argelés, and their man-servant had charge of another, a few yards down our street. They were certainly an industrious, striving family, and had many strings to their bow. They kept a *cabaret*, or wayside inn, where wine, not beer, 'was drunk on the premises;' but, except on the market-day, it was not much frequented, and I found no annoyance to speak of from it. Jacques was a guide to strangers and a *voiturier*. They had a small shop for soap and candles, and thread, &c., chiefly managed by the aunt; and the mother made pastry and cakes of various kinds for sale. They had all been very civil and kind to me; and notwithstanding my English ways, I think they liked me; so before I left, I shook hands with them all round, and, moreover, gave them a lesson in scouring floors with Keeper's brush, by which I am afraid, as the custom is new to Argelés, they would not profit. I really was sorry to say good-by to them. After I had packed my wee bag, I carried it down to M. Armiral's shop, and then I strolled through the market, and found out Marie's stall, and bought a sponge-cake, which the good-hearted girl wanted to give me as a *souvenir*, and which was very good too; and then Keeper and I wandered up and down lanes, and sat on walls looking at the beautiful mountains, till the market of Argelés closed, and it was time to get into M. Armiral's coach. It was night when we reached Bagnères, and I was glad to get to my new lodgings and to bed.

October 16th, 1862.—I had such a pleasant walk yesterday. You cannot imagine how beautiful this country is now, in autumn, when the changing leaves, with their crimson and brown and pale yellow hues, contrast so beautifully with the spring-like verdure of the emerald meadows. Down between mountain passes or sombre chestnut and oak woods one gets glimpses of lovely green valleys watered by clear streams, and under the trees grow the beautiful large bugle; the delicate-fringed, sweet-scented dianthus springs from the rocky ledges of the mountains; and there are so many other flowers, and everything looks so gay and bright, that as I walk along I am involuntarily reminded of some lines out of one of the old poets, which I was fond of repeating in my youth—

> 'The winter here, a summer is—
> No waste is made by Time—
> Nor doth the autumn ever miss
> The blossoms of the prime.'

I found pink centaury, the larger and the lesser scabious, tormentilla, wild reseda, and a little low-creeping potentilla, that at first sight I took for a strawberry.

The view from the Bédat is exquisite. One looks upon mountain piled behind and upon mountain, with such lovely little valleys dotted over by trees, and white cottages nestling under chestnut trees and copses, cresting picturesque ledges of rocks lying in their green depths and hollows. · As I came down again from the top, I gathered quite a *gerbe* of flowers; and when I got to the chestnut trees, instead of turning down the road to Bagnères, I went upwards through a long lane at the back of Salut—where I gathered a quantity of the beautiful wild spindle-berries—and came out into some green fields forming a sort of natural terrace in front of Castel-Monné and the Monné.   Several white farmhouses, surrounded by orchards, lay scattered about; high hedges of wild box-trees sheltered the green meadows from the wind; and as I sat resting on the thick, fine grass, with Keeper at my feet, and basking in the sunshine, arranged my beautiful bouquet, I could hardly believe it was not the early summer-time, and the illusion was completed by the bleatings of some young lambs, who were frisking beside their mothers on one of the sunny banks.   An indescribable feeling of holy calm and peace, such as I have not felt for years, steals over me as I wander alone among these mountains—a sense of the majesty and the power of God such as I never before experienced; and, like the Apostle on the Mount, I feel inclined to say, ' Master, it is good to be here; here let me build a tabernacle.'

When I got home, I made my room look really pretty with my wild flowers.   Madame —— kindly lent me all the flower-vases in the house, and I put three on the sideboard and one on each table, besides those I took her for her *salon*.   That on my book-table was so pretty that I must describe it, dear reader.

It was made entirely of the lilac-fringed pinks, and the spindle-berries, and you cannot think how beautifully the pale-pink capsules of the spindle-berries, with their four bright orange seeds, one in each cell, harmonized with the delicate lilac dianthus.   I wonder that Ruskin has never written about the 'Complementary Colours' of flowers.

There is such a thing; and the French lady's *maître d'hôtel* was right, when he excused himself, as he put a less beautifully-arranged *bouquet* than usual in the centre of the dinner-table, by saying, 'he had not had time that day *to study its composition.*' I was always fond of grouping flowers from my childhood; and my mother, who had always nosegays in her room, entrusted the making them up to me, as, she said, I made prettier *bouquets* than she could.

We had not a great variety of flowers in that old-fashioned vicarage garden, and I was sometimes at a loss for contrasts. When flowers grew scarce towards the close of summer, the everlasting peas were in full beauty. Growing round the two cherry-trees, a rich mass of Magenta colour, they looked beautiful; but they marred every nosegay I put them into. Those everlasting peas were my *cauchemar*. It was years before I found out what other flowers would harmonize with them; but when I lived at Hampstead, I discovered that they made an exquisite nosegay mixed with the flowers of the lime-tree, after most of the dark-green leaves had been cut away. Their pale, tender, yellow-green is the complementary colour that the deep-red of the pea requires. Its own young leaves and tendrils are of somewhat the same shade, especially when the sunlight glances through them—for Nature, or, rather, Nature's Almighty framer, always mingles, both in animals and plants, those colours which harmonize best together. The only exception that I know of to this rule is in the monkey tribe, some of whom seem actually made for the purpose of disgusting.

CHAPTER XIII.

I WENT to-day along the beautiful upper terrace cut through the wood of Mont Olivet, from whence one has a lovely view of the valley of Bagnères, besides delightful peeps at the blue mountains through vistas cut among the trees. I found here, for the first time, the delicate ivy-leaved campanula, a creeping plant, whose slender stalk is scarcely thicker than one of my hairs, and bears several small bells of the loveliest pale cerulean blue. It twines round the stalks of the long grass, or creeps under the furze, drooping from the bank in low, graceful festoons. I found dodder also. Do you know that pretty little parasite? It looks like tangled threads of red silk, thrown carelessly upon the heath and furze, and has a delicate blush-coloured flower, like a minute *Hoya*, and like it is honey-scented, and covered with a sort of honey-dew. I fancy it is not very common in England, for though I have been a flower-seeker all my life, I never met with it except at Tunbridge Wells, where it grows on the upper common above the town, not far from Dr. Cummings's cottage.

From Mont Olivet I turned into the high road to La Bassère, followed it a little way, and then struck into a footpath across a field, below a wooded hill, on the right-hand side. There was a very pretty bit of woodland scenery here; it only wanted a few cows grazing to make it quite a subject for a painter. Nearly at the foot of the hill the meadows were divided by a little brook, forming endless

pools and shallows and windings, overshadowed by alders,
and bridged in its widest part by one large slab of unhewn
stone, so slightly to all appearance poised up on a large
roundish one, that as I crossed it I wondered whether it
might not give way under me and give me a sousing in the
water. Keeper—who always takes care to keep at a
respectful distance from me out of doors, except when we
are both tired out and lie down to rest on the grass—
would by no means adventure his precious carcase upon it
while I was there. He put a paw on the stone, looked
cunning; drew it off, and scampered to the other end of
the field. Once he got as far as the middle, but upon my
turning to call him he ran away again. His coyness
irresistibly suggested a ducking. A wash does him good
now and then, and go into the water he won't; so I walked
up towards the opposite wood and sat quietly down on a
felled tree. Now Mr. Keeper thought himself safe, and he
came and lay down beside me. Alas! he was once more
deceived by his faithless mistress. I caught him by the
scuff of his neck, carried him, fighting and scratching like
a rabbit with his hind feet, back across the brook, sat down
under the alder bush, and laved him well in the deep pool
at its root. As soon as I let him go he shook himself,
whisked his tail in defiance, and bounded off into the very
muckiest part of the swamp, as much as to say, 'You've
had your fun and now I'll have mine.' Nor would he
come back or approach me or cross the brook again till
he saw me half way up the wooded hill opposite, when he
dashed after me. I followed a narrow path out through
the low brushwood and met some peasant women who were
gathering dead boughs to burn, and dry fern leaves to
fodder their cattle, and they told me it would lead me to
the next village, called Pouzac. Here and there the path
was a little wider, the sun shown in upon a dry sandbank
under some holly trees, and the little lizards ran in and

out of their holes, or stopped an instant to look timidly at
me, and then waggled off as fast as they could. They
seem to live in communities, for one scarcely ever sees a
solitary one; but I am told they are very pugnacious, and
often have terrible battles with one another. They are
always a dull brown and ash colour, never green as in Italy
and Germany, and are singularly like crocodiles, if one may
compare small things with great ones. After I got out of
the wood I came to a meadow, bordered by grand old chestnut trees. The ground beneath them was sprinkled all over
with the beautiful flowers of the meadow saffron. In the
wood at the side of this meadow I noticed our common
garden shrub, St. John's wort, and also that creeping kind
which bears a large handsome golden-coloured flower, and
is often called the rose of Sharon. I wonder this plant is
not more cultivated, for it is one of the few that grow well
under trees. I remember a show place at Torquay where
the shrubbery was absolutely carpeted with it, and whether
in or out of flower the effect was very good. It is an ever-
green, and never grows in a straggling untidy manner, but
of one uniform height, forming a compact dark green
carpet.

A peasant who was at the far end of the meadow came
up to see whether I was not gathering up his chestnuts—
for though the crop had been got in, a few missed ones
still hung on the trees or lay on the ground—and seemed
much relieved to find I was only pulling crocuses. He
asked, ' What I was going to do with all those flowers?'
as I am often asked. The peasants here cannot understand one's taking pleasure in a thing merely on account
of its beauty. I inquired the way up the hill; he pointed
it out, and I began the ascent. I had not gone far, when
a man leading a cart overtook me, and we fell into talk.

' *Madame est Anglaise?* '

' Yes.'

'What did Madame think of the country?'

'It was beautiful as heart could wish; Madame had never seen a finer country.'

'Yes, the country was well enough, and one could get a living in it; but then one must work hard for it. How did Madame like the people?'

'Madame thought the people a fine race, and always civil and kind; but she did not approve of the women working in the fields—they did not work in that manner in England.' *

'It is the custom here, that.'

C'est la coutume, appears to the Pyrenean an unanswerable argument.

'May be so,' said I; 'but it's bad policy. In the first place, it destroys your women's health and good looks—they are old at thirty.'

'Yes, that is quite true—they are quite old at that age.'

'And in England they are still young and pretty, because they do not work in the fields.'

'But they *must* work here—people must work hard here to get a living.'

'They must work harder in England, where every necessary of life is so much dearer. But there is no economy in your women doing field work; they not only get old soon, but their health is ruined; you have to send for the doctor, and to pay for medicine; and besides all that, you actually spend more money in various ways than you would do if your wives remained at home. Your houses are neglected and dirty, because, when the wife

---

* It appears from the returns of the last census that Madame only showed crass ignorance of the real state of her own country in asserting that women did not work in the fields in England as they do in the Pyrenees, merely because they do not do so except a few days' weeding, hay-making, or harvesting in the year, in the county (Yorkshire) in which she lived most of her life. This women's field-work is *a disgrace* to two nations that call themselves *civilized!*

M

goes home at night after a day's hard labour, she is too tired to clean it up.   For the same reason, you never have a comfortable meal.   When the Yorkshire labourer comes home, he finds a good supper ready by the fireside for him, and his children awaiting his return with clean-washed hands and faces, hair nicely combed, and clean pinafores on ; his kitchen and hearth all clean swept up, neat and comfortable, and a good fire burning in the grate ; while you come home to a cold hearth and a dirty house.   Then, as your wife is working all day afield, she can neither mend your clothes, nor make her own or her children's ; so, for want of timely repair, your clothes wear out and you have to buy new ones ; and, last and worst of all, your poor children often meet with dreadful accidents and get lamed for life, or burned to death, because they have no mother at home to take proper care of them, and then again the doctor has to be sent for ; so that, if you put all these expenses together, I think you would find you saved more if the women stayed at home and attended to their own proper work.'

'There may be truth in that,' answered the peasant ; ' *mais que voulez-vous ? c'est la coutume.*'

I don't believe anything but an *ordonnance* of Govern-ment, forbidding women to work in the fields, would put a stop to this practice ; and it is so demoralizing, that the subject is worthy the Government's attention—it forbids a great many more innocent things.

Then the peasant next asked if I had seen Le Camp de César.   The view from it was *magnifique ;* and if I would accompany him to the top of the mountain, he would direct me to it.   He was going nearly as high to set potatoes.   Potatoes grew well on the mountains ; and last year, when all the potatoes in the lowlands were blighted, there was not one touched on the mountains.

This tallied with what I had always thought, that the

disease arose from a superabundant degree of moisture in the soil.* When I was a child living near York, the potatoes grown on the dry sandy soil, which abounds in some places there, were very superior to those grown on the clay. The oxen dragged the cart slowly up one of the zigzag roads cut in the mountain, which at a distance look like a huge pair of idle-tongs laid on its flank; and as he went along the peasant told me the names of some of the smaller mountains. There was the Twelve o'clock Mountain, so called because, when the sun rested just above that, it was always twelve o'clock; and the Four o'clock Mountain, and many others. But numbers in this range have no name; and when they have, the peasants do not always know them. '*C'est la montagne*,' is often the only answer you can get to a question about their nomenclature.

We reached the brow of the hill at last, and before turning into another road, my friend directed me to hold on towards the top of the hill, where I should find a road that would lead me to Cæsar's Camp, and see a most magnificent view; 'And don't forget,' added he, 'that *I* told you how beautiful it was, and took you up this mountain, and told you the names of the Twelve o'clock and the Four o'clock Mountains; *but put* ME *into your book*, since you say you came to this country to write a book about it, and say, "The peasant I met near the Camp de César told me all this."' I laughed, and promised I would; but, alas! he forgot to tell me his name, and I to ask it,—so I cannot immortalize him.

About half-an-hour's good walking brought me to the farmhouse called Cæsar's Camp, which once belonged to an Englishman, and had been a very pretty semi-French,

---

* I was told in France that if beans were planted with potatoes in the low lands, the beans prevented *the disease*, by absorbing the superabundant moisture.

semi-English cottage of gentility. It stands upon a sort of natural platform on the very brow of the hill, with a fir wood sheltering it behind. A pretty garden has once clearly sloped from its front.

> ' Near yonder copse where once a garden smiled,
> And still where many a garden flower grows wild.'

The Englishman's 'modest dwelling' still stands; but ah! how changed and degraded. I went up to it, and peeped in—no one seemed at home. The paper was torn down from the walls, enough only remaining to show it had been papered. The floor of what had been the drawing-room was covered with maize, while on the ceiling above was the circle and hole from which a chandelier had evidently once been suspended. The other apartment, which the peasants made their kitchen, was even more destroyed and more dirty; and in both, and on the stairs—for both door and windows were wide open—the fowls hopped and cluttered, and flew about as they liked; while outside the house was a sort of dry midden on what had been a smooth grass-plat, where the pigs lay basking in the sun. Yet when the Englishman left it with a sad heart, forced by heavy losses to seek his fortune in a strange land, where he found death instead, there was a comfortable, elegant house, with every necessary outbuilding for a farm. But the peasants could not use the outbuildings for their fowls and cattle, and the house for themselves, but must needs live in the same state of dirt and squalor that they would have done had they merely had one of the hovels in a mountain summer pasturage.

The view from the front door was a perfect panorama of mountains. Bagnères was hardly to be seen, though one knew where it lay. Rock was piled upon rock, and mountain upon mountain, till the farthest off melted into the distant haze of clouds, sublimely beautiful. A lame

boy came up to the door while I stood gazing, and seemed
at first surprised to find me there. I said I had come to
see the beautiful view; and he replied that many people
did, and there was another equally beautiful from a seat
in the fir-wood behind the house. I bought an apple from
him to refresh myself with, which I gathered myself from
the tree, for I could not have touched anything out of his
dirty hands, and then I went to the spot he indicated. It
was curious how completely different this view was from
the other. That was all mountains—this stretched over a
wide level expanse towards Tarbes. I sat down for a few
moments on a circular bench, surrounding an immense
round table of slate, scrawled over with innumerable
names, to drink in its quiet beauty. I could not help
thinking, also, much of the family that had once sat on
that bench admiring the same view. Many a merry party
had, doubtless, gathered round that table in former days,
when the rich Englishman bought the property, built a
house on it, and brought home a fair young bride to be
its mistress. There they lived a few years in peace and
prosperity, and children were born to them; and then
some speculations of the husband failed, and the young
wife sickened and died; and he re-married, and struggled
on a year or two longer. But his second wife was reck-
lessly extravagant—a drag, and not a help-mate—and he
was forced to leave her, and go to America to try and
redeem his fortunes there ; and there he fell ill and died,
away from the home he had built and delighted in, from the
wife who had injured his fortune, and the children he had
loved. After his death, his creditors claimed the estate,
let it to a peasant, and it became what it is.

I gathered some sprays of box from what was once the
avenue hedge. The wind and the frost had turned the
leaves to a burnished-coppery hue, which is very beautiful
when the sun shines on it, or in a nosegay mixed with the

large purple bugle, or the lilac autumnal crocus. There is a wide road leading from the fir-wood, and winding below it, down the steep hill to Pouzac, which, no doubt, was the carriage road to the Camp de César in its palmy days. I went down it, passing some fine old chestnut trees in one of the sloping hollows of the hill side, and walked on till I reached the village. It has two towers. One decorates the Mairie, the other adorns the village church. The church is rather handsome, and a wooden gallery runs all round its tall, square tower (from which rises an extinguisher spire), where one may stand and look out over the distant country. The little boy, who showed me the church, was very anxious I should go round it, and assured me '*qu'il n'y avait pas de danger;*' but I felt giddy and dared not adventure. I had a pleasant walk home through the maize fields and meadows, having before me one of the loveliest views to be seen about Bagnères, of the dear, pleasant little town, lying among green meadows at the feet of the mountains, and got back in time for dinner. By the way, I wonder why the Bagnèrais are so dilatory in cutting the maize. At Argelés, they were reaping it long ago, and it looks quite ripe here also.*

* Some years ago, I am told, there were visible traces of a Roman encampment on this hill-top, from whence it derived its name, Camp de César. They have all been destroyed.

CHAPTER XIV.

IT rains to-day, and a thick mist, as dense as a London fog, hides the mountain peaks that I usually see rising distinct, and clear, and verdant, behind the houses on the Coustos ; so I have piled up my fire with logs to make a cheerful blaze, and am about to crouch down beside it, and study old myths and legends, if Keeper, who always considers the very front of the fire as sacred to himself, will let me. Keeper retreats very discontentedly to a mat made of the stalks of the Indian corn, which I bought for myself, as there are neither carpets nor hearth-rug in these lodgings, but of which he has taken entire possession. When the cobs are gathered, they are plaited together while the stalks and leaves are pliant, and suspended from the balcony roofs, exposed on one side to a current of air. They keep better thus than in a closed granary, and look very ornamental and pretty besides. As they are wanted, the strings of maize are taken down, and the cobs cut off them, and the plaited band left, serves to make mats, which when new, are white-looking and pretty, and wear well. Every part of the Indian wheat seems valuable ; the tender leaves are stripped off the plant while it is yet growing, as fodder for the cattle, and the ears seemed to ripen best when thus exposed to the sun and air. The mattresses throughout France are made of the inner husk, or soft leaf, enveloping the cob. They make the cleanest and softest mattresses I ever slept on ; and even poor people usually have the case washed, and refilled with fresh leaves, once a year. The very refuse of the cob is service-able, and is sold after the grains have been shelled off with a knife, under the denomination of *charbon blanc.* It burns out very rapidly, of course, but throws out great heat, and is very useful in lighting a reluctant fire.

Now for the legends—

The Serpent.

'There is a terrible and mysterious serpent, who figures in all early mythologies and legendary lore, and whose existence is probably derived by tradition from the old serpent of the Bible history. The fear and the dread thereof seem coeval with the human race, and an instinct rather than the result of reason. The tradition of the fall has doubtless been handed down to father and son, grow-ing ever more hazy and indistinct, and enlarged, or altered, by each generation, till it becomes no longer recognizable.

'Even at this day the shepherds of the Bigorraise valleys believe the serpent to be endowed with an extraordinary power to do harm. They say that as soon as the cock has laid his eggs he buries them in a dunghill, whose heat hatches them, and thence comes out the frightful cocka-trice, whose breath, like flame, draws everything to it that he may devour it. Not only beasts and birds thus become his prey, but even little children.

'Now the largest serpent that was ever seen, crawled upon the *plateau* of a beautiful green mountain, at whose base, surrounded by others of sublime and lofty forms, so as to form a wide amphitheatre, stretched a valley so calm and beautiful that it soothed and enchanted the saddest heart. Large flocks of sheep and cattle fed in the emerald meadow of this paradise, bounding gaily under the watch-ful care of their shepherds and the loud-barking* snow-

---

* The Pyrenean sheep-dogs equal the largest Newfoundland in size; they are very sagacious and tractable, and usually snow-white. I have

white dogs. But, alas! a horrible fate befell them all. Shepherds, watchdogs, and flocks, drawn thither by some mystic and irresistible force, rushed up to the magic *plateau*, and became the prey of the hideous reptile; and this had gone on for a long, long time, and innumerable victims had been devoured, so that the whole country side was filled with tears and lamentations.

'Now there was in the village of Arbouix, which is built on the side of that green mountain, a man who had great courage, and was as subtle as he was brave, and he resolved to deliver the country from the monster. To this end he established a forge in the most hidden depths of the mountain and forged iron, and when it was red-hot he laid it, at the hazard of his life, in the serpent's way, and then hastened to hide himself. The monster, who was gliding about seeking prey, seeing the hot iron lying there, aspired it, as he did everything else, and by means of his fiery breath drew it up into his mouth, and swallowed it at one gulp. But the hot iron set his entrails on fire, and he drank so much cold water to quench it that at last he burst. The water which he had imbibed gushed out and formed a lake, and that is the lake of Isabit. Then the inhabitants of Arbouix, in testimony of their gratitude, gave to their deliverer the right of pasturing his flocks without payment on the slopes he had freed from the monster, and his descendants enjoy the right to this day. And they took the ribs of the reptile and used them to build a church, believing that it would be pleasing to God; but as soon as the church was built, hail fell incessantly. Then the people saw that the serpent's bones were accursed, and ought to be burnt, so they made a bonfire of them, and as soon as they were consumed the hail ceased.'

been told they are uncertain in temper, but I never heard of an accident caused by them during the nine months I spent at Bagnères.

Bos de Bénac.

'In the reign of the most Christian King, Louis IX., of France, there lived at Bénac, in Bigorre, a Baron named Bos, who went to join the Crusaders, and he said to his wife, as he bade her good-by, "I have taken the cross for our Lord's sake, and I go to the Holy Land to fight against the infidels. If it please God I shall return home, but if I do not come back again before seven years are passed, thou art free, my wife, to take another spouse." Then he embraced her tenderly and set out.

'The years passed away and yet Bos did not return, and there wanted but three days to complete the seventh year. The lady of Bénac had wearied of watching for tidings from the Holy Land; and believing she should never see her husband again had nourished other thoughts, and had promised her hand to the Baron d'Astugue as soon as the seven years should have expired. The good knight Bos de Bénac had followed the King Saint Louis, by whom he was much beloved, and he had fought right valiantly, and killed a great many Saracens for the good of his soul ; but at last the French army was defeated, and Bos de Bénac was left for dead upon the field. He was carried away captive to the Land of Egypt by the infidels, who set the brave knight to keep their flocks, and beat and ill-used him because he was a Frank and a Christian, so that he wished to die. Now one day as he lamented to himself, and thought of his lady and the fair castle of Bénac, a black man with two horns on his head and the feet of a goat stood suddenly before him. Bos was so accustomed to see black men that he forgot to make the sign of the cross. So the black man—who was the devil himself—said to him, sneeringly, "What have you gained, Bos, by fighting for God? He leaves you the servant of my Nubian slaves. The very dogs in thy castle at Bénac are better treated than thou. Thy people think of thee as dead; and to-morrow thy wife re-marries. As to thee, good knight, thou mayest go and milk thy cows."

'Then Bos lifted up his voice and wept, for he loved his wife passing well. And the devil pretended to pity him, and said, "Only give me a drop of thy blood, and I will carry thee home to Bénac before the marriage takes place."

'But Bos answered, "Nay; for my blood belongs to my Lord, who shed His for me, and I owe it Him to the last drop."

'"Then," said the devil, "at least thou wilt promise to be mine. Thou canst do no less if I take thee so long a journey, and bring thee to thy castle of Bénac before thy wife marries the Baron d'Astugue?"

'But Bos refused this also.

'"Well," said the devil, "but if I take thee thou must own I deserve something for my pains. Promise me, therefore, that thou wilt give me something in exchange for my help as soon as thou shalt arrive at thy castle."

'The baron was very eager to get home in time to prevent the marriage, so he promised the Evil One the reward he asked.

'Then the devil took Bos upon his shoulders, and the grip of his hand was like an eagle's talons, and he went quicker than the wind. He flew through the clouds with Bos upon his back, and they traversed mountains and rivers and seas like a flash of lightning. And as they thus journeyed, he tried to persuade Bos to give himself to him, and tempted him, saying, "Surely thou oughtest to give thyself to me, for I could let thee fall into the sea, down among the fishes: but I love thee so much that I will take thee safe home to Bénac."

'But Bos was a man who knew no fear, and he merely answered, "Go on; and take me whither thou hast promised."

'They traversed a wall of clouds and stood upon the Peak of Anhie, and at the same instant the lightning separated the mass of vapours, and Bos saw a phantom as tall as a pine tree, enveloped by red clouds, with a face that flamed like fire. A violet aureole waved and flickered round his head, the thunders growled beneath his feet, and his body shone like white lightnings. The thunderclap burst—the mountain peak crumbled—the rocks fell down and smoked, and Bos heard a voice like thunder shout,—"Bos is come back; Bos is the friend of our master!"

'A moment afterwards Bos was before another mountain, which he knew by the light of the stars. It was Campana, which always rings before misfortune happens to the country.

'Without knowing how, Bos then found himself within the mountain, and saw that it was hollow to the top. A huge silver bell hung from the highest vault, and a troop of black goats were attached to its iron tongue, and Bos understood well that these goats were devils, for their eyes were like glowing charcoal, their horns pointed and crooked like Syrian swords, their bristles waved in the air like the branches of trees, and their tails wagged like that of a dog. They all glared fiercely upon Bos, and danced about him like wills o' the wisp; and then they formed into a long line and ran forwards, and the huge bell rang—ding-dong—ding-dong — dong! and a loud voice thundered above the sound of the bell, and Bos seemed to hear it to the bottom of his marrow, and he trembled like a man in drink as he heard the bell toll out—"Bos is come back; Bos is the friend of my master!"

'Then he felt himself lifted up again, and he was at the foot of Bergouz, before a stone-door he had never seen before. The door opened of itself, with a sound sweeter than the carol of a bird; and they entered a hall of crystal, a thousand feet high, which glittered as if the sun shone on it. Bos saw there there little women as high as one's hand, sitting on agate chairs. They had eyes like the clear, green waters of the Gave; their cheeks were as red as the rose without a thorn;* their white robes were like the mist above cascades, and their scarfs the colour of the rainbow; and they spun, turning their spindles so fast that the wheels could not be seen: and when they saw the baron enter, they rose, and cried, with their silvery voices—

' " Bos is returned! Bos is the friend of our master! Bos, we will spin thee a robe of silk instead of thy Crusader's mantle!'

'At last, poor Bos, trembling with a cold sweat at these awful sights, was carried to the door of his own castle of Bénac, and there the devil placed him on the ground, and said, sneeringly—

' " Now, then, good knight, go, seek thy loving wife."

' Then he laughed, with a sound like that of a tree rent by the storm, and disappeared, leaving behind him a strong smell of sulphur.

' The morning dawned cold and frosty, the ground was wet, and the wretched Bos shivered under his rags, when a gay cavalcade came up to the castle portal. The ladies were all clad in rich brocade, and the knights in their harness of polished steel, over which they wore chains of gold, and they were all mounted on palfreys with scarlet housings, led by pages in black velvet. And last of all came an escort of men-at-arms, whose cuirasses glittered in the sun. It was the Baron d'Astugue, who came to wed the fair Châtelaine of Bénac; and he and the whole train entered the courtyard of the castle. Bos also hastened to the portal; but the warder put him back, saying—

' " Good friend, return at noon, and thou shalt have thine alms with the other poor. "

---

* The rose without a thorn is indigenous on the mountains near Luchon.

' He went out, therefore, and sat down upon a rock, and
thought how the Baron d'Astugue was going to take from
him both his wife and his lands : and when he thought
thereon, he wept.

'All the poor in the neighbourhood came by-and-by to
beg alms, and Bos went into the courtyard with them ;
and as he crossed the moat, he saw in the water his own
face blackened by the hot sun of Egypt ; his hair all
rough and uncombed like that of a wild beast ; his wasted
body, and fierce, haggard eyes ; his sackcloth garment
covered by an upper coat of goat-skin ; and knew he
looked more miserable and hideous than any beggar there.
As he entered the great door of the courtyard, his dog
came up to him, and knew him again, and fawned on him
joyfully, and licked his hands ; and Bos stroked him, and
called him by his name ; and his favourite courser heard
his voice in his stall, and whinnied in his stable for joy.
But when he reached the hall where the Baron d'Astugue
and the company feasted, his wife knew him not. She
sat by the side of the Baron d'Astugue, and smiled on him
as she had often smiled on her husband. Then he went up
to her, and said that he was Bos de Bénac, her husband ;
but she turned away, saying she knew him not ; and the
Baron d'Astugue ordered him to be driven from the hall.
Then Bos cried out, mournfully—

' " My horse whinnies in his stable at the sound of my
voice, and my dog knows and fawns on me ; but my wife
will not own me for her husband."

' And he took from his breast half of a diamond which
they had divided together before they parted, and as the
lady of Bénac had kept her half, she put the two together,
and they fitted exactly ; and she knew, and acknowledged,
that Bos was her husband and lord. And while the guests
looked at one another, wondering what they should do—
for they saw plainly there would be no wedding now, and

the Baron d'Astugue would fain have chased poor Bos away, and the lady grew pale as death, for she had forgotten Bos, and given her love to the Baron d'Astugue—the devil suddenly appeared among them, and claimed his reward. One may guess how frightened everybody was! Only the Baron de Bénac did not tremble, because he had a great heart; and he answered the devil—

' " Be it so: thou wert to have something from the feast—here, take this plate of nutshells for thy recompense."

' At these words the Malicious One, who had reckoned on receiving one of the aliments which preserve man's life, and which are therefore in the country called the " Grace of God," seeing his desires frustrated, went into a horrible rage. He made an enormous bound, and bursting the thick wall of the seignorial chimney, flew through it with a cry of fury. Since that time no one has ever been able to repair the chimney, however carefully they try; and it is said, that this breach in the wall could be seen still when the Revolution began, after which the castle was entirely destroyed.

' However, the baron, whose heart was touched by so strange an adventure, and who was uneasy both about his wife and his own civilities to, and intercourse with the devil, determined to become an anchorite.

' " Adieu, forgetful wife!" said he. " I go into solitude, where I shall only remember God."

' The Sire d'Astugue, deceived in his expectations of uniting his fortune to the rich portion of the Lady of Bénac, followed his example; and the lady was left without a husband. But the devil, still angry at the trick played him, six hundred years ago, comes back to the old castle of Bénac under the form of a white dog, and torments the peasants who inhabit its ruins.'

THE SHEPHERD WHO WAS 909 YEARS OLD.

' In the valleys of Arize, where stretch the wide green
pastures, from whence rises the Pic du Midi de Bagnère,
there lived in ancient times a very old shepherd. He fed
his sheep upon the sweet green grass of the hills, but he
had never seen snow upon the mountain. When he had
attained his nine hundred and ninth year, he saw the snow
fall for the first time, and beholding it he knew that his
end approached, and called for his two sons. They who
knew how very old he was, and had sometimes looked with
wonder upon the long beard of moss, which hung from
their father's chin as from an old fir-tree,* tried to renew
his strength by bringing him wine. The old man wet his
lips therein, and he wet them again.

' " What fruit is this made from ? " asked he.

' " It is not made from the fruit of the bramble," replied
his sons, smiling.

' But the new and generous liquor only gave him momentary pleasure, and warmed his old blood for a minute.
It was merely the flaring-up of a lamp just before it dies
out. And when the first snow fell, it snowed without
ceasing.

' " My sons," said the old man, " I am dying. Nothing
can now keep me among you. This is my appointed end.
I knew it, for it was foretold me long ago. These white
flakes are my winding-sheet, which unfolds, and spreads
itself. But for you, take courage, and when I am no more,
follow as your guide this fair heifer with the tinkling-bells.
She will lead you to the region of the hot springs, to Bagnères. Go wherever she conducts you, and stop where she
stops."

---

* A moss whose fibres resemble human hair hangs from the lower
branches of the old pine trees. I gathered some in the pine woods of the
Col d'Aspin.

'The old shepherd, the patriarch, the ancient of ancients, the great master of healing, the inventor of powerful remedies composed of simples, and the milk of the flock—died, after having thus spoken, amid the soft sounds of the falling snow which was to be his shroud. Then his sons, seeing the heifer set off alone, followed her at once in pious obedience to their father's commands. She went first, and they followed, until they came to the marvellous thermal springs known as the waters of Bagnères. And it snowed still. Then the heifer, whose faintly-tinkling bell could scarce be heard because it got continually choked up by the falling flakes, went on and on, without stopping; a superior spirit guided her. And descending the banks of the Adour, then a torrent rolling down golden sand, but which now only washes along great stones and water tumultuously together, she stayed her feet in the place where now rises the rich and pleasant village of Montgaillard. There the sons of the old shepherd stayed also, and the snow fell no more. A rock above the village preserves the form of the heifer, and the memory of this event, and from that time there has always been snow on the mountains. But the corpse of the great pastor did not remain unsepulchred. He was piously interred, and a slab of white marble placed over his grave, on which unknown characters seem to be engraved. In time his virtues, his wisdom, even his very name, were forgotten, and sacrilegious persons violating the sanctity of the grave, took away the marble covering. Immediately it began to rain, and the rain kept falling—falling day and night forty days without ceasing; then they were obliged to restore his stone to the angry spirit.'

N

CHAPTER XV.

I WONDER if my reader knows what a *palombe* is? I did not till this morning. It is a wild pigeon resembling those of our dovecote, but larger, and with rather bluer feathers. At least, so the three I saw to-day in the Bagnères market appeared to me. When I went home and spoke of them, Madame —— said I ought to go and see the *Palombières* —everybody went to see the *palombières*. Of course I went. The *palombières* are a row of trees at the top of a high hill above Gerdes, which is reached by a very round-about, long, but pretty walk, by going down the street leading to the Toulouse road; and when you get nearly opposite M. Lavalette's pretty house, going up through a chestnut wood on the right-hand side, and a long, dreary lane, ending in a wood above Gerdes, which you leave as it were behind you, following the upward path that, shortly after quitting the trees, winds up a very steep hill, at the top of which are the *palombières*. When I got there I found nets stretched from tree to tree; a man concealed by a little hut under the trees—made of boughs with their leaves on—was watching them, while another man, perched at the top of an immense long pole, kept a look-out for the *palombes*. I had the patience to wait above an hour, but the *palombes* were inflexible; they would not come and be caught. I cannot say I was sorry, for I hate to see any-thing put to pain; and I merely went to the *palombières* because the catching these wild pigeons is a sort of feature of Bagnères life.

After waiting in vain all this time, the man in the hut asked me if I would like to see how they were caught, *when they did come.* If I would give half a franc the man at the top of the pole would show me. I assented; indeed I pitied the poor fellows for their weary, disappointing watch, and would gladly have given them three francs could I have afforded it. The man at the top of the pole then threw down a piece of wood shaped somewhat like a bird, which, coming swiftly down with a whirring noise, rudely imitates the swoop of a hawk, and frightens the pigeons into the nets spread among the branches. These *palombes* breed in Spain, and usually come to Bagnères about September and the early part of October, sometimes in large flocks, but this year there had been very few. I thanked the men, paid the half franc, and walked on over the brow of the hill.

The view from a little above the Palombières is magnificent. One sees Bagnères below the wooded heights of the Bédat and Mont Olivet; a little to the left, the Adour flowing past Gerdes and Asté to Campan; while above these white villages rise a darkly-wooded hill, that partly hides the Penne de Llhéris (so renowned for flowers), the Pic du Midi, and Mont Aigu. Crossing the meadows behind the Palombières, the view is grander still—mountain rises above mountain, a sea of hills—and the sun gleaming in the hollows, and the passing clouds, casting here and there long grey shadows, render the scene exquisitely lovely. I met some peasant women here, herding sheep; the sheep of the Pyrenees are not timid, but, on the contrary, sometimes aggressive. One of the young rams, displeased at the appearance of Keeper, came up, and butted rather savagely at me; the women called to him by his name like a dog, the younger taking him by the head and pulling him away, upon which, he nestled up to, and rubbed his head against, her, just as a dog would; but if I

approached, he butted again, as if he were resolved to protect his mistress from all strangers.   They told me, the
wood that clothed the descent of the hill on which we stood,
led to a village called Bagnos, and that it was about three
miles off.   I called Mr. Keeper, and set off to walk thither.

In summer it must be a very lovely walk; the road
winds along a hill side, through a pleasant wood, and
wherever there is an opening, one sees the blue mountains
towering aloft the trees, or catches a glimpse of distant
hills bounding distant valleys; but now the branches were
nearly bare—the dead stalks of what had been lovely
flowers, bent, dry, and withered, to the long, dewy, fading
grass—and the gossamer, full of raindrops, glittering in
the sunlight, hung a fairy fabric against the sides of the
banks.   When I had passed through the wood, I came to
long green lanes; many of the edges were of wild holly,
thickly covered with beautiful scarlet berries; under their
shelter the flowers still lingered.   Beneath the hedge-rows
I gathered a large bouquet of sweet-scented wild pinks,
blue scabious of the larger kind, *marguerites*, spindle berry
and holly berries.   In a field peasants were making hay,
and I asked the way to Bagnos, and reached it in about
half-an-hour.   The road was pretty good all the way to
the entrance of Bagnos, when it became full of ruts, and
filthy.   I went to look at the church, which is not worth
seeing, and then I sat down on a low wall in front of a
farmyard, in the middle of the village, to rest.   The owner
of the farm came out to have a talk with the *Anglaise*, and
two or three women gathered round, to whom he translated what I said, into patois.   He had been a soldier.
The becoming one seems to me a very good thing for these
illiterate peasants, now there is no war, since it is an education.   The men who have *served* are always better informed and less prejudiced than peasants who have never
quitted their village.

This man put very sensible questions to me. He wished to know, how people of his class lived in England, and if they were better or worse off. I have never been in the extremely wretched Midland districts of England, where men, women, and children, according to 'Punch' and the statistics, *are worse lodged than pigs.* In my beloved York-shire, *our country gentlemen deem it a duty incumbent on the owners of landed property, to see that their cottage tenants are well lodged,* and in Lancashire and Cumberland, as in the Pyrenees, most of the agricultural working class are small landowners, owning a garth or two, and the cottage they live in. Therefore, *without intending to say what was false,* I told my Bagnos friend, that the English cottages were far tidier, and more wholesome and clean, than those of the Pyrenees, being well drained, and having glass win-dows. His cottage, and many others around, had only *wooden shutters,* and were unglazed.

Alas! what a sad thing it is to reflect on—how the selfish luxury of the few, not merely embitters the whole life of others, but positively forces them into crime. *What sense of modesty or decency can there be in a peasant family, obliged, by want of room, to sleep six or eight of all sexes and ages in one room?* And where the sense of decency and self-respect is once lost, the whole character becomes speedily degraded. In my opinion, *no man has a right to be the owner of a large estate, without fulfilling the duties his position entails on him.* He is God's steward, set by Him over his poorer brethren, and will assuredly have one day to render a strict account of his stewardship. *He has no right to accept the pleasures and the emoluments of the office and to shirk its duties.* Every soul corrupted by a life spent in misery, filth, and vice, caused by inability to attend to the common decencies of life, because a proper dwelling, within his means to rent, is not provided for him: will be required of the proud gentleman, who, in life, had his grooms, his hunters, his packs of hounds, his 'ordered gardens great,' his stately mansion with its twenty, thirty, or forty rooms—by the Lord and Master of both.

I told the Pyreneans gathered round me, through the medium of my interpreter, that they ought to try and keep their houses and the approaches to them a little cleaner; and I am bound to say, they listened civilly and deferentially; but no one person likes to differ from all his neighbours, and thereby gain their hatred and ill-will. It is the government who must make proper drains for every house, and force the people to attend to the decencies of life, as it is the government that has compelled the people to do what they would never have done for themselves, and has made good roads from village to village. They are very sensible of the benefits the present Emperor has conferred on them by laying down this regulation,* and, probably, if their villages were once well drained, would be equally grateful for that. But in endeavouring to inculcate a higher civilization, the *government ought to begin with the schools and school children. Every school in every village ought to have all necessary conveniences attached to it, and strict cleanliness ought to be enforced on the children; from them it would spread to the parents.*

It is delightful to see how much the services rendered to the country by Napoleon III. are appreciated by these peasants. If the Emperor is not popular among a set of idle, worthless men, who see in war and revolution a chance of elevating themselves, and belong to the class of people who would burn down their neighbour's house to roast themselves an egg, the industrious and thinking classes revere and love him. I am a great admirer of his wonderful genius; and, so long as he keeps peace with

---

* The regulation that there must be a road wide enough for two carriages to pass abreast between village and village. For which most wise and beneficent law the people have to thank his Majesty Napoleon III.

England, most sincerely wish him long life and prosperity; and it always gives me pleasure to find how popular he is, when, as is my custom, I have a chat with the peasants I meet in my walks. They speak of him with absolute affection.* 'He has done us good,' say they. 'We voted for him because we loved his uncle. He did us good, too; and the nephew has been our best friend. Why, the people in Paris wanted to tax corn more, and the Emperor said, "If you do, there will be an army three days hence at the gates of Paris;" and so there would have been. There would have been another revolution. We want a man like Napoleon III., and I hope he will live long, and that his son will reign after him.'

I came home tired enough, but charmed with my walk, which I recommend everyone who visits Bagnères to take.

November 10*th*, 1862.—To-day and to-morrow are, I understand, fair-days. There are three fairs in the year— St. Barthélémi, the day after Pentecost, and this. The principal articles of merchandise to-day are old clothes. To-day the peasants come down from the hills to exchange their summer garb with the *fripiers* of Tarbes, and other neighbouring towns, for winter clothes; or to sell the coarse, home-spun cloth they have themselves woven. From the top of the Place des Coustos, and half-way down the Allée des Platanes, there is no getting along for the crowd. The buzz of hundreds of voices, perhaps I ought to say thousands, reminds one irresistibly of that of a beehive; but there is little of gaiety in the scene. An English village feast, with the women flaunting in gay-coloured ribbons, and many-hued dresses, is a far prettier sight.

The costumes of France have nearly departed, and what

---

* This does not apply especially to the inhabitants of Bagnos. I heard the same warm expressions of gratitude from peasants belonging to Bagnères, Pouzac, in short, from every peasant proprietor I conversed with throughout the Pyrences.

remains of them is precisely what is most ugly and least picturesque. The mass of clustered peasants collected in Coustos, on which I look down from my gallery, resemble a swarm of bees, not only in their hum, but in their sober colours. Their suits of brown, the jacket cut like an English sailor's vest, and trowsers, are generally of the dark-brown hue, which is the natural colour of the undyed wool. Here and there the sombre hue of the crowd is relieved by a blue *beret*, or cap, a scarlet or green sash, an immaculately white shirt front, and a flaming waistcoat, or a red umbrella. The older men walk about, stick in hand, with a brown woollen nightcap on their heads, and a huge, rather picturesque covering, also of undyed brown wool, which is a sort of hybrid between a great coat and a capuchin's cloak, and more comfortable than either. It would tell well in a picture, but is ugly enough in real life. How odd this is, by-the-by, that a dilapidated, untidy, unrepaired cottage, with the thatch hanging in shreds, old clouts or wood filling up the broken casements, a few ragged clothes suspended between bare poles to dry, and a tumble - down garden wall and ruinous pigsty, should make a prettier picture than what is far pleasanter to the eye in reality, a comfortable modern house, and its trim flower garden. The Pyrenean garment in question consists of an ample cloak with sleeves, with a cape reaching to the waist, and a capuchin's hood, which covers the head and most of the face. In this he walks about almost secure from weather as to the upper part of his person, as a snail in his shell; and except that the colour is different, resembles not a little, a walking sentry-box. No doubt such warm clothing is necessary for men who spend days, and even nights, herding their flocks on the snowy mountains; but I must say it rather amused me the first rainy day after my return to Bigorre, to watch from my gallery a man employed about some repairs that

were making in a house opposite, shovelling earth and
lime, and wheeling stones, and digging in one of these
portable pent-houses.   I could not help thinking how one
of our broad-chested, herculean-limbed, hardy navvies, who
work in all weathers in shirt sleeves, and with open breast,
or at most a fustian vest and jacket, would have laughed
at the sight.   I have myself often gardened in heavier
rain, in my usual dress.

The costume of the women is as sombre as that of the
men, only here and there a few scarlet or white capulets
gleam like tulips among a bed of brown fritillaries.

I have been out to the fair.   The elm trees in the Place
des Coustos had garments that clearly once belonged to
ladies hanging from their lower boughs instead of leaves.
Further on, a group of peasant women were examining an
old petticoat, turning it inside out, and holding it to the
light, to discover rents and stains.   There, second-hand
sheets and towels were unfolded and displayed at full
length, by seller and buyer.   There were rows of old
shoes and boots, all apparently shining in Warren's im-
mortal blacking, 'to gar them leuk amaist as weel as new.'
Peasant women walked about with thick home-spun woollen petticoats on their arms, gathered, but not sewn, into
a waistband, that they might be arranged to fit any
purchaser.   Before others, were heaps of *chiffons* of all
sorts, bodies of gowns, stray sleeves, faded ribbons, soiled
blonde, odd stockings, bits of lace and work.   One heap
always consists of cuttings of furniture, which the peasants
buy to make thick, warm caps, for their children, which
they always wear till four or six years of age.

Some of this damask is very elegant in design, and the
colours being new, are most brilliant.   There were also
several stalls of the staple manufacture of the country,
shawls, quilts, mittens, hair-nets, and other articles knitted,

of Pyrenean wool ; and the space in front of M. ——'s
door was filled up, as it is every sale day, by groups of
market-women, chaffering over huge bundles of dyed and
undyed wool, for knitting stockings. There was one stall
of knick-knacks. Some of them were made of the marbles
of the country, and were really pretty ; but the prices
were enormous. In fact, one sees nothing in foreign
countries that one cannot buy *far cheaper in London.* I
had the curiosity to ask the price of a pair of glass ear-
rings. ' *Six francs,*' was the reply ; but perhaps this price
was asked out of respect to my *chapeau Anglais.* Certainly
the French and German shopkeepers, and market-women,
look upon us as a nation of fools, possessing more money
than wit. Files of horses and mules were also led up and
down the streets, for this is also a horse fair. I saw, however, nothing to interest or amuse me in the scene, so I
returned home.

November 11th.—There was a perfect tempest of wind
and rain last night, and the large trees in the Coustos
creaked and groaned like the masts of a vessel. When
day dawned the mountains were clouded over, and torrents
of rain, sleet, and snow have poured down at intervals all
day. A sad fair time. Nevertheless, the booths of yesterday have been re-erected, and a good many peasants are
higgling and bargaining, chattering and scolding, under the
shelter of huge umbrellas. I think I never saw so many umbrellas in one place before—conspicuous among them are
one or two bright red ones. Some of the peasants drive
in, in strange, long, heavy carts, formed apparently of
nearly half the trunk of a tree, with a long and very thick
plank on each side. One miserable little ass has just gone
past, drawing one of these vehicles, and in it I counted
nine persons. What a load for the poor animal! Truly,
man in all grades of life has small mercy on the useful
beasts that are his slaves.

I meant to have gone and seen whether this second day's fair were better worth looking at than the first, but the weather never clears for more than half-an-hour, and I detest walking in the mud when I can avoid it. I spent the evening with Madame T——. Old M. La C—— came in, and I mentioned the number of peasants I had seen in the cart drawn by one poor ass.

'That is a common sight,' said M. La C——; 'I have often seen more people than that in a cart drawn by one poor ass,—the peasants have no mercy on their cattle. And look at their oxen and cows! They let the poor things' hides be covered with cow-dung, so that every step they take must pain them and fray the skin. But what can you expect? They do not keep themselves clean—is it likely they will care for their cattle? Go into their cottages—they are filthy beyond description. Men, women, children, dogs, fowls, and sheep often sleep in the same room; and they go about bare-legged, treading in all manner of dirt, and go to bed without washing it off.'

Such is a Frenchman's account of the peasantry!

CHAPTER XVI.

BAGNÈRES DE BIGORRE.

November 22nd, 1862.—No more beautiful nosegays of wild flowers. I came home on Monday with such a beautiful *gerbe* of sweet-scented *Dianthus, Scabious, Cistus Marguerites*, and berries of all kinds. The day was quite summer-like, and I spent most of it in my gallery, where I sat without hat or shawl on, making moss baskets for my flowers, and arranging them afterwards. The next day was cold and sleety—as unlike Monday as May is to December; and when I got up on Wednesday, the terraces and roofs of the houses, and the *Coustos* were several inches deep in snow, and the mountain-peaks glittered white in the sunshine. The fault of the Pyrenean climate is these sudden changes. One hardly knows how to dress; for one day it is so warm that a thin muslin would be pleasant wear, if not strictly appropriate to the season, and the very next perhaps, one is shivering over a log fire, wrapped up in a thick shawl. I often wonder that doctors should send consumptive patients abroad. First, the invalid has to encounter a lack of all the customary comforts of an English home, which is very trying. It is true the rich can obtain even most English comforts—what will not money obtain? but the poorer and the middle class have much inconvenience to endure. I hear continually in England that such a person is recommended to try a warmer climate. It is become a fashion to abuse the English climate, and to speak of it as if fine days were few and rare, and the land was generally enveloped in fog.

In my girlhood I looked forward to going to 'sunny France' and the glorious clime of Italy, as I looked forward to being a grown-up woman as a sort of entrance into Paradise. Growing-up and sunny France have both proved to be mere delusions. I have a notion which I will only venture to whisper to you, dear reader, as it is treason against all received dogmas and opinions—it is that the climate of Italy will prove a delusion too, if I am ever rich enough to try it.

I have now been three times in France, for periods varying from seven months to thirteen, and twice in Germany for about six months at a time, and I must honestly confess that go where I would, from Paris to the Pyrenees, or on the grape-clad slopes of the Rhenish provinces, I have never seen any difference between the climate abroad and that of England, except that the summers and autumns are hotter and last longer than our English ones, while the winters are shorter and more variable in temperature. One feels the cold more when these sudden changes of temperature occur; and I declare that I saw fog, and sleet, and rain, and hail, and snow, and dull days everywhere, just as I used to do in England. When mist came down from the mountains upon rare occasions at Bagnères, I have been as unable to thread a needle, to work, or to read at one o'clock in the day, as in a London fog. When I say that I do not see that the climate abroad is better than in England, I am immediately told that this is '*une année exceptionnelle*.' It is very hard and very strange that I should never travel except in *une année exceptionnelle*, and I believe that 'Mr. Burchell' would have uttered the word ' *Fudge!*' if he had been told that we had no sun in England, or that foreign lands were so much more favoured by Heaven as to climate. For my part, if one could choose, I like an old-fashioned English winter—hard frosts and deep snows in their season—and then a warm, genial spring, and a glowing summer and autumn.   We have no hot April and May and September, such as I remember in my childhood, and no such hard winters, in England now. At the same time I must admit that there is a purity and clearness in the air of France and Germany that is most exhilarating and delightful; and *it is in this, and not in the weather, which is as variable and uncertain abroad as in England, that the true superiority of foreign climates consists.*

As soon as the snow had partly melted away from the high roads and fields I hastened to ascend the Bédat, that I might see how the range of the Pyrenees looked in snow. I have just returned from my expedition, and want words to express how beautiful and grand they were.   The day was balmy and mild, and the sky a clear deep blue, unknown in England.   From the signal-staff on the Bédat I looked, as I sat, upon a magnificent panorama of hills piled upon hills, and mountain towering above mountain in solemn, sublime majesty, all keenly glittering, white, clear and distinct and pure as angels' robes, against the blue of the summer-like sky.   They seemed the throne of God—the visible image of His unspeakable purity, His power and majesty and might.   Does the all-pervading spirit of the Almighty rest peculiarly upon the mountains? It was on a mountain that God talked to Moses; to a mountain Christ often retired to pray; it was on a mountain that He was transfigured before the eyes of his wondering and awe-struck disciples; and there is something elevating and ennobling even to poor, weak humanity in the solitary mountain-top.   One feels for the time lifted above earth and earth's petty cares and vanities—nearer to heaven and to God.

I like Bagnères very much as a winter residence; in short, since I was forced to give up my little Hampstead cottage, and thrown poor and solitary upon the world, I have never liked any place so much. It is a *lovable* place. I don't wonder mountaineers are always so attached to this country. These glorious mountains soon become to one dear friends. I could be well content to end my days here if I could afford to buy a farm with some chestnut trees near it.

CHAPTER XVII.

BAGNÈRES DE BIGORRE.

January 22nd, 1863.—January is come and well-nigh gone too, and winter is nearly over. On the whole it has been a very fine one, and I have enjoyed it greatly, notwithstanding the sudden change from summer warmth to snow and frost. To-day the air is quite soft and balmy, and like the rest of the Bagnères world I have been up to La Côte, *i.e.* the side of a hill above the town on the road to Toulouse, to see the peasants dance. To-day is the feast of St. Vincent, the patron Saint of Bagnères, and the people are all in holiday costume, feasting and dancing. You cannot imagine what a pretty sight it was. Fancy a regular drop scene for a theatre. A green meadow by the road side, in the middle of which three *ménétriers*, or fiddlers, were seated in chairs placed upon a deal table, fiddling away merrily to two or three hundred peasant lads and lasses, all decked out in their holiday suits. The men in their neat self-coloured brown jackets, vests, and trowsers, with clean white shirts, and gay neckties of the newest fashion—the girls chiefly in their neat-fitting dark gowns, white or coloured aprons, with deep pockets in them, and *mouchoirs* as varied in colours and blending of shades as a bed of tulips, and this gay, pretty picture framed in as it were by a background of snow-covered mountains. It was thoroughly foreign and theatrical.

The Pyrenese are passionately fond of dancing, and although the priests reprobate it, and even refuse the sacrament to those who have been at a ball, take advantage of every holiday to pursue their favourite amusement. They usually dance remarkably well, their movements are never awkward, and always accord with the measure. Why is it that the English working classes are so much more clumsy and vulgar than French people of the same rank? I can only repeat my idea, that it is because the French peasant respects himself, and is not ashamed of being a peasant. While the Englishman is always trying to impress you with the idea that he belongs to the class above him, whom he apes in dress and manners, and thereby only succeeds in making himself vulgar and ridiculous. Only one large double quadrille, or a very long country dance, was danced at a time; the rest of the company stood, or sat on the ground looking on.

I sat some time on the road-side bank talking to a young and rather pretty peasant girl beside me. I hoped to see some of the national dancing of the country, a *branle*, or a *saut*, and I asked her if any would be danced. '*L'on ne danse que les quadrilles, ou les contre-danses,*' said she, very indignantly. It was clear she felt huffed at my supposing anything so vulgar and old-fashioned as a *saut* or *branle* could be danced in that polite and fashionable assembly. Poor human nature! It is the same everywhere, among the Browns, Smiths, Ledburys, and De Robinsons of Islington and Pentonville, and here among peasants dancing in a meadow by the road side, and would as soon be accused of absolute crime, as have it supposed possible that its ways and fashions differed from the ways and fashions of the Tuileries or St. James.

Most of the English families in the town came to look at the dancing, and among them two pretty English girls, with their brother, who won all hearts by joining in the fun; the young ladies dancing with some of the lads, and the young man with two or three of the lasses. It is a pity the travelling English do not oftener lend themselves to the

o

customs of the country. The French are so sensitive to haughty demeanour, and so grateful for courtesy and kindness, and *unlike* vulgar English people, they do not presume upon it. At an out-of-doors fête at Coblentz, I have seen a German countess of high lineage, dancing with a tobacconist from the town. There was no assumption in the one, and no vulgar obtrusive familiarity in the other. St. Vincent's is a very great fête to the Bigorrais. Everybody asks their friends to dinner, and the peasants dance for two or three days in the meadows during the daytime, and in a large room at night. The ball at La Côte began at three o'clock in the day, and I am told will last till dark. There was a small public-house adjoining the field where the dancing was going on, where numbers of the young men were sitting drinking—for drinking is as common a vice in the Pyrenees as it is in England. Some of them had beautiful voices, and they sung several glees and part-songs most harmoniously.

After I had sat about an hour looking at the dancing, I rose to return home, but thought I would first stroll up the hill to gaze on the snowy mountains, and while I was ascending it, a band of more than thirty young men issued from the public-house and came up arm-in-arm, in two long rows, singing most exquisitely. I was quite alone and no other creature on the road except Keeper and myself, but I felt no fear. The Pyrenean peasant is always courteous.

I went a day or two ago with Madame T—— to see an exposition of priestly vestments, worked for the priests of poor parishes by a society of ladies, who are affiliated with a similar society in Paris, which provides them with elegant designs, and charges itself with making up the embroidery when done. I assure you this needlework was very beautiful, and as I examined it I could not help thinking that similar embroidery applied to the less holy use of decorating curtains, sofas, and table-covers, might be made a means of supporting many distressed gentlewomen in England, as it costs next to nothing and is very effective. I even had a vision of working a table-cover myself for Her Royal Highness the Princess of Wales, and requesting Miss Parkes to allow it to be exhibited at the office of the 'Englishwoman's Journal,' in order to set the fashion. But, alas! the means on which I had calculated did not come, and my scheme fell to the ground. Truly does Shelley say—

> ' Such thoughts of good
> Oft come and leave us in our solitude.'

The thing, however, is feasible, and may perhaps some day be taken up by other hands. Mademoiselle Féraud, the *présidente* of the society at Bagnères, was very kind, and explained the whole process to me. The beautiful work is entirely composed of *chiffons*. The sole expense incurred by the society is the cost of the silk on which it is *appliqué*, and the sewing silk, beads, gold thread, and braid employed in the work. The ladies of the society give themselves, and beg from their friends, old velvet bonnets, silk and satin gowns, remnants of ribbon, milliners' and mercers' clippings, &c.; the smallest article being turned to account. One of the most magnificent vestments was embroidered with parts of what had once been a lady's worked Canton crape shawl. The next handsomest was, as Mademoisselle Féraud informed me, fabricated out of an old black velvet bonnet. It consisted of *fleurs de lys* of black velvet, bordered with a gold thread — *semé* upon rich white *moiré* silk. The pattern having been decided upon, the materials to be used are cut out in little bits, neatly tacked on the silk—any foundation could, of course, be used; merino, cloth, or whatever material was thought best suited for curtains, table-cloths, &c.—and fastened down with gold or silk braid in one mode of work, and crossed all over with coloured silk in regular lines in the other, but two stitches or modes of embroidery being used. It is far more quickly done than floss-silk embroidery, and far cheaper, while equally beautiful and effective.

How much is annually wasted in a great city, that might employ and maintain thousands if rightly employed! I remember reading in the account of a 'refuge,' that a lady connected with it once asked a milliner to contribute the odds and ends of rubbish in the workroom which she had habitually burnt every Saturday night, and these bits—*the produce of one workroom in one week*—were given to a poor woman who had sought shelter at the refuge in the deepest distress. She manufactured them into caps, which were sold for three shillings, and since that time this poor widow has been enabled to maintain herself and her two children in tolerable comfort, by making up the remnants given her by one milliner into cheap caps. If there were a depôt where old dresses, gauzes, laces, gloves, and ribbons could be received by a competent lady manager, who would also supply patterns procured from Paris, all these things, which are now wasted, might be turned to good account. The educated woman, with her refined eye and artistic taste, could convert a part of them, in the seclusion and retirement of her own house, into costly and delicate embroidery, and the others might be made into caps, bonnets, jackets, children's frocks, &c., and sold at a moderate price to the shops; the receiving, sorting, and giving-out these materials and work patterns, and the disposing of the work when done, giving respectable homes and maintenance to one set of impoverished ladies, while the work itself furnished means of support to others.

So again with our markets. In England the cooks throw away the tops of the celery, and the outer leaves of the cabbages; in France they are all put into the *pot au*

*feu** for soup.   The French, too, make an excellent soup
from a *purée* formed of potatoes, to which a very little meat
is added.   If some of the idle boys and girls in the streets
of London were employed to go round to the market-stalls
and greengrocers and collect the cabbage and turnip leaves,
the onion and celery tops, and small potatoes they throw
away as refuse, and others to collect remnants of meat and
bones from the butchers, and carry them to poor women
selected for the office, these women, once properly taught
to prepare soup and savoury stew from such remnants,
might keep a humble sort of *restaurant,* where the very
poor and starving might always get a basin of good wholesome soup, or a plate of savoury stew and a piece of bread,
for a penny or a ticket.   I would make a moderate charge
for the soup or stew, both to supply the bread, and to pay
the boys who collected the materials and the women who
cooked.   It has been found by the Shoeblack Society that
the plan of collecting rags that were formerly burnt from
house to house answers; why should not a society be
formed for collecting the waste of our markets, our houses,
and our butchers' and bakers' shops, and turning it also to
good account for the starving and destitute?

Among the priests of poor parishes to whom vestments were
given, was the Curé of Uzer, a small village lying on the left
hand of the Toulouse road.   Thither I walked one day with

---

* *Pot au feu.*—The *pot au feu* is used in all French families, from the
very highest to the lowest.   It is a brown earthenware vessel with a cover,
which is filled with a sufficiency of water, and placed close to the fire as
soon as it is lighted.   Into this pot the bones and fragments of bread and
vegetables remaining from yesterday's meals are thrown, and to it are added
from time to time stray bits of butter or grease, or meat, fowls' feet and
heads—anything in short, from a cabbage-leaf to an onion top.   The hedges
and fields are ransacked for wild sorrel and other vegetables, and this constant feeding of the ever-simmering caldron goes on all day—bean-husks,
peas-cods, stalks of spinach—all we think *refuse,* goes to the *pot au feu*
abroad, and in our great London hotels, whose proprietors know its value as
excellent soup.   So a first-rate cook told me.

Keeper, along a beautiful winding road, whence there were delicious peeps into green shady valleys, watered by clear streams and environed by mountains. On arriving at Uzer I went, as is my custom, to look at the church, which is no way remarkable, and when I came out I met the Curé talking to a woman in the churchyard. He recognized, and invited me in to rest, telling me he should like to know me, as he was sure he should soon make me a *bonne Catholique.* I laughed, and followed him; the woman, with the freedom of a peasant, accompanying us. The good old priest led me into a cabin little better than any of those inhabited by the labourers around. His bed and a shelf with a few books, stood in a recess of the kitchen, and a table on which he could write was the only furniture distinguishing it from the merest hut. 'Here I live,' said he, smiling, 'nor do I desire better. I have lived here twelve years, and am as well lodged as my predecessors, the apostles. But you must be tired. It is a long walk from Bagnères to Uzer. You must at least eat a piece of bread and drink a glass of wine with the poor priest.'

I declined the bread, but accepted the wine, for I was thirsty, while Keeper, always in mischief, occupied himself in hunting for the cat.

'Nay,' said the Curé, 'that I cannot permit. Thou art a pretty dog, but my cat is my friend and companion.'

So Keeper's mistress held him by main force, struggling and scratching with his hind feet, while the Curé and the woman who entered with us and the priest's *bonne* caught the cat with equal difficulty, and shut her up in another room, and then we settled ourselves again for a chat.

'Your religion is only three hundred years old,' he began, striking his staff upon the ground. 'What is three hundred years? The *Catholique* religion dates from the Apostles; yours, from your adulterous King Henry VIII.'

'*Ecoutez-le! Est-il savant? Monsieur le prêtre sait tout*,' cried the admiring women.

'But answer me,' he went on; 'is it so, or not? Do I speak truth? Does not your Reformation, as you call it, date from *Henri Huit?*'

'Impossible to deny it,' said I.

'*Voyez donc—Monsieur le curé avait raison!*' cried the women.

'And why have you left the Church of Rome, and for what? For a church that is no church.'

I could have answered—'Because your clergy made themselves *princes and not priests—because Rome defiled herself with innocent blood—by luxury, and by crime;*' but I would not. I could not defend *myself* without wounding *him;* so I was silent.

After awhile he took me to see the garden of the *presbytery*, for the cottage was his parsonage. It was of a piece with the house — a mere square plot of garden ground, full of cabbages, peas, and onions, with two or three common pansies, on the edge of the borders, of which he seemed very proud, and *all* of which he desired his *bonne* to pull for Madame, if Madame liked flowers. I would not have them all pulled, but I took a few, not to wound him by seeming to undervalue them; and then, thanking him for his hospitality, I withdrew.

I honour these poor priests, whose lives are spent in poverty and seclusion, and in leading a poor and ignorant population to good. Their power over the minds of their parishioners is great—for their lives are pure—and their practice agrees with the doctrines they preach. I honour, too, the nuns, who labour in nursing the sick, and teaching the poor, or who take charge of young infants while their mothers go out to work. There is much in Catholicism that is noble, real, and true; and while I cannot assent to all her doctrines—the lichens which have overgrown the original temple—I cannot help looking forwards to a time when all religions and sects shall be fused into one, and all men shall know the Lord, from the least to the greatest ; for ' the knowledge of the Lord shall cover the earth, as the waters cover the sea ;' and believing that these men and women are also, in their generation, doing a good work, and labouring in the great harvest-field of the Almighty. If they were not, He would not so long have suffered them.

CHAPTER XVIII

I HAVE just been enabled to compare the way sick people get treated in lodgings in France with the treatment they receive in English lodging-houses; it is just the difference between six and half-a-dozen. I went on Sunday to church, and took a walk afterwards. In the evening I had a pain in my foot, of which, as it was not very severe, I took no notice. When I took my stocking off at night, I found a little blister, the size of a pea, in the middle of a long white line, crossing the whole foot, which was very painful to the touch. The next day it was worse, and by the fourth day it had enlarged to a regular abscess, the size of half-a-crown, whose constant discharge and great pain confined me entirely to bed. Marie, the maid, brought me my coffee as usual, and inquired what I would have for dinner that day.

'Nothing, Marie, thank you; I am too ill to eat.'

'Too ill to eat!' shouted Marie, colouring up with anger. 'Too ill to eat! Then you may get a *garde malade* to wait upon you—who you will—for I won't. I've something else to do than to wait on sick people.'

'Marie,' said I, 'I don't want much waiting upon. When I am well and about, you have my two rooms to keep clean, and my fire to light; you cook my dinner, and make me coffee twice a day. Now I am too ill even to have my bed made; all you have to do, therefore, is to light my fire, to dust my room, bring me water, and

make me some coffee twice a day, as I have no appetite,
and cannot eat meat.'

' It's well you want nothing,' bawled Marie, wrathfully ;
' if you did, you wouldn't get it.   I'll bring you coffee
twice a day, that's all; but—' coming up to my bed, and
pushing a red face close to mine, and shaking her fist—' if
you ring for anything, mind! I'll send Jean! I won't
come, not I.   I'll send Jean—n—n!'

I had long suspected Marie of what the French call
' *faisant l'anse du panier*'—making a handle of the basket,
i.e. charging me more for everything she bought than she
gave. *Now, I was sure of it ;* for there could be no other
reason for her flaring up into this violent rage, when I
said that I could eat no dinner, but that she lost the half
franc's profit she had calculated having upon it.   I know
very well most of my friends would say I ought to have
bought everything myself.   Those who have been like me,
obliged at one time of their life to live upon a small income, know that one is *compelled to submit to these pecula-
tions*, to prevent the greater expense and inconvenience of
continually changing lodgings.

Whenever I spoke to Madame —— about the price of
food, she always asserted it was the price *Marie* said ; if
ever I bought anything in the market myself, it gave
Marie mortal offence ; and *Marie*, who was a good cook, and
made *them* comfortable, ruled both Monsieur and Madame
——. My lodgings suited me in other things, and I tried
to economize the three or four francs a week *I knew Marie
overcharged me*, by various other small savings.   When
Madame came upstairs to inquire after me, I told her of
Marie's insolence ; but, as I expected, she made a hundred
undeserved excuses for her. I passed a dreary time, confined for nearly three weeks to my bed, and for thirteen
days too ill even to rise to have it made.   Marie, who did
nothing for me but light my fire, replenish my water-jugs,

and bring me coffee twice a day—doing that little in the most unwilling manner, and usually repeating, as she went out of the room, slamming the door after her—' *Oui, vous ferez mieux de ne pas sonner, car je n'y viendrai pas.*'

Madame —— had long been in the habit of spending her mornings in my sitting-room, Marie having requested that I would invite her to do so, 'because,' said she, ' *Madame ne veut pas dépenser son argent, elle ne fait pas de feu toute la journée, et elle se rend malade ; à son âge elle a besoin de se bien chauffer.*' I thought so, too, and as I could not do without a fire, I invited Madame, though I well knew she could afford to have as many fires as she had rooms, to come and warm herself by mine. Now, therefore, that I was ill, she came as usual, and brought her work, and sat by my fire, so that in fact I was not so ill off as I otherwise should have been with that ' *bon cœur, Marie,*' as Madame used to call her. I liked Madame in those days, and her *économies* used to amuse me, and I kept to the plan on which I started—to vex myself about nothing—and considered Marie, in the light of *a model*, sitting to me for her portrait—a mere study of character. Once I was very much amused. I have stated how Madame had cheated me out of the window-curtains which were in the rooms when I engaged them, in order to save their wear and tear, and washing during the winter. One day she came in as usual to work by my fire, trailing six or seven yards of dimity behind her, and sitting down by the window, began with melancholy looks to cut, and patch, and shape—

' *Mais qu'est-ce que vous faites donc, madame,*' said I mischievously, seeing perfectly well from my bed what her work was.

' *Je fais des réparations*' (a deep sigh); 'I mend the curtains that belong to these rooms—I had put them *dans le grenier* against spring, when I meant to have them washed clean, and put up before *les étrangers* came; and, *voyez-vous!*' holding them up—' *les rats me les ont tout mangé.*'

I couldn't for the life of me help laughing outright. She would not let me have them; and Nemesis had avenged me in the form of a rat. However, Madame was kind to me in her way. She used to bring me apples and pears, and books to read. She was always willing to show any kindness that did not cost money, but to save had become an instinct with her. It was stronger than she was.

A strange thing happened one day as she sat with me. We were talking of the sorrow that there is for everybody in the world, in some form or other, at some time or other of their lives.

' Yes,' said I; ' and not only for human beings, but for animals, as St. Paul says, " the whole creation groaneth and travaileth together, waiting for the restoration of all things." If one considers it—how sad it is that there should be so much pain and death in the world from the inferior creatures preying one upon the other, as they do. Ah! this is a dreary world!' As I spoke a robin perched upon the railing of the gallery outside my window, and resting there for a moment, looked almost wistfully in, with its large black eyes, and then fled away. It had not been gone an instant when a hawk flew to the very spot, and he also rested on the paling and looked in at the window. I called to Madame —— to drive him off, and frighten him away, but could not persuade her to move. And, after a second or two, he flew off in the same direction as the robin had done. Was it not a strange commentary on the conversation we had just been holding? As I looked at the fierce, bold, beautiful bird, I almost felt as if he were Satan himself in visible form, triumphing in his power to injure and destroy me, and the creatures I pitied. There is no promise more soothing to my feelings or more beautiful, than that the time will come, 'when the wolf shall lie down with the lamb; and the weaned child put his hand on the cockatrice den;' 'when there shall be no more sorrow, because there will be no more sin.' 'For the *earth shall be full of the knowledge of the Lord, as the waters cover the sea.* Amen, Lord Jesus, even so, come quickly.'

I am well now of my abscess, and able to walk about again, but the consequences of my illness do not end with it. Marie has taken a violent dislike to me. I believe she is afraid Madame —— likes me too much.

'*Madame —— va lui léguer toute sa fortune,*' said she, spitefully, one day.

'Madame —— has nephews and nieces, Marie,' said I.

'*Oh! elle en a bien assez pour vous, et pour eux.*'

In short Marie has taken it into her head to turn me out of the house, and I have no doubt will effect her end. I know I could get plenty of lodgings quite as good, and better furnished, for the same terms, but I hate changing; and every change, if only to the next street, is a waste of money, so, if I can, I shall rub on till the season draws near.

March 14th, 1863.—I have been at a very gay ball, and I absolutely went to it in my plain black mousseline-de-laine dress, for I had no other. The English gentlemen gave a ball on the 10th March, to all the English residents at Bagnères, in honour of the Prince of Wales' marriage, and sent me an invitation among the rest, and as the note stated that 'high dresses would be worn,' I determined to go, and make acquaintance with my country folks.

The room was very prettily and appropriately decorated, with the arms of England and Denmark surrounded by what looked a wreath of moss, but was in reality a wreath of box, and the crossed flags of the two countries above them on one side of the room, and on the other the arms of France wreathed with box, and the French ensigns above them. The musicians were screened off by a hedge of *lauriers rose* and orange trees, and orange and oleander trees formed a sort of bower at the end of the apartment, where the principal English ladies were seated. I felt a little awkward at walking in by myself among so many strangers, for I knew no one. The rule at Bagnères is for the stranger to call upon the English residents, and I did not know this, and called on no one. I afterwards learned there had been some talk about calling on me, but that M. Frossard, the French Protestant pastor, knowing I came with the intention of writing a book on the Pyrenees, had given it out, I was too busy to enter into society— from M. Frossard himself—which was quite a mistake, however, as I should have been very glad of English acquaintances. I was not long left in the corner I had selected. On entering the ball-room, Mr. Bradstreet, one of the oldest English residents in Bagnères (I think his family have lived there twenty years), came up and shook hands with me, and expressed his pleasure at seeing me there. We exchanged a few words as to the pretty decorations, and then he took me up to the top of the room, and introduced me to the Countess of Carnwath, and his own wife and sister. I spent a very agreeable evening in talking with my new acquaintance and looking at the dancing, and thenceforth I was free of the English society in Bagnères. There was a good sprinkling of French gentlemen and ladies among the English; and as almost all the lady-dancers were young and pretty, it was a very pleasant sight to look upon. I like to see people enjoy themselves, and felt very glad I went.

A day or two after, Lady Carnwath invited me to dinner, and all the other English families called on me as soon as I got into my new lodgings; for Marie became so insolent, that I was obliged to quit Madame ——'s the week after the ball. From the time of my illness Marie had shamefully neglected my rooms, and as they were neither washed nor *ciré*, they were full of fleas—and one day I hired a woman to scour them at my own expense; but when she came, Marie refused to allow her to go upstairs, pretending the day was damp, and the floor would be spoiled by wetting!

'*Vous ferez mieux*,' said she, '*de vous en aller; c'est moi qui vous le dis.* You may stay till the end of the month if you choose it, but no longer—I've been told to tell you so.'

'I don't take warnings from servants, Marie,' said I; 'I hired the rooms from your mistress—not from you—and I shall make any arrangements I think needful with her.'

So, after breakfast, I sallied forth, and speedily found other lodgings, which I engaged; and then returning home, I requested to speak to Monsieur ——, and quietly handed him myself (as I could neither trust Marie nor Jean to deliver it) a note, in which I politely informed him of my intention to quit his apartments that day week. After this, Madame paid me no more visits, but held herself stiff and stately if I passed her in coming in or going out, and merely acknowledged me by a bow. I wished to part on friendly terms with the ——s, after being there so long; but Madame and Monsieur chose to make a quarrel of my departure, Why they should, I don't know, for I certainly had been a good, quiet lodger to them, and put up with Marie's insolence till I could stand it no longer. I don't envy Madame if she has that woman about her when she becomes sick and infirm; she will have an awful tyrant.

My new lodgings are clean, light, and airy; but, alas! though they profess to cook for me, they don't do it. I am half starved—for Ma'mselle does not choose to cook anything properly, except an omelette, which takes only five minutes to make, and is no trouble to her.

CHAPTER XIX

FRENCH writers seem unable to trace with certainty the origin of the prescribed and unhappy race named Cagots; but all the authors I have consulted, Baron Taylor, Lagrèze, Deville, &c., assert that they must by no means be confounded with the Crétins. Like the *goître*, cretinism is a *disease*, to which, from various causes, some families are more subject than others.* The Crétin in Béarn and Bigorre is, unhappily, an object of dislike. His outward appearance is uncouth and repulsive, often hideous; his awkward shambling gait, misformed limbs, thick protruding lips, from which the saliva is often flowing, and unintelligible mutterings, create, even in the mind of the humane, an irresistible feeling of disgust. I have seen several.—The poor creatures are generally, if not always, harmless; yet I felt it almost impossible to look at them. I had to tell myself again and again that they were God's creatures as well as myself, and that their physical and mental defects only rendered them the objects of a tenderer compassion. Probably they are born with some organic defect, for, happily, they seldom live long. They seem to me to be most frequent in those towns and villages where the inhabitants are the dirtiest and most degraded

---

* It is well known now that the *crétin*, or idiot, is susceptible of improvement, both by the results of the Bicêtre at Paris and the Hospital for Idiots near London; in both which institutions these unhappy beings have been proved to be capable of learning various useful trades. It is a pity that similar hospitals should not be founded in every province in France and every county in England.

P

in their habits. I saw several in Argelés and Asté, only one at Bagnères de Bigorre, where the people are rather more cleanly; but I was told that one belonged to a family of five, *all Crétins.*

The Cagots, on the contrary, seem not to have been a people originally marked with disease by the hand of God from their birth, but with reprobation and hatred, as the descendants of an invading race, by the original owners of the soil. Deville states that Clovis having conquered the Visigoths at the battle of Poictiers, where their wise king Alaric perished, some of the vanquished fled into Spain, while others, confiding in the generosity of the conqueror, bowed to the yoke, and became scattered throughout the kingdom. But Clovis tried to protect them in vain. The clergy, burning for revenge on account of the ill-usage they had received from Evaris, one of their kings, and disliking them as Arians, neutralized all his efforts, without regard to that gospel which commands Christians to return good for evil. They refused them the holy sacrament, and the rites of sepulture, forbade them to enter into the churches by the same door, or to use the same *bénitier* as the faithful, or to appear in public without the mark of a goose foot upon their clothes, as the sign of the leprosy with which they proclaimed them to be infected; and as they could not deny that they were a handsome, well-formed race, they declared '*qu'ils avaient la lèpre en dedans;*' and, to crown all, gave them the name of 'Cagot,'* dog of a Goth, from Ca, or Caas, the *patois*, or Béarnais idiom for a dog. They were treated as slaves. They were condemned to follow the profession of wood-cutters (*bûcherons*), their touch was accounted pollution; and by one of the ancient *fors*, or customs of Béarn, the testimony of *one Béarnais*, was held equal to that of *seven Cagots*. Does not

---

* Throughout Béarn and Bigorre *ca* is still the common term for a dog, *chien* being rarely used among a people who habitually speak patois.

this remind one of the still more cruel and unjust American statute, by which the evidence of a negro is not received against a white man. This universal reprobation in the course of long centuries of misery, semi-starvation, and filth, necessarily ended by degrading them physically. From a fine, healthy, athletic race, they became scrofulous and diseased, but they are not to be confounded with the Crétins. Before the Revolution, there were still families who were pointed out as Cagots, though no sign of leperism existed about them. Their enemies pretended to distinguish them by the round shape of their ears, and the absence of the lobe. *Now*, the term is frequently applied to the poor, diseased, and idiotic *Crétin.*

Goître is fearfully common in the Pyrenees, and it is chiefly the women who suffer from it, though I have (but rarely) seen men with very large ones. The learned dispute as to the cause of this deformity—some referring it to the use of melted snow for water, as in the colder parts of Switzerland—others to the presence of *talc* in the water. The scientific and excellent French Protestant pastor of Bagnères, M. Frossard, well known by his ' *Tableau Pittoresque et Scientifique de Nismes,*' his graphic and amusing ' *Lettres écrites de l'Orient,*' &c., says, in his ' *Guide du Géologue dans les Pyrénées Centrales,*' ' some learned men attribute goîtres to the presence of talc in the waters. It is a fact, that those places where this hideous deformity reproduces itself most frequently, and with the greatest intensity — *St. Mamet, près Luchon, Gerdes et Asté, près Bagnères de Bigorre, Davantaigue,* in the valley of *Argelès,* the valley of *Azun,* &c., are eminently regions of talc.'[*]

* M. Frossard adds, 'When will a society be formed for the extinction of *goîtres* in this country?' Ah! how many human evils might be put an end to if men would only live more for others and less for themselves—if the great principle that it is everyone's duty to work for the amelioration of humanity were once generally recognized and acted upon by all. God alone

Without disputing the dictum of those far better able to judge of its cause than myself, I cannot help attributing goîtres, in a great degree, to the continual strain upon the muscles of the neck, from the immense burdens the women carry on their heads, and the fact that it is generally women who suffer from them, seems to support this theory. I have frequently seen peasant women carrying heavy loads of wood (which an Englishman would have had difficulty in merely lifting) on their heads, down steep mountain paths. I once tried the weight of *one* when the bearer laid it down for a moment to rest herself—for a woman I am tolerably strong in the arms, but I could not trail it along the ground, *nor even move it*. Yet this poor delicate-looking, half-starved woman—far slighter built and less than myself, carried it a couple of miles down a mountain-side, so steep, that I, carrying nothing, could scarcely preserve my equilibrium.

I walked one day to the village of Asté, and, as my custom is, entered the church to look at it. I always kneel down and pray when I enter a Catholic church, for two reasons—first it is the house of God and therefore sacred ; next, my doing so prevents the worshippers present from feeling hurt or wounded, when I afterwards walk round to inspect it. As I came out, a peasant girl, who no doubt took me for a Catholic, dipped her fingers into the *bénitier*, and touched mine with holy water, and after we got into the street, offered to show me a beautiful view from some fields behind a gentleman's house. When we reached the spot we sat down on a garden wall to rest, and I then noticed that my companion had an incipient goître.

'You have a tendency to goître,' said I to her, 'though

can destroy Satan and the evil he has brought upon the world ; but if men would but unite as brethren, they could bind the spirit of evil by their united efforts, as the Lilliputians bound Gulliver. Most of the misery on earth is caused by the selfishness—the cruelty—and the ambition of man, who lives only for *self*.

not more than I had myself at seventeen. I wish I had
the prescription which cured me here with me and I would
cure you.'*

'Ah! I wish you had!' cried she eagerly. 'Can't you
send for it? I would take it at once. I had no goître till
last year. I went last summer as servant to the *Hôtel de
Paris*, and I had to carry out dinners. *It was carrying the
heavy dinner box on my head that made the nerves of my neck
swell*, and I have had it ever since. The work was too hard
for me, and I left as soon as the season was over.'

'And what do you do now?'

'I work in the fields.'

'How much can you earn a day by that?'

'About a franc (tenpence).'

'And you find that easier than house-work? You would
not have dinners to carry out in a private family.'

'No; but I prefer to work in the fields.'

Thus it is; there are no real good servants in the
Pyrenees. Few families keep more than one, or at most
two maids; and servants do not, as with us, go out as
little girls, and learn their work under experienced and
efficient domestics. They go when they are grown up,
and disinclined to learn, straight from the fields into
domestic service. They pick up a little knowledge of
cookery and house-work; but they retain their lazy,
sluggish, filthy habits, their love of independence, and
their custom of loitering and gossiping in the market, or
on errands. Well may the men say they are '*oisives et
bavardes*.' Their work is not done, but slurred through.

* This prescription was given me by an uncle who was a very skilful
medical man, who lived in the mountainous district of Wales, and had in
his time cured many *goîtres* by it. The chief ingredient was calcined sponge
made into lozenges, with a little honey. One of these was to be placed
under the tongue on going to-bed at night, *and not sucked*, but allowed to
dissolve as slowly as possible. The result was a perfect cure. To be efficacious this remedy should be taken at the *commencement* of the swelling.

If they spill any water on the chamber floor, or the passage, they never wipe it up. '*Ça ne fait rien. Ça se séchera bientôt.*' They empty the slops out at your window, to trickle down the roof into the gutter, or on to the balcony; and the more anything *requires cleaning,* the more obstinately they refuse, with an air of ineffable disgust, to clean it. When I used to see those vulgar, coarse Pyrenean girls, standing with flashing eyes and open mouth, wondering that I should ask them to do anything so horrid, and contrasted them mentally with our neatly-dressed, *lady-like* looking maids, who do all these things as a mere matter of course, and would deem themselves disgraced if such needful work were left *undone,* I used to feel out of all patience. Those hands that lately spread dung on the fields, now disdain contact with any soil. Your room is half swept and undusted. You point it out. '*Ça ne fait rien.*' If you insist on amendment, and complain, woe to you. They tell you you may be thankful they are *honest*—they don't want to be told their work, &c. They are *hard mistresses, not maids.*

To return to the girl I met at Asté. I asked her if she were married?

'No; and I will never marry.'

'Why?'

'Because *les hommes sont méchants ici, ils vont au cabaret, et boivent, puis ils retournent chez eux et battent leurs femmes.*'

The men on their part, say '*Les femmes sont méchantes ici, elles sont oisives et bavardes.*'

I believe both parties. I have frequently met men in a state of inebriety; and it is said the women are too often given to drink also. One of their own *patois* songs on the change of the *coutumes de Lavedan* (or ancient laws), more than hints, that provided the *ci-devant* heiresses have plenty of wine, they will not mind losing their rights of

first-born.* I give the verse as an example of the *patois*
dialect, with its translation :—

†' Lon lengatye de las d'Azun,	' Le langage de celles d'Azun
Que'n-ey mes dous et mes segur,	Est plus calme, et plus *positif*,
Pourbu qu'ayen bi—	Pourvu qu'elles ont du vin,
Noun hars nad chagrin.	Elles n'ont aucun chagrin.
Es datz-en bère tasse	Donnez-en donc une tasse ;
Bèt safè amigous	Allons, petits amis,
Si n-ètz amourous	Si vous êtes amoureux
Coupe tey en amasse.'	Vidons la coupe ensemble.'

How would you like a Pyrenean damsel for your maid,
my fair readers ?

* The *coutume de Lavedan* was that the first-born child inherited the
estate, whether male or female. This law is abrogated, and property now
descends to the first-born son ; or the father, by portioning off his other
children in his life, may select as heir the child he thinks most likely to
keep the property together, or whom he prefers to the others.

† 'Celles d'Azun,' *i.e.* of the heiresses of Azun.

CHAPTER XX.

THERE are *two* idioms, or separate languages, in the adjacent provinces of Béarn and Bigorre. The Bigorrais accent is harsh and untunable, notwithstanding the multiplicity of vowels, at least when spoken by the peasants; of the other, hear what Rivarès says:—

'Few idioms can compare with the Béarnais in richness and harmony. The verbs are extremely numerous, and there are many for expressing the same idea by modifying it. Thus, beside the verb *brusla*, burn, there are *cresma*, *creseca*, *ary*, *ardé aslama*, *ahouega*, whose force augments *successively*, and most substantives can be made into verbs. From *taüle*, *table-taüleya*, to remain at table; from *ardit liard*, a farthing, *arditeya*, to gather a little money; from *pot-a-kiss*, *pontiqueya*, to give kisses, &c.

The innumerable synonymous substantives allow of a great variety of expressions, enabling the speaker to select the fittest, and render them strong, or soft, at will. The gender can easily be modified, and many are indifferently employed for both masculine and feminine. Thus, *gourg*, or *gourge*, a collection of water; *clot*, or *clotte*, a ditch or grave; *arram*, or *arame*, a branch of a tree.

All substantives and adjectives have, besides, diminutives and augmentatives, which attach to the words at the will of the person using them, either agreeable or disagreeable

* Most of this chapter is quoted from Rivarès, from whom also most of the music and songs are taken.

ideas. The diminutive is formed by adding *et* or *ette* to the end of a word, to express joy or pleasure ; *in* or *ine*, to express friendship, tenderness, or love ; *on, ot,* or *otte,* to express pity or contempt. The augmentative is formed by adding the syllables *as, asse.* It serves to express hatred, disdain, ridicule, or some disagreeable idea. Thus *henne,* a woman ; *hennette,* a pretty little woman, pleasant to sight ; *hemnine,* pretty little woman, that one loves and cherishes ; *hemnon,* or *hemnotte,* poor little woman, that one pities or despises ; *hemnasses,* disagreeable or hated by one—*i.e.* people even say *hemnass-asse,* to increase the strength of the expression.*

The Béarnais are full of deep religious feeling, though they allow the clergy small influence over their minds, and like the inhabitants of the Pyrenees generally, have a most especial devotion for the Holy Virgin. Bétharram, Héas, Sarrame, attract at certain times of the year such crowds of pilgrims, that a stranger would rather believe he was in the midst of a fair than in places which have been looked upon for ages with respect and veneration. The inevitable disorders which arise when so great a multitude congregate together, are rather a cause of scandal than of edification, and for this reason the priests somewhat dis- countenance the faithful from these pilgrimages. In re- turning home the pilgrims unite in bands, singing, as they take the homeward path, to their different villages ; while others, provided with *mirlitons,* play the wildest accom- paniments to these chants.

'The custom of assembling and watching together, during Advent, and especially before Christmas, has given birth to innumerable songs, many of which are composed

---

* Much of what follows is extracted from 'Chansons et Airs populaires de Béarn,' par F. Rivarès, a work much prized by the French, and now out of print and difficult to obtain. It was procured for me by the kindness of the excellent and learned M. Frossard, pastor of the French Protestant Church.

of couplets alternatively in French and Béarnais.' The
' Noël,' by Andichon, is an instance of this: the angel
speaks French, the pastor replies to him in *patois*. In
translating this 'Noël,' I have been obliged wholly to
abandon all attempts at rendering it in the same metre as
the original, the lines being often so excessively short,
that in English they would have degenerated into mere dog-
grel. I have, therefore, given a paraphrase of it, adhering
as closely as possible to the thoughts, but altering the
rhythm entirely. These short abrupt lines, and the frequent and sudden change to others of ten or eleven
syllables, rather remind one of the old poems of Lovelace
and Withers, but often want their grace and sweetness.
The thought is often indicated rather than expressed in
many; and were a literal translation attempted, it would
sound utterly bald and poor. When I have given both
music and words, I have adhered as closely as possible to
the metre of the original.

' A people so lively and fond of pleasure as the Béarnais, were sure to give themselves up with ardour to the
amusements of the Carnival.' Nevertheless, there are few
songs connected with it of any poetical merit. But
Rivarès gives so curious an account of a custom nearly
obsolete at Pau, that I transcribe it. It still exists in full
force in other parts of Béarn, and also in Gascony. This
is the trial and condemnation of the Carnival,* on Ash-
Wednesday:—' His advent has been celebrated by songs,
and cries of joy; but, woful example of the fluctuations of
popular favour, he is now exposed to the hatred of the
same persons who exalted him to the skies a few days ago.
He is a fallen monarch, and his reign is ended. At a
fixed hour, which has been loudly announced beforehand,
a crowd of masks throng into a theatre prepared the previous day. The judges take their seats, the advocates are

* Carnival is represented by a stuffed figure, like our Guy Fawkes.

at their posts.   The unhappy *Carnival* arrives on a cart
drawn by an ass, and surrounded by *gendarmes*, and most
grotesquely dressed.   He is lifted into his place—the
accusation is made—the witnesses against him examined ;
he is defended by his lawyers, but in vain.   He is condemned to an ignominious death—usually to the double
torture of fire and water.   Some of the by-standers address
him in mocking songs, others deplore his fate.   In this
manner he is conducted to the bridge, when, after a
harangue suited to the gravity of his functions, the pre-
sident of the court executes the sentence he has himself
pronounced, by setting fire to the accused's clothes, and
precipitating him thus flaming into the river.

> ' Adiü praübé, praübê, praübé,
> Adiü praübé Carnabal ! '

' The mountaineers' custom of traversing the streets in
a company divided into bands separated by a considerable
distance from each other, and the members of each band,
holding each other by the arm, is well known.   The first
group sing a verse, which the second repeat from the distance.   No words can give the picturesque effect of these
chants, generally of a mournful cast—which seem as if
repeated by the distant mountain echoes.   How often,
seated on the edge of the road leading to Eaux-Chaudes,
towards sunset, have I listened attentively to this sweet
and touching music.   The breeze of evening brought to
my ear the entire couplet, and, like a faint murmur, the
voice of the farthest singers.   At other times the different
parties seemed lost in the winding path that sank deep
into the hollows of the mountain, and the most profound
silence reigned in the valley.   All at once they reappeared
at some angle of the road, and their voices again reached
me, softened and prolonged by the distance, till at last
the sound ceased entirely, leaving me plunged in sweet
and tender reveries.'

This custom used to prevail at Bagnères also, and gave much pleasure to the visitors; but the present *Maire*, Monsieur d'Uzer, has forbidden all singing in the streets, and thus deprived both the people, and the strangers who throng the place during the season, of a very great enjoyment. I often mentally quoted Shakespeare's well-known lines, when I thought of this act of petty tyranny:

> 'The man that hath no music in himself,
> Nor is not moved by concord of sweet sounds,
> Is fit for treason, stratagem, and spoils.'

'The Montagnards' national dance is the *branle*.* Youths and maidens hold each other by the hands, singing and executing different evolutions at the same time, accompanied by cries and bounds. The most nimble dancer is placed at the head of the *branle*, and every one imitates the proofs he gives of strength and agility as well as they can. There are, as may be imagined, innumerable *branles*, but they are all formed on the same model. Some consist of the same burden, repeated alternately by lads and lasses: others are rather longer. Among the first, is " *Gageat ! pastoure rencountré à l'oumpre de la rose;*" and the interminable Odyssey of *Capitaine Salies*,† whom the poet takes up as he jumps out of bed (*Capitaine Salies, de bon Maty se lhéba*), to conduct him through such a crowd of adventures, that the legs of the young girls of Laruns, accustomed as they are to rough exercise, and the strong lungs of young men who converse with each other from the heights of opposite mountains, can hardly succeed in following them to the end.

'When a dance is to take place the fiddlers traverse the

---

* I wonder whether the *brawl* danced by our ancestors and immortalized in 'The Long Story,' is derived from this?

> 'The grave lord-keeper led the brawl,
> The seals and maces danced before him.'

† This song of Capitan Salies relates a predatory inroad of a Capitan Salies on the lands of the Lea family.

village streets playing their *utis*. Few young men resist this clear invitation, and the *yougadous* (*i.e.* fiddlers), who set off alone, soon find themselves at the head of a numerous company, increasing every moment, which they conduct to the grand *place*.* But the girls have not yielded to the temptation; they dare not show so openly their passion for dancing. They will come later, and in succession. " *Yougadous ú saüt !* " Fiddlers, a spring! The flageolet sounds "*Muchichou*" or "*Monein*," and numberless quadrilles are formed for executing a *saut Basque*. This characteristic dance is borrowed from our neighbours, but has acquired such rights of citizenship in Béarn, that while preserving the name, which testifies its origin, there is neither great town nor small village hamlet where it is not had in honour. It is danced exclusively by men. Their severe grave air and stiff bearing recall the military dances of the ancients. Often holding their sticks in their hands, they add gestures to the figures. People press round the best dancers, and the crowd, who are always warmly interested, applaud the nimble and ridicule those whose inexperience spoils the quadrille, or whose fatigue forces them to quit the circle. A person must have both agility and strength to execute a good *saut*.

' "*Muchichou*" has no less than eight burdens or choruses, which are twice repeated, and the figures of which, always different, follow one another like those of a ballet. I have seen a quadrille composed of a dozen vigorous young men successively reduced to three or four, then to two,

---

* As Rivarès' book was published in 1844, it is probable that many of the customs spoken of no longer exist in full force. Every year some old *coutume* dies out as the people become more *fashionable*, for fashion and hoops have invaded the mountains, *and conquered*, though cleanliness is still kept at bay. The priests of the present day, unlike the younger *Despourrins*, disapprove both of theatres and dances, and, as respectable people informed me, refuse the Sacrament to those who frequent either. Nothing, however, can stay the people's inordinate passion for dancing, and they dance every Sunday in the meadows at Carnival time, and on all feast-days, holidays, and weddings.

finally to one, who, bathed in perspiration and breathless, danced on, finding in his vanity and the frenzied acclamations of the mob strength to execute the most brilliant *sauts*.

'"*Jean-Petit*" is rather a game than a dance. A circle is formed, in the midst of which stands a singer, armed with a long stick. The first burden is danced like a *branle*, but at the second he says "*dap lon pé*," "*dap lon dit*," and at these words the dancers are obliged to strike the ground in time, with foot or finger, or whatever part of the body is indicated, and rise promptly enough to execute a *pirouette* on the last notes of the air "*Ataü, danse Jean-Petit*"—thus dances Jean-Petit. It is clear that when a mischievous singer chooses to designate the back, for example, instead of the foot or hand, it needs singular quickness to rise in time for the final pirouette. He who is behindhand is stimulated by blows with the stick. This is an understood thing, so that no one thinks of taking offence; besides which, the time of retaliation soon arrives.

'I,' concludes Rivarès, 'have only spoken of the Béarnais and their customs as connected with popular songs and dances, but I believe an interesting book might be written on the subject, though I am obliged to content myself with a very brief and incomplete notice of it. Another will perhaps some day do for these original manners and quaint usages, what I now do for our songs.'

This book, which would be so desirable, remains still, so far as I know, unwritten. Ancient habits are fast dying out, and the stranger passing rapidly through the country, or even residing in it for years, but never mixing with the peasants, has no chance of becoming familiar with their customs and way of life. Pity that some man of genius like Rivarès does not arise to collect together, into one pleasant volume, the ancient customs and traditions of the Pyrenees, and let us know how people amused themselves, and thought and acted, in the times of Henri IV. and *le bon Réné*.

The preface to Rivarès' book is full of interesting information as to customs formerly universal in these mountains, but now nearly as obsolete as others of which, but for his brief notice, and that of a few other old and rare authors, all memory would soon be lost. As he pathetically says :—' I say it with regret, *Notre Béarn s'en va tous les jours* —manners, language, songs, customs, all are melting away ; in a little while we shall be morally, as we are topographically, only a department of France. One hardly finds now in a few distant villages the old customs, whose observation at their weddings and funerals seemed as necessary to our fathers, as the benediction of the priest. *Tout le monde devient Franciman*, a rare and ridiculous exception forty years ago ! The young men have cut their long hair, the *causse* (knee breeches) no longer outlines their athletic limbs. The women of the plain have replaced the rich and graceful folds of the *coyfe* by the handkerchief of the *grisette*. The whole valley of Aspé has repudiated the national *costume*, and if it yet survives in that of Ossau it is modified every year, and will soon disappear entirely. The national songs are going out of vogue also, and are replaced by villanous French romances, whose airs and words equally mangled, inflict a double torture on the ear.

· The scope of my work being principally to make known the most remarkable of our national airs, I was much restricted in the choice of songs. Nevertheless, we possess a great number of very curious ones which are not set to original music, or which is of sufficient merit to be admitted into this collection. To collect these ballads would be a new and different work, more interesting perhaps than this, inasmuch as it would give a complete idea of poetry that deserves to be known, and would produce a book that would have no small intrinsic value. We have songs that are really popular, upon the invasion of the Moors; others recall the battles fought under Henri IV. The first of our poets, our favourite author, him of whom we are most proud, is Despourrins. Virgil and Theocritus have not in our eyes more charms, sweetness, and passion. Nothing can be more touching than " *Là haut sur las Montagnes ;* " or more original than " *De cap à tu soy Marion,*" which Louis XV. delighted to hear sung by the famous Jéliotte." Despourris was born at Accous, in the valley of Aspé, in 1698. His ancestors were shepherds. One of them having made a fortune in Spain, bought the Abbey of Juzan on his return home and was ennobled. Pierre, the father of the poet, served with some distinction and obtained the king's leave to add three swords to his arms, in memory of a triple victory over three foreign gentlemen with whom he had quarrelled. An anecdote will prove his coolness of temper. The poet, being at Eaux-Bonnes, sent his servant home one day to get his sword. The old man let the messenger take it and depart, but suspecting an affair of honour he followed him closely. On his arrival he heard that his son was shut up in a room with a stranger; ran to the door, and heard the clash of arms within. He stood still, stoically awaiting the issue of the combat, and when the young Despourrins rushed out hastily, he found his old father listening, with his sword under his arm ready to take his place had he succumbed.

'The poet had two brothers, one of whom was Curé,* the other Vicaire of Accous. Both were musicians. Every Sunday they assembled the young people of their parish in the court before their house, and from a window they played joyous *branles*, while the young folks danced gaily till the bell tolled for vespers, when everyone followed the good

* Our terms are reversed in France—the *Curé* is the village priest, the *Vicaire* his assistant.

pastors to church. In 1746, Despourrins inherited property from the house of Miramon, and quitted Béarn to establish himself in the valley of Argelés, where his new domains were situated. His family subsists there still.'

Rivarès continues—' We possess a great number of airs far from remarkable in themselves, but which borrow interest from the curious customs which have consecrated them. The public will probably be glad to have a few details concerning these customs, whose antiquity is so great that we are quite ignorant how they originated, or what their meaning may be. I begin by the marriages.*

' On the morning of the day designated for the wedding, the guests arrive on horseback, and are saluted on their entrance by firing off pistols. Each individual brings a present, as fowls, fruits, wine. A table is spread, around which the men only sit down. When the time draws near for conducting the bride to the altar, she enters and places herself in the middle of the room, leaning her arms upon the back of a chair. Everyone then advances, kisses her cheek, and places an offering in a plate placed upon the chair before her. The whole party then mount on horseback, the bride, behind one of her relations, heading the cavalcade. This is the moment when they chant the song :—

> " Sourtit, sourtit, lous ahumats."†

and each improvises couplets to the air, which are repeated in chorus. It is, in fact, a sort of framework for criticism or praise, and the village humour usually exercises itself at the expense of those whom the train happen to meet on their road from time to time. The young men shout the curious cry known under the name of *hilhet*, and which, like an Indian war-cry, cannot be rendered in writing. Pistol-shot succeeds pistol-shot—discharges, *hil-*

---

* The wedding, funeral, and other customs of Béarn, differ from those of Bigorre, as will be seen later.

† Go out, go out the smokers, *i.e.* of tobacco.

hets, and noise, being in proportion to the wealth and position of the bride and bridegroom. But suddenly the leader of the cavalcade stops short at a turn in the road. A long red sash* has been placed across it, and four men armed with guns stand menacingly at either end. On one side is a table surrounded by numerous lads. This is *la ségue* (*la ronce*), (the hedge), and at this sight everyone prepares to pay the customary toll, and pieces of money rain upon the table. Then the tollkeepers offer nosegays, the road is strewn with fresh herbs and branches, and the guardians of *la ségue* fire off their guns, and join the wedding party. Woe to him who has been remarked as parsimonious in his offering; he is followed to the church-doors by hootings and insulting couplets, while the air resounds with improvised verses in honour of those who have proved their generosity. They reach the church at last, when the bridegroom and his party have already arrived, and during the ceremony flutes and tambourines incessantly play the national airs. On coming out of church the two wedding parties separate, the bride being reconducted to her paternal home where dinner has been prepared. After the repast is over, two of the principal guests are deputed to the husband's father to inquire if it will·be convenient to him to receive his daughter-in-law. During this time, the young men post themselves on the road armed with large bottles, and *force*, rather than invite, all who pass to drink with them to the healths of the new married couple.

'But here come the ambassadors with a favourable answer, and the bride must bid a last farewell to her mother, to all recollections of childhood, and all the pleasant and dear habits of the young girl. . . . It seems as if the guests sought to drown her grief by noisy exclamations,

---

* The Pyrenean men wear a red or green worsted sash wound round the waist, instead of braces.

songs, *hilhets*, and pistol-shots, "*qué partén coum la brume*," as, accompanied by her father and friends, she departs for the home of her husband. On arriving they find the doors carefully closed. Nobody to be seen outside, not a sound to be heard within. They knock loud and long. At last the master of the house opens the door, and asks—

' " What do you want ? "

' " We bring you," replies the father of the bride, " a maiden who is to become the mistress of your house."

'Permission to enter is then formally refused—fresh requests for admittance are made by the party without— and at last terms of compromise are agreed upon ; the conditions being mutually debated. The bride's friends will give poultry, wine, a leg of mutton, and the maiden's godfather will bestow a bridal gift. When these matters are arranged, the doors open, and the *cortége* admitted into the house, find the husband's friends who invite them to sit down around a perfectly bare table. Then begins a dialogue, chanted between the two wedding-parties—the bridegroom's and that of the bride.

' The new-comers defend themselves as well as they can, and this strife of improvised couplets is often both witty and full of good sense. Meanwhile the godfather's present has been placed upon the table. It is a pyramid of nine loaves of bread surmounted by a cheese, into which is stuck a tree-branch, bearing nine apples. Then everyone sings "*Aü nousté poumé*," &c. ; and at the end of each verse, the godfather gravely takes an apple from the bough, and lays it on the table ; when he has plucked the ninth apple, the time has come for leaving the maiden in her new home. The bride and groom are conducted with great ceremony to the nuptial chamber, and seated in two chairs at the foot of the bed. The company keep a profound silence, and the father of the bride retires with his friends. No more songs, no more *hilhets*—sadness shadows every face—they have left there a well-beloved maiden, whose future is uncertain.

'But, to make amends, what tumultuous joy—what quips and pranks in the house of the bridegroom! Restraint is banished, and gaiety too often degenerates into licence, The guests dance all night, and the bridegroom is often obliged to purchase a little repose; but do what he will, he cannot avoid "*la roste*," and its accompaniment of quizzing. In the middle of the night, there is a knocking at his door —to refuse to open would be useless, as custom gives the right of breaking it open upon the least hesitation or delay. Four young men carry in an arm-chair, upon which a sort of Guy is seated, dressed in white. His apron and white cotton nightcap denote that he is a cook, who comes to offer the new married couple a dish of his cooking; and he gravely carries upon his knees a huge jug of highly-spiced wine, in which swim bits of toasted bread (*rostes*), to both of which the bride and bridegroom are forced to do honour.

'Funerals offer one remarkable peculiarity. No sooner has the sick man breathed his last, than his body is extended at length upon the floor of the chamber, and surrounded by a crowd of women, who pray and watch it,— giving vent at intervals to plaintive cries and frightful groans: the wife of the deceased, and his nearest relatives, improvising chants, in which his virtues are celebrated. These testimonies of grief and affection follow the dead to his last home; and the moment when earth is first thrown upon the beloved remains, is marked by an explosion of cries and lamentations. Nevertheless, *l'aürost* (as this chant is called) often contains something other than praises, and is rather a judgment than a funeral oration; and the relatives and the clergy have often been scandalized by improvisations, more calculated to lower the character of the deceased, or that of the survivors, than to excite regrets for the departed. *L'aürost*, which I reproduce, is an example of this kind. It has been rigorously transcribed from an improvisation of "Marie," formerly surnamed " *la blague, la blanche*," on account of her beauty, the most celebrated chanter of *aürosts* in the valley of Aspe. Her great age, the vivacity of her imagination, her character exalted by the habit of frequenting sorrowful scenes, and the high idea she attaches to the performance of her functions—all resemble those of the Pythoness of old.'

Mr. Maxwell Lyte, of Bagnères, the well-known photographer, told me of another curious funeral custom which he witnessed in one district, I think, at St. Gaudens. He was breakfasting with a friend at the small inn there, when their attention was attracted by a crowd of people in the street. Going to the window to ascertain why it had collected, they saw, what to them seemed a hideous and unnatural sight : the crowd were following the corpse of an ugly, withered *old* woman of seventy, who was dressed out like a young girl for her first ball, and borne on an open bier to her grave. On her grey hair was a wreath of flowers ; her neck and arms were bare, and she was decked out in satin, and tinsel, and finery, making her poor, faded, shrivelled features look all the more repulsive and hideous.

It is the *coutume* of the place that when a woman dies unmarried, she shall be borne in full dress upon an open bier to the grave.

' Take care, Miss Eyre,' added Mr. Lyte, mischievously, ' that *you* don't die at St. Gaudens ! '

It is difficult, if not impossible, to break through one of these *customs* without exciting a popular tumult.

' *C'est la coutume du pays*,' is to the Pyrenean an irrefragable argument for the continuance of any time-honoured folly or inconvenience whatsover. Before I visited the Pyrenees, an opera used to seem to me ' an excellent piece of fooling.' The music and the acting were beautiful in themselves, but the idea that anyone ever scolded, made love, died, or 'went mad to soft music,' seemed to me preposterous. It does not seem so to me now. The Pyrenean peasant's life is an idyll, beginning and ending with song. Are they merry, they sing; are they melancholy, they comfort themselves with music; does anyone offend them, they vent their indignation by holding him up to ridicule in a *charivari* song, of which the air as well the words are often improvised, and which will hand the memory of the culprit down to posterity. I met a little boy once in one of my walks, who was piping most melodiously—he stopped bashfully as I came up—but a little praise and some *sous* soon made him recommence.

'What are you singing?' said I.

'It has no name—it is a *charivari* the boys made on a man in our village.'

The peasants sing as they go and return from their pilgrimages; they sing as they return in bands after husking the maize at some neighbouring farm; they sing at weddings and at funerals, and when the '*tir au sort*,' the drawing lots for the conscription took place, the poor young lads who drew the evil card, relieved their sadness by song. It was touching to see them go arm-in-arm along the streets of Bagnères, with the fatal card stuck in their hats, singing plaintive farewells to the girl they loved, to their mountain-home, and their families; and then, with eyes made bright by unshed tears, bursting out into some spirit-stirring *chanson de guerre* about *la patrie* and honour. One honoured the poor young fellows for the manliness and courage which were evidently so difficult at that trying moment, and my eyes were wet many times as I heard the refrain, '*Nous partirons demain.*'

I WENT through the meadows at the back of Monsieur Lavalette's pretty house, La Côte, to-day. I wish I was rich enough to buy that estate, which, with the house, is to be sold for about two thousand pounds, and live upon the produce of my farm and garden, and rear ducks and chickens, sheep and calves. Alas! I have missed my true vocation, not by my own fault, but my aunt's. I was cut out to be a farmer's wife, to skim cream, see to the butter-making, make jams, currant wine, and seed-cakes, and doctor all the old women in the parish. Woe is me! I am the square woman in the round hole, and my *angles* are always sore from rubbing against its sides.

M. Lavelette's house is fitted up inside with English comforts, for his brother, who built it, married an English wife; and when he took me over it one day, I longed for means to purchase it more than ever. The windows command one of the finest views about Bagnères. If I had it, I should set up a school for the rough children in the Rue de Toulouse, and try to teach them a little English cleanliness and decency.

There is a very pretty walk behind it, past several other farms, which brings one out across the railway line to the village of Pouzac. As I walked past an old quarry, I was startled by an exquisite small blue flower growing among the brown withered grass. I gathered it, and found it to be the *gentianella verna*, which I had never seen before. It is not above two or three inches high, scarcely as tall as thyme; and its glossy, oval-pointed, green leaves are about the same size. The flowers are five-lobed, and of the deepest blue, relieved by a little white eye at the base; it grows rather plentifully on La Côte, and looks like small blue stars scattered among the grass, which it seldom overtops. Farther on, near the next farm, I found sweet-scented white and purple violets, and a large bed of blue periwinkles. The beautiful little gentian is too short stemmed to put in water; but it makes lovely nosegays, if patches of it are carefully cut out of the turf, and placed in a *terrine*, or common brown saucer or plate, and the earth hidden by moss, which has the property of keeping water sweet. In this way, delicate flowers may be kept for a week or two, fresh blossoms opening as the first ones wither and die.

From these fields, there are such lovely views of the town of Bagnères, and the snowy mountain peaks above. I went there one day with a lady,—whose rich endowments I often envied, for she excelled as an artist, a singer, and a musician, besides being a very good linguist, and very quiet and unassuming withal, as all really clever people are,—to sketch them, that is to say,—*she* sketched, while I sought for flowers. I don't know how I shall ever bring myself to leave Bagnères. I like the place better every day, and I have met with so much kindness from the French Protestant pastor, M. Frossard, and his sister, and the English families resident here, that Bagnères seems more of a home to me than any place I ever lived in, since I was forced to give up my dear little four-roomed cottage at Hampstead.

I was sitting writing one day, when the singing, sketching lady came to ask me if I would join her and two other ladies, and our English clergyman, in a drive to Escala-

dieu. I was only too happy; and we set out. A merry
party we were, though one poor lady was clearly in the
last stage of consumption; but her sweet temper, and
bright, cheerful, hopeful character, perhaps also the nature
of her disease, prevented her feeling low or anxious about
herself. I had walked nearly to Escaladieu before, and
should have reached it but for that Keeper. Doubtless the
mountain air had made him hungry, and seeing some
fowls in a field of maize, he rushed after them, and caught
one. He seems to have got it into his dog's noddle, that
fowls in a farm yard are human property, whom it would
be sinful to touch; but *fowls in a maize field are feræ
naturæ*, expressly for him, Keeper, to eat, and he runs after
them in the most hardened manner, never exhibiting the
smallest symptoms of penitence when he is punished for
doing so. On this occasion, he caught a fine black
Spanish fowl, with a scarlet comb, that reminded me of
my dear Hampstead poultry. Out rushed a peasant with
a. gun—whether loaded or not I know not—vowing he
would 'shoot that dog for killing his fowl.' 'No; don't,'
said I, 'for he's mine, and I'll pay you for the fowl.'

He still swore and threatened, and seemed ready to
shoot me as well as Keeper; however, at last I got him to
listen, and comprehend that his fowl would be well paid
for, as was only just. 'But,' said I, 'I will only pay you
on one condition—that you give the dog a good beating,
which will make him remember that he is not to chase
fowls again;' to which the peasant agreed. But now came
a fresh difficulty. Keeper knew well enough he would be
punished, and kept at a respectful distance, from which
neither calling nor coaxing could induce him to swerve.
At last I went into the cottage, and sat down as if going
to stay, cruelly practising upon his affections, to his un-
doing. When he saw I did not come out again, he came
to seek me, and I laid hold of him instantly. 'Can you

give me a cord?' said I. The peasant looked for one—
'*Il n'y en avait pas.*' 'Oh, yes!' said he, correcting himself; 'there was a piece tied to the fryingpan.' But
where was the fryingpan, do you think? Why, *under* the
bed. He pulled it out—there was no string. 'Ah!' said
he ; '*Ce n'est pas celui-ci—c'est l'autre.*' *L'autre* was *in*
the bed.

There were two beds both unmade in this hovel, which I
should think had never been swept, far less washed, since
it was built. The floor was inches thick with dust, and
strewn with boots and shoes, and pots and pans, and sticks
for firewood, and cobs of Indian wheat not yet tied together
and hung up, and the fowls ran in and out among all, and
sat upon the beds or perched upon the tables, and did as
they liked—it was Liberty Hall.

Well, the fryingpan string was a mere packthread. So
mine host went up to the *grenier* and came down with a
rope. But like all bullies he was a great coward, and clearly
afraid to touch the dog. So *I* had to tie the rope round
poor Keeper's neck, and then *I* had to make him fast to
the shafts of a cart which stood in the yard, and then the
peasant took a switch and began to belabour him, while I,
armed with another, stood by. Poor Keeper sprang howl-
ing to me for protection. Alas! I only gave him a blow
with my switch. Then he grew furious, he sprang at the
peasant and certainly would have bitten him if he could
have reached him. I stayed till he had had, for the first
time in his life, a real good flogging, and then I untied
him from the shaft and paid the man three francs for his
fowl. I had scarcely done so, before another peasant came
with a fowl in *his* hand. He asked the first what I had
paid for the black fowl, and then demanded as much for
his, which he said Keeper had chased also.

'That is true,' said I, 'he did chase it, but he did not
catch it, because we came in here.'

'O yes! he had caught it—here was the place where the feathers were torn out.'

I looked and saw very clearly that the poor fowl's feathers had been *pulled out* to make it look as if it had been injured, and I knew very well that though Keeper had run after it while I was parleying with the owner of the black hen, I had run after him and prevented him from following up the chase, the fowl moreover flying into a tree.

'I shan't pay you for feathers you have pulled out of your fowl yourself,' said I; 'I can swear my dog never touched your fowls, they flew away into the trees, and I called him off; I was quite willing to pay Monsieur for his fowl, because it was really injured.'

'*Killed! Killed!*' cried the first peasant, pathetically, 'my best fowl! such a layer! I would not have sold it for *ten francs!* (I knew very well he would have been glad to sell it for *two*) it layed me an egg every day, it was the best fowl I had—you ought to give me more.'

'Can't,' said I; 'and indeed I think you are a gainer by my dog's misbehaviour. I have kept fowls, and that hen is an old one. She is a good deal torn, poor thing, but she has no bones broken, and it's my belief, indeed I am sure of it, that she will live, if you take care of her for a day or two, and so you will have both the fowl and three francs.'

The peasant insisted upon it he should be obliged to kill her—she could not live, and she was worth more; but I saw he did not think so, and was in reality well content with his bargain, and as they saw I was inflexible, and that no more could be got out of me, the owner of the fowl that *was* injured, and the owner of the fowl that was *not* injured, let me depart. As for the convict he was led home with a rope round his neck, and every time we passed a fowl I gave him a slight tap and reproached him with his sin— 'you *will eat fowls,* will you?' Upon which the hardened

sinner put his tail down between his legs and assumed a
penitent air for a moment or two, but five minutes afterwards it was insolently curled up as high as it could curl
and he was wagging it about and dancing up to me as if
we were on the best of terms with each other.

Thus it was that I never reached Escaladieu.

The drive between Bagnères and Escaladieu is renowned
for its beauty. It has everything scenery can have to
make it lovely, except a lake. Wood and meadow, and the
tranquil river winding in silvery coils through all; and behind, and at one side, the long, long range of the Pyrenees,
the lower mountains green with spring—the high peaks as
they generally are even in summer, white with snow, and
in front on a high monticule frowns the grim old ruin of
Mauvezin, as it is pronounced, from *mal* or *mauvais*—*voisin*,
bad neighbour, as doubtless the maurauding barons who
once owned it, were to all the valleys around. Old annals
tell that more than one of the potent barons of 'the good
old times' commanded that every peasant who did not
pull off his cap as a sign of homage, in passing the Seig-
neurial Castle, should receive a blow from a sword. The
Pyrenean peasants were always a fearless, independent
race, and often refused the salute, which led to cruel out-
rages on them, often ending in death.

We had a very pleasant drive, and my companions
amused themselves by imagining how they should figure
in my journal—*pretending modesty*, and hoping I would
only put them in as Mrs. N—h, Miss G—s, and Mr.
B—b—r, and Mrs. P—r—s, and I promised, laughing, not
to come nearer to the names than this, and, as you see,
have kept my word.

By dint of a franc's persuasion the driver took us up the
steep hill to Mauvezin, where we got out and walked up to
the foot of the castle, and sat down and looked at the view,

stretching over a fertile expanse, gay with the tender green of the sprouting wheat, relieved here and there by the cerulean blue of the flax fields now in full bloom, the river winding between woods and meadows, and the mountain frame that walled all in ; and Miss G—s and Mrs. N—h sang duets very sweetly, but as for Mr. B—b—r, by some strange concatenation of ideas, best known to himself, he chose that lovely spot to tell us how butchers killed calves, when with one consent we clapped our hands to our ears and refused to listen. It seemed a strange idea, especially for a gentle, refined, intellectual man—but I think now I can follow his thought—it was—how ill such intense beauty as that of the scene before us, accorded with all the suffering there is on earth, even for the animal creation. 'All things groaning together,' as he quoted from St. Paul, but we were too merry to be moralized to—even by our clergyman, and would not allow him ' to improve the occasion,' by an impromptu sermon.

I say nothing of the Castle of Mauvezin, because there is nothing to see in it. It is a mere shell, with no architectural beauty whatsoever.

CHAPTER XXII

I HAVE just returned from such a pleasant excursion with Lady Carnwath and her daughter, Miss Sharp, Mrs. and the Miss Claytons and Miss Bradstreet, to the top of the Monné. Two or three of the party walked; Lady Carnwath had engaged donkeys for the more delicate of the party, of whom I was one. We had a most lovely day, the sun shining down into every hollow among the hills, and giving to every tree and bush, and crag, that peculiar aërial clearness and delicacy of colouring, which pen cannot describe, and which Turner's pictures so well render. How can I paint the scene with my poor pale colourless words, as we wound slowly up the mountain, every turn showing us a lovelier view than the last. In about an hour and a half we reached the top, and the whole valley of Bigorre, with all the adjacent mountains, above which the Pic du Midi de Bigorre towered pre-eminent, lay spread before us like a map. The top of the Monné is a narrow level platform thickly covered with heath and short scrub. We got off our donkeys, turned them loose to browze under the care of Marie, our guide, and then walked the whole length of the terrace, admiring the view; after which we sat down to enjoy a good luncheon. We had filled a bottle with pure water from a spring half way up, which Marie the guide pointed out, and we had flasks of wine with us. It is curious how these springs of delicious water gush out of the hard rock so high up. There are several springs on the Bédat as well as on the Monné, and probably upon most mountains. After luncheon we all began to search for flowers. The rhododendrons were not yet in bloom, but we found the globularia nudicaulis,* a pale blue flower, somewhat resembling a scabious, but with a much shorter stem, without leaves on it—quantities of daffodils and the large gentianella, with its deep azure cups of lapis lazuli blue, a pale yellow wallflower,† the growth of whose flowers, and their size, resemble the common white alyssum, the biscatella, and the dwarf arbutus. And again I remarked the beautiful contrast of the yellow daffodils and the mountain wallflower, with the rich deep blue of the gentianella.

After our return home I went to drink tea with Mrs Alexander, 'the most beautiful hymn-writer of the day,' as she is justly called in the preface to the ' Lyra Anglicana.' One volume of her ' Hymns for Children ' has gone through *thirty-two editions*, the other two volumes which contain her finest poems, and among them ' The burial of Moses, a poem worthy to rank with ' Hohenlinden,' and ' Ye Mariners of England,' are not so well known. I have often observed that mediocrity is more widely appreciated, and more easily obtains success and fame than true genius. And the cause is obvious. The greater part of the world have merely average abilities, and cannot of themselves recognize the beautiful and the true ; they require to have it pointed out to them again and again by critics, till at last the merit of the work becomes a literary canon, which it would be crass ignorance to dissent from. It took nearly thirty years to establish the fame of Shelley and Wordsworth as poets, but Martin Tupper succeeded in making a name at once. *Everybody could understand him.* A

---

* *Globularia nudicaulis*, Philippe.

† *Erisimum Ochroleneum*, Philippe. The flower-stem, and flowers grow exactly like those of the white *alyssum*, and are of a lovely chrome yellow or sulphur colour. The Biscatella, like a miniature flowered Erisimum, but much taller in growth.

century hence, I suspect Wordsworth and Shelley will be read more than ever, and no one will know the name of Martin Tupper. And so it happens that Mrs. Alexander's highest work, the 'Poems from subjects in the Old Testament,' is less known than her 'Hymns for Children.'

Where can there be more exquisite harp-strains than these from 'The Burial of Moses'?—

> 'That was the grandest funeral
> That ever passed on earth;
> But no man heard the trampling,
> Or saw the train go forth—
> *Noiselessly as the daylight*
> *Comes back when night is done,*
> *And the crimson streak on ocean's cheek*
> *Grows into the great sun;*
> *Noiselessly as the spring-time*
> *Her crown of verdure weaves,*
> *And all the trees on all the hills*
> *Open their thousand leaves;*
> So without sound of music
> Or voice of them that wept,
> Silently down from the mountain's crown,
> The great procession swept.'*

What can be more truthfully tender and *motherlike* than these from 'The Warning Angel'?—

> 'Cometh the Angel of the Lord full often
> And standeth by our homes,
> Not in his visible presence bright,
> Passing from Gilgal's paling height,
> With word and power, and arm of might,
> Yet evermore he comes.
>
> 'Perchance he takes death by the hand and standeth
> Low knocking at our door—
> We miss one little lambkin's bleat,
> The gabbling voice so wild and sweet,
> The tottering of uneven feet,
> Along the nursery floor.

---

* The italics are mine.

'Perchance he comes with sickness in his quiver
And stirreth all the deeps
Of our whole inward life, and tells
Where in our bosom's secret cells,
In its green grove some idol dwells—
Some sin unheeded sleeps.'

But I shall never have done if I go on picking out for you the beautiful verses that haunt my memory, and that I catch myself repeating unawares as I sit alone on some hill-side overlooking a world of mountains, or lazily reposing after a long scramble beside some clear bubbling fountain or tiny streamlet, with Keeper at my feet, and my fingers curling his velvet ears.

It is good to go alone into the mountains, and hold there communion with God, but it is better still when one has the privilege of communion with His highest, noblest work —a far more sublime and magnificent thing than mountain, or lake, or sea—when one meets those angels in mortal garb to whom God has given great powers which they use for His glory and the good of the world.

People have such a strange, wild idea that all authors are proud, and cynical, and all authoresses conceited and unfeminine. I only know that among all my acquaintance the most gifted with intellectual power are the most tender, indulgent, lovable, and natural; the most truthful, and the readiest to help the unfortunate.

It was a great delight to me to know Mr. and Mrs. Alexander, and to see them at home in their family, and one listened with willing attention to Mr. Alexander's eloquent sermons, because one knew his life to be a practical comment on his doctrines.

I went with Mrs. Alexander this evening to the church of the Carmelite friars, where there was a grand ceremony. The church (which as well as the monastery adjoining is newly erected) is a very handsome building, and was brilliantly lighted up, but I do not admire the tawdry

R

decorations of blue and white chains, cut out of *silver paper* and suspended from the ceiling in front of the altar, nor all the bouquets of tawdry artificial flowers. The ceremony began by a mass, and chanting; then the friars all came out one after the other, looking very picturesque in their monkish costume, which consists of a close gown of brown serge, coming down to their bare sandaled feet, and a hood and tippet of very white cloth over their shoulders. They wear this dress summer and winter, and both legs and feet are always bare, but I have seen them occasionally wearing hats, though I believe it is against the rule. The crown and the lower part of the head where it joins the nape of the neck, is shaven quite clear by the Carmelite monks, leaving a fringe of hair about half a hand's breadth in width all round the head, which looks at a distance like a turban, and the whole costume is very striking and becoming. The Roman Catholics always have an eye to *effect*.

Each monk bore a large lighted taper in his hand, and they placed themselves in two parallel lines in the middle aisle, in such a way that one on the right holding his taper in his right hand, the one facing him held his in the left, so that they resembled living chandeliers. One of them then ascended a sort of temporary pulpit placed in the aisle for the occasion, and chanted a service in Latin, to which the monks responded, bowing their heads till they almost touched the ground. There was something solemn and affecting in the ceremony when, at its close, each silently put out his light, and they all again defiled one after the other through the communion rails to their cloister, and were seen no more. Not understanding Latin I could not follow the service, but the putting out of the tapers one after the other seemed to me to be strangely significative of human life. Is not that also a long and often a gloomy procession, when the light of one torch-bearer after another is put out? A friend had accompanied us instead of Mr. Alexander, who stayed behind to prepare his Sunday's sermon, and as we stood behind the Carmes he pointed out to us the extreme repulsiveness of most of their faces. Most of them had a very bad expression, they were men from whom one would instinctively recoil. Mr. —— had just returned from a tour in Spain and Portugal. He told us that in those Ultra-Catholic countries, not a monastery or nunnery remains. The brethren and the sisterhoods have been all expelled on account of the extreme dissoluteness of their lives.

'What the sisters of charity, too?' exclaimed I.

'Yes,' he said; 'they were found to do more harm than any other community—from the mischief they made in families by their gossiping and prying into private concerns.'

One only of the Carmes was a dark-eyed, melancholy-looking, but interesting and almost handsome man. I wondered whether he was Monsieur de Cayhuzac. This gentleman was a member of one of the first families of Tarbes. A disappointment in love led him to assume the monastic habit, and his magnificent voice used to draw great crowds to the Carmelite church. On one occasion the lady he had loved came to hear him chant, and on recognizing his voice, fainted away. It was said in Bagnères that the affection of the young people had been mutual; but that though M. de Cayhuzac was very rich, the lady's father preferred a still wealthier suitor, to whom he compelled his daughter to give her hand. I don't know whether monks flirt, but I heard that Monsieur de Cayhuzac was very popular among the French ladies, and that they were for ever calling at the convent-door with rolls of music for him, or asking him for music to copy.

The rule of the Carmes is very severe. They eat no meat and drink no wine all the year round. They sleep on an iron bedstead without mattress, having merely a little straw on it, over which is one blanket, and they have one other as a covering.   Their rooms are the smallest possible cells, with tiny little windows not larger than a common-sized sheet of writing paper when unfolded, and just hold a bed, a chair, and a table.   They have no fireplace; nor do the Carmes, I was told, light fires in their refectories or parlours, but there is a fire in one apartment, to which all the brethren are admitted in turn, to warm themselves once a day.   It is also said that they scourge themselves with a heavy whip every Friday. When, however, one spoke to any of the townspeople or the peasants about the severe rule of the Carmes, the invariable reply was—'*Ils ont assez de bon vin dans leurs caves—tenez.   J'ai vu avec mes propres yeux de gros tonneaux de bon vin qui venaient de Bordeaux, et qu'on faisait entrer chez eux.*'

One of the Carmes was a music-master—a man, it is said, of infidel opinions and licentious life—'*un homme à bonnes fortunes.*'

The story goes that as he was one day playing on the organ in a Catholic church where he was organist, the Virgin Mary appeared to him in a vision, upon which he fell senseless to the ground, where he was afterwards found lying like one dead.   When he came to himself, his whole character was supernaturally changed.   He entered a Carmelite monastery, and devoted all the wealth he had acquired to building the church and monastery at Bagnères. There is a Carmelite nunnery in the same street as the monastery, with a chapel of its own.   The abbess died while I was at Bagnères, and I went with a friend to see her lying in state.   We had to sit for, I should think, three hours, during which the Carmelite brothers were saying masses for her soul, and every now and then going up to a side grating of iron, on one side of the altar, which separated the nunnery from the chapel, behind which the body lay, and asperging it through the rails with a long brush dipped in holy water. At last the ceremonies ended; the crowd left the chapel, and we entered the nunnery, and asked if we might see the dead abbess. The portress was very civil to us, and having obtained the sister's permission, took us back into the chapel and inside the communion rails up to the side-grating, through which we saw the body of the late abbess stretched upon a bier, with her feet towards the altar. She was so muffled up we could not see whether she wore the dress of the order or not. On her head was a wreath of artificial roses; and tawdry artificial orange blossoms, such as one sees on bride-cakes in confectioners' shops at home, were strewn over the white satin quilt that covered her body. Her hands seemed to be folded, as if in prayer, and on her breast was a little gilt ball surmounted by a cross. She was seventy-two or three, I was told, but did not look near so old. Probably her face was rouged, for the cheeks were red. Being a cloistered nun, even her dead body could not be removed beyond the grate until it was carried to the grave. I saw the funeral procession go past the windows of my lodging to the cemetery next morning. After the bier, over which was a black velvet pall, edged with white, came all the Carmelite monks, with lighted tapers in their hands, and a vast concourse of the devout Bagnérais followed behind, attended, of course, by all the idlers and children.

One of the Carmelite nuns is said to be very beautiful. Her family were greatly averse to her entering a convent, but nothing could dissuade her. I was told, that for two days before she was professed she sat full-dressed at the grating, talking to anyone who liked to visit her, and that some were bold enough to try and dissuade her from the step she was taking, but failed in the attempt. After profession, a nun is dead to the world, and sees no one except the members of her own family, and that at rare intervals, and by permission.

While I was at Bagnères, one of the sisters had the toothache, and it was necessary for a faculty to be sent for to Rome, giving her a dispensation to see a dentist or surgeon, and have her tooth taken out! It seems to me that these sisters take a very mistaken view of duty. One of them was an only daughter, rich, young, and beautiful ; her mother's death grieved her so deeply, that she took a distaste to the world, and retired into the Carmelite nunnery, *leaving her poor paralyzed father to the care of servants !* No nun was professed while I was at Bagnères, but I saw a Carmelite monk take the vows. The novice sat on a high chair at one side of the altar beside the prior or abbot and two other monks, and the rest of the brethren sat on chairs within the communion rails, with their backs to the assistants. One of the brethren preached the profession sermon, in which he dwelt, upon the difference between the precept or law which was for all, and the counsel or advice meant for the few, who could receive it, by the Bible. He quoted Christ's words, and proved, to his own satisfaction at least, that according to them, celibacy was a higher state than marriage.

After the sermon, the postulant was asked whether he would observe 'the three vows of poverty, chastity, and obedience all his life,' and kneeling before the abbot, he placed his hands in those of his superior, and in an inaudible voice took the vows. He then prostrated himself, the shroud was thrown over him, and a hymn was sung ; after which the shroud was taken off, and he again knelt before the superior, who put a wreath of white roses on his shaven head. The wreath was too large, and there was something droll in seeing the prior take it off, and bend in the wires to narrow it; after which, he replaced it on the head of the new monk and kissed him on each cheek. The two other principal members of the brotherhood, as I supposed them to be, by their sitting apart from the rest, with the prior and the novice, did the same, and then, still wearing his crown, he went to the row of monks by the altar rails, knelt down before each in turn, and received from them on each side his face the kiss of brotherhood. This terminated the ceremony. The side door by the altar opened, and the new monk followed the others into the cloister. The Carmelite monks are not so strictly cloistered as the nuns of the order. No woman—not even a mother or sister—is admitted within the walls; but the brethren are allowed to pay visits at stated times, and to hold intercourse even with the interdicted sex. They usually go out two together. I often saw two of them pass under the trees of the Coustos to the opposite house where the lawyer of the convent lived, from my window, while at M. ——'s, and I have more than once met a single Carmelite brother in travelling; on certain days also they take long country excursions, and once or twice I saw two or three of them with large wide-awake hats on, promenading on Mont Olivet.

As no woman is allowed within the 'Monastère des Carmes,' so no man is allowed to enter the 'Couvent des Carmélites;' but, of course, accidents will happen, and repairs are required in nunneries as in other houses. I was much amused by a story my mantua-maker told me: her cousin, a carpenter, was sent for to do some repairs in the convent, and the prioress came to speak to him about them, accompanied by the young and beautiful nun I spoke of before, who was the youngest sister in the convent and not yet twenty. The rule is, that when absolutely obliged to speak to a man, the sisters should wear their long black veil down, so as to hide their faces, and it was strictly observed on this occasion—only—the young sister's veil *blew aside by accident* several times, and my cousin said, continued my informant, '*qu'elle était si jolie—si jolie—que c'était un plaisir de la voir.*'

I dare say the sight of a masculine visage was a treat to the poor nun also, although he was but a poor carpenter.

CHAPTER XXIII.

I HAVE just been such a lovely walk with Miss Le G——
and Miss C——. We went past Mr. Geruzet's *chalet*,
towards La Bassère, turning up a lane by the water-mill,
instead of going up the hill quite to La Bassère. Almost
as soon as one rounds the shoulder of Mont Olivet, the
rare flowers began to show themselves. The hedges are
full of white, blue, and pink hepaticas, Jerusalem cowslips
(*pulmonaria officinalis*), the chocolate-coloured (*geranium-
phæum*) pennywort (*hydrocotyle vulgaris*), large celandine
(*chelidoninm majus*), and the common, but beautiful, white
stars of the stellaria. In a ditch on one side of the road,
I found a variety of the common arum, with larger leaves
than usual, prettily streaked, and variegated with straw
colour. Soon after passing the mill, we gathered quantities
of a greyish-blue, scentless hyacinth, often cultivated in
old English gardens, the *scilla, lillo-hyacinthus.* We
passed up a wild, picturesque mountain gorge, with a
clear stream brawling beside the pathway, and taking this
streamlet for our guide, followed it till it lost itself in the
meadows, and we all agreed we had never had a prettier
walk. The sloping bank on the left-hand side was frequently covered with bushes of wild box, whose dark,
glossy green leaves contrasted beautifully with the pure
white stars of the hepaticas, which covered the ground with
their lovely blossoms. They are a fairy-looking flower
thus seen growing—not in a trim flower garden out of

black mould—but scattered thick as spring buttercups among the green grass. The little stream was thickly fringed with alder and ash trees, and at their foot, almost in the water, often grew large cushions more than a quarter of a yard across, of a curious parasite flower, the *Clandestina rectifolia*, which grows on the decayed roots of trees. It is usually a dark brownish purple, with stamens of the same colour, but some few were pale lilac; and it has no leaf or stem. The flowers, which a good deal resemble a salvia in shape (only that the hood is rather more prolonged), grow out of a lengthened white calyx, and so close together, that a pin can scarcely be thrust between them. We cut up large round patches of it, and carried them carefully home, planting them in *terrines*, surrounded by moss, and I edged mine with another most lovely flower that I saw here for the first time—the yellow wood anemone. It grows like the white one, springing from the centre of a leaf, but the leaf is a brighter, tenderer green. Under the hedges, too, we found the delicate, fragile Euphorbia, *Thalictra Ranunculoides*. Its tender green leaf is not unlike that of the pretty pink *Spectabilis*, which has been so favourite an ornament in our drawing-rooms of late years, and the transparent white flower also somewhat resembles it at a distance, though both are infinitely smaller, the whole plant being scarce a foot high.

It is somewhere among the woods above the mill in this lane, and on Llèris, that the beautiful *Dentaria digitata* grows. I did not succeed in finding the plant myself, but Lady Carnwath kindly gave me a specimen of it. It is a shrubby, handsome plant, whose stems grow about two or three feet high, with palmated leaves, a good deal resembling those of the American creeper, and of a dark lustrous green, that makes them look almost artificial. The flower, rising from among the leaves, is like honesty, lilac coloured and cruciform. It is well adapted for the garden, in which it is frequently cultivated by the Bigorrais. I do not know whether it would bear the English climate.

As I walk through the woods and fields here, I cannot help thinking that most of our old-fashioned garden flowers have probably been brought to England from the Pyrenees during the wars between our early Plantaganet kings and the French. Perhaps some stately dame, or some fair damsel, who had admired the Hepatica in the green lanes and woods of Bigorre, took seeds of it back with her when she returned to her Island home—the gentianella, the Jerusalem cowslip, the geranium phœum, the columbine, the scilla hyacinthus, Solomon's seal, the starch, and the tassel-hyacinth, the fritillaria, and many others that I cannot at this moment recall to memory, are all common flowers about Bagnères.

There is another lovely flower, the *Erinus Alpinus*, to be found in this same delightful lane. When I first saw it on the rock, I thought it was a primula, an illusion which vanished as soon as I gathered it. It has a small serrated leaf, and bright rose-coloured or purple flowers, sometimes, but rarely white ones, growing on a stalk like the alyssum, but infinitely smaller, and clings to the rock on which it grows almost as close as moss. The flowers are five-petaled, each petal being heart-shaped. The rocks round this La Bassère lane are covered with it, and it always grows where its lovely colours add fresh beauty to the landscape. At the top of the lane, there is a spring oozing out between some large, mossy, greystones, into a natural basin, whence a slender rill trickles away through the grass to join the stream that runs all the way beside the footpath. It is a quiet, secluded nook. High hedges and trees grow up behind it, and in front, on a green slope, surrounded by its orchard, stands a solitary white farmhouse.

The sward near this spring is covered with daisies. Blue forget-me-nots grow in the little pool, and on the stones whence the water issues, glow golden moss, and purple and pink erinus, and a flower no less lovely—the *Pinguicula grandiflora*. It has glaucous, pale green leaves, that look as if they were, but are *not*, transparent, clinging closely to the rocks like a green star. The flowers are shaped like a violet, but have a much slenderer, longer, mouse-coloured stalk, and are usually of a bright, rich, deep purple; but I have found some the colour of old port wine, and some of a greyish lilac. Both these flowers bear transplanting well, and will live a week or two in a terrine filled with moss, if taken up carefully with the earth round their roots. Cowslips and great numbers of the purple orchis grow on the high bank behind the farm; and there too, in the early spring, I found the snowdrop in abundance, as well as in a little wood behind the chestnut-trees after passing the *Tir au Pistolet*, on the way to the *Bédat*, and drooping gracefully from the bank of the stream, above a mill-dam near Asté. The *cyclamen*, or dog-tooth violet, is another of the lovely spring flowers that grow in the neighbourhood of Bagnères; it is to be found near the Palombières, and in a little valley above Asté.

But with all these treasures, I miss two flowers, that probably from early association, I think lovelier than any. There are no beds of sweet-scented bluebells under the trees, and no 'primrose on the river's brim.' What the Bagnérais, and even M. Philippe, the botanist, call the primrose, is our oxlip, which, as every English country child knows, is a very different flower. Even the cowslip is rare, growing plentifully only in the fields near Asté, at La Bassère and at Grip. I found also in the La Bassère

Lane the *orchis bifolia*, London pride, of two kinds, golden moss, and the Welsh poppy.

How often, as I walked about Bagnères, I wished that it had pleased God to endow me with artistic power. What exquisite lessons of light, and shade, and colour an artist might learn from the sites selected by wild flowers, and their harmonious contrasts. I use the word *selected* advisedly, for I can scarcely think that it is *by chance* that one always sees those flowers growing near each other, whose hues blend or oppose each other with the most perfect beauty. Thus, one usually finds the rich purple orchis growing most plentifully among golden cowslips, and here at La Bassère, at the foot of the ash-trees, close to the purple clandestina, drooped the elegant, pale-yellow cups of the Welsh poppy. Alas! it grew on the opposite side of the clear mill stream. To leave it ungathered was impossible. I dare say, no lover of wild flowers will be surprised to hear—that there being no gentlemen present—

' I kilted my kirtel
A little aboon the knee,'

and waded right across the stream for it.

The time fails me to tell of the delicate *Scilla verna*, a little, pale-blue squill, scarcely so high as my finger, and with only three, or at most, five, flowers on its stem, found near Asté and on Mont Olivet. Of the large blue columbines towering above the tall grass as spring advanced—columbines of a deep clear, blue colour, and a size such as I never before saw—of the purple irises, that were *said* to grow wild, but which, as they only grew in one hedge near Asté,* were clearly ' a garden flower grown wild,'—of the white star of Bethlehem that grew in such quantities in

* Monsieur Philippe, the botanist, afterwards told me that the purple iris did *not* grow wild in France.

the fields near the irises, and of the elegant, purple *Campanula patula*. But my readers will be weary of flowers, and I want to sleep, for it is near twelve.

I went again to-day alone to my favourite walk up the little secluded valley near La Bassère. Fancy tall, steep hills hemming you in on either side, and between them just space enough for a narrow rippling stream that turns two or three mills in its course, and a green meadow beyond it; to the left, another defile, walled in by stony mountains, and a small flock of sheep, and their shepherd and dog winding slowly up the rocky road. It is quite a painter's glen. Farther on one comes to a narrow lane bordered on one side by wild box, which, in early spring-time perfumes the whole air by its rich spicy odour, under whose shade grow hepaticas, blue, white, and pink, and innumerable other lovely wild flowers; while on the opposite side of the pathway, the clear stream grows wider, ripples over stones shaded by alder and ash-trees, which skirt a rich meadow with grass of the most vivid green, prankt over with oxlips, marsh marigolds, and ladies'-smocks, and backed by a low range of wooded hills, which keep all the loftier mountains out of sight. Farther on still is a white farmhouse on a high, steep bank, shaded by an orchard, and a plantation of trees behind it, under which the ground is literally carpeted with flowers.

I wandered there alone to-day, and something of the intense delight I used to feel in my childhood in looking at wild flowers returned to me as I beheld the purple orchises gleaming crimson in the sunlight, fringing, as it were, the green slope above; and that exquisite fairy flower the *Pinguicula grandiflora*, growing like a slender stemmed purple violet from a starry centre of tender green leaves. I could not help thinking what a strange mixture of good and evil this world was, and how singular it was that there should

be so much sorrow in so beautiful a world. My thoughts
at last shaped themselves into verse. I was gathering a
nosegay that I meant for Lady Carnwath, who always
kindly sends me a specimen of any rare flower she finds—
and so I dedicated these verses to her, and took them to
her with the *terrine* of *pinguiculas*, *erinus*, ferns, and yellow
pimpernel. I assure you my *terrine* was lovely, and I
saw all the people in the Place des Coustos gazing at it
admiringly, as I carried it along.

EARTH'S EDEN.

'Twas in a garden full of flowers
　　And fruits, pleasant to eye and taste,
In Eden's paradisial bowers
　　That the first man was placed.

'Tis an old tale—yet ever new,
　　And full of import deep—
How that one slight observance due
　　To God—man failed to keep.

How for his sake, God cursed the earth—
　　Still sound those accents dread—
' Thistles and thorns ' it still brings forth,
　　And man still toils for bread.

Man toils—Alas ! even children* toil—
　　And dreary vigils keep ;
Seeing the great wheels whirl and moyle,
　　Half dead for lack of sleep.

Toil—ever toil—beneath the sun,
　　What breaking hearts still cry;
Lord, let me earn, by labour done,
　　My daily bread, or die !

Oh, dreary world ! ' Briars and thorns '
　　Hast thou indeed brought forth ;
What dark nights, following dreary morns,
　　Have passed o'er thee, O earth !

---

* This alludes of course to the children employed in manufactories.

Yet—lest man's heart sink in despair—
  Changed as thou art, and cursed,
We dimly trace in all things fair,
  Thy glory at the first.

The grey mist still, the mountain's height,
  Doth as a robe enfold ;
Still in a flood of crimson light,
  Setteth a sun of gold.

Still—making music as they run,
  Dash down a thousand streams—
Green valleys glisten in the sun,
  Faint, lovely, as in dreams.

And still when fall the vernal showers,
  The messenger of God ;
The flower-angel leaves Heaven's bowers,
  To deck with bloom the sod.

Invisible to human sight,
  Yet may his steps be traced ;
For flowers spring up beneath his feet,
  Where stretched a wintry waste.

He strews the seeds, ripened in heaven,
  Of flowers in mead and grove ;
Fair types to man in mercy given,
  Of that fair world above.

Perfect in form and hue, each one ;—
  Lilies of whom Christ said—
That 'in his glory Solomon
  Was not like these arrayed.'

Pale wind flowers, bending down anew,
  Each time the spring gales breathe ;
And purple violets, wet with dew,
  In the thick lush grass beneath.

Kingcups, like streaks of sunlight gold,
  Glimmering beneath the trees ;
Cowslips, that gem the open wold,
  And purple orchises.

Bluebells, whose rich perfume recalls
   Youth's fleeting, joyous dreams ;—
Flowers spring, where'er his footstep falls,
   By mountains, groves, or streams.

Illuminated letters, ye—
   In earth's great missal—book,
By angel hands written, that we
   May on your glories look.

And read in those fair characters,
   Still bright with Eden bloom,
Of that bright world beyond the stars,
   That heaven from whence ye come.

I hate Latin names. It was the beauty of the *Pinguicula* more especially that brought these ideas into my head ; but how can one bring *pinguicula* into a verse? However, in very truth, flowers always have seemed to me at once a relic of Eden, and a warrant of Paradise.

CHAPTER XXIV.

I WAS sitting writing yesterday, when I received a wee note from Mrs. Nash, a lady whose acquaintance I made at Bagnères, which acquaintance was further cemented by my lending her 'The Queen's Pardon' to read. She had been seven years in Australia, and like Mr. Howitt and others who have been in that country, said my descriptions of Australian life were graphic and living, down to the 'plop plop' of the kangaroo, which so entirely described its way of leaping.

The note was to say she had hired a carriage to go to Luz, St. Sauveur, Gavarnie, and Cauterets, and if I liked to join her she should be glad to give me a seat in it, and I should have no other expense than my food and beds at hotels, and the horses and guides I required for expeditions. Of course I gratefully accepted such an offer, and we set off the next day.

The weather was beginning to change, it was the 2nd of June, and the summer is the rainy season *en la Montagne*. Unluckily, too, that very morning I found on getting up that I was about to have a violent attack of lumbago. To give up Gavarnie, however, was not to be thought of, so when the carriage stopped before my door in I got. We had a beautiful drive from Bagnères past Lourdes to Argelés, and I was glad to see that beautiful valley in the early summer time, and be able to contrast it with what it was when I first visited it in the end of autumn. It is incomparably more lovely in summer, when every meadow and reach among the shallows of the Gave are emerald green.

As leaving the valley of Lourdes, we entered the valley of Argelés, we were aware of a peculiar rich, sweet, aromatic scent, which we afterwards discovered arose from the box-wood covering the rocks on our right hand. Among these rocks I soon descried a small, delicate, white lily about a foot high, resembling a very small garden white lily— *Lilium anthericum*' (Philippe). Our good-natured driver got down and gathered me a handful, and Mrs. Nash, who is fond of flowers as I am, and a better botanist, and I, admired its delicate scent and texture on a nearer inspection. We reached Argelés about midday, and lunched at the *Hôtel de la Paix*, outside the town on the road to Pierre-fitte.

The *Hôtel de la Paix* is thoroughly Pyrenean. That on the left hand of the road, the new built hotel, is clean and pleasant looking. Of course the apartments let well and it is always full, though the owner has made the common mistake of turning the windows of the principal rooms *to* the dirty, narrow, little street, instead of to the glorious view over the valley to the mountains. That on the right, opposite, where all the cooking is performed, is in the old Argelés style, close, suffocating, and dirty. We could not lunch in the first, because there was no room vacant, and were shown into the common *salle à manger* of the second, where all the *voituriers* and farmers come to Argelés market were tabled. The day was hot, the atmosphere stifling, and the noise insupportable. We asked to be shown into a bedroom and requested to have our food up there. No, they could not let us, '*à cause des mouches.*' It would bring flies about to soil the white furniture. Mrs. Nash remonstrated, I backing her. At last the hostess relented and gave us our dinner in her own bedroom, which was on the ground-floor and adjoined the kitchen, for which we were very thankful, and I am bound to say we had an excellent meal at a moderate price. A roast fowl, young peas, potatoes, bread, and wine, *à discrétion*.

We had finished our repast before the horses were sufficiently rested. So we strolled down the road to Pierrefitte, leaving orders with the driver of our vehicle to follow and take us up. I found quantities of the *Poa vivipara* on the top of the old stone walls. It is a singular little grass, every seed is a perfect little bulb, which germinates even while hanging to the parent stem, and it is very curious to examine a tuft of it and see each tiny bulb with its tiny crown of leaflets sprouting at the top, before it shall fall off to the ground and there root.

In about half an hour the carriage overtook us and we went through Pierrefitte down the beautiful road I have before described, to Luz, where we were to sleep that night at Madame Cazaux's *Hôtel des Pyrénées*. We ordered tea and a roast chicken on our arrival, and while it was preparing went to see the Templars' Church—the new church built in memory of the Anchorite, *Ambroise de Lombez*, and the bridge of St. Sauveur.

The sun had long set, and the evening was fast closing in as we passed through the meadows between the hill of the Hermitage and the bridge. It was light enough, however, for me to gather two, to me, new flowers. One resembling a delicate teasel, but of a paler and more cerulean blue; the other, a kind of vetch, whose pink but rather rose-coloured flowers growing from a white bladder-like sheath, had a gay and singular appearance. This is the *true ladies'-finger*, and I now understand the meaning of that trivial name which had often puzzled me. A lady's-finger should be white with rosy tips like this vetch *Anthyclus vulneraria* (Philippe and Withering).

I cannot tell you how grand that single arch, springing from rock to rock over the vast chasm, looked in the moonlight; how beautifully the black masses of shadow, contrasted with the hushed silvery light; nor paint the rippling light of the moonbeams on the water, while the moon herself moved on in calm majesty through vaporous clouds above, and little stars peeped out from the white edges of grey clouds. It was a sight to *feel*, not to talk of. One of those sights which hush the soul into sublime repose and make one for a time forget the troubles of earth.

We went back to our inn, and as I passed along the usual open corridor looking on the court to my bedroom, I had the misfortune to slip on a solitary unexpected step in the middle that broke its level uniformity, and wrenched my back most violently. This completed the lumbago I had felt symptoms of in the morning, and the next day I had the greatest difficulty in moving. I could not put on my own boots, and our driver was fairly obliged to lift me into the carriage.

How on earth was I to ride to Gavarnie? Mrs. Nash suggested that a hot-bath might benefit me, so she stopped at St. Sauveur that I might have one. The spring at Sauveur is a tepid warmth, not so hot as those of Wiesbaden, but the water is much pleasanter, and has the same soft satiny feel as the celebrated baths of Schlangenbad. It seems very gaseous. I noticed while in it that my skin was covered all over with very minute grey-coloured bubbles that looked like small particles of quicksilver. When I rubbed them off with my finger, they all rose to the surface of the water, and the moment I lay still they settled on me again. The bath woman said they were caused by the gas in the water. I stayed in my bath about twenty minutes, and certainly came out rather relieved. St. Sauveur is said to be very efficacious in rheumatic complaints. However, I had to be lifted into the carriage again by Fachau, our civil driver. We drove as far as the little village of Gèdre, where saddle-horses had been ordered for us the day before.

Leaving Fachan to bait those which had brought us, and mounting on horseback (I being lifted on my horse), set out, with a guide apiece, for Gavarnie. We passed through a village and then up a grand mountain gorge. Rocks were piled upon rocks in wild profusion, and whole beds of broken stones lay scattered around; while above and on all sides the mountains reared their sublime heads erect, stern, and immovable; still bearing on them the impress of the Almighty hand that moulded them into their present form æons of years ago. Here and there in a hollow of their vast flanks, a shady wood, or two or three green meadows nestled, and a white cottage peeping out under trees, a few sheep, browsing under the care of a shepherd and his dog, or one or two of the fawn-coloured deer-like cattle, couched in the thick grass, gave life and variety to the scene, which else was wild, savage, and sombre in the extreme.

The rocky mountain road was *worse* than usual, because several gangs of men were employed in making it *better* against the expected visit of the Emperor and Empress, who, it is reported, are to visit the Pyrenees this summer. There were a good many Spaniards among these labourers, easily distinguished by their handsome features, dark eyes, and swarthy complexions, as well as by their picturesque costume, which consists of velveteen breeches, decorated by ribbons and open at the knee, so as to show their purfled white drawers, a crimson or green sash round the waist, and a gay-coloured handkerchief bound round the forehead, leaving the upper part of the head bare.

It seems strange to me that in these hot climates, where sunstrokes are common, at least among the English visitors, the Spaniards should only cover the forehead and lower part of the back of the head and never wear a hat.

I suppose it is the *costume* of that part of the country from which they come, for those that sell scarves, cambric handkerchiefs, and chocolate in the *Place des Coustos* during the season, wear the well-known, high-pointed Spanish hat, as also velvet jackets of a peculiar form, gaily decorated with braid and tassels, and white stockings knit in ribs or some intricate pattern, which does much honour to their wives and daughters' ingenuity, with lace boots, or more frequently the *espartilla*, or hempen sandal.

These workmen were blasting the rocks to make the new road, and the explosion, reverberated on all sides by the mountains, was very grand. In one place the old road had been so narrow, that there was only room for one horse to pass between the cliffs at a time, and even this narrow passage was so blocked up with huge fragments of the blasted rock, that our horses had to pick their way very carefully.

I had not mounted a horse for twenty years, and I must plead guilty to being very nervous as we rode along this rough path, sometimes scarcely passable, and generally paved with loose stones, which slipped and rolled under the horses' feet, and often winding along a narrow shelf of rock, with nothing to prevent one rolling down the precipitous side, into the Gave that roared at the bottom of the gorge. Just in the very narrowest and most blocked-up part, between two great masses of rock, the horse Mrs. Nash rode stumbled and fell. I saw her legs graze the sharp rocky fragment that impeded the passage, and thought they must be broken by the weight of the animal, but before horror left me power to cry out, the pony righted himself, and she rode on clearly unhurt, while I thanked God inwardly for what was almost a miraculous preservation.

This part is called the Chaos, or Peyrada, and as Murray says, 'looks as if a mountain had tumbled to pieces.' It was refreshing, after passing this wild and savage scenery, to ride through a narrow lane bordered by flowery meadows on each side, to the village of Gavarnie. I noticed, as we rode along, numerous plants I had never seen before, but refrained from asking my guide to gather any till we should return. We reached the village. I was lifted off my horse, for I was helpless, and the guide led us into a dirty little cottage on the road-side, whence we emerged through a cabbage garden, on to a green sunny slope, and right before us rose the *Cirque de Gavarnie*. The winter snows were beginning to melt, and the ledges of the *Cirque* showed bare and distinct in the sunlight, rising one above the other like the tiers of a theatre, and flanked on either side by walls of snow. At its base lay a grand glacier, a sheet of pure white snow, but already beginning to melt toward the edges, and streaming away in conjunction with another torrent of melted snow that rushed dark and turbid down the mountain to the left, into the green valley below.

The celebrated Brèche de Roland, which the legend says was cleft through the solid rock by the famous Paladin Roland, to enable him to pass over into Spain in pursuit of the Moors, was pointed out to us, just discernible from where we sat. Parties often ascend to the Brèche in summer, and those who sit astride the rocky wall may boast that they have one leg in France and the other in Spain. It is through this *brèche* and similar mountain passes that the wandering Spaniards, who frequent the watering-places of the Pyrenees, bring their wares, in order to evade the custom-house duties, as some of them told me. The old woman through whose cottage we passed pointed out and named the mountains—The Vigne Male, the Cylindre, the Tours de Marbouré, and many others.

' *Comme c'est magnifique !* ' cried we.

' *Oui !* ' answered the old cottager, sadly ; ' *C'est grand,*

c'est beau, mais c'est bien triste. The snow melts from the
glaciers, and falls and kills the poor peasants who are
working near. *Mon pauvre homme* was killed in this way,
with several more, twenty years ago. Twenty years! I
was young then; a gay young girl. I had not been married two years; now I am an old woman; but I remember
how sad it was when they brought the bodies home, and
my poor man's among them. *Ah! mesdames, croyez-moi,
c'est un triste lieu en hiver!*'

Poor woman! we pitied her, and did what we could to
console her, by giving rather more than we should have
done had we not known her sad story, for which she was
very grateful; and she retreated and left us to ourselves to
eat our luncheon, after pulling down some linen that was
bleaching on the rocks and spreading it on the grass, for
fear '*les dames*' should take cold, out of gratitude, and did
not whine or bother us for more money, according to
Pyrenean fashion. After our repast we again mounted our
horses and rode homewards, and as we passed the meadows
I made my guide gather me some of the rare plants. I
never saw fields so full of flowers as these. There was the
common forget-me-not, but growing to a height and luxuriance I never before saw; nor did I ever see before any
forget-me-nots 'so deeply, darkly, beautifully blue.'

Their rich turquoise absolutely dazzled one, as the sun
shone on them. Then there were quantities of the elegant
globe-flower (*Trollius*, or *Ranunculus globosus*); viper's
bugloss; burnet, crimson-tipped in the light; squills (*Lilio-
Hyacinthus*); the teasel-like *Phyteuma spicata*, the leaf
of which is used by the Parisians for salads; vetches, the
tall-branching salver-shaped purple *Campanula patula;* the
ox-eye daisy, known to the French by the more poetical
name of *Marguerite;* purple orchises, and tway-blades;
corn-rattle, and the three common kinds of campion; the
slender-fringed ragged robin; the beautiful tall white

Potentilla rupestris, with its strawberry-like blossoms and leaves; *Asclepia Vince-toxicum* (*Dompte-venin*); the *Valeriana montana ;* the chocolate-coloured *Geranium-phœum,* and many others. I saw a shrub that looked like our common cotton-bearing willow, but with white crinkled flower-petals falling very much down, in a hedge, and gathered it as I rode past, and M. Philippe afterwards told me it was the *Amelanchier communis.*

As we went along, our guides told us that the schoolmaster of Gédres was a great botanist, and had collections of all the rare plants found thereabouts, so on dismounting at that village we went to him, and he showed us some of his herbariums. I could have remained looking them over for hours, but Mrs. Nash felt oppressed by the atmosphere of the schoolroom, from which near a hundred scholars had just been dismissed; and besides, we had to return to Luz for tea, so we gave him a trifle and bade him adieu. He told us he was making a collection of all the plants in that neighbourhood for Mr. Lyte, of Bagnères, who seems much and justly liked and respected by the French, for he patronizes them in the best possible way—by employing them.

These self-taught botanists and naturalists are to be found in nearly every small town in the Pyrenees, and are of the greatest possible use to science, by preserving and describing any rare plant, insect, animal, or fossil that their more ignorant neighbours would otherwise have destroyed or cast aside as worthless. I wonder the liberal and enlightened French government does not bestow a small pension upon each of them. Anyone wishing to procure dried plants of this district can obtain them, all properly prepared and named, at the school-house, from M. Bordère, Instituteur, Gèdre. His wife seemed almost as good a botanist as himself. As we drove home I noticed again a beautiful plant, with oval hairy primula-shaped leaves, from the centre of which, as from a primrose root, grew single-stemmed flowers, with rarely more than one flower on a stem, of the most brilliant lilac hue, the stamens forming a point of bright orange colour, like the nightshade and potato, which last flower it much resembled, except that the blossoms were solitary, and the petals all separate. This was the *Raymondia Pyrenaica* (named after the celebrated Alpine traveller Raymond), and is rather rare. In Philippe's 'Flore des Pyrénées,' it is said to grow 'on damp rocks and in damp valleys, in the Oriental and Central Pyrenees, at Pratto-de-Mollo, Rocca Galiniera, St. Sauveur, the whole valley of Luz up to Gavarnie, Lac d'Or, Esquierry, Sarrancolin, and the Cirque d'Arbison.' However, we did not go to all those places, and only found it on rocks between Gèdre and St. Sauveur.

Before starting this morning I tried to purchase some brown terrines, such as I paid twopence apiece for at Bagnères, which sum was double their real price, but seeing I was an *Anglaise*, the mistress of the crockery shop at Luz demanded *half a franc apiece for the smallest*, upon which I scornfully retired *sans terrine*. What was to be done? To spoil good-humoured Fachan's new *voiture* was impossible; impossible also to let my beloved flowers die. I had set my heart on carrying some of those beautiful lilac flowers to the neighbours with whom I exchanged specimens of plants at Bagnères, so I folded up some old newspapers in the form of a tray, and I pinned them again in the quadruple folds of an old dressing jacket I had taken with me, and arranged them in wet earth in that, leaving space for the beautiful *Raymondia*, which I put among them as Fachan gathered it. We took this in the carriage to Cauterets and back to Bagnères; no water ever leaked through it, and all the flowers lived well except the globe-flower; so well that Mrs. Nash took a small terrine with a *Raymondia* in it with her to Switzerland, when she left Bagnères.

THE next day we left Luz for Cauterets, which we reached about noon, passing up the beautiful gorge between St. Sauveur and Pierrefitte, and I was glad to wind once more in broad daylight up that grand road the Col du Limaçon, and see again the narrow secluded valley of Cauterets, where I had spent such a pleasant week the autumn before. We got out at the 'Lion d'Or,' a clean and comfortable inn, and engaged rooms for the night, and then mounted two horses, engaged for us from the hotel at Luz over night—not as I should have liked, of my friend Canon, but of another guide, Bararum or Barare, a hunter and guide like Canon, *de première classe.* I have written his name so badly in my note-book that I cannot make it out clearly. He gave us good horses, and was very civil and intelligent, and something of a botanist to boot. I needed a careful guide that day, for though when once lifted on to it I could, strange to say, bear the motion of my horse better than that of the carriage, I could not turn or help myself in any way, had any accident occurred.

We were as unfortunate in our day as we had been lucky yesterday. It was grey and hazy when we left Luz, and a thick mist veiled the tops of the mountains. We hoped it would clear off, but it grew denser and denser every moment; and as we rode up past the hot springs of La Raillère, following the course of the torrent upwards, we could only just dimly trace how grand the scene would have been *if we could have seen it.* The path wound among, and at the base of, rocks, shaded by lofty pines, the Gave falling in torrents over the rocks at our side, and throwing up clouds of snowy foam and thundering and roaring in the ravine below. Every turn almost brought us to a larger *chute*, and each fall differed in sublimity and beauty from those before it; but we could only just see the stems of the pine trees and the white foam curling over the rocks; the branches and heads of the pine trees, and the summits of the mountains, were alike lost in a dense cloud of mist.

There was something eerie in this ride; I was sorry not to have seen the Pont d'Espagne in all its beauty, for the melting of the snow on the mountains, our guide told us, made the fall peculiarly grand at this season, but not sorry to have travelled through the wild wood and rocky passes in that gloomy mist. It reminded me of the ride through the wood in Undine, and I almost fancied I heard Kühleborn sweeping in his wrath through the forest. We reached the little platform of green grass, with its little summer-house, under which were tables and chairs, and a small hut where they are housed by an old woman who goes up to the Pont every morning, and returns to Cauterets every night, and who supplies visitors with cheap wine, spirits, glasses, and plates. We gave her a trifling remuneration for the use of her chairs, tables, and glasses, but drank none of her wine, having taken flasks of our own, as well as provisions, both of which we shared with our guides.

Our poor jaded horses were tied to the railing that divided the platform from the Gave, and had nothing; so I gave them each a good large lump of bread, which they ate very gratefully from my hand, while we regaled the old woman with sponge-cake, which she seemed to enjoy as much as the horses did their bread. Then we walked across the narrow wooden bridge dividing the two lower falls; as to the upper one, which our guide said was far the finest, *it was invisible.* All we could see was a clear, intensely green water, boiling and seething up into wreaths of the whitest foam, *whiter* than any snow I ever saw, and the stems of the pine trees sprouting from the rock. I have never anywhere seen water so beautiful as that of this Gave de Cauterets. It is the richest, the most intense, blue-green, like that of the malachite shading into aqua marina and chrysophras.

We rode home much quicker than we had ascended, and my good-natured, civil guide seeing how fond I was of flowers, gathered me some lovely Alpine primulas and several sprays of rhododendron, which, however, was not quite in bloom. Oh! I should like to see the Pont d'Espagne on a clear, bright day, a fortnight hence, when all the rhododendrons, with their rich lilac and pink blossoms, will contrast so beautifully with the sombre hues of the sapins and Scotch firs, the green waters of the Gave, and their wreaths of white foam.

By the way, I don't understand why the bridge over the upper falls is called Le Pont d'Espagne; it is a decided misnomer, inasmuch as it is *not* near the Spanish frontier at all.

We slept that night at Cauterets, and just before we retired to rest our guide came to be paid, and brought me, as he had promised, one or two dried plants, among them the *Ixia Bulbocodium* and the *Pulsatilla* or *Pasque Anemone,* which he said only grew on the tops of the highest mountains.

The habitat of flowers in the Pyrenees seems the reverse of the same flowers in England. With us the daffodil grows in woods and by water; in the Pyrenees it abounds most on the mountain tops. There is a rarer and more delicate daffodil which I am told abounds on the cliffs at Biarritz, and which grows on the Mont Olivet side of the Bédat, while the common daffodil occupies the opposite height on the other side. This is the *Narcissus Bulbo-codium*, or petticoat daffodil, so called from its resemblance to a lady's hoop. It is a delicate pale yellow, and the narrow coronal of petals might almost be likened to ends of ribbons floating down the petticoat. The flowers are solitary, or nearly so, and the pale glaucous green leaf is very short, and makes no show, there being only two, three, or four to each plant, instead of their growing thickly like those of the *Pseudo-Narcissus*. The *Pulsatilla*, also, grows on the open moorland in Yorkshire : here, it seems, it is found only on the mountain tops.

We returned next day to Bagnères, and in accordance with my request, Mrs. Nash kindly consented to lunch and bait the horses at Lourdes instead of Argelés. I wanted to explore the lake, and if possible to see the *Osmunda regalis* in flower. M. Philippe had told me it grew in such quantities at one end of it as to force the waters to retreat in the opposite direction. While luncheon was preparing, therefore, we set off for the lake, following in the wake of two or three parties who were clearly going on the same expedition. The town and castle of Lourdes, the latter of which is very strongly fortified, look very imposing from this road, with the mountains towering up behind them.

Mrs. Nash, however, was not a good walker, and seeing an avenue of roses leading to a farm, with two very inviting arbours, one on each side close to the gate, she ventured in, declaring she would rest there, while I went on to explore, past the Gendarmerie Impériale. I followed the parties before named, and soon came to the lake. It is interesting to geologists, as rising in a basin formed among the mountains and fed by no visible source, and to the botanist, because many rare plants grow on its banks ; but not to the artist or the traveller in search of the picturesque. The basin of low land in which it lies is perfectly flat, and only a low line of hills on the opposite side is visible, the mountains not being seen from it, and it looks more like a large marshy pond in the midst of flat marshy meadows than anything else. The *Osmunda* grew at the other end of the lake, and I had not time to go and seek for it, as I knew Mrs. Nash would not like to be kept waiting, or to have the fowl we had ordered for luncheon overcooked; so I went back as fast as I could, having had nothing but a dusty hot walk on a broiling day for my pains. Mrs. Nash in her arbour had had far the best of it, and when I came up, I found her quite recovered from her fatigue, and holding a gorgeous bunch of rare roses in her hand. The polite owner of the rose avenue had come, begged her to *repose* in his arbours as long as she liked, taken her down the avenue, showed her his finest roses, and gathered some of them for her, desiring she would herself pluck as many of the others as she chose. Certainly the French people are very kind and polite.

We drove home after lunching at the inn at Lourdes, where the fare was good, but the people uncivil; they would not give us a room to ourselves as we had at Luz and Cauterets. I wonder the Pyrenean innkeepers have not found out by this time, that travelling English, especially ladies, do not like to dine or lunch in a hot, stifling *salle à manger*, where there are some twenty or thirty tables, occupied, perhaps, by *voituriers* and peasants. The only other occupants of the *salle* at Lourdes were a French baron, dining with Monsieur le Curé. They did not annoy us in any way; but the low ceiling of the room, its close proximity to the kitchen, into which we could see, and the intense heat and odours arising from cooking the various comestibles, annoyed Mrs. Nash so much, she declared she would never go there again—I thought she was right.

We reached Bagnères about six o'clock, and to show the untidy, indolent habits of the Bagnérais, I found my

rooms exactly as I had left them three days before—the bed
still unmade — the slops yet in the basin — and all the
flowers which I had left in the vases, pulled out and strewn
on the floor of the *salon*, which Mademoiselle *intended* to
sweep the following day (as she had settled it in her own
mind we should be absent four days)—no one in the house,
and not a drop of water to wash my hands in, after my hot,
dusty drive home.   I felt rather angry and provoked, but
I knew there was no use in making any complaint.

French women *invariably* put off doing their house-work
to the last possible minute, letting any idle gossiping or
amusement take up their time instead; therefore it is
always *ill-done*, and the houses half-dusted and slovenly—
except when they belong to rich people, for money can
purchase *anything* — it can even buy cleanliness in the
Pyrenees.   However, in about half-an-hour Madame and
Mademoiselle (the latter of whom waited upon me) returned,
and then came a host of apologies—'they did not expect
me that day ; they had been to a sale,' &c., &c., with
which I was fain to be content.   The Pyreneans are so
kindly in general, one wishes tenfold they had English
or Dutch habits of order and regularity.

CHAPTER XXVI.

THE LEGEND OF THE LAKE OF LOURDES.

THERE is a pretty legend regarding the origin of the Lake of Lourdes.* It runs thus:—

GOD AND THE LAKES.

There was a time, many ages ago, when the Lord God walked to and fro upon the earth, to behold the things that He had made. He wished to see whether men obeyed His laws, and were kind to one another, showing hospitality to the poor and the stranger, as He had commanded. Therefore, taking the form of a poor old man, He entered one evening into a town of Bigorre, which was the first Lourdes. And I have been told that this poor old man

---

* There is a somewhat similar story told of the formation of the lake of Wensleydale in Yorkshire, which is of unknown depth. It is said that one day a wayfarer, scantily clothed, hungry, and pennyless, but of noble and engaging aspect, came thither soliciting alms and shelter. He sought in vain, and then turned eastward down the vale. Without the bounds of the city lived an aged couple, too poor and mean to be allowed to take up their residence within the town. The stranger entered their dwelling, and ere his tale of woe could be told they placed before him the best their house afforded, namely, a bowl of milk-cheese and an oaten cake. Having satisfied his hunger, he bestowed his benediction upon their basket and store. Beneath their roof he passed the night, and on the morrow repeated his benison, which was attended with the effect of making his hosts increase from that day in worldly wealth. Being then ready to depart, he turned his face to the west and uttered this malediction,—

> 'Simmer-water rise, simmer-water sink,
> And swallow all the town but this little house,
> Where they gave me bread and cheese and *summ'at* to drink.'

Immediately the earth made a hissing noise, the stream overflowed its banks, and the city was buried in a deep flood. On a calm day *it is said* the spires of the churches and the tops of the houses can yet be seen. A similar tale is recounted of Lough Neagh in Ulster. *Vide* 'Chambers' Edinburgh Journal,' No. 177, new series, May 22nd, 1847.

went from house to house, all through the town, beseeching everyone to give Him something to satisfy His hunger; but everyone refused to help Him, so that, finding
He could get nothing to eat, through the wickedness of
the men of that place, He looked around, and saw a miserable cabin, the only dwelling-place at which he had not
implored succour, and He went there. In this hut He
found only two women and a little child that lay sleeping
in its cradle; but as soon as He entered, the poor women
forestalled His request, saying—

'Poor man! What can such as we do for thee? for we
are as poor as thou art, and have nothing. Howbeit, come
into our house, and sit down and rest thee a little, and if
thou wilt wait awhile, there are two cakes which we have
kneaded of ryebread baking under the ashes—when they
are enough done, we shall eat them, and thou shalt have
thy share.'

And the Divine poor man taking the seat the women
offered, sat down before their hearth, and warmed his
limbs, without speaking a word. But the two cakes which
were hidden under the cinders began to spread themselves
—and they grew wonderfully large—for wherever the Lord
shows Himself, everything prospers, and poverty is changed
into abundance — so the cakes became very great. When
the two women judged that they had been baking long
enough, they stooped down and took them from under the
ashes, and wondered much to see how large they were.
Then they divided them, and gave their guest His part as
they had promised, while they tendered Him all the kindness it was in the power of two such poor women to offer
Him. He assumed an air of mingled authority and bene-
volence, and said to them—

'Women—because of your charity, I will now save your
lives, for this town shall be swallowed up immediately with
all these wicked people who dwell therein.'

Then He commanded them to leave their house and follow Him, and they obeyed trembling, carrying with them all the wealth they had—the beautiful child asleep in its cradle.   When they had gone a good way off, the ground upon which the town stood suddenly sank with all its fine houses and rich buildings, and the people that dwelt in them, and the waters gushed up from the earth and covered them like the Deluge, and formed a lake.   No living thing there escaped with life, but the three inhabitants of the poor cottage.   And long, long afterwards, another town was built beside the lake of Lourdes, and was called by the same name as the first town, Lourdes.   But as a memorial of all this, there is to this day on the water-side, an open cradle of stone, which seems as though still waiting for the beautiful child who once slept in it.   And those who look earnestly on the surface of the lake when its waters become shallow, can sometimes even now see the spires and pinnacles of the great buildings, and the roofs of the houses which adorned the drowned city.

Many curious popular customs formerly prevailed in Lourdes.   When there was a storm, for instance, all the bells in Lourdes were rung; a signal, previously agreed upon, warned the Curé to repair to the church.   And will he, nill he—he was obliged to perform exorcisms, and commence a procession, whether it occurred in the night-time or by day.   In vain the Curés protested against the dangers of these nocturnal processions—in vain they appealed to their bishop, prejudice was too strongly rooted in the hearts of the populace and they insisted on adhering to the ancient custom.   An annual collection was made to pay for the ringing of the bells during storms, and it is but within the last few years that the ringing has been forbidden; but the ringers, doubtless that something may remain of the good old custom, continue the yearly collection.

In Toulouse, in the 16th century, Awakeners traversed the streets of the town, crying—

‘ Réveillez-vous, vous qui dormez, ‘ Awaken you who sleep,
  Priez Dieu pour les trépassés.’   And pray God for the dead who weep.’

In Lourdes also, until the Revolution, the monks of the Hermitage, true awakeners, went through the sleeping town at all hours every Friday night, crying in a slow and melancholy tone—

‘ Vous qui dormez, ne dormez pas si fort,*
  Que plus ne vous souvienne de la mort.’

Whenever a baptism takes place, all the children in the town hasten to crowd round, shouting untranslatable *patois* cries, upon which money and fruits are thrown to them in all haste, as the only way of stopping their mouths. When a marriage occurs, that the populace think fit to disapprove of, they make a *charivari* (equivalent to our term ‘riding the stang’). Throughout France it has always been so customary to punish second or ill-assorted marriages by a *charivari*, or explosion of popular contempt, that even queens who re-married were not exempted from the insult. The custom was continued in spite of the decrees of Parliament and excommunications of councils, at Paris, to the end of the eighteenth century. Had the *charivari* at Lourdes been like what is usual elsewhere, it need not have been noticed, but this is what goes on every day in the heart of the town.†

If a stranger, whether male or female, marries and settles at Lourdes, all the neighbours on the arrival of the couple,

* *Anglicè*—
  ‘ You, who sleep, sleep not so fast,
    Lest you forget death comes at last.’
† If the reader compares the marriage customs of Lourdes with those of Béarn, he will find considerable difference in them.

unite to form what is called *La sègue*, the hedge. A red sash is held across the bride and bridegroom's door; two files of young men range themselves on each side to open a way for the wedding party, and as soon as it appears, everyone hastes to offer the bride and bridegroom bouquets of flowers, after which they present to them a waiter on which are a bottle and a glass. The offer of wine is rigorously required by the laws of politeness. This concourse of neighbours spontaneously collecting together, and associating themselves with a family festival, would be touching, were it disinterested. But the stranger pays dear for his right of entrance! If his means allow, he must invite all these eager welcomers to a good dinner, at which they feast joyously in honour of the new married couple, who, sore against their will, are obliged to defray the expenses of the festival. Unhappy is the wight who in such circumstances has the temerity to attempt to bargain with the young men *de la haie!* An infernal concert of frying-pans, kettles, bells, and all sorts of discordant instruments will serenade his doors every night with indefatigable perseverance, deafening his ears, disturbing his rest, and holding the miser up to public contempt and ridicule, while the idle and the curious, of whom there are always plenty, will increase the crowd and the noise.

If the police tries to interfere, the *charivari* disappears at their approach and becomes invisible. No sooner do they turn their backs, than it reappears full gallop. If driven out of the town, it takes refuge on the lofty rocks which dominate it, and the horrible uproar recommences with fresh fury. And the people of Lourdes say that the custom is a just and rational one.

'With us,' say they, 'the relations of neighbourhood are sacred. A neighbour is almost one of our kindred. On the smallest accident occurring, he hastens to assist. In the slightest sickness, he is willing to watch the sufferer;

he will not allow others to bear the coffin of the dead to its resting place. His disinterested help is given without shrinking in all the accidents of life. Is it not just, therefore, that he should be indignant at the avarice of the stranger, who while willing to accept his help in time of trouble, is not willing he should share in his joy? The people are frank. They show their sympathy or their hate openly, and give flowers to the first, a *charivari* to the others.'

It is probable, however, that this fashion springs from an old custom, so long disused that most are ignorant that it ever existed. Formerly *les forains* who intermarried in the town were received *voisins*, but they were obliged to swear fidelity to the laws, and to pay a sum for letters of neighbourhood (equivalent to our freedom of the city), which were drawn out for them.

The mountaineers long believed in fairies and sorcerers; indeed, many of them do so still. The faith in good fairies has apparently nearly worn out; but they still believe in the malevolence of sorcerers. Only a few years ago, when any disease was incurable by medicine, the relatives of the afflicted person believed him to be bewitched. A spell had been cast over the house, and to free themselves from it, they received a part of the furniture, and burnt the bed in which the invalid had *not* obtained a cure, in a kind of *auto da fe;* and in order effectually to banish the spirit of evil by the spirit of good, they called in some devout person who had a reputation for sanctity, hoping the prayers of the good would counteract the wicked spells of the sorcerer.

The medical men of Lourdes have, at last, with great difficulty, put a stop to the superstitious remedies that used to be administered to the sick, when medical art seemed unavailing. They have another prejudice yet more dif-

ficult to root out. The people are persuaded that if a
stranger accidentally dies away from his own part of the
country, he must necessarily receive the honours of sepulture in the *commune* or village, where he has drawn his last
breath. To give this hospitality to the dead, is in their
eyes a most sacred duty, and could not be violated without
exposing themselves to the anger of God, which would
manifest itself in the course of the year by a plague of hail.

A young attorney of the valley of Azun was drowned in
the lake of Lourdes. His family wished to bury his remains in the village where he was born. It was found
impossible to do so. The whole population of Lourdes,
usually so tranquil, rose in tumult. The voice of the ma-
gistrates was not even listened to, their firmness was of no
avail, their courage in opposing the popular commotion,
nearly cost them their lives, and the family of the dead
man withdrew their request, fearing that blood would be
spilt over the coffin, in the collision that would have been
inevitable had they persisted. Nevertheless, the people
were not appeased, till they had assured themselves with
their own eyes, that the corpse really reposed in the grave
in Lourdes, and that they had not been duped by a feigned
interment. The heads of the tumult were called to
account before the *Maire* for their conduct; but their
punishment took less effect upon them, than a singular
circumstance which, occurring at that precise time, was
well calculated to show the people the absurdity of their
prejudice. This event was followed a few days afterwards,
by an unusually frightful storm of hail, which fell over the
town, and caused disasters unknown before in the memory
of man.

In a great part of the Pyrenees, especially in the valley
of Lavedan, consisting of the smaller valleys of Azun,
Davantaigue, Batsouriguère, Casteloubon, Estremede
Salles, Pierrefitte, and St. Savin, the ancient *fors* or

customs obtained.* Landed property passed *to the first child born in lawful wedlock, whether son or daughter.* But in Lourdes, the law changed between street and street. The rules regarding the rights of succession varied with the quarters of the town. Two neighbouring houses obeyed different legislations. Thus in the street Du Bourg, *the eldest of the sons* was heir by law to all the property of his father and grandfather, to the exclusion of the daughters (Art. 8, du Commune de Lavedan). In other streets, *the eldest, although a girl,* excluded the younger children, whether boys or girls, from succession. The Revolution of 1789, by abolishing these contradictory laws, did great service in a country naturally unprogressive, and which especially needs a clear written law.

Lourdes was at one time in the possession of the English, but Gaston Phœbus, Count de Foix, cruelly murdered the governor whom Edward the Black Prince had placed there, and seized the castle. On the 22nd of January, 1594, the estates of Bigorre were convoked together at Lourdes, to consent to a loan. They then solemnly declared peace, and submitted to Henri IV., and Bigorre was reunited to France.

The castle of Lourdes was long the Bastile of the Pyrenees, in those atrocious times, when any cruel father, or relative of consequence, could obtain from the French court a *lettre de cachet*, and consign an unfortunate young man to years of imprisonment and suffering without trial, and without appeal. Lagrèze cites two touching instances of this kind, though I cannot understand the false delicacy which makes him abstain from

---

* Before 1789 the province of Bigorre was divided into two parts, one obeying the written law, the other the *coutume* or *for*. In 1769 the parliament of Toulouse decreed that parents could choose among their children the one of either sex they thought best of as heir, after providing according to law for the other children. I was told the decree obtains to this day in Argelès.

giving the name of the prince implicated in the first:—
'Among the prisoners who have left most remembrances,
was a Mazarin, Duke of Valentinois. He had as his rival
in love, a young prince whom it is useless to name. Unfortunately, the two gallants met one day before the lady's
door at the same hour. The prince cruelly abused his
strength against the young duke, who was paralyzed by a
sense of the respect due to the son of his king, and seizing
him, hurled him to the bottom of the staircase. The fall
broke the duke's leg.

'This adventure made some noise at court. The prince
was placed under arrest in his palace. The Duc de Valentinois was sent to the castle of Lourdes, to be cured both of
his broken limb and his passion.' Think of sending a man
who had sustained so grave an injury two hundred leagues
along such roads, and in such carriages as there were then!
He passed some years in confinement. ';The parish register
is lost, and had it been forthcoming,' says Lagrèze, 'no
doubt the history of these young victims, snatched secretly
and suddenly from society by arbitrary power, would have
been in as laconic a style as that of destiny.'

' *The first care of despotism is to stifle in oblivion the secret
of the arbitrary sufferings it imposes.*' Never was a truer
apophthegm penned. Whether ruling over empires with a
rod of iron from the throne of absolute power, or domineering over one unhappy family, *tyrants always seek to stifle
even the very cries of their victims.* It is a sin worthy of
death, in their eyes, *to dare to complain or to weep.** 'Popular
memory has preserved an intense horror of *lettres de cachet*,
but has forgotten the names and history of most of the

* *November 28th*, 1863.—While I revise this sentence, its truth is singularly exemplified by the barbarous decree lately promulgated by Russia,
which forbids relations even to wear mourning for the Polish victims, and
punishes any infringement of this tyrannical and cruel law, by sending the
mourners to the gibbet, the torture, or Siberia. Would to God that He
would make bare His sword, and avenge the Poles for the exterminating
war carried on by Russia against them!

victims who suffered from them ; probably neither of them
were often known. But one still more lamentable history
than that of the Duc de Valentinois is yet remembered.
A young nobleman, of distinguished talents and extreme
susceptibility of character, appeared destined to occupy a
brilliant position at court. The future seemed apparently
unrolling before him the brightest prospects. He was
happy in the world, in the lustre that his father's name
shed over him, happier yet in his home, and in the affection
of the tenderest of mothers. He had met a heart worthy
of his own, and his love, his first love, was returned. But
all these brilliant prospects vanished like a dream.

' His mother suddenly died when everything seemed to
promise that her life would be long spared to bless him.
His father soon sought consolation in a second marriage, and
the new wife tried to despoil the unfortunate son of everything, and even of his father's affection. The feelings of
the family with whom he had hoped to ally himself, seemed
to chill towards him as his position became less brilliant.
Every fresh day withered one of his hopes, or brought him
a fresh sorrow, but the love of the woman he worshipped
remained to him still. She was his consoling angel, and
his only happiness now was to mourn the past with her,
and hope for a brighter future. One evening, without
knowing why, without being informed whither he was
going, without being able to bid farewell to her he loved,
he was seized, and dragged far away from Paris, to this
barren rock in the centre of the Pyrenees. His mother-
in-law had made use of her credit with the minister of the
day to obtain a *lettre de cachet,* by which means she freed
herself from the unwelcome presence of one whose sole
crime was to have a right to the affection and the riches of
her husband. The young prisoner, shut up in the dungeon
of Lourdes, knew well whose hand had struck the blow.
He had more sensibility of soul than fortitude, and his

courage entirely forsook him. In the midst of fellow-prisoners, who strove to forget their misery by idle amuse-ments, he was never seen to smile. He kept aloof from all, and when he could give way to his feelings in solitude, his tearful eye showed the utter desolation of his soul.

'Well might his thoughts be sad. No ray of hope shone through the darkness of his lot. Disinherited of his father's tenderness, and followed by the blind hatred of his stepmother, who could hold out a helping hand to withdraw him from his living tomb? His sudden dis-parition would always be a mystery to his beloved, and the explanation and colouring that might be given to his absence would be fatal to her love for him. When days had followed days, and years succeeded years, would not a time come in which her fidelity, vanquished by a long, vain waiting for one who could not come, would at last yield to the solicitations and prayers of the family, whose only hope she was, and make her take another husband?

'The Commandant of the Castle was struck by the pro-found affliction of the young man, whose gentle and noble manners attached all who came near him; but yet it was not without difficulty that he learned from his prisoner the secret of his misfortunes, for he had never uttered a com-plaint. But when the heart is brimful of sadness, sooner or later it must overflow into the soul that has won its con-fidence by true and generous sympathy. The governor being enlightened as to the young man's secret history, himself implored his pardon, and the minister finding how he had been deceived, deeply regretted that he had allowed himself to become the instrument of the mother-in-law's wickedness, and ordered the poor prisoner's instant release. The reparation came late, the captivity had been long. Did the young lover find his beloved still faithful to her promises on his return to Paris? and were the wounds of his heart healed at last by a marriage with her he had desired so long? No one knows. No memory of him remains in Lourdes but that of his never-ceasing tears and his grief.'

Lourdes was the last strong place held by the English, and they were driven out from it in 1426 by Jehan, Comte de Foix. But the old hatred of the invaders has not yet quite died out. In this present year of 1863, I have seen peasant women turn aside, and spit as they passed me—a common French mode of testifying execration, even among ladies; for Madame T—— has told me her sister-in-law used to do it as she passed her.

'Lourdes,' says La Grèze, 'is a small and very ancient town of the province of Bigorre. It is the *chef-lieu judiciaire* of the 3rd *arrondissement* of the *département des Hautes-Pyrénées*. On one side it is dominated by a pyramidical mountain called the Pic-du-Gers, on the other by a rock surmounted by a fortress.' The ancient name of the town was Lapurdum; as to the derivation of which, many learned and ingenious hypotheses have been maintained. La Grèze dedicates a page and a half to them. I prefer to quote from him the old fabulous legend.

'Once upon a time, long ago, there was a Queen of Ethiopia, who was named Tarbis. One day she took it into her head to make war upon Pharaoh, King of Egypt, and, brave woman as she was, herself led on her armies. Pharaoh, on his part, prepared to receive the visit of the young Amazon suitably. He had about him a young man full of courage and wisdom, who later —— but at that time he 'was quite in his good graces—it was General Moses. Pharaoh made him Commander-in-chief of the Egyptian troops. Moses was already famous, and before fighting him, Tarbis had a curiosity to see him. She demanded, and obtained, an interview. But lo! on beholding him, the queen felt her heart moved by very different feelings to those an enemy ought to inspire. She

became suddenly and violently in love with him. Resolved
to sacrifice everything to her passion, she thought nothing
would be easier than to satisfy it, and she offered Moses
her hand and her throne. He refused both! He was
already engaged to Séphora, the daughter of Jethro, and
he was not a man to sacrifice his engagements to ambition. The young queen (we are not told whether she was
pretty!) was not accustomed to contradiction, and her
unhappy passion troubled her reason. When she found
Moses would not share her throne, she resolved to abdicate
it; but being ashamed to reappear in her own land after
a refusal so humiliating to her charms' (no doubt it was
while Moses wandered forty years in the desert), 'she
also,' says the legend, 'undertook a voyage which did not
last so long, but which led her to a greater distance. She
came to the banks of the Adour, at the foot of the
Pyrenees. The country pleased her. Besides, one tires
of everything in time, even of wandering. So she built a
town, which yet bears her name, Tarbes. This is not all.
She had a sister whose name was Lapurda. She wished
to have her settled within an easy distance, yet not too
near to herself. She sent her to build the castle of
Lourdes, which took its old name of Lapurdum from
her.'

During the time that the Romans had possession of
the country, this town was called Lapurdum; probably it
was in reality founded by them. There is yet a *métairie*,
or dairy-farm, called Strade, (belonging to the family of
La Fitte, one of the most considerable in the country,)
whose name as well as the vestiges which yet remain,
prove it to have been an ancient road. It is supposed to
be of Roman construction, and was some time back the
direct road from Lourdes to Tarbes.

In 1844, the French engineers, while making excava-
tions in the half-moon of the fort, discovered, at the depth

of three *mètres* from the surface, a marble capital, of the
Corinthian order, and a sepulchral inscription, which runs
thus—

D. M.
PRIMVLVS PRIMI
SIBI ET VXORI
RECVNDO FIL
ISSIMO.

The perpetual-secretary of the *Académie des Inscriptions
et de Belles-Lettres à Paris,* M. le Baron Walckaenna,
translates the inscription thus:—

Aux Dieux Manes,
Primulus, fils de Primus,
Pour lui, pour sa femme,
et pour Secundus, son fils
très chéri.

Thus the Roman occupation of the castle of Lourdes is
proved.

‘ The Saracens,’ says Fleury, ‘made a last attack upon
France in the year 732. *Abderame attaqua en personne
l'Aquitaine, se fiant à la division qu'existoit entre les Francs,
car Charles Martel y étoit venu, l'an 731, pour faire la guerre
à Endes, qui eut peine à souffrir son autorité. Abderame entra,
l'année suivante, dans cette province désolée, et ayant d'abord
passé la Garonne il ruina la ville de Bénéarne (aujourd'hui
Lescar), Oléron et Auch. Il prit Dax et Lapurde, que l'on
croit être Bayonne. Il ravagea le Comminge et le Bigorre.’*

There is an ancient legend perpetuating this invasion of
the Saracens; and not far from Lourdes there are some
fields yet known by the name of ‘ Lannes Mourines ’— *i. e.*
‘ Landes des Maures.’

‘ After Charles had broken the innumerable forces of
the Saracens in the plain of Tours, as a hammer breaks
iron, the conquered retired, flying towards our country.
They seized several forts, and attempted the conquest of

Bigorre, at first with some success.   But a priest of Tarbes, prebend of St. Jean, named Missolin, essayed to stop the progress of the infidels.   The people rose at his voice; and with holy ardour armed themselves to defend their country and the faith of their fathers.

'This Christian hero perished a martyr to his zeal. But his blood was not sterile.   From the heights of heaven he seemed to protect the Bigorrais in the terrible strife in which he had himself been engaged before leaving the world.   A great and last effort was made to avenge his death, and a glorious victory delivered our country for ever from the presence of the children of Mahomet.'

'This battle is not mentioned in history.   Our fore-fathers did not write the high deeds of their great men, but they were honoured by the national gratitude.'

'For more than a thousand years a white marble eques-trian statue of Missolin, decorated the peristyle of the church of Arcizac, and every year, on the 24th of May—the anniversary of his festival — the young girls orna-mented it with ribbons and garlands of flowers.   This traditional ceremony was only interrupted by the Revolu-tion.   The eighth century raised this statue to Missolin, looking upon him as a saint: the eighteenth century broke and destroyed it, although the saint had been a hero, and the saviour of his country.'

Here is another old legend of these wars with the Sara-cens, taken from the archives of Pau, by Lagrèze, and translated from the original Latin :—

'As the life of man is fugitive and fragile, to prevent the memory of the taking of Mirambel from perishing, we will relate it to posterity. In those days, Charlemagne, King of the French and Emperor of the Romans, had seized the whole country of Florra, except the castle of Miram-bel. For a long time he had besieged it on three different sides—from the side of Ferragut, that of Hyppolyte, and that of St. George's. Mirat, Lord of Mirambel, had been often summoned to surrender, and become one of Charlemagne's knights, after he should have received baptism; but he replied, that so long as he could possibly defend himself for a single day, he would yield to no mortal whatsoever. Therefore, the king, fatigued with the weariness of so long a siege, thought of retiring. But Sainte Marie, the Mother of God, our Lady of Puy en Velay, invoked by humble prayers, worked a miracle of grace. An eagle, seizing in his talons an immense fish from the Lake of Lourdes, had left it untouched upon one of the highest parts of the castle, which yet bears the name of the Eagle's Stone.

'The captain, justly surprised, sends it immediately to Charlemagne, with a message to the effect, that the emperor deceived himself if he thought he should reduce him by famine, while his fish-ponds furnished him with such fine fish. The king on its receipt was quite disconcerted; but the bishop of Puy, guessing the truth, reassured him, saying, " Prince, the Mother of God—Holy Mary of Puy, begins to work marvellously;" and the king answered, " Even so be it ! " Then the bishop, as a good servant and ambassador of the said Lady, the Holy Mary, went to seek Mirat, and among other words addressed these to him :— " Mirat, since thou wilt not surrender to Charles the Great, the most illustrious mortal in the world—since thou wilt not acknowledge a master, acknowledge at least a mistress. Surrender thyself to the most Holy Lady that ever was— the Mother of God — Sainte Marie du Puy; I am her servant, do thou become her knight."

' At these words, Mirat, already enlightened by a ray of grace from above, said to him, " I lay down my arms, and I deliver up myself, with all that belongs to me, to the Mother of the Lord, Sainte Marie du Puy; I consent in her honour to embrace Christianity, and to become her knight

U

—but you shall understand, I engage myself freely, and I will, that my country shall hold of her alone, both for myself and my descendants."

'The bishop, who was a good diplomatist, took in his hands a handful of hay from the meadow, where he stood with Mirat, and added, " Wilt thou then grant nothing in sign of homage to the Mother of God ?   Offer her at least these blades of grass, to show that thou art become her vassal."

'Mirat said, "I will not take counsel of thee—I will grant, that I will."

' " So be it," replied the bishop.

'Then he returned back to Charlemagne, and asked the king his pleasure.   The king having convened his council, made this reply: " It pleases me that homage be rendered to our Holy Lady of Puy, and I ordain that it shall be so."

' The bishop then went back to Mirat, and agreements were drawn up, as it has been said, with the king's consent. Mirat and his soldiers putting garlands of hay upon the head of their lances, in token of the surrender of the place, prostrated themselves at the feet of Sainte Marie du Puy, making litter of this hay in honour of the Mother of God. Mirat obtained the title of knight for himself and his children. He was baptized by the name of Lorus, all his goods were remitted to him, and he resumed possession of Mirambel, and, according to the custom of gentlemen in those days, gave his name to the castle, which thereafter was called Lordum (Lordes).   This happened in the year 778.'

The Castle of Lourdes was long held by the English, who, according to the usage of that time, made it a stronghold, whence they issued out from time to time to pillage and devastate the country.   The Black Prince came to visit it, and as Froissart relates, he said to Pierre Ernault or Arnaut, of the country of Béarn, cousin of the Count de

Foix, 'Messire Pierre, sith I am come into this country, I make you castellan and captain of the Castle of Lourdes. See, therefore, that ye look after this castel, so that ye may render good account to my lord, my father, and to me.'

'Pierre Arnault and his six captains made in Bigorre, in Toulousain, in Carcassone, and in Albigeois, many tournays and forays; for as soon as they were out of Lourdes they were in the country of the enemy, and they crossed other, riding and running over that country, and put themselves at those times full thirty leagues from their fort; and as they went they took nought, but when they would come home nothing escaped them—and brought in those times so great plenty of cattle and so many prisoners, they knew not where to lodge them; and they made all the country pay a ransom, except the country of the Count de Foix; but in that, they dared not take a hen without paying, from a man who was the Count de Foix's man, or had his safe-conduct, for and if they had angered him, they had not endured.'

'But the Count de Foix entered into secret arrangements with the Duke of Anjou to deliver up the Castle of Lourdes to the king Charles V.; wherefore he sent for his cousin, Pierre Arnaut, to Orthez, who had thereupon many imaginations, and knew not if he should go, or let alone going; all things considered, he said that he would go—for he dared nothing anger the Count de Foix. Before he departed, he called to him his brother, Jean de Béarn, and said to him in presence of all the garrison, "Jean—my Lord the Count de Foix has sent for me, and wherefore, I know not—but sith it is his will that I shall go and speak with him, I shall go—and I doubt greatly that he will require of me to yield the fortress of Lourdes; for the Duke of Anjou hath not entered into his country of Béarn, and I know not what treaty they have had together; but I tell you, that so long as I shall live, I shall yield this castle only to my natural lord, the King of England. I will, Jean, my brother, at this time, that I establish ye here my lieutenant, and that ye swear to me by your faith and gentleness that ye shall hold this castle in the form and manner that I hold it, and that neither for death nor for life shall ye make default."

'Jean de Béarn took the oath required, and the knight, Pierre Arnault, set out for Orthez, and was well received by the count, who made him sit at his table, and showed him such fine semblance of love as he could; and after dinner, he said to him that he must speak to him of many things, and commanded that he should not depart from the castle without taking leave. The third day, the Count de Foix spoke in the presence of the Viscount de Bruniquel, the Viscount de Couzerans, the Lord Auchin de Bigorre, and other knights and esquires, and said to his cousin, "Pierre, I have sent for ye, and ye are come. Know, therefore, that my Lord of Anjou has great ill-will to me, because of the Castle of Lourdes—and my lands would have been harried if I had not good friends among his horsemen. He has opinion that I sustain ye, because ye are of Béarn, and me likes not the ill-will of so high a prince as the Duke of Anjou. Therefore, I command ye, insomuch as ye can do much against me, by the faith and lineage that ye owe me, that this Castle of Lourdes ye shall render unto me."

'And when the knight heard those words he was sore astonied, and he thought a moment to know what answer he should make, for he saw well that the Count de Foix had a set will. Howbeit, all things considered and thought over, he said—

'"My Lord—Without doubt, I owe ye faith and lineage, for I am a poor knight of your blood, and of your land, but for the Castle of Lourdes, I shall not render it to ye. Ye have sent for me, ye can make of me that ye will, but

I hold that castle of the King of England, who put me there, and established me, and to him only shall I render it."

' When the Count de Foix heard this answer, his blood stirred in felony and anger, and he cried, drawing his dagger—

' " Ho! false traitor! Hast thou said this word? Thou wilt not? By my head, thou hast not said it for nought."

' Then he struck the knight evilly with his dagger many times, and there was no knight or baron who dared hinder him.

' The knight said—" Ha, my Lord, ye do not gentleness; ye sent for me, and ye slay me."

' But the count stayed not, but after he had given him five wounds with the dagger; and then he commanded that he be put in the moat, and he was put therein, and there he died of those wounds.'

The crime was useless as crimes generally are. Jean de Bigorre remained faithful to the promises he had made to his brother, and the brutal outrage committed by Gaston Phœbus only increased his hatred to the Duke of Anjou, and this prince was obliged to renounce the hope of conquering that fortress. The choice made by Arnault was confirmed by the King of England, and Jean succeeded Pierre Ernaut as Governor of Lourdes.

There is another pretty legend regarding a lake I did not visit, the Lac de Lhéon:—

' Once upon a time in the early days of the world, the Lord God often took upon Him the form of a man and descended to earth, and walked about among men. Now one night He was belated at the hour when all creatures seek repose, in a village high up in the mountains of Bigorre. He called to beg hospitality at the doors of many rich people, but one and all refused to take Him into their houses, and He could find no shelter except in

the hut of a poor cowherd. And as the cowherd had
nothing to set before the poor traveller for supper, he
generously killed his only calf, and made it ready, and
set meat before Him. And God said to the poor cowherd—

'"My dear host, put aside all the bones of that calf except this one, which I will take."

'The cowherd obeyed, and when they had supped, He
laid the bones of the calf in a row at one end of the hut,
and the two laid down and slept. At daybreak the cowherd arose and went out, and he saw his calf whose flesh
they had eaten the night before, eating the grass before the
hut; and he had got all his bones, except the one which
the Lord God had taken, and which sounded merrily in a
great bell that hung round his neck.

'But the village, with its wicked and inhospitable inhabitants, was swallowed up entirely, except the cabin into
which the Lord God had entered, and in its place there
was a great lake, whose clear waters were as blue as the
sky. That lake is called Lhéon.'

The man in the moon and his fagot of sticks is also a
Pyrenean, as well as an English legend.

'Everyone knows that holydays and sabbaths were
much more strictly observed formerly than they are now.

'Well, once upon a time there was a man who worked
every day without respecting those days which should
have been kept holy, and this offended God, and He said
to him—

'"I pardon thee the past; but henceforward only work
on those days when it is lawful to work."

'This man, however, paid no attention to the words of
God, but worked on without regard to the sacred days. He
had sinned thus three times, and the third time he was
carrying a bundle of thorns on his back, when God appeared, and said to him—

' " What did I say to thee ? Did I not command thee to observe the holy days, and to suspend thy work on the Sabbath ? Thou hast not obeyed me ; now, therefore, I will withdraw thee from earth, and exile thee either to the sun or the moon ; choose to which thou wilt go."

' And the man answered: " What now shall I do? Shall I choose to live in the sun or in the moon ? I know not."

' The Lord came to his succour, and said to him ; " The sun is a burning fire, and the moon is ice."

' Then the man having thought a moment, replied, " The heat of the sun frightens me ; since I *must* choose, I would rather go into the moon."

' " So be it," said the good God, and He transported him thither.

' And because all this happened in the month of February the man was called February ; and because he never would repose on holy days, the man has now no repose in that planet, which is for ever in motion.

' It is not difficult when one looks at the moon to see him in it, still loaded with his fagot of thorns. It is his shadow that is on the moon's surface—he himself is in the middle of the moon. But it cannot always be seen, for the moon herself is first invisible, then she appears, but seems very small, then she grows bigger, and at last her immense countenance looks down upon men. It is at that time, and while she is on the increase, that the shadow shows itself, and the prisoner reveals his punishment to the earth. And the punishment will endure. But when the world ends—when the stars shall fall from heaven—February, purified by repentance, will resume, with his name of man, the freedom of the skies.'

CHAPTER XXVII

BAGNÈRES TO GRIP.

I HAVE been on another pleasant excursion to Grip. The Miss Chapmans were going to drive there with Mrs. Nash, and kindly offered me the vacant seat in their carriage. It was a lovely afternoon, and the drive up the valley of Campan enchanting. The fields at St. Marie were one mass of gay flowers. There were pansies, hyacinths, orchises, campions, *campanula patula*, columbine, the tall *persicaria, geranium phæum,* and in some places the grass was perfectly blue with the elegant flowers of the *viola cornuta,* so called from its long spur or nectary. This violet has no scent, and in its growth and leaves more resembles a straggling field pansy than a violet. It is, however, a true violet; its flowers are as large as those of the dog violet, and the same lovely blue, but, pansy-fashion, numbers of blossoms grow on the long branching stems. They look beautiful in the grass, but do not make so pretty a nosegay as many less lovely flowers, because it is so difficult to arrange them on account of their straggling, branching form.

Farther on, after we had passed the inn at Grip, little Gerald Potter and I must needs get out of the carriage to scramble after a beautiful white flower I saw on the edge of a rock. We could neither of us reach it, after many vain attempts to do so, so we contented ourselves with such way-side flowers as we could gather, and then ran after the carriage, which Gerald seemed to think had been swallowed up bodily; he could 'see all down the road, and there *was*

no carriage there ! ' His little heart began to fail him at
the thought of being left alone with a stranger, but I
cheered him up, assuring him it was only concealed from
our view by the black rock in front, and that when we
turned its shoulder we should certainly see the carriage.
So it proved. 'There it is! there it is!' shouted Gerald,
joyfully, and he bounded forwards to rejoin his aunts. The
first time I went with this same party to Grip we had
divided, that Mrs. Potter might take a place in our carriage, her driver not being sufficiently accommodating to
take her on to the cascades, in consequence of which some
of us saw the lower falls only, and this time we were all
determined to see the upper falls.

I would advise anyone to be very careful in making an
agreement with the Bagnères *voituriers to take them to the
cascades of Grip*, for if Grip only is specified, they take
them merely to a wayside inn at the entrance of the *commune*, or property of the village, for the village is distant,
and the cascades above a mile off, up a very steep hill.
The *voituriers* always say the road is bad, and their horses
cannot go up it, whereas the cascades are not half the distance of the Col d'Aspin, nor is the ascent, up a most
excellent road, half so fatiguing for the horses. It is certainly a very steep pull, and for that very reason it is
better to drive up than to walk. The upper falls are far
the most picturesque and beautiful, and to-day they were
quite enchanting from the exquisite contrast between the
snowy foam of the water and the beautiful rose-coloured
rhododendrons which clothed every rock and hillock, while
the dark firwoods, above which towered mountain peaks,
added grandeur to beauty.

There were a great many workmen employed in constructing a new road to Baréges—one of those wonderful
roads which are the glory of the Pyrenees; and a young
man (in the hope of a fee) offered to show us the new road,

and where the bridge (for which the workmen were now digging, or rather *hewing*, the foundation through bush-wood and rock) was to be thrown over the torrent ; and so take us down to the lower falls, which we wished to re-visit, that we might compare them with the upper. One of these men told me he had been an old Peninsular soldier, under the first emperor, and was nearly ninety years of age. He was a fine stalwart old man, and did not look much above fifty; but our guide said it was all true. I wished I could have given him something ; but alas! it is all I can do, under present circumstances, to pay my way, and reserve means for the impending journey to England. *I dare not be generous now*, and this being obliged to stay my hand so often, when I would willingly give, is one of the bitterest pangs of poverty.

Every inch of this road was full of fresh beauties. Gerald bounded among the rhododendrons, which glowed like fire in the rays of the setting sun, and wished to gather them all, and his elders were little behind him in plundering. So large a bouquet was collected that it had to be transferred to the guide to carry for us to the carriage. The pale bright blue columbine grew here and there among the rhododendrons, adding beauty by contrast, and no one who only knows the columbine of English gardens can have an idea of the beauty of this cerulean blue flower of the Pyrenees. I have often remarked how much the growth, form, or colour of plants is affected by the soil and climate of different localities, so much so, as sometimes to be hardly recognizable as the same.

When we got to a certain bend of the road, Mrs. Nash called to us to turn and look back, saying 'the scene before us now was exactly like a Swiss view, though the Pyrenees in general had a peculiar characteristic beauty of their own, unlike that of other mountain scenery.' I also had repeatedly observed the extreme difference of the colouring

and aërial distances here from those of our Lancashire and
Cumberland mountains.   The green hues of the little valleys, and the pastures scattered along the mountain sides,
are much softer and more vivid than in England; but
mountains and distances are all of a more neutral greyish
tint, and there are none of those rich deep-blue shadows,
thrown across rock or mountain, which are so gloriously
beautiful in Cumberland.   It is twenty years since I saw
those mountains, lakes, woods, and fells ; but the Pyrenees, beautiful as they are, do not seem to me to equal
the lake scenery on the whole, though we have nothing
like the grand chain of mountains visible from the Col
d'Aspin.

I remember Wordsworth told me he considered ' the
English lakes quite as beautiful as the Swiss ones;' because, said he, ' though the Swiss ones are on an infinitely
grander scale, yet, as the human eye can only take in a
certain extent of vision, it can only see a part of the Swiss
landscape ; while it can take in a complete and perfect
view of our lakes, and their surrounding mountains.'

The view Mrs. Nash called on us to admire, was that of
a winding road, losing itself between two steep, precipitous
hills thickly clothed with dark firs, while just where they
seemed to meet, rose a high cone covered with snow, and
flecked here and there with green-blue shadows.   We.
scrambled down a narrow path under the brushwood to
the lower fall, but remained of opinion that the higher
ones were the most beautiful ; and then we walked through
the meadows and hamlet of Grip towards the carriage.

On our way, we met a peasant with a copper pot in his
hand (nearly all the utensils of the Pyrenees are of copper
and brass, *fer blanc* or tin being excessively dear), and
asked him for milk.   He uncovered the pot, and gave us
some of the most delicious I ever tasted.   I have never
drunk such milk as on these two visits to Grip; but, as

usual, the glasses brought were so filthy we had to rinse them two or three times in the running stream before we could use them, and the peasant wanted a *franc* for about a quart of milk, which he would have sent six miles to Bagnères, had we not drunk it, to be sold for three *sous.* We had given him half a franc, considering we were paying him very handsomely; but he grumbled exceedingly, and said, 'If he had known it, we should not have had the milk at all; and he would take care to make the next party pay for it beforehand.' We, on our side, went off grumbling at the Pyrenean peasants, who, whatever may be their other good qualities, are described even by French authors as 'very avaricious, and never losing an opportunity of extortion.' When we got out of ear-shot, our guide—doubtless to ingratiate himself, and unloose our purse-strings for his own benefit—said, 'It was very dear—and he sends it every day to Bigorre, and sells it for only three *sous* the bottle. But he is *un avare ;* and yet he is a very rich man—he is the landlord of the hotel at Grip.' That dirty, mean-looking man the owner of a large landed-property, and a good way-side inn! Such are the Pyreneans.

When we reached the carriage, just as I expected, the man who had been our guide for some hour and a half, was not satisfied with the *franc,* the price of *half a day's labour,* which one of the Miss Chapmans gave him. There was, however, more excuse for him than for the rich peasant at Grip. He and his fellows were working *en corvée ;* they were doing government work, for which they were not paid, a fortnight's work in the year being required from every peasant as a kind of road tax.

As we drove home, we stopped that the driver might gather me the beautiful white flower. It proved to be the *epipactis ensifolia.* It grows under the trees, and is about a foot and a half in height, having long lanceolate, striated,

alternate leaves all the way up the stem, surmounted by a
spike of white flowers rather apart from one another, and
of the purest white, that look at a distance like lily bells.
When you examine it more closely, there is a faint tinge
of pale yellow at the inner part of the lower lip. Altogether it is a most graceful and elegant plant. I do love
white flowers, they seem to me more pure and perfect than
the gayest coloured ones. As we passed through St. Marie,
on our way home, Gerald and I got down again to
gather the *viola cornuta*. I found also the white *potentilla*,
and the teasel hyacinth, and one true narcissus; but as it
grew near a cottage, I suspect that in this instance the
root had been thrown out of the cottage garden. It is,
however, indigenous both in England and in the Pyrenees.

I have found the whole end of a large meadow near
Abergavenny, covered with it. I believe, in fact, that
most of the Pyrenean flowers are to be found in England,
Ireland, Scotland, or Wales; but what is rare with us is
common here. The fritillary, for instance, grows in some
parts of England as well as on the Mounné, in the Pyrenees.
Miss Emily Chapman gave me her beautiful columbines
when we got home, and the next day I arranged my
flowers into the largest and loveliest bouquet I had ever
yet made, and took them to Lady Carnwath, followed by
admiring eyes all down the Coustos. But as for the
epipactis, that I carefully dried, in memory of my last
visit to Grip.

After all, I am but half a botanist. I hate long Latin
names, whose harsh, foreign sound appears to me to mar
the endearing *homeliness* of the flowers, whose greatest
charm is that they stud every copse and lea, and are
associated with one's earliest and dearest memories; and
I especially hate dried flowers, which seem to me like the
dead corpse of what once was fresh, sweet, and beautiful.
Who, if they could, would like to keep a friend's corpse
dried like a mummy?

CHAPTER XXVIII.

'THE superstitions of this Celtic race are numerous, and many are the legends and myths related by the peasants round the wood fire at night. Sometimes they tell how a shepherd went into a cave in the mountain, and, to his astonishment, saw some magnificent silver plate, which he hastened to envelop in his smock-frock, and carry home. But unfortunately, when he went out of the cavern, a red cock went out too, and followed him so obstinately, that the poor man, thinking to appease him, threw him, one by one, all the pieces of plate he was carrying off, till his smock-frock was quite empty, upon which the evil bird disappeared.'

'Or how another shepherd, wandering alone on the banks of one of those lakes that rise on the summits of the loftiest mountains, whose grand and solitary waters, blue as the sky, are surrounded by bare and jagged cliffs, saw of a sudden before him a heap of gold shining in the sun, over which a red goat seemed to keep a watchful guard. For you must know that every kind of treasure is guarded by a goat of supernatural kind, and that they are obliged to expose their buried riches to the beneficent rays of the sun three times in every year. The shepherd, dazzled by the vision of so much treasure, ran hastily to fetch one of his companions; but when they both arrived at the place where it had been, they saw nothing but the mist on the mountain.' They say, also, that when the heroic Bigorrais chased the hated English from their

country, those implacable foes avenged themselves by
casting a spell over the mines of precious metal they had
worked, which should prevent the Bigorrais from making
use of them. There are flying deer, too, among the
mountains of Bigorre, whose apparition sometimes startles
the lonely herdsman in the full noon day, as they rise
from the ground, straight as the handle of a sickle, and
are lost in the clouds of heaven. They have wings like
fire, which make so great a wind when they are agitated,
that men at a distance are thrown down by the blast, and—
marvellous children of another world—a perfect diamond
adorns their foreheads.

'Sometimes, too, under the blue vault of heaven, a fire-
coloured serpent, with a more brilliant diamond on his forehead than that which shines on the bishop's finger, is seen
to ascend into the air, and there can be no doubt that it is
the expression of the will and power of Satan himself, the king
of all pomp, and the arch-mage of all beautiful delusions.'

'"Let the mountain shepherd, who opened to me the
golden folding-doors of legendary lore, speak," says Eugène
Cordier; "he will tell us the story of his own life:—"

'When he was yet but an infant, at the breast, he became ill, and wasted away daily, refusing his mother's
milk. In great anxiety about him, she went to consult a
priest, and this priest was a clever man. "Make haste,"
said he, "before your child withers still further, to empty
the pillow upon which he sleeps, you will then find out the
true cause of his illness." The good mother opened the
pillow, and found, to her surprise, that the feathers it was
filled with, were joined and linked together, so as to form
a long and compact chain, which it was impossible to
break. She threw away the enchanted pillow, and the
child recovered.

'But from that time he has always had spirits in his path.
If he endeavours to penetrate into a mine where ore is

supposed to exist, his torch is instantly extinguished—or a goat runs up and strikes him with its golden horns. If while he is herding the flocks the rain falls in torrents, and he seeks a shelter under the white rock which over-hangs the side of the mountain—there is a frightful noise as if pans and caldrons were knocked together by invisible hands. The fern rustles and speaks, as he walks over it—the hollow earth gives forth dismal groans—and the wind whispers menaces—but where would *he* be more tranquil?

'Already aged, under these constant terrors, he passed one day near a fountain, when an old maid, who was drawing water there, looked strangely upon him. He hastened to turn his back to her—but the evil eye caught him on the loins. "Peter," she cried, "are you sure you have not got sciatica?" Alas! from that moment, he felt a frightful pain, which is dragging him slowly to the tomb.'

But there are means by which malignant influences may be averted. The juice of a branch of alder, gathered on the 1st of March, and squeezed into the Paschal holy water, is an efficacious talisman: and if cattle languish and die, from the effects of an evil eye, it is an urgent necessity to spin a dying toad at the end of a bit of pack-thread in the stable. But who can hinder the angry neighbour who is a witch from stopping the flowing of the water in which the linen is washing, by a single gesture? And who can preserve himself from the deadly effects of unknown sorcery?

'There was a girl in the valleys, that brought a child into the world, whose father refused to marry her. The faithless man was seeking another alliance. The forsaken mother, listening to no feeling but her burning thirst for revenge, had recourse to magic arts. She made such powerful conjurations, that her seducer first fell sick—then his sufferings increased—and his body became as full of holes as a sieve. Pain and remorse brought him back to his mistress; he came fulfilling her most eager desire—to offer her his hand. The woman forgave, and tried to save his life, as she had tried to take it—but it was too late— the terrible witchcraft ran its course.—He died.*

'Sometimes a shepherd, eager to enrich himself at any rate, goes at midnight to a spot where three roads meet, and asks for the price of his black hen, but ah! how many a one has had cause to repent it. The devil, thus called for, appears. If the person who summons him can bear his terrible appearance and fantastic conversation, it is true that he sometimes departs, leaving behind him a considerable sum of money! but, if fear is shown, he darts forward, and throws over his visitor the skin of a were-wolf— a white skin, like that of the great mountain sheep-dog. How many times has the belated peasant been tormented by the dumb, silent, circling of these were-wolves. In vain he takes up a stone, and throws it at the animal—the

---

* I cannot help believing that evil wishes to one-self or another do give a certain power over human beings to the spirits of evil. In my father's house at Hornsea we had a servant called Jane Beswick; she was seduced by our next door neighbour, a young butcher named Michael Burn, under solemn promise of marriage—he wishing 'that his legs might rot off if he did not marry her.' After the birth of a child, however, he refused to fulfil his promise, and I got the unfortunate girl a place in the family of an old friend. Michael Burn then engaged himself to his cousin Nancy Straker, but just a little before the wedding was to take place, his mother, with whom he lived, sent in to our house one night to borrow a foot-bath, as her son had come home from Beverley fair complaining of violent pain in his legs, and she thought bathing in hot water might do him good. When the foot-bath was brought back next day, he was worse. The doctor was called in, but Michael languished for months, and became a perfect cripple, upon which his cousin Nancy refused to marry him. It is a fact *that the bones of his legs did rot, and several of the smaller ones actually worked out.* In his pain and remorse he wrote to Jane Beswick, and she came over and married him. 'Of course I wished to marry him after what had happened,' she said, when people wondered at her doing so. However he never recovered, but went on crutches for about two years, when he died. The singular thing was the sudden fulfilment of the curse he had imprecated on himself—he had nothing the matter with his legs when he went to Beverley Market—he rode home as usual on horseback—complained of intense pain on entering the house, and became a cripple from that day.

stone hits the beast who does not bark, but continues his magic round; he fires his gun—the ball flattens, and returns towards him; he utters a cry of despair—the were-wolf looks at him, and his voice dies in his throat.

'This magic dog has a peculiar hatred to the canine race. If he meets a real dog, he stands up on his hind feet, lassoes him with a whip loaded with balls of lead, and flays him miserably.

'The were-wolf is a glutton. One of them used to go every night to a lonely dairy-farm, and uncovering the vessel that contains the milk of the herds, lap it all greedily up. One night he was surprised, and received a violent blow on the reins with a hatchet. The next day there was a man dead in the village.

'Some shepherds one day found a white skin suspended from a tree. Guessing that it was some sorcerer's left-off garment, of which he had contrived to rid himself, they lit a fire of leaves, and threw the skin upon it. But it began to crackle, and made three leaps of a prodigious height, after which it allowed itself to burn away. If anyone sees the were-wolf appear by night, it is prudent to wait silently till he departs; for if anyone speak or even only open the mouth, the simple vision becomes a frightful reality, which stands upright, and struggles with the indiscreet speaker. Evil is his fate, if he prove weakest in the strife; the were-wolf throws his skin upon him, and while the poor chatterer is constrained to go on four feet, and to wander about all night under a form unworthy of an honest man, the wicked sorcerer rejoices that his nocturnal enchantment is finished, and that he has regained henceforth the form of a man.'

'Strange superstition—the terror of the peasant—and once the belief of the entire people—workman, citizen, noble, and judge! Bodin cites a decree of the parliament of Dole, of the 18th January, 1574, condemning to the flames one Gilles Garnier, who having bound himself by oath to serve the devil, had been changed into a were-wolf. Shall I speak of the presages drawn in the valley of Argelés from the bleating of calves. Shall I tell how the woodcutter of Ferrières when afflicted by a painful wound, sought to learn the cause of his disease by blowing through a ram's horn into water which threw up air bubbles? It is true that in a report drawn up towards the end of the last century, I find these words which go far to explain many of these beliefs:—"The inhabitants of Arbéos (aux Ferrières) are illiterate; ignorance and rusticity are their heritage. There are scarcely four inhabitants among the whole population who know how to write. And I must add, to the shame of our age, that up to the moment of which I write, vaccination is almost unknown to these exiles from civilization."

'But it is not only,' continues Cordier, 'the relations of the middle ages, which have traversed time in the memory of the people, there are cotemporary histories, more or less strange, the heroes of which exist, and with whom the curious traveller can converse if he likes to do so.' Two miracles were recently related to me in one of the least known, and most neglected valleys of Bigorre, the valley of Ferrières:—

'A young girl grew weaker every day, the victim of a witch's evil practices; her tongue unnaturally lengthening, fell down on her bosom, and marred her opening beauty. Tall, thin, and pale, her great black eyes burned with sombre fire, and she bent under the magic influence like a fading plant. No remedy benefited this unknown disease; the doctors lost * the little Latin they know in these out-of-the-way places, where Latinity never reaches. She sank slowly, as if mined by a secret wound,—in a word, she was

---

* 'Perdre son latin' is an untranslatable French proverb.

dying. She was at last persuaded to undertake a journey
to Jacca in Aragon, and was conducted to the procession of
the celebrated and beneficent Ste. Oroise, upon which the
young girl's tongue shrank up visibly and went back into
its natural place; her drooping figure gently straightened;
her complexion cleared; from pale it became white, tinged
with roses; her eyes shone only with the modest fire of a
pure youth. The witnesses of the miracle beheld the frail
flower recover all its pristine beauty, and the caressing
words and admiration of the young men fell on her like
the soft breeze falling on a rose that has been beat about
by the furious blast of the east wind.

'A child in the same valley of Ferrières had also suffered from the same evil eye. He was then at school in
the holy place of Betharam. No one knows how this innocent was in a moment transported into a forest near Pau.
What is sure is, that he opened his eyes like one awaking
from a deep slumber, and thought he had fallen asleep
while out walking. Some one happening to pass by, he
inquired the way back to his school, and was laughed at
to his face, because the person he questioned naturally
imagined him to have played truant. However, he obtained
sufficient information to enable him to find his way back
to Betharam, where he related his adventure, which caused
great surprise, and prayers were offered up for him. But
after this the child was never well; he had sudden
attacks of frenzy, he foamed at the mouth, his blood-shot
eyes rolled wildly, he writhed, and twisting himself about,
dropped to the ground senseless; the doctors thought him
attacked by the falling sickness, and treated him for that
disorder; but far from benefiting by their remedies, his
attacks increased in number, and became more and more
severe. His father was then advised to take him to Jacca,
and father and son went thither; but scarcely was the
child in the presence of the relics of Ste. Oroise, whose body

is all entirely preserved in the church, except the head,
than he screamed frightfully, threw a frothy saliva over the
faces of those who were near him, and even on the holy
altar, and used the most blasphemous and horrible language. He could scarcely be retained in the temple, and
five or six strong Spaniards held him down with difficulty;
while, strange to say, the child who had never before heard
a word of Spanish, began suddenly to speak it with the
utmost facility, using it the better to insult those who
forcibly detained him. He even addressed the priests in
Latin, and abused them grossly, but correctly, in that language; and what is still more extraordinary, he conversed
in Basque* with the men of that province (for people come
from all parts of the world to the shrine of Jacca), horrify-
ing them by fearful blasphemies, expressed in the purest
Basque dialect. The poor father, stupified and ashamed
that the demon should bestow the gift of tongues on his
son, only that he might make so scandalous an abuse of it,
knew not what to think, and prayed the blessed Ste. Oroise,
yet more fervently, to work a miracle in his child's behalf.

One morning that the relics were exposed to the
people with more than ordinary pomp, while the young
Ferrarais was held down by force near the holy reliquary,
the resistance he had hitherto offered to his best friends
suddenly ceased, his countenance lost the expression of
blind rage and fury, his hallucinated look was directed upwards to Heaven, with an expression of angelic piety. The
people who held him loosed their grasp, and thus left to
himself, the child who till then had writhed in convulsions,
as if tormented by the flames of hell, now looked like a
cherub out of paradise. At the same time occurred a singular and undeniable fact, which is related in the archives
of the Saint Oroise—one of the child's boots fell off of its

* Basque is said to be the most difficult of all languages, and is supposed
to be the same dialect as that of the ancient Carthaginian.

own accord, leaving him with one foot bare. No one knows if the demon quitted him by the heel, but the thing was so evident and probable, in the eyes of the witnesses present, that it was agreed that the boot should be placed in one of the repositories of the sacristy, in testimony of the miraculous termination of so frightful a case of possession. Since this pilgrimage, the young Ferrarais, it is averred, has neither foamed at the mouth, howled, rolled his bloodshot eyes fiercely, or twisted himself about on the ground in convulsions, or uttered foul blasphemies, or had any return whatever, of fits. I have seen him, as well as the young girl, whose marvellous cure is still the subject of the pious conversations of the country.' Thus says M. Eugène Cordier, in his 'Légendes des Hautes Pyrénées,' in 1855, a work now out of print.

CHAPTER XXIX.

No words can describe the lumbering agricultural implements used by the Pyreneans. One would think they inherited them from the Celts, their ancestors. Their carts
are often the rough stem of a tree, with a few boughs nailed
at each side, set upon wheels. The ploughs are small and
light, and a woman generally follows the ploughman and
breaks the clods after he has turned them with a hoe, or
may be seen spreading the manure among the furrows with
her hands. It is impossible to estimate *the demoralization*
to which women's working with men, whether in English
collieries or Pyrenean slopes, occasions.

Bigorre is a fertile country, and were its lands properly
tilled would be still more productive. Its crops are corn
of various kinds, and especially maize, or Indian corn
(which is often sown as a second crop on the same land
from which a previous crop has been taken), peas, beans,
mangold-wurzel, carrots, turnips, vetches, hemp, and flax.
Chestnuts are also a *récolte*, they are not considered as a
fruit, but as an article of food, and are commonly sold
ready roasted and stripped of the husk in the markets.
They are also often parboiled; the rich adding a small
quantity of vanille to them in boiling—at least this was
done at M. ——'s, where I lodged. I did not like boiled
chestnuts, but Keeper approved of them exceedingly, and
ate them greedily, while he did not care for roasted ones,
because they were not so tender.

The fields on the lower grounds are almost all water-meadows, and in the autumn about November or December (for the Pyrenees are blessed with a second summer, called St. Martin's summer, and October and November are generally far warmer and more beautiful months than July, August, and September, which are the rainy season); the water is turned on to fertilize and freshen the grass which has been parched and burnt up by the long months of hot weather. This enables the cultivator to have several crops of hay, for they do not allow the grass to go to seed as we do, apparently. Anything so beautifully green and fine as these meadows are till quite the middle of December, I never saw. They can only be compared to the fine verdant lawns in front of an English gentleman's house. One part of their farming system struck me as singular. They manure the grass in February and March, just when it is beginning to spring. I cannot think the system a good one, seeing it is contrary to nature. Providence provides the earth with a warm coating of dead leaves, to defend the tender buds from the inclemencies of winter, which, gradually decaying, mix with the mould and enrich it when the spring rains set in. To me this practice was a great annoyance; the meadows were rendered ugly and inodorous just at the loveliest season of the year, when in England one sees them all sprinkled over with yellow cowslips, orchises, primroses, and ladies'-smocks, while

> 'The wild marsh marigold glows like fire,
>   In swamps and hollows gray.'

And I question whether it is not bad farming into the bargain. On the sloping lands too, the heavy equinoctial rains to which this country is subject, and which alternate with snow storms, must wash a great deal of the dressing away. I have often thought we have too many and too high hedges in England—albeit a neglected old hawthorn hedge, with

long branches of the wild rose hanging from it, and clematis, honeysuckle, briony, and wild hops twining among
it, and golden, yellow, and purple vetch straggling up the
sides, be a very lovely thing to the poet's eye and heart,
and that it is to the immense number of close hedges in-
tersecting all the fields, and preventing a current of air,
that we owe so much blight. In England our fields, our
gardens, our very hedge-flowers are attacked by innumerable insects, which of late years have increased frightfully. In my childhood, except upon the beans, currant
bushes, and rose trees, this plague of *aphides* was, comparatively speaking, unknown. Now it infests everything,
while caterpillars of all kinds have multiplied in the same
manner. *There must be a cause for this. What is it?* I
believe it is the absence of a free, thorough circulation of
air, for the reason that all greenhouses, which by their
nature are close, are all thus infested. Yet we have mil-
lions of little birds who live upon these insects.

During the summer and autumn I spent in Germany, I
seldom heard the song of a bird except the nightingale, or
saw one; while with us, they flit from bush to bush, and
one cannot walk out without seeing hundreds. It was a
peculiarly, wet, unfavourable season, yet there was no
blight, except upon the vines, either in the gardens or in
those large, wide, orchard-like fields, divided from each other
only by a trench, or a low turf wall. It is the same in
France. In the nine months I have now spent here, continually rambling in the fields, and entering every garden
I could, I have never seen any aphides.* Yet certain field-
flowers are peculiarly liable to be attacked by them—at
least in England. I attribute this to the paucity of hedges.
A French hedge is a laughable thing to English eyes. It
is sometimes made of quickset, planted far apart, with the
branches intertwined *au jour*, like a kind of lace or lattice-

* After writing this I saw some upon a species of wild sage.

work, and may be a yard high, and every twig is sedulously pruned off that it may preserve its thin lace, wire-like appearance. I notice this hedge only on the lands of careful farmers, who no doubt think they have a perfect clipped fence *à l'Anglaise*. What purpose it serves except that of division, I cannot conceive. A cow or a horse could easily break through or leap over it. The palings are as absurdly slight, even those meant to protect the railway lines from the incursions of cattle. Sometimes they are made of split stakes, each about the breadth and thickness of two of my fingers, with a similar rail across, or of sawn wood of equally slender dimensions.

French practices seem in most things the opposite of English ones, and the advantage does not *always* lie on the French side. Whatever we in England think ought to be strong and large, the French make slight and small. It is in vain that you point out that owing to this, the convenience in question is rendered well-nigh useless—' *C'est la coutume ici*,' is all the reply. Excelling us in all things that strike the eye, as in painting, anatomy, architecture, public fountains, and last, not least, bonnets, caps, artificial flowers, ribbons, and silks, in the country villages the French are far behind us, in the common decencies and comforts of civilized life—they all go upon the principle of the farmer's wife, in Elizabeth Hamilton's clever and useful work 'The Cottagers of Glenburnie.' 'Ou, it'll joost du weel aneugh, there's nae use in mak'ing sich a fash.' 'I canna be fashed,' was a favourite saying with myself and a girl companion, after we had read that book ; we said it in fun, but it seems the genuine expression of the French heart. Does your servant make a slop in your room ? she cannot be fashed to wipe it up, it will dry in time, ' *Ca ne fera rien.*' When she sweeps, the dust is left in little heaps, till it suits her convenience to take it away, and I have known it thus lie *two days* in a large respectable house. If you object that the draught from the open window will blow it away, and that it was no use sweeping, unless the dust were also taken away, the French equivalent for 'I canna be fashed,' is on their tongue directly, ' *Oh, ça ne fera rien.*'

I have heard there is a dust-shovel in Bagnères. I believe it to be a myth; I never saw one in any French house I ever lived in, except in Paris. How that dust is ever taken away remains a mystery to me. Doubtless it is an Eleusinian mystery not to be revealed to the common herd of women. I have watched the sweeping, I have followed the maid and her broom to the very verge of my lawful domains, *mon appartement;* she always made some excuse to go downstairs and left it, ' *Cela ne fera rien,*' she would take it away by-and-by. Never yet could I detect a French *bonne* in the act of clearing away that dust. My private opinion is that they gather it up in their hands, and thus throw it away.

But ' *Retournons à nos moutons.*' Sheep constitute a great part of the wealth of the Pyrenees, and a pastoral life is here no fiction. But I am sorry they have abandoned the crook, which, besides looking picturesque, must really have been useful in hooking down nut and apple boughs, and as a staff, and leaping pole, across the mountain springs, and up the rough steep hill sides. Almost all the sheep have large twisted horns, and I notice three pure colours, white, black, and a sort of dark brown, from which the neat useful dark-brown undyed cloaks, *capulets*, vests, rowsers, and gowns, usually worn by the labouring population, are made. The shepherds do not keep the breeds separate, so that one sees a white lamb with four black feet and a black tail, &c., ring-straked, speckled, and brown sheep.

The mutton of these sheep is generally very small, and excellent in flavour. I have bought legs whose bones were not thicker than a lady's forefinger; I paid for each thirty *sous*, about fifteen pence. It is common here to *piquer* a leg of mutton with garlic, that is, small holes are drilled into it before roasting, and a small kind of garlic resembling a very young onion, inserted therein. If I had been told of this plan beforehand, I should have declared it was an abomination, but when my first tiny leg of mutton came up dressed in this manner, I ate it without thinking about it, and found it to be a decided improvement, giving the whole joint a high gamy flavour. They do the same thing to lamb, which I think spoils it. Another way of dressing a leg of mutton here, is to stew it whole in *vin ordinaire*, together with some ham, a little butter, a *little* garlic, mushrooms or *ceps*, and a little salt ; a *little* burnt sugar is added to colour it, and it comes up to table a rich brown colour, like a roasted hare, and is a capital dish.

But do not suppose you can always have mutton at Bagnères. No. In January the *Maire* issued an order that every butcher should have beef in his shop, since which time we have been restricted to beef, lamb, pork, and veal, which latter seems the staple food all the year round. In England we make our soups of beef; here all soup is made of veal. Lamb, and pork, the last especially, are dear in the Pyrenees. Game is very scarce. Poultry and ducks nearly as dear as in London. Geese are fattened like an English prize bullock, and distended with yellow fat, are to English eyes most disgusting. To roast them would be impossible; the French eat them cut into pieces, and stewed in their own grease; it must be a dish fit for Laplanders, as they must taste like train oil. They are as dear as in England. Venison I never saw. A stray izard or chamois may be killed now and then, but they become rarer every year, as the mountain heights are more and more invaded by visitors, and will soon become extinct. Buck wheat and millet are a good deal cultivated, and the corn made into cakes. The millet is made into oblong rolls of paste, about the size of a rolled pudding, and sold in this form in the market. These rolls of paste are cut into thin slices, fried in butter, and covered over with powdered sugar, and taste very well. Semolina is also a good deal sold in the market. Fruit and all kinds of vegetables are very plentiful and cheap, but Bigorre is not a fruit country, being too cold. The yellow peaches and grapes come from Pau and the district about Tarbes, while the oranges which are of a very large kind, and dear, come from Spain. These oranges have still their fresh acid taste in March, when they are quite over with us in England. Potatoes are cheap and good, and are much cultivated on some of the mountain slopes where wheat will not grow, and those grown on this dry soil are always free from the disease which attacks those planted in a damper soil.

The potato is sometimes called the *parmentière* in France, from *Parmentier*, a celebrated chemist, who first succeeded in bringing them into common use. They had been grown for some time in the country; but a prejudice existed in the people's mind against them. They grew them occasionally, as a cheap food for their animals, and that was all.

Parmentier was born the 17th of August, 1737, at Mont-Didier, a town in ancient *Picardie, Département de la Somme*, of an honourable but poor family. In 1780 he commenced a series of laborious examinations into the qualities and uses of the potato, and finding it contained a great deal of nutriment, endeavoured in many ways to bring it into common use as an article of diet. It was a difficult matter to ask the great and the rich to eat a food that had hitherto been scarcely thought fit for pigs; but he proved that it contained a delicate and wholesome farinaceous matter of extreme whiteness, which might be made into the most exquisite dishes, or mingled with flour into excellent bread, and would even give a good brandy.

He invited his friends to dinner, and gave them twenty dishes, all prepared with this precious vegetable ; and by degrees the thing got talked of, and people began to believe that potatoes *might be good.*

For some years the cereal crops had been very insufficient in France, and the people suffered much from scarcity of bread. In 1785, they were in a state of absolute famine. There was a vast arid, uncultivated plain, called Sablons, near Paris. Parmentier had it planted with potatoes, and persuaded the Lieutenant of Police to set a guard of soldiers over it during the day only, in the hope that the people would steal them by night when they saw them considered so valuable a crop as to be guarded by the government. He was right in his conjectures. Every morning people came to tell him that large quantities had been stolen during the night. He was delighted, and recompensed the informers liberally, who went away quite stupified at a man's rejoicing over the loss of his property. But the prejudices of the people were conquered; and from that time the potato became a common food in France. Parmentier also persuaded Louis XVI. to wear a *bouquet* of the potato flowers at a public festival, and that helped to bring it still more into fashion.

The potato gives six pints of pure brandy for every hundred pounds of potatoes; and the liquor being kept some months in new barrels, and slightly coloured with burnt sugar, is equal to common brandies. It is easily made : — A hundred pounds of potatoes must be well washed, cooked by steam, and bruised by a cylinder. After 225 pounds of well-water has been first added to them, four pounds of barley-meal are then put into a barrel or tub, and upon this is poured 25 pounds of boiling-water; this water is stirred about, and the crushed potatoes are then thrown in, and the whole well mixed together. Six or eight ounces of yeast, together with six

ounces of good brandy, are next added, and the whole
well mixed again; the barrel or tub is then covered up,
and the mixture left to ferment quietly. The fermen-
tation generally lasts five or six days. It is known to
have ceased, when a clear liquid only remains, on uncovering the tub. It is then decanted off the lees, and
distilled. This liquor is known by the name of *Cohobé*.
The lees, or refuse, after distillation, is employed in feeding
cattle, who drink it eagerly, if mixed with water; and
cows thus fed give a quantity of milk. I copy these details, however, from Deville. I did not hear of *cohobé*
being much used in France.

M. Cadet de Vaux also discovered that potatoes helped
to make an excellent paint. It gives the paint consistency,
and has not the inconvenience of animal glue. This is the
recipe: — A pound of potatoes, two pounds of Spanish
white, four pints of water. The potatoes are cooked by
steam, crushed while in a boiling state, and then mixed
with *two pints* of hot water, which mixture is passed
through a horse-hair sieve. The Spanish white is then
mixed with the two remaining pints of water and added to
the potatoes (more water may be added if necessary).
This paint is laid on with a brush, like that made with
glue. It is a beautiful milk-white. It can also be coloured
grey, by adding porphyrized (*sic*) charcoal; yellow, by
adding ochre, &c. Two coats may be laid on without
difficulty. It holds perfectly either on walls or on wood;
it is neither liable to shell off, nor to fall off like dust;
and it does not cost *deux centimes* (a halfpenny) the square
of six feet.

Acorns also are a crop, the pigs of each village being
driven into the woods belonging to it to feast upon them
in their season. Nuts and walnuts are cheap, and plentiful. One or two people in Bagnères keep silkworms for
profit. M. Villeneuve, the proprietor of the *bonbon* and
wine-shop, usually makes about a hundred a year by his

silkworms, though the mulberry-leaves on which they feed have to be brought from a great distance, as there are none in Bagnères. He lets the insect emerge from the cocoon, and lay its eggs, which are sold under the name of '*La graine de vers de soie.*' The silk sells, of course, as an inferior article, and is made into the kind of stockings called spun silk in England.

There are one or two paper manufactories at Bagnères, and another at Pouzac. The paper made is chiefly of a coarse, inferior kind. A coarse, common kind of cloth, and a strong linen, are manufactured in most of the mountain farms, as they used to be in England seventy years ago, for family consumption. Even among the gentry most of the stockings worn are knit by hand. The knitting of the Pyrenees is renowned for its beauty, and some of it is almost as fine as lace. The finest specimens I saw of Pyrenean were at the shop of Madame Costellat, near the Place des Coustos. There also I saw specimens of the *Crêpe de Baréges,* which Murray says is manufactured at Bagnères, but I could not hear of any manufactories of it in the town, though I inquired. Madame Costellat had merely scarves of it.

Knitting is the staple work of the female population of the town; and as one walks up the *Rue de Toulouse,* and sees the groups of dirty women sitting before their doors, knitting the most intricate and gay-coloured patterns, from some thirty or forty different coloured balls of worsted that lie in their laps, or roll upon the muddy ground, one wonders how those delicate fabrics can ever come out so clean and beautiful. The colours are, I believe, all dyed in grain, and the shawls washed after they are finished. I saw some scarlet ones undergoing that process. The patterns from which they are knitted are worked in cross-stitch on canvas, and look like any other cross-stitch flowers.

Turning boxwood is another Pyrenean industry. It is

made into cups and balls, glove stretchers, silk winders, candlesticks, &c. I have seen some of the women making rosaries; they do it very quickly, stringing the beads on to a ball of fine wire, and twisting the wire into a loop as they break off every bead separately; like *crochet*, it seems to be done by a turn of the wrist, and I should think the knack must be acquired in childhood. Straw plaiting does not obtain, as hats and bonnets are not worn by the multitude. I went all over Bagnères in vain, to try and get a yard or two of straw plait to enlarge my hat. The beehives are not made of straw as with us, but of a coarse, light, basket-work, which is afterwards coated with clay and cow-dung. The basket-work all comes from Tarbes, Pau, or Toulouse.

The crockery is of the very commonest description; it is a coarse brown ware, and not half so pretty as the grey-and-blue kind manufactured in Germany, and common also in the Bordeaux market. Marble is cheap and common; the thermes or public baths are built of marble, and the door-posts and lintels of nearly every house in Bagnères are of marble. A great variety of very beautiful kinds, pale-rose, green, white, and veined are found among the mountains, and the valley of Campan especially is celebrated for its marble quarries. Marble works abound in every part of the valley of Bagnères, the Adour turning innumerable wheels, and being apparently more considered and valued as a 'water privilege' than as a lovely romantic stream; but the principal works are those of M. Léon Geruzet. He kindly showed Madame —— and myself over them one day before I left her, and we saw very beautiful tables, vases, altars, and ornaments manufactured from the rarest varieties. What struck me most, was the exquisite finish of many of the carvings, executed from models, by his workmen, who had never learned to draw. The French are, undoubtedly, *born artists*.

Y

CHAPTER XXX.

I went yesterday to the Col d'Aspin with my kind new friends, the Miss Chapmans, their sister Mrs. Potter, and her children, Mrs. Paris and her two little girls. We were a very merry party. *Cela va sans dire*, where there are children—for their quick, keen sense of enjoyment gives zest and life to everything. I wonder whether the far-famed Swiss views are finer than the chain of the Pyrenees seen from the Col on a clear day? However, the weather was not propitious, and had I been alone, I should certainly have given up the expedition. As I stood at the window awaiting the carriage, a sudden gust of wind blew the dust up and whirled it in the air, and the birds uttered that peculiar chirp, which is always the certain herald of rain. One of our party, however, was about to return to England; she did not like to give the excursion up, so we went. We drove along the lovely vale of Campan, and then, instead of going on to Ste. Marie, took the road to the right, which wound among the hills to Paillole. It was a regular ascent all the way, and at every step, the view grew wilder and grander till we reached the inn of Les Quatre Vesiaux, which stands on a small plain at the foot of the Col, with a meadow in front of it, closed in by mountains clothed with dark pine woods, called here *sapins.*

There are plenty of wolves in these woods, and sometimes, in very severe winters, they come down even to Bagnères. Some winters ago, the servant of an English lady who lived in the heart of the town, on opening the house-door at five o'clock in the morning, to go to early mass, was frightened by two pair of fierce green eyes glittering in the dark—two wolves stood there. Fortunately they are very cowardly, and, unless pressed by severe hunger, always run away. Still, I should not like to meet one.

My friends had taken all the materials for a good break-fast with them, and, though we had all had one breakfast before starting, the mountain air had made us quite ready for another. We ordered a jug of hot milk, four cups of coffee (we had chocolate in a bottle), an omelette, and a dozen boiled eggs; bread, butter, and everything else we had of our own; for this and *le service* they charged us *five francs and a half*—quite enough, we thought. I dare say, they would have charged French people only three. It is quite time English people left off their foolish habit of paying more than the prices of the country. The doing so does not make them a bit better liked, and it is hard upon other travellers, who are also English, but have not the same means, and yet are expected to pay *à l'Anglaise.*

After we and our horses* had breakfasted, we began to ascend the steep winding Col through a wood of magnificent *sapins*, from whence we *ought* to have had splendid views; but, alas! a fine drizzling rain came on, and we were ob-liged to have the hoods of the two carriages up for a while, and when it ceased to rain, a rising mist half veiled the mountains from our sight. The sun never came out for more than a momentary gleam the whole day, and as it was an expensive excursion—twenty-five francs for each carriage, which included everything except our private

---

* It is not usual for the party hiring a carriage to pay for the food of either the driver or his horses; these items are included in the charge made for the carriage, which is always high enough to cover all. As in one place I lodged at, the house of a man who let out horses, I had the oppor-tunity of learning practically that there were two tariffs of charges, one for the English visitors, the other for the French residents.

breakfast at the inn, and we could not all of us afford to come again; it was vexatious. There was, however, no use in grumbling—we were all ready to be pleased with what we could see, and though we were disappointed in not seeing the Spanish Pyrenees (I missing them for the *second time*), we all enjoyed our day thoroughly. It was what painters call a grey day. The effect of the large moving masses of mist now veiling a whole mountain, now rolling heavily off, and showing the peaked crest or part of one side glittering white and keen, or of a rich mossy green, against the grey rocks, was very grand.

When we got to the *Col*, an ill-favoured peasant forced himself upon us as cicerone; he would tell us the names of mountains *we could not see.* Nothing of the long chain of mountains that ought to have been visible, could be seen, but one near inconsiderable hill, and the Tourmalet. But we could look down into the valley and village of Aspin and trace part of the road towards Luchon, and beyond that a wall of mist shut everything out. Again it began to rain, and most of the party retreated to the carriages, but three of us were sure the mist was clearing off, and would at all events, walk a little farther to the edge of the hill. It did, in fact, clear a little, and the view of the valleys below the *Col* in that soft grey light was inexpressibly lovely. So lovely that I and Miss Chapman would go farther on yet, leaving the other lady to return alone. We went down the road a good way, and looked into two green vales. There I saw a great many daffodils in a field below the road. My companion said she would sit down and wait for me while I gathered some, and I ran down to them. I never saw anything more beautiful than that plain of flowers. At a distance only daffodils were visible, but when we got to them we found the ground covered with innumerable large blue gentianellas also, forming the loveliest contrast with their pale yellow; and among them, here and there, grew two orchises I had never seen before, a bright crimson one with golden spots on the lip, and a pale green one * with small crimson spots, which had a very faint delicate scent; both kinds grew close to the ground, and their stems were close sheathed in the long pale green leaves. There was also another plant (*Gentiana lutea*), not yet in flower, with a rounded leaf, crimped longitudinally. I never saw such beautiful daffodils before. Their cups were much longer and larger, and the side petals far paler and almost twice as large as is usual. The leaves also were larger and thicker. The gentianellas, on the other hand, were not nearly so deep coloured and lovely a blue as those on the Monné, which I attributed to their being more exposed, and growing on a marshy plain, for the few we had seen peeping from under the heath on the road side, as we ascended the *Col*, were the true *lapis lazuli* blue. I gathered a few and returned to Miss Chapman, but we had not gone far towards the carriages, when we met another of the sisters, and her little boy, coming to seek us, and we agreed to go back to the daffodil field.

We were busily gathering flowers when a peasant came up, and said it was his field, and we should either pay him something for them, or leave them; we were injuring the grass by treading on it. It was not true, for cattle were browsing in the field, and moreover the daffodils nearly covered it, and we demurred. The man insisted. We might give what we pleased, but something we must give —he was poor.

' If you own this field you are richer than I am,' said I ; ' I have no land.'

' But you have money, or you would not be travelling here.'

---

* *Orchis sambucina.* The other died before I could ascertain its species.

'I earn my bread by writing books, as you earn yours by working in the fields, and I shall put in the one I am writing about this country, that the peasants on the Col d'Aspin want one to pay for the wild-flowers that God has planted there, and which are no use to them. You are the first Frenchman who has ever asked me for such a thing as money for wild-flowers.'

'*N'importe, vous me donnerez ce qu'il vous plaira, mais je veux quelque chose.*'

I felt in my pocket. 'I have only quatre sous,' said I, handing them to him. He took them with half a laugh —saw he had an obstinate woman to deal with—and departed, and we remained to gather gentians, and admire the extreme beauty of the panorama around. Now and then the fleecy clouds of mist rolled off for a moment, but soon from the depths of the valley it came up like a dense grey wall, hiding everything from our sight, and we hastened back to the top of the Col, where our hungry companions, tired of waiting for us, had, as the children informed us, 'dirtied all the plates, and eaten everything up;' which being Englished, meant that *they* had dined. There was plenty left, of course, and we fell to, and the others began by helping us, but the appetite with which we ate, awakened theirs, and they all gathered around, and we had a very merry repast. Our ill-favoured, gaunt, discontented, self-constituted *cicerone*, a woman who was knitting, and five ragged, barefooted boys, standing for full half an hour watching us with curious eyes. I had taken a roast leg of lamb with me, and as no one would help me to eat it, I cut off a large slice and sent it with a roll to the man, by one of the children. Then we sent the remains of the cold chickens, half the lamb, and some bread to our two drivers; and lastly, I called the girl and the five boys, and we gave them the leg of lamb and a long roll, with which they retreated to a stone opposite, where they devoured it, each taking a bite in turn. I suppose they were not possessed of a knife, as I concluded they would be, when I gave it them whole. A gaunt, hungry shepherd's dog came behind us, and ate up the bones we threw away, but drove away a younger and leaner cur than himself, *as human dogs who are beginning to make their way in the world, sometimes drive away still poorer strugglers.*

By the time we had dined, and packed up the dinner things again, the mist had turned to rain. We were glad to have the hoods of our carriages put up, and to drive homewards as fast as we could; but as soon as we began to descend, and left the magnificent prospect which we had *not* seen behind us, the fog and rain lessened. The distant landscape remained veiled, but it was fine around us. We put down the hoods of the carriages, and I and the children got out to gather asphodels. Our English garden asphodel is a very ugly affair, but Pope knew what he was about, when he wrote of—

'Meads of flowery asphodels.'

The asphodels here are a transparent white starry flower, growing on a tall, smooth, green stem, about as thick as my finger; and except that their colour is brown, the un-blown ones resemble a gigantic head of asparagus. They bear a spike of flowers about a yard or a yard and a half high, the lower buds opening first. The flower has six transparent white petals, each of which has a long, narrow, brown line up the middle of the *back* of the petal, but dimly showing through its transparency; and when they are freshly gathered, the orange tips of the stamens reflect, as it were, a kind of flame colour in the centre of the white corolla, which has both a singular and beautiful effect, that I never observed in any other flower, and which it loses, though the tips of the stamens retain their orange hue, after being a day or two in water. The leaves are about the colour of the daffodil leaf, but more pointed, and twice as long and large. When these fields of asphodels are in full bloom, they must be very beautiful. The root is tuberous, and grows precisely like that of a dahlia, only that the tubers are very much smaller, being little thicker than one's finger in the middle, and tapering off to a point.

When we got near Ste. Marie, it was clear and fine, and again *we children*, the old child and the young ones, got out to gather the beautiful blue horned violet in the rich grass meadows. If we had been asked to pay for our flowers here, we could not have grumbled, for we had no right to climb the hedges and get into fields growing for hay; but who could resist such violets? and they do not grow near Bagnères. We got, also, some white narcissi from a stray plant, taken along with manure into the field I suspect, though the narcissus does grow wild near Campan, I believe. We noticed, also, in the meadows hereabouts, great quantities of a little yellow pansy, which some of the party said was very common in Switzerland; orchises fringed the banks, and the beautiful pink-fringed lychnis marked out the course of the meadow runnels; lastly, to crown all, we got some white potentillas, of a kind I had never before seen growing wild.

It was seven o'clock before we drove into Bagnères; the baskets that had held our dinner were full of gentianellas, daffodils, and asphodels. The little children had large bouquets of Alpine violets, and the big child had one hand full of asphodels, and the other of violets, as after setting down her companions, she drove in solitary state to her own door.

'*Quelles belles fleurs vous aviez quand vous revintes du Col d'Aspin!*' said the butcher's wife to me, when I went to buy Keeper's dinner there this morning as usual.

Need I say, that despite fog and rain, I enjoyed my day thoroughly. So did my companions. There was not a look of real vexation, or a cloud on anyone's face the whole day. I never was with a merrier party of big children, and little children. It is good to be children again sometimes, and pleased with small pleasures. Yesterday, at the *Col*, the heat was really oppressive, the air was so close ; to-day it rains heavily, and after shivering half the day in despair, I ordered a fire. There never was such a changeable climate as this, and yet it seems to suit asthma and consumption in the early stages.

CHAPTER XXXI.

My English friends have sometimes inquired of me what
kind of people the Pyreneans were. Here is their
character, as I myself observed it, *and as it is drawn by
French writers.* The peasants are astute, close, and avaricious. They grow rich by saving up *sous*, and often buy
up the property of families who have been expatriated
for political offences, or which has been brought to the
hammer by the extravagance of the owners. But they do
not, upon this, alter their habits or mode of life, as an
English *nouveau-riche* would. The decorations of the
Seignorial *château* fall to pieces, the gilding becomes
tarnished, the paper on the walls hangs in fragments, or
the costly arras, covered with dust and spider-webs,
moulders silently away; the windows remain uncleaned,
and by degrees the panes drop out, and the *parquet* floors
are undusted, unwaxed, and unswept. The new lord and
his family live in the kitchens, and keep their corn in the
richly-decorated *salons* and bedchambers. They breakfast,
as before, on *pâte*, a sort of porridge made of maize flour,
previously grilled in the fryingpan, and dine, except on
fête days, on *soupe aux choux*, or *aux haricots*. The children
run about in wooden *sabots*, or barefooted, and the wife in
a faded, soiled *mouchoir* headdress, and dirty gown, twists
thread from the distaff as she herds the pigs; and yet
that wife brought a fortune to her husband, and each of
her six children will have also from five hundred to a

thousand pounds, while the favourite child will inherit the estate.

'Disinterestedness,' says a French traveller, 'is not a mountain virtue. In a poor country, money is the first necessity. Beggars swarm in the Pyrenees. I never met a child that did not ask alms, from four years old to fifteen; this is their trade, and nobody is ashamed of it.' The same writer gives an amusing instance of their dexterity '*in shearing an egg*.' A friend of his desired the servant to sew a button on to his trowsers. In the evening she entered the room, pantaloons in hand, and said, with an undecided, anxious manner, as if she feared her demand would be disputed, '*C'est un sou*.' The master, without speaking, took a *sou* from his waistcoat pocket, and laid it on the table. Jeannette went on tiptoe to the door, recollected herself, came back, took the trowsers and showed the button. 'Ah! it is a beautiful button! (a pause). I had not one in my box (another, longer pause). I bought that one at the grocer's, *c'est un sou !*' She looked up with anxiety; the owner of the pantaloons, still without speaking, laid on the table a second sou. It was clear there was a mine of sous in that quarter. Jeannette went out, and a moment afterwards re-opened the door; she had settled her plans, and with a shrill, piercing voice, and wonderful volubility, she cried, 'I had no thread. I was obliged to buy thread. I used a great deal of thread; it was very good thread. The button will not come off again, I sewed it on strongly. *C'est un sous*.' The master pushed towards her a third sou. Two hours after, Jeannette, who has reflected on the subject, reappears. She prepares breakfast with minutious care, wipes up the slightest slops, softens her voice, walks gently, and is most ostentatiously attentive; then she says, in the most obsequious and winning manner possible, 'I must not lose —you would not wish me to lose; the stuff was hard, I

broke the point of my needle.   I did not know it before,
I have only just seen it.   *C'est un sou.'*   The master drew
forth the fourth *sou*, repeating—

> ' Ce peuple est innocent : son ingénuité
> N'altère pas encore la simple vérité.'

Take courage, Jeanette, you will gain a fortune, my child.
Happy the husband who shall conduct you, candid and
blushing, under the roof of his ancestors !   Go and brush
my pantaloons.'

'They are as great bargainers as beggars.   You can
scarcely cross a street without meeting a guide who prof-
fers his services to you.   If you are sitting upon a hill,
three or four children, fallen apparently from the clouds,
bring you butterflies, stones, curious plants, or nosegays of
flowers.   If you go near a stable, the proprietor comes out
with a bowl and tries to force you to buy some milk.   I
stood looking one day at a young bull, out came the owner
and wanted to sell it me.' *

Pierre Gaston Sacaze, the shepherd, poet, botanist, and
geologist of Aas, near Eaux-Bonnes, in his *patois* poem—
' A Promenade to Gabas '—relates, ' that being with some
gentlemen on the mountain, they were overtaken by a
sudden and violent storm, which tearing up fir-trees,
beech-trees, and great stones, flung them upon the route,
and rendered it impassable.   The travellers did not know
what to do, the only safe road was through a small meadow
surrounded by stone walls belonging to Jean Doulet.
They turned their horses' heads thither.   Out rushed Jean
Doulet, forbidding them to go through his heritage, and
they were forced to purchase the right of passage *by a
double napoléon.'*

To set against this eagerness for gain, the peasants are
kind and civil to the passing stranger, and seem pleased if

---

* See ' Henri Tain,' a French writer.

one enters into conversation with them. Crime and violence are rare; and I felt no fear when miles away among
the mountains with no guard save Keeper. Was I not
there, as in the city, under the protection of God? They
are often, also, scrupulously honest, notwithstanding their
avidity. Nicolle, after relating that a mountaineer made
him pay ten sous for having walked on his grass at
Bun, relates that the same day a traveller from Eaux-
Chaudes by the Col de Tortes, to Cauterets, being warned
by the clink of metal that the lock of the portmanteau he
carried before him on his horse, had given way, and the
purse within sprung open also, examined both, and found
he had lost twenty-five louis, which he had *sown* along the
road he had traversed. His guide turned back to look for
them. Wherever he passed, the pieces of gold had put the
people on the alert, and as he went on relating what had
occurred, each individual gave up what he had found—
here two pieces, there three—farther on ten, till he had
the whole of the twenty-five in his hand. And all these
people were poor, hard-working peasants, who found it
difficult to gain bread.

'How lucky you were,' said some one to the guide.

'Bah!' replied he; 'I knew I should find them.'

He could not have given his compatriots higher praise.

Deville speaks of their love of bargaining. 'When a
father, who has marriageable daughters, observes a lad
paying attention to one of them, he asks his intentions,
and if the word marriage is pronounced, goes at once to
the young man's father to inform him of what has occurred. If he approves the match, both parents go to a
ca'aret, pour vider la bouteille, and it is while striking the
glasses together, in sign of good fellowship, that they
settle what each will give his child, and conclude the affair.
When the principal points are arranged, a day is named
for signing the contract. On the day appointed the friends
and neighbours of both families meet together, and the

dot is agreed upon.   Here the most comical discussions arise.   Every object, every piece of cloth, which is to form part of the household linen of the future bride, is the cause of contention.   There is a battle about every rag and *chiffon,* and a marriage is often broken off, because an apron, or a pair of *sabots,* is refused.   I was witness to one such rupture.   A young man and girl were to be married, and all the preparations had been made, when they came together to Tarbes to buy the wedding-ring.   The girl wanted a gold one, the young man thought silver good enough.   A discussion arose between them, and the wedding was broken off for four francs.   On another occasion, when the contract was signed, the mother of the bridegroom bethought herself of counting over the linen of the bride.   A towel was wanting.   She counted again, it was certainly missing.   There were reclamations on one side, and evasive replies on the part of the girl's mother, who, to shorten the discussion, added, that if they were not satisfied with what there was, the marriage should not take place.   Both parties rose, and were about to separate, when the notary solved the difficulty by saying *He* would give the towel.   He actually gave it, and thus a marriage was concluded, which had been on the eve of being broken off for thirty sous (about fifteenpence).'

'The godmother of the bride is expected to give the wedding-shift, which is generally very pretty, being trimmed at the hem with lace or flounces, according to the fortune of the giver and the receiver.   The eight days before the grand day are spent in preparations for the feast, which are ordinarily very ample.   The direction of it is usually confided to the Curé's housekeeper, or the cook of some rich countryman.   Rich peasants send for a cook from the nearest town.   It is a great affair to them.   Most of them date their existence from their wedding repast.   Events, age, *nothing* effaces *that day* from their memory.   It is the stand-point of comparison for all the succeeding feasts at which they may assist, and even very old people remember its most insignificant details. As soon as the destined day dawns, the village fiddlers hasten under the bride's windows, and serenade her with village airs. Officious girls also join her, after having laid all the neighbouring gardens under contribution for wedding bouquets, to give the coming guests. When the bride's toilet is completed, which does not take long, as there is no luxury of dress among our mountaineers, the *nobi** and the *nobie*, each conducted by their godfather and godmother, armed with huge bouquets, repair first to the Mairie, and thence to church, followed by the wedding train, marching two and two, each donzellon giving his arm to his donzelle. The Curé unites the couple, and afterwards preached to them a sermon in *patois* which he received from his predecessor, who received it from his, who had it from the one he succeeded, to whom also it had been transmitted.'

' When the ceremony is over, the party return to the bride's house, and on entering she takes a plate which she holds between her hands, kneeling modestly on a chair or stool placed for her. The husband advances first, traces a cross upon her forehead with some pieces of money which he holds in the right hand, kisses her on each cheek, and puts his offering into the plate. Each of the assistants then gives the two kisses, and pays tribute; and the collection thus made is generally abundant, especially if the parties are much beloved. The money serves to defray the expenses of the feast. When all have given, and the *nobie* is *étrenné*,† the party sit down to the festival. Two

---

* Dead godfathers or godmothers are replaced by substitutes. The groom is called *nobi*, the bride *nobie*. While the wedding festivities last every young man invited is called *donzellon*, every young girl *donzelle.* It will be seen that the Bigorrais wedding customs somewhat differ from those of Béarn.

† *Etrenné*, given gifts, equivalent to our Yorkshire handselled.

badly-joined planks placed upon stakes driven into the floor, and covered with a resplendent white cloth, form the table, and are loaded with dishes enough for four times the number of guests assembled. Six chairs placed on each side, and two at the ends, support other planks on which the party take their seats, the seat of honour being reserved for the Curé, when he vouchsafes to assist. As the peasants do not understand the art of carving, and the meat is generally tough, any citizen invited, or the *Régent* (or schoolmaster), the first person in the village after the Maire and the Curé, is charged with this office, as it is supposed he must be genteel enough to know how to acquit himself properly of this onerous duty. Unhappy man! No sooner has he served round the *bouilli*, than a neighbour asks for a little fricassee. He helps to some, and at once most of the company hold out their plates. The fricassee despatched, he hopes for a little respite, no such thing—some one who has refused fricassee, wants a chicken leg, and by the time it is cut off, all the empty plates of the fricassee eaters fly back for something else. The poor carver has not swallowed a mouthful, while the rest have partaken of five or six dishes. His only chance is to seize the moment while they are drinking—when the good wine cheering all hearts makes their tongues wag. Then he hurriedly repairs lost time by vigorously attacking the remains of the dishes which he has taken care to heap around him. As the repast goes on, the gaiety increases, but it is rarely that it passes the bounds of decency. The Curé, who is generally present on these occasions, would be offended at any such breach of good manners, and soon put a stop to it. Wine is not spared. But there is no intemperance. After dinner everyone rises, and each donzellon giving his arm to his donzelle, the party *promenade* round the village while some place is prepared for the dance, which is to terminate the festival, and to which amusement they all give themselves up with thorough and hearty enjoyment.

Some Curés object to dancing, innocent as this diversion is, but in vain. The flock regret to go against the commands of their pastor, but dance none the less.

In cases of a second marriage, the *caillaouari* (*charivari*) takes place nightly before the intended bridegroom's house, for a week or a fortnight, and he is happy if he does not also find his door hung with horns. A man of the department *des Hautes Pyrénées*, who re-married within a month of his first wife's death, was obliged to pay a hundred and fifty francs to his tormentors, before he could get rid of the frightful noises made every night before his doors. It is supposed that this custom had its origin in times when there were fewer women, and when each man wishing for a helpmate, he who took more than his share, was held up to shame and reprobation.

Man is physically stronger than woman, and this physical force is sometimes wrongly used, and a man beats his wife, 'which,' says Deville, 'although not according to strict rules of propriety and right feeling, has in it *nothing unnatural*, or contrary to the law of Nature, which seems to indicate that the weaker shall succumb to the stronger, but the laws of Nature are reversed, when the opposite case occurs, and the wife thrashes her husband. How is this abuse to be suppressed? To punish the wife does not appear noble to the Bigourdans, for while disapproving the violation of the bond between husband and wife, they cannot help admiring her courage and audacity. They prefer, therefore, to shame the weak and craven husband, who has submitted to such chastisement. Whenever it is publicly known that a husband has allowed his wife to beat him, those who are in his own rank of life, meet in masquerade on the public *place*, and send a deputation to the house of

z

the victim, which conducts him to the meeting.   There
they blacken his face with charcoal, and mount him on an
ass with his face to the tail, which they oblige him to take
in his hands.   In this fashion a man leads the ass through
all the streets, the rider being received everywhere with
shouts of contempt and derision, the *cortége* stopping every
now and then to sing, through speaking trumpets, a *patois*
song alluding to the circumstance, whose burthen is *Eh !
rou lan la l'azou qué courrera*.   This farce was particularly
common during the three last days of the carnival.   The
authorities have taken steps to put an end to it, and it is of
late years more rarely practised, and only in the villages.'

In 1818, when Deville wrote, and even it may be said in 1863, since I saw in a journal, while resident at Bagnères, the trial of two women for beating a third, whom they supposed to have cast a spell upon the child of one of them, sorcery was still an article of faith among the Pyreneans. 'Nothing,' says he, 'is at once more amusing or more painful than to listen to the conversation of five or six women collected round the burning brands, while the boys and girls of the village listen open-mouthed. Jeanne relates, that going one day to market, she could not return home until very late, and as she left the town she saw a pretty little white cat, which she fancied had lost itself, and resolved to have it. She caught it, wrapped it up in a table-cloth, and put it under her arm to bring home. She was rejoicing in her find, when lo! just as she reached the village and was exactly opposite the house of a woman who was well known to be a *bronche* (a witch), she felt the cat loosen itself from her arms, and spring lightly on the ground, saying, in a very soft voice, "*Thank you, Jeanne;*" and how, half-dead with fear, she ran as fast as she could to her own home, and told her husband, who was as sure as she was, that the little white cat was neither more nor less than a *bronche.*'

'Marie, in her turn, relates, that she knows from one of her friends, that some time ago a woman in a neighbouring village being forced *de faire au four* (a provincialism for baking), early, got up about midnight, or half-past, opened her bedroom door and crossed the yard, when lo! in the moonlight she saw the form of an immense dog, which rising on its hind feet advanced towards her to seize her with its fore paws. At this sight her hair stood on end, a cold sweat covered her body, and her knees seemed to bend under her. She could not cry out, much as she wished to do so; however, she had yet strength to drag herself to her room, when with much difficulty (for she was so frightened she could scarcely speak), she related what she had just seen to her husband. He got up directly, loaded his gun with a good charge of powder, and two balls made of the wax of a paschal candle,* went out, fired at the *loup-garou,* and brought him to the ground. What was his astonishment when going up to the place where he was lying, he found, instead of the immense dog that he had seen sweeping the ground with his tail, a man lying there all his length, whom he recognized as a neighbour, and who said, in a pitiful voice, "*I am much obliged to you, neighbour—you have saved me from a sore thrall.*"†

'Lastly, Annette, who never doubted that there were sorcerers for a moment, and wishes to convince her auditors of the fact also, tells them that a woman she knew had the misfortune to have one of her daughters taken to a sabbath by a witch, and this is exactly what the little girl related the next morning. The witch, after having frequently caressed her and given her sugar-plums, coaxed her one day into her room under pretext of giving her a doll, but really with intent to enlist her into the service of Belzebub; for as soon as they got there, forgetting her promised gift, she asked instead if she would like to go to a dance. On her saying yes, the witch went to the hearth, lifted up one of the bricks and took from underneath a pot of very white ointment. After having washed herself, she put some of

---

* A bullet made of a paschal candle is *infallible* against were-wolves.
† *i.e.,* you have delivered me from the power of evil spirits.

this grease on the end of her finger and anointed her own hands and those of the little girl. This operation performed, she put the pot back into its place, and all at once they both found themselves transported to the spot where the witch's sabbath is held, having both passed through the key-hole of the door. It was a great hall, in which she recognized many persons no one would have suspected of being there. The devil, dressed in red, with two horns of enormous size overshadowing his forehead, presided over the assembly, and received them both with marked attention. He inquired what would give them pleasure, and promised to grant them everything they could desire, provided they were faithful. Each took an oath to be so, and then they all gave themselves up to joy and revelry, which did not finish till one of Monsieur Satan's *corps* announced that day was dawning, when each person returned home by the same way they had come.'*

'About two years ago,' says Deville, further on, ' a woman died at Tarbes, in the firm conviction that she was bewitched, because she was almost completely paralyzed. During her illness, she tried all sorts of extraordinary means to discover the sorcerer. Whenever any one visited her, the servant instantly reared the broom behind the door in such a manner that the twigs or the hairs were uppermost, and the end of the handle upon the floor. This would prevent the guest from going out again, if she was a witch. A person who told fortunes by cards had taught her a number of uncouth magic words, which she made every one repeat who visited her, being quite persuaded that whoever could not say them after her was a witch. One day an empiric gave her a singular remedy against witchcraft. He ordered one of her petticoats to be suspended before the door of her house. Two women, armed

* C. Deville's 'Annales de la Bigorre,' 1818.

with rods, were then commanded to beat it till some one should ask why they beat it so ? None but the sorcerer could make that demand. The floggers set to work, and the rods fell upon the unhappy petticoat with a rapidity beyond belief; but as nobody asked wherefore, they got tired, and were obliged to leave off, and the bewitcher remained unknown. After this poor woman's death, some of her friends who had shared her belief, opened her featherbed to see if it contained the charm which had caused her death, "when," said one of them, "to our great surprise we found a crown of beautifully variegated feathers,* of a thousand colours." These plumes were so artistically joined, without anyone being able to perceive what held them together, that they were sure it was the effect of diabolic art, and that the deceased had died from the practice of wicked arts. Unable to recall her to life, they resolved in some manner to avenge her on her hidden enemies by burning their work. And to render this vengeance more complete, they selected the hour when the hideous crew of witches are believed to attend their sabbath, as well as a spot where four roads met.'

'Having put the feather-crown in a paper bag, and furnished themselves with a fagot and a few handfuls of straw, they set out towards midnight to the place. They laid the fire, amid signs of the cross and amens, put the enchanted crown upon the log, and lit it with a wax candle that had been blessed, which they took on purpose, and as soon as the straw was fairly in a blaze they ran away as fast as their legs could carry them, frightened at their own temerity. Having run about thirty yards, they turned for a moment to look at their sacrifice; the flames which rose into the air made them hope it would be consumed; and

---

* It is usual in France to *wax* the ticking of a featherbed.' The heat of the sick woman's body had melted the wax, and thus stuck the feathers together.

they regained their homes content. But as soon as daylight came, they returned once more to the sacrificial spot, and to their astonishment found the sac of paper, with its contents, untouched in the midst of the cinders, and not even singed. Frightened to death at the sight, they both ran away, more firmly persuaded than ever of the power of sorcerers.'

The Bigorrais are very fond of dancing, and excel in the art. During the Carnival, the young men and maidens meet every Sunday in some of the meadows to dance to the sound of the *tambourin*. This is not the instrument we call a tambourine, but a sort of lute with six strings. The player performs on it by striking it with a short stick, made on purpose, with his right hand, while his left holds a fife, which he blows at the same time. Sometimes there is a fiddler instead, and sometimes both these kinds of music. I cannot say much in favour of the fife and *tambourin*, the two together produce a squeaking, dismal sound, far worse than that of a bad fiddle badly played. However, they serve to mark the time of the dances. In most countries the *gentleman* pays for the *lady*. 'In many parts of Bigorre,' says Deville, 'and especially in the valley of *Azun*, it is the girls who pay the fiddlers, and they also invite the cavaliers to dance. It often happens, likewise, that when the girls go to the public-house, which they sometimes do (but only among the mountains), the lady pays for her lover, instead of his paying for her.'

Another favourite amusement of the Bigorrais, is, *La Pastorale*. *La Pastorale* consists in acting plays, and the peasants' mode of doing this appears to resemble that of Bottom and his companions. It is Voltaire's tragedies that are chiefly in favour; an honour on which he hardly calculated when he wrote them.

The young men's amusements are, throwing the hatchet, a large stone, or an iron bar. Every Sunday after vespers, they collect in some spot beyond the village, and challenge one another to feats of strength. Each puts down ten or fifteen *sous*, and the sum thus collected goes to the most adroit—he who has many times thrown the bar, axe, or stone, the farthest. Ninepins seems also a favourite game; and to English eyes there is something rather absurd in seeing a set of grown men—and often two or three young women among them—bowling down immense ninepins. The French are more easily amused than we are. I have often on Sundays seen grown men playing at ball in the street.

Pilgrimages are still fashionable among the peasants in most parts of France; and if Deville's account be true, and he says he speaks from actual observation, ought to be put down by law, as leading to demoralization. *Héas* and *Betharam* are two of the favourite shrines. The devotions last two days; and so many people congregate, that even by putting them pell-mell together, in the houses of the neighbouring villages, two or three thousand persons remain without a place to rest in. They pass the night in the meadows, under the trees, and even in the streets, joining together in groups of four, six, or eight.

The pilgrims almost always go in couples, a man and a woman together; and the journey, amid religious and profane songs, is as gay as can well be imagined. The *pélerine* takes the arm of the *pélerin*, on setting out, and does not quit it till their return home; such a degree of intimacy reigning between them, that they even share the same couch. 'I have seen,' says Deville, 'scenes which decency does not permit me to recall to my readers.'

'There is a fountain at Betharam, which, according to tradition and popular belief, cures all diseases; but its waters have only a temporary virtue. They are only remedial twice in the year. On the 23rd of June, at midnight, when the dew falls heaviest, and the air is in-

supportably cool, those who believe in its efficacy plunge
into the water, or bathe the part affected with a linen rag,
which they afterwards hang as a memento on the neighbouring brambles. Without this last formality the waters
would be useless. The consequence of these immersions
is, that he who was paralyzed in one arm becomes paralyzed in his whole body. On the 8th of September, at
midday, is the other time when pilgrims visit the fountain. The road leading to it is exposed to a burning sun,
the pilgrims arrived bathed in perspiration, and in that
state uncover themselves to apply the wet rags, or to bathe
in the fountain. Deville saw there an octogenarian, who
was rheumatic in the shoulders from age, and had also
some pain in the chest. She had journeyed to the Holy
Well in hopes of cure, and was just taking off her shift to
bathe in it, when he represented the danger she was incurring so forcibly, that she desisted. I do not doubt,'
says he, 'that her sudden death would have been the
result, had she persisted.'

What the Americans call a 'husking frolic,' is another
amusement of the Pyrenean peasant farmers and their
families. They meet at one another's houses to strip the
maize cobs of their husks, spend a merry evening in the
operation, and return to their village in bands late at
night, singing the part-songs in which they so much excel.
' It is delightful,' said a *Bagnerais* to me, ' as one walks
home from a friend's house on a fine autumnal evening, to
hear the sweet, plaintive, or joyous songs of the returning
maize-huskers in the distance, blending with the ripple of
water, the rustle of the breeze through the trees, and the
wild wail of the wind.'

THE *patois* of Bigorre differs considerably from that of Béarn, which is far more liquid and sweet; but both are true and very rich languages, not mere dialects.

'The *patois* spoken in Bigorre,' says Deville, 'is a corruption of the old Roman language, with a considerable sprinkling of Greek and Celtic words. It is sonorous, rapid, beautifully expressive, and very imaginative. More liquid than the French, because many of the words are formed chiefly of vowels, and *every* letter is pronounced; it is the language of every-day life. It is spoken in the markets, in fields, in families, and even in society, when strangers are not present, by the gentleman as well as the peasant. The peasant's children learn a little French at school, but it is always a foreign language to them. In the idiomatic *patois* they are at home. It is the language of their childhood, the first sounds that struck their baby-ears.'

I found it no easy matter to obtain any of the popular airs of the Pyrenees, with the words adapted to them. The people learn them in infancy from their mother's lips, and by far the greater part are not even noted down, but transmitted orally from one generation to another. They have a wonderful talent for music, which seems to come as naturally to them as speech to others, and an equal talent (as I was told) for improvised verses. Every event that takes place in a village becomes the subject of song and verse. If it is ludicrous or disgraceful, it brings down a *caillaouri*, or *charivari*; if it is of a sorrowful or pathetic nature, it will be handed down to posterity by means of a mournful air.

I inquired at all the music shops for Pyrenean songs, but without success. I asked my few French acquaintance, but in vain; until M. Frossard, the excellent French Protestant pastor of Bagnères, who is also a man of the most varied acquirements, a scientific geologist, an eloquent preacher and writer, and a clever artist, procured for me from a literary friend, a copy of '*Rivarès' Chansons Populaires de Béarn*,' a work long since out of print. From this book I chiefly derived the music and songs contained in this work. A few others were procured for me by the kindness of other friends.

Rivarès (a *Béarnais*) calls his collection ' *Chansons Populaires de Béarn*,'* but they are quite as popular in Bigorre; and Despourrins, the Burns of the Pyrenees, was born at *Accous*, which I believe is in Bigorre, and not in Béarn.

I have selected from his work those airs which seemed most commonly sung; and of these, the beautiful one of ' *Les haut sus las Montagnes*,' seems the greatest favourite with all ranks of Pyreneans. Many of the songs to which these airs are adapted are real poetry; and as Rivarès gave a French translation of all those he published, I was enabled to translate a few of them. In all those of which

---

* It is really a pity that so interesting and charming a book should not be reprinted. M. Rivarès is clearly a man of great taste and genius, and by collecting these fugitive songs and their music has conferred a great boon upon his country. But there are numerous other songs and airs of which no collection has been made : and it is to be lamented that good grammars and dictionaries of the various old idioms of France (several of which are not merely *dialects*, but real languages, as the Béarnais and the Bigorrais) should yet be a desideratum. I wonder that great linguist, Prince Lucien Bonaparte, does not turn his attention to the publication of good grammars and dictionaries of the various French languages, instead of publishing the song of Solomon in the different English dialects, much as I, a Yorkshire woman, and a great admirer of the raciness of that familiar speech, feel glad that his Royal Highness should have felt interested in printing specimens of that and our other country dialects.

I have given the music, I have endeavoured to preserve the *metre* of the originals. In those selected as exemplifying local customs, or for their poetic beauty, I have been obliged to take a few liberties. *A single word in patois will express a whole sentence*, and had I strictly adhered to the measure, that which was beautiful in the original would have become mere doggerel in a literal English translation. I have done the best *I could*—if not the best that could be done; and I must beg my readers to have patience with me, remembering my difficulties were great. I had no great means to spend in prosecuting my researches, and buying books, and I found it impossible to procure a good grammar, while no *patois* dictionary is yet published, and I did not remain long enough in the country, or mix sufficiently with the people, to acquire their language orally. I think, however, I have done enough to prove to my readers that there are great treasures of true poetry and exquisite melody hidden, like the wild flowers, among the sequestered mountains and valleys of Béarn and Bigorre.

LAS HAUT SUS LAS MONTAGNES.*

By Despourrins.

On the Mountains Above.

A shepherd forlorn on the mountains above†
Sat bitterly weeping, beneath the beech grove,
And bemoaning the change that had come o'er his love.

'Light heart! wandering heart!' moaned the lover forlorn;
'All my love, and the tenderness of that love born—
Was it these, cruel maid, that drew on me thy scorn?

'Since thou 'midst the great art accustomed to go
My poor little cot, in the valley below,
For thy high-flying thoughts is a story too low.

---

* The literal translation of Las haut sus las Montagnes is, 'There high up on the mountains.' A peculiar favourite with the Pyreneans.
† The measure imitated from the original.

'The time when we herded together is o'er ;
Thy proud sheep with mine will mingle no more,
Or come near, with their horns, but to topple them o'er.

'Of riches I boast not, nor honour, nor birth ;
I am but a shepherd.   But are riches worth
The true love that has not its equal on earth ?

' And poor as I am, love, and mean, and all that,
I'd not give my old bonnet, so shabby and flat,
For any proud gentleman's finely-laced hat.

' The riches of this world bring sorrows untold ;
And the finest young lord, with his silver and gold,
Has not more than the shepherd content with his fold.

' Farewell, tigress hearted ! without love—go find
Some rich and great suitor that's more to thy mind.
Thou wilt ne'er meet another so faithful and kind ! '

BEROUYINE, CHARMANTINE.

DESPOURRINS.

My beautiful, my charming one,
My heart's delight, my sun ;
Oh, wherefore so much rigour show,
    My gentle dove !
Wherefore such bitter looks bestow
    Upon thine own true love ?

The little Loves are flying round thee :
Nought on earth can drive them from thee !
Round thee fluttering, night and day,
    They try thy heart to move ;
Thou wilt not listen what they say—
    Thou wilt not love !

The Pleasures to thee offer feasts—
Sweet Smiles are their invited guests ;
And on thy lips and eyes would stay,—
    Sweet company !
But from thy heart, if driven away,
    Will doleful be.

That thou may'st know how dear to all
Thou art, flowers for thy festival
Are gathered, and the sweet-toned flute
    Awakes the vale :
But, if thy heart remaineth mute,
    With what avail !

How can'st thou be so proud, who art
Well known to have a gentle heart?
Alas ! in vain the God of Love
    Thy beauty gave ;—
If nought thy icy heart can move
    To pity those it doth enslave !

Farewell, dear maid,—good night !
Within thy heart, oh might
Him whom thy scorn has grieved, be placed,
    By some soft dream in sleep,
That wakening thou may'st love at last
    Him who for thee doth vigil keep ! '

THERE'S A YOUNG LAD I'VE MET.

DESPOURRINS.

There's a young lad I've met, and the handsomest youth
    In the village, who pays me his court :
His heart undivided, his faith, and his troth,
    He has sworn me a hundred times over, in short.

The neighbouring girls may be fair—but it's me
    He prefers ; not the least complaisance
Does he ever show to them.   His manners are free.
    He treats them with indifference.

He brings me each morn violets wet with dew showers ;
    He scatters my pathway with armfuls* of flowers ;
And if I should e'er be o'ertaken by sleep,
    No harm comes to my flock, for he watches my sheep.

He has always, to please me, new songs, as a treat ;
    He can play the flute deftly : his voice is so sweet—
How pleasant the time will with him pass away—
    Never dreary or dull—but a year like a day.

---

* Armfuls in the original.

The moment he's leisure, the instant he's free,
  He leaps rocks and streamlets to hasten to me ;
He has no wish to wander—he's fond of his chains—
  And delights to share with me my joys and my pains.

When I see his soft looks I feel fainting with love,
  If ten thousand lads sought me still faithful I'd prove.
I'd fain offend none, but go search through the town :
  He's the King of the Shepherds, and shall have the crown!

A FUNERAL DIRGE.

CHANTED BY MARIE LA BLAGUE (THE FAIR).

From Icherauna I came down :
  I know not by what road I pass'd.
I could not see that pathway lone,
  Cousin, in hastening here so fast.

I reached, at last, the open plain :
  I heard the church bell toll :—
'Is it to-day the feast of some saint ? '—
  ' It is for thy cousin's soul.'

' This night I left my home,
  Where I ought to have been—not here.
They are burning charcoal at home ;
  There is no dishonour there—

' No dishonour in earning their bread :
  As the priest his—by mass and prayer.'
(*Before the house.*)
  ' Ho ! cousin ! where have they made thy bed ?
  Those who long wished to see thee there ! '

The maid servant was sweeping up manure in the courtyard at the time Marie entered it.)
  ' Where is the graceless wench
  Who works on a day like this ?
For shame and decency's sake, methinks,
  Thy Sunday's hood had not been amiss ! '

The widower, to make her keep silence.)
  ' Where is the widower sad—
  Who has never let fall a tear ?
Of consolation he has no need ;
  He wished for this many a year ! '

'This sacred wedded room
   For nine months she never came nigh
Until she entered it yester morn—
   Entered it—but to die!'

(*It was reported she had been killed by a blow with a chair.*)
   'This silent murdering chair
     Accuses no one—none!—
   Don't wipe the ground so, there;
     The blood shows what thou'st done!'

(*Before the corpse.*)
    'Bring me a linen winding sheet!
     That for the dead—not silk—is meet.
    Piteous your state, cousin so wan;
     You, who were wife to a holy* man!'

(*The husband's property had belonged to an abbey.*)
    'For being an abbot's lady gay
     Your cheeks are hollow and pale to-day.'

(*The curate is before the house.*)
    'Sir priest! the son of old Bedous,
     Look here—reflect—see justice done!
    Send for the justice! Look not thus,
     For here there has been cruel wrong.'

    'From Peyronère to Oleron
     Never before such deed was done;
    From Oleron to Peyronère
     Never was done a deed so drear.'

(*The funeral train begins its march.*)
    'While I was on the abbot's ground
     I spoke not a word—breathed not a sound;
    But now that I am in the open street
     I call him adulterer—as is meet.'

(*The curate tries to silence her.*)
    'Pray God, you who can do it, and keep
    Silence, and let the afflicted weep.'

(*The curate insists on her silence, and pushes her with the cross.*)
    'Sir priest! sir priest! if you feared God
    You would not make of the cross a rod.'

---

* She calls the husband a holy man ironically, because his lands had formerly belonged to a monastery, for which reason he was nicknamed the abbot.

(The curate—' Let us say the prayers for the dead.')

    ' Sir priest, the curate of little winning,*
      Asks a farthing for every prayer he'll say ;
      If he hears in the dish no money ring,
      Not a pater he'll mutter to-day.'

(Before the grave.)

    ' Farewell, cousin ! a long adieu :
      Without farewell you have left me here,
      But I've a thing to beg of you :
      Give my love to my mother dear ;
      And God grant that she be with you this night,
      In the realms of endless joy and delight.'

SONG BY GASTON PHŒBUS, COUNT DE FOIX.†

CONTEMPORARY OF EDWARD THE BLACK PRINCE.

    These mountains rising so high above,
        Lullaby,
        La, la !
    Forbid me to see where dwells my love,
        Lullaby,
        La, la !

    If I hoped to see her, or meet on the heath,
        Lullaby,
        La, la !
    I would swim the wide river, fearless of death,
        Lullaby,
        La, la !

    These mountain heights will seem to lower,
        Lullaby,
        La, la !
    As I draw nigher to my lover,
        Lullaby,
        La, la !

---

* ' Gain-petit, little winning.' Marie calls the curé by this name ironi-cally, implying he is priest of a very poor parish. The money to pay for a funeral is collected in a dish.

† The air of this song is celebrated as very beautiful by all the French writers. I cannot say so much for the words, but I have rendered them as exactly as I could, and as nearly as possible in the same metre.

MOUN DONS AMIE S'EN BA PARTY.

DESPOURRINS.

_____

MY GENTLE LOVE IS LEAVING ME.*

My gentle love is leaving me ;
　He goes to La Rochelle.
What shall I do, left here alone ?
　Oh, cruel soldiers tell.
Oh ! I shall die, thus forced to part
From him who was my life and heart.

Wit and good manners both he had—
　And had abundantly ;
My shepherd was a handsome lad—
　The flower of shepherds he.
He stepped so stately in the dance :
He has not left his like in France.

Upon the day he drew the lot †
　He said to me, 'My fair,
To serve my lord the king were joy,
　Except for thy despair.
Thy tears, my darling, break my heart,
And make it worse than death to part.'

Then kissing me he said, with eyes
　Brimful of tears, 'Good night !
Remember, sweet, thy faithful love
　Who goes in arms to fight,
In hopes by gallant deeds to prove
Worthy the treasure of thy love.'

Of lovers the most loving, I—
　Unhappy girl—have lost ;
And without pleasure, life, or love,
　Must my best days be passed.
Flowers and ribbons, all adieu,
I am alone—and need not you !

The scissors that my love gave me,
　And the gold ring so gay,
Safe in my breast I carry them
　Hid since that fatal day.
I water them with tears each day,
Until my tears all dry away.

_____

* The measure is imitated from the original.
† Was drawn by lot for a soldier, according to the French law.

Great God! who seest my heavy grief,
  And knowest my heart is sore,
Oh, give that saddened heart relief—
  My bonny love restore.
Let me but see his face again,
  And when thou wilt—take Madelaine!

LA PLUS CHARMANTE ANESQUETTE.*

DESPOURRINS.

THE CHARMING EWE LAMB.

For the charming ewe lamb lost,
  Shepherds, come and comfort me;
Not long since gambolling on the grass,
  Not now in my fold—ah! me!
Ah! some savage beast of prey
  Has carried her from me away;
Or perhaps the foolish thing
  Wants to see me following.

I kept her in the meadow green
  In the sweet time of flowers;
She was my favourite of the flock—
  I petted her for hours!
With kisses ate her up—was none
  Caressed like that beloved one:
And, as the most beloved and dear,
  Handfuls of salt I gave to her.†

Of all my flock, so beautiful,
  She was the flower and pride;
And those who saw how fine her wool,
  'Thou happy shepherd!' cried.
But, alas! I lost my lamb!
  If not restored, too sure I am
My heart will be so full of sorrow
  That I, too, shall die to-morrow.

---

* The measure imitated from the original.
† The Pyrenean sheep will follow the shepherd all over the field for salt, which is frequently given to them, and of which they are exceedingly fond.

Wander, sheep, then, where ye will ;
　Quit your wretched shepherd's side ;
There's the salt-bag, here's the crook—
　Heaven give you pastures green and wide !
In the meadows down below,
　Brother shepherds of the plain,
If you meet my wandering ewe
　Bring her to my fold again.

Echo ! who repeatest still
　The sad sounds of my complaint,
Tell me on what rock or hill
　I shall find the joy I want.
Rocks are not so hard but they
　Would my sorrow do away ;
And could they my grief but know
　Would have pity on my woe.

DE CAP A TU SOY MARION.*

DESPOURRINS.

I'M THINE FOR EVER, MARION.

I'm thine for ever, Marion ! †
By thy gentle manners won :
Bound captive from the hour we met—
　　　So softly, oh !
　　　So sweetly, oh !
That I am in torment yet ;
And will thee, nill thee, I must love,
Till the grass grows my head above.

Never feel I such a pleasure
As when I can see my treasure.
When those charming eyes I spy,
　　　Softly smiling,
　　　And beguiling,
Ah ! for love of them I die !
And when thou speak'st, the dulcet sound
Deeper yet my heart doth wound.

* The title literally means, ' From the *head* I am all thine, Marion.'
† The measure of the verses is imitated from the original, on account of the music.

No fine palace can I give,
But a cot where thou may'st live ;
No rich buildings there will be ;
　　　No ornament,
　　　Save hearts content :
Brave folks content with poverty.
But ah ! within that little cell
What happiness and peace will dwell !

Can we not live contented, sweet ?
Unenvious of the rich or great ?
No life a shepherd's life can match !
　　　His sheep he feeds,
　　　Has all he needs,
And from each hour some joy doth snatch !
And when his flock's safe in the fold,
He straight forgets the storm and cold.

My God ! how sweet my life would prove
If thou wouldst but accept my love.
No king would be so blest as me !
　　　Thee I'd obey,
　　　And love alway,
Ever still caressing thee
So much, that thou wouldst try in vain
Not to love me in turn again !

———

A NOËL OR CHRISTMAS CAROL (PARAPHRASED).*

By ANDICHON.

The Angel.

Shepherds, rise—the Lord doth call !
To your Saviour hasten, all.
The God of thunder gives you peace !
Henceforth sin and war shall cease !

———

* The measure of this Noël was so irregular, that in English it would
have sounded like a mockery of holy things. It is a characteristic of Pyrenean poetry to vary the lines from long to short. The *sense* of the lines is
strictly adhered to. In the original the angel speaks in French, the shepherd replies in *patois*.

Shepherd.

Leave me quiet—let me dream—
Trouble not my wearied brain !
Leave me quiet—let me dream—
On thy journey go again.
Of no sentinel I've need :
What to me's thy news, indeed ?
Leave me quiet—let me dream !

The Angel.

Who can sleep, when God doth make
Such new wonders?   Thou must wake.
Join thy songs to ours ;—let earth
Echo back our thankful mirth.

Shepherd.

Leave me, once again I pray.
If thou mak'st me leave my bed—
Leave me, once again I pray,
Lest I make thee run with speed.
If I leave my bed, indeed,
Thou in vain for grace may'st plead !
Leave me, once again, I pray !

The Angel.

Hither come ; your homage bring
To this new-born babe, your king !
To the Saviour, as a gift,
Those proud stubborn hearts uplift.
Fearless rise, nor heed your rest,
Nor sorrow more, for ye are blest.

Shepherd.

Blest ! that can we never be !
Bliss is not for such as we !
Sad and dreary is our lot :
To poor shepherds joy comes not.
What strange jesting may be this,
That a child should bring us bliss ?

The Angel.

His soft voice shall kings obey ;
Demons fierce confess his sway ;
Hell her weapons shall lay down
Before the Conqueror, on His throne.
To the Redeemer's sweetness bow
The strong heart, the lofty brow.

Shepherd.

I will rise; but take thou heed,
If thou boastest false indeed,
Thou perhaps may'st chance to find
That which is not to thy mind.
Worthy men break no one's rest
For a silly joke at best.
I will rise; but take thou heed,
If thou boast, thou'lt pity need!

The Angel.

Open, then, those half-closed eyes;
Look up, behold the opening skies!
See what light is flooding earth:
Hear the songs of cherub mirth.
The God of mercy breaks man's chains;
His hand shuts out both sin and pain!

Shepherd.

God! what see I? What a sight!
Is that Heaven that shines so bright?
Ah! a Saviour must appear
Since God's kingdom seems so near!
Heaven opens! I must be
Saved from death—from sin set free!

The Angel.

Hither come and banish fear;
Doubt no longer—hasten here!
Your defence—beneath your eyes—
New born, unlocks to you the skies:
Doth your innocence restore,
That ye may be blest once more.

Shepherd.

Yet I fear—for mortal ear
Never yet such strains did hear.
Yet I fear—so many run
To that village farther on.
When I see their ardent zeal
I fear; strange tremors o'er me steal.

The Angel.

In that village, poor and mean,
Christ, the Holy Child, is seen.
By His poverty He teaches—
You the lessons that He preaches.
He a manger chose that ye,
O men! might learn humility.

Shepherd.

Ha! What sayest thou? It can
Never be believed by man!
What will all those shepherds do,
If they find the Saviour so?
Ah! Great God! Who will be able
To see the Godhead in a stable?
Ah! What sayest thou? Can it be
That Christ puts on humanity?

The Angel.

He that has a faithful heart
Believes that which I impart;
But the rebel stands aloof—
Questions, doubts, and asks for proof.
If you would believe, go seek
Him of whom the Scriptures speak.
Wait no more, but seek the Child
Whom God and man hath reconciled!

Shepherd.

Farewell, angel! I will haste
Where the little Child is placed.
If my speech and thoughts were wrong
I shall know it before long.
Farewell, angel! There's the star
That has guided us from far.

CANZON D'ESTELLE.*

Roussignoulets atay sat bous,
     Prado per zou sies pas plus bero,
Margalidettes, parpallous
     Sarneats pas les oueils d'Estelle

---

* I give this song because the air is very pretty. I am not, however,
sure that the words are either Béarnais or Bigorrais patois; on the contrary, I believe them to be Gascon. The Countess of Carnwath kindly
copied the music for me.

Ey perdet le plus bel pastourel,
  Que fasio moun bonnier pécaire
Qui ferez comme l'agnet
  A qui le loup rabi sa maijre.

Au bord d'eau gardou tout flurit
  Et tout parsemat de violettos
Ton bendras plus paoure méuil
  Coueille de flores per las fillettos
Ou foun d'eau bos le loun d'eau jour
  N'entendrey plus toute pensivo
Les ers et las cansons d'amour
  De la bouès douce et ta plaintivo.

Bé siet urousés aouserons
  Connéchet le maou d'Estello
Sentisset pas que las douçous
  D'uno tendresse mutuello,
Abets pas de cruels parents
  L'amits faous d'amourous boulatyés
Cautet tous tem et siet contents
  Aimeto l'aygnetto et l'oumbratye.'

FRENCH TRANSLATION OF CANZON D'ESTELLE.

Petits oiseaux, taisez-vous,
  Prairie pour moi ne sois plus belle,
Paquerettes et papillons,
  Ne charmez plus les yeux d'Estelle.
J'ai perdu le plus beau pasteur
  Qui faisait mon bonheur, malheureuse,
Je ferai maintenant comme l'agneau
  A qui le loup ravit sa mère.

Au bord du jardin fleuri
  Et tout parsemé de violettes,
Tu ne viendras plus, pauvre ami,
  Cueillir des fleurs pour les fillettes.
Au fond du bois, tout le long du jour,
  Je n'entendrai plus tout pensive
Les airs et les chansons d'amour,
  De ta voix si douce et plaintive.

Soyez heureux, petits oiseaux,
  Vous ne connaissez pas les maux d'Estelle,
Vous ne ressentez que les douceurs
  D'une tendresse mutuelle.

Vous n'avez pas de cruels parents,
    D'amis faux des amours volages ;
Chantez toujours, soyez contents,
    Aimez les petits ruisseaux et l'ombrage.

LE PORTRAIT DE MA BERGÈRE.

Sé counnéchets, ma bergère ?
Qu'ey béro coum lou lugra—ouéro, ouéro,
Qu'ey béro coum lou lugra—ouéro la !

Sa taille ben ëy ta fino,
Qué la pouyres empugna—ouéro, ouéro !
Qué la pouyres empugna—ouéro la !

Ses poupettes soun mes blanques
Que la néau d'eau hougara—ouéro, ouéro !
Que la néau d'eau hougara—ouéro la !

Sus sons oueils, l'amour qué llhébo
Sus sons co, nous ba paousa—ouéro, ouéro !
Sus sons co, nous ba paousa—ouéro la ! '

TRANSLATION.

Connais-tu ma bergère ?
Elle est belle comme l'étoile du matin—regarde, regarde !
Elle est belle comme l'étoile du matin—regarde-la !

Sa taille est si fine
Que tu pourrais la prendre à poignée—regarde, regarde !
Que tu pourrais la prendre à poignée—regarde-la !

Son sein est plus blanc
Que la neige de la lande—regarde, regarde !
Que la neige de la lande—regarde-la !

Sur ses yeux l'Amour se lève
Sur son cœur il va nous poser—regarde, regarde !
Sur son cœur il va nous poser—regarde-la ! '

ESTELLA'S SONG.

Little birdies, sing no more!
  Meads for me no more be bright:
Easter-flowers* and butterflies
  Charm no more Estella's sight;

For I have lost the bonniest lad,
  Who made me happy night and morn,
And now I wander like the lamb
  Whose mother cruel wolves have torn.

To the blossomy garden-hedge,
  Beneath whose shade the violets grow,
No more, alas! thou'lt come, poor friend,
  To gather flowers for lasses now.

Sing! Be happy, little birds,
  Who know not Estella's woe!
Ye feel nothing but the sweets
  Of mutual love—no griefs ye know.

Ye no cruel parents have;
  No false friends—no faithless lovers!
Then sing, birds, sing! content and gay,
  By running brooks and woods, blest rovers.

MY LOVE'S PICTURE.

Dost thou know my shepherdess?
She is fair as the star of morn—behold, behold!
She is fair as the star of morn—behold her!

She has got so small a waist
Thou could'st span 't wi' a hand—behold, behold
Thou could'st span 't wi' a hand—behold her!

She's a neck that's whiter by far
Than new fa'en snow on th' moor—behold, behold!
Than new fa'en snow on th' moor—behold her!

From her eyes sweet Love doth dart!
He will fix me on her heart—behold, behold!
He will fix me on her heart—behold, behold her!'

---

* *Paquerettes* are, I believe, *marguerites*, or ox-eye daisies.

DE CAP A TU SOY MARION.

LÀ HAUT SUS LAS MONTAGNES.

ADAPTED TO THE PIANO.—RECUEIL DE FREDC. RIVARÈS.

UN SAUT.—YAN PETIT.

BEROUYINE—CHARMANTINE.

DESPOURRINS.

MY BEAUTIFUL—MY CHARMING ONE.

CANSON D'ESTELLE.

Rous - si - gnou - lets   a - tai - sat-

bous,   Pra - do - per   you   siés pas plus

bé - ro,   mar - ga - li   det - tos,   par ... pal-

lous, Sa - moats pas plus lës oüeils d'Es - tel ~ - - -

lo Ey per-dut lé plus bel pas-tou - rel qué fa -

sio moun boun hur pe - - caï - - res! A - ro fé -

2 B

ney   cou - mo l'a - gnel   à   qui lè

loup ra - bis s'a may . . . . ré,   a - ro fe -

rey   cou - mo la - gnel   à   qui lè -

rall.

loup ra - bit ca may - - - - ré.

PYRENEAN SHEPHERD'S SONG.

Adagio.

La haüt sus las moun - ta - - gnes û Pas ton

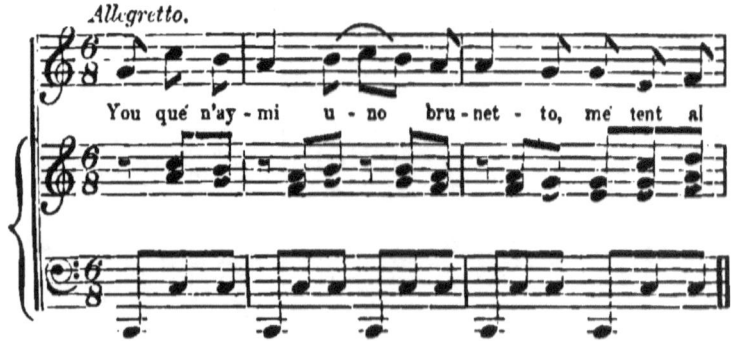

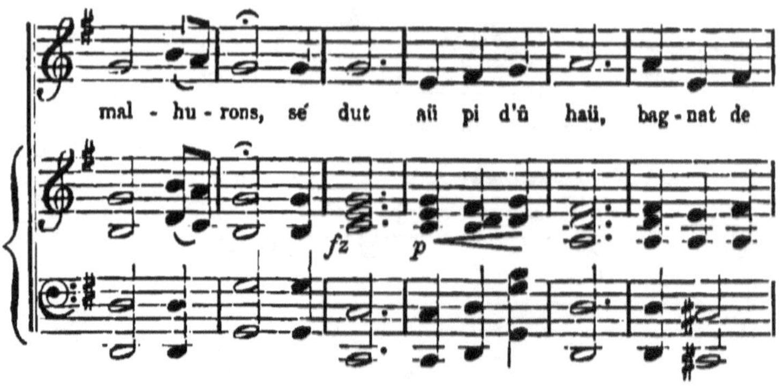
mal - hu - rons, sé dut aü pi d'û haü, bag - nat de
fz p

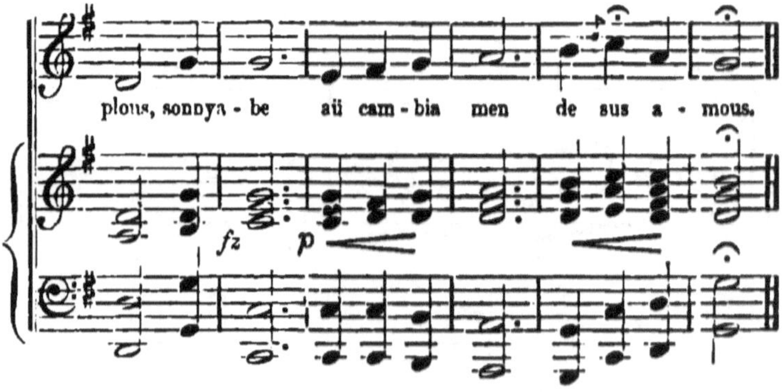
plous, sonnya - be aü cam - bia men de sus a - mous.
fz p

CHANSON PATOISE.

Allegretto.
You qué n'ay - mi u - no bru - net - to, mé tent al

co me tent al co. Mès que-nan cou

di si de may-ma mo rem-bi-

o taou Cen-deu-mo.

1.

Moi j'aime une brunette,
Elle me tient au cœur,
Mais quand je lui dis de m'aimer
Elle me renvoie au lendemain.

2.

Lou lendouma quonan la baou bésè
Perlin conta
Mahé lou mema coumplimens
Et quin malhur! Amou næubien

.2.

Le lendemain quand je la vais voir
Pour lui conter fleurette,
Elle me fait le même compliment.
Ah! quel malheur! Amour ne vient point.

3.

Sen soun troubados més quounaté
Quonan refusat
Lous airés deans plus bels flingalrés
Pus quonan äymat
Hillettes non digat yamey
D'aguer aïguetto non biourey

3.

On en a vu plus de quatre
Qui ont dedaigné
Les chansons des plus huppes,
Elles ont ensuite aimé.
Fillettes, ne dites jamais,
De cette eau je ne boirai pas.

LE PORTRAIT DE MA BERGÈRE.

Sé caun - né chets ma ber - ge - ra? Sé caun - ne - chets
ma ber - ge - ra? Quey ve - ro coum lou   lu - gra   oue - ro
oue - ro   quey bé - ro coum lou   lu - gra   oué - ro   la.

MOUN DOUX AMIE S'EN BA PARTIR.

AÜROST, OR FUNERAL CHAUNT.

BRANLES D'OSSAN.—CAPITÈNI SALIES.

PEYROUTOU.—UN BASQUE.

DE LA PLUS CHARMANTE ANESQUETTE.

AQUERES MOUNTINES.

COMPOSED BY GASTON PHŒBUS, COMTE DE FOIX, COTEMPORARY OF
EDWARD THE BLACK PRINCE.

CHAPTER XXXIV

BAGNÈRES DE BIGORRE—A BATH À LA RUSSE—
A RIDE TO LLHÉRIS.

I LEAVE Bagnères next week, if all be well, and was re-
gretting I had never been able to accomplish the ascent to
Llhéris, when a lady I knew slightly invited me to join
her party to go there.

My back is still stiff after my fall at Luz, and the riding
to Gavarnie and the Pont d'Espagne afterwards, though
somewhat better for a Russian vapour bath I took a day or
two ago, but I could not resist the temptation. Before I
tell about our expedition, let me give an account of the
bath.

Did you ever, dear reader, go into the wash-house in the
middle of a washing-day ? Well, it is like what you felt
then, '*only more so*,' as the Americans say. You undress
entirely, tie an apron round you, and are conducted by
Madame Balet, the bathing-woman, into a square room,
with a marble bench to sit on, at the upper end. The
room is full of steam like a wash-house, through which you
dimly see a bell-pull, and two water-cocks in the wall, and
Madame Balet tells you that if you feel *rather* faint, you
must lave your face, and sprinkle yourself with cold water
from the cocks, but if you feel *fainting*, you must pull the
bell, and she will fetch you out. You seat yourself as desired, on the bench, and think how very disagreeable a
Russian bath is, but that as you *are in*, you will endeavour
to bear it. So when Madame Balet re-enters at the end of
five minutes, you bravely say, in reply to her inquiries, that

you're very well, and *not* faint a bit, upon which she immediately goes, *and puts on more steam.*

Now you begin to understand the sensations of a lobster boiling alive in a pot—(how *dare* people imagine they have a right to treat God's creatures with cruelty, however low their place in the scale of creation?)—but you haven't time to moralize because you can't breathe, and must dash cold water over your face to relieve the awful sense of suffocation. And you wish in your heart you had *not* taken a vapour bath. Just then, in comes Madame Balet for the third time, and inquires how you get on.

'Oh, very well, thank you, the bath is rather hot—but I'm very well.'

' *Vraiment !* ' says Madame, incredulously, and in a tone which sounds like cruel mockery to your ears—for the truth is, you are *half-boiled*, only you don't like to own it. Other people take Russian baths, and why shouldn't you? So you brave it out. But ah! you never foresaw that cruel woman would heat the furnace ten times hotter. Now you can't even see the water-cocks close to you for the dense vapour—it is thick as a London fog. You could cut it with a knife. You gasp for breath—hold on by the railing in front of the seat, and grope your way to the water-cock to lave your face—but it is all in vain. You are *boiling—your lungs are scalded—your eyes are scalded—you feel as if both would burst*—you *can't* stay any longer. Yes you will—other people do—never say die—people say it's a cure for rheumatism—it's worth a disagreeable sensation to get that back cured—you will stand it a little longer—*that is, if you can.* No, you can't—you'll faint if you stay another minute—you ring the bell, but see no one —only a voice sounds deadly through the dense steam— and asks in an aggravating manner, *if you're comfortable !*

'Oh! I'm fainting, take me out; I can't stay another moment.'

2 c

'I thought so,' says Madame Balet. 'You've been in above twenty minutes; many can't stay in half so long.'

Out you go to the room where you undressed, dry yourself, and pop into bed. Madame Balet heaps you up with clothes, and leaves you there for half an hour to cool; after which you dress and walk home.

Madame Balet knew I was not rich, and she refused to take anything for her attendance upon me. I would far rather have paid her; but I felt I ought not to deprive her of the pleasure of doing a kindness.

I must introduce Madame Balet to my readers, for she is a picture. 'She is a native of Arles,' and 'all the Arles women are very handsome,' says M. Frossard. She certainly is, and has both a very fine open, winning countenance, and a very fine figure, which her pretty neat costume sets off. Her dark hair is confined by a broad black ribbon round the top of the head and comb, but she wears one ringlet on each side of her face. A velvet band clasps her full white neck, which is concealed by a very fine muslin handkerchief plaited in many folds, over this is a black merino jacket, made half high, her skirt is coloured. It is a pity *costumes* should ever die out, they are so becoming, and add so much life and variety to a crowd.

Madame Balet has a very beautiful complexion. She told an acquaintance of mine who was much freckled, that she would cure her freckles as she had cured her own, by an infallible remedy. This was to wash the face on going to bed at night, with an infusion of *fennel water*, which was to be washed off the following morning with fresh strawberry juice. I have not tried the recipe, and cannot speak to its effect.

Having dressed, I walked home, and kept quiet indoors the rest of the day, and the next I was free from my rheumatism. I doubt, however, whether that scalding is good for the chest and lungs.

The day appointed for ascending Llhéris, dawned bright and clear, and by nine we were all assembled at the door of a house belonging to one of the party where we had agreed to meet. The donkeys, and a horse for the one gentleman who went with us, came soon after, and we set out. We rode through Asté, and past a ruined castle, concerning which I have never been able to learn more than that *c'était brûlé il y a longtemps—longtemps de cela*, and up the side of a steep mountain. It was not till we got to the top of this that we saw what is called Le Penne (Celtic, head) de Llhéris, rising higher still, and really began to ascend Llhéris itself. We wound up another steep bank, slowly and painfully on foot, sending the horse and asses, which could not drag us up so steep an ascent, forwards, with our two boy guides. Then we remounted, and rode through a shady wood, over a steep hilltop, and emerged on to a grassy plateau, with a tall white crag on one side of it, and a high steep bank on the other. This was the plateau of Llhéris, and the white rock was the Penne.

I do not know that it is so, but the depression in the middle of the summit gave me the idea that Llhéris is an extinct volcano. There are volcanic influences still at work in the Pyrenees, for there are often earthquakes at Bagnères, but they never do any harm. I was awakened one night by one, and hearing the furniture and the house shake, and the windows rattle, while my bed rocked as if heaved upwards, with an oscillating motion, I thought, sleepily, 'it must be an earthquake. Well, if it is, I cannot help myself. I am as safe in God's hands now as at any other time.' So I said a short prayer for my own safety, and then prayed to God to keep me and all in the house and town safe, and fell fast asleep again. Next day I imagined it was a dream, for no one spoke of an earth-quake; but the day following I met a peasant in the woods who asked if I had felt the earthquake the night before last, and added, 'probably there has been a great battle somewhere. During the Crimean war, there was always an earthquake here, when a battle was being fought.'

When I went home, Madame —— told me 'she had not liked to speak to me of it lest I should take fright, and leave Bagnères; but that there had been two distinct shocks, one at twelve o'clock in the day, which the noise and commotion of the Saturday's market prevented most people from feeling, but which she and her husband had distinctly perceived; the other at a little past eleven on Saturday night, which alarmed her so much, she got up and went to seek protection from *le voisin*'—so husbands are called in France, from the custom of husband and wife occupying neighbouring rooms. She added, 'earthquakes are frequent here, but I never remember any mischief done beyond an old house and a shed being thrown down some years ago.'

This plateau on the top of Llhéris was covered with a short beautiful purple labiated flower, like, but *not* a small salvia—the *horminum pyrénaienne*. On the road-side, I found one plant varying to white. We rode on to a spring where we dismounted and lunched. It was not the best spot we could have selected, for it was damp, from the trampling of the cattle who came to drink, and dirty from their odour, but Monsieur (he was a Frenchman) ruled, and the cloth was laid on that spot among the dried cow and sheep dung. After our repast we scrambled up towards, but not on, to the Penne. On the steep bank grew innumerable tufts of the lovely chrome-yellow *erysimus*, and a most delicate and exquisite little flower I had never before met with, growing close to the ground like the lilac *erinus*, and having also a five-petaled flower, but each petal being of a roundish oval form. Its hue was a chalky, dead pure white, the buds and centres of the flowers being tinged with a delicate pink, like that of a shell. The flowers grow eight or ten upon one foot stalk, like the *erinus* or *alyssum*. This charming, pure-looking little flower, is not common, its name is *androsace villosa*.

As we walked downwards to get our asses, a little below the spring where we had dined, I found the *orchis latifolia*, which resembles the purple orchis a good deal, but has a long purplish leaf at the back of every flower that is not distinguishable from the flower till you examine it closely. Among the places where Philippe states it is to be found in his excellent *'Flore des Pyrénées'* (a work no visitor to the Pyrenees who loves plants, should neglect to purchase, and which may be got best of the author, at his *'Cabinet d'Histoire Naturelle,'* in Bagnères), is the *Pic d'Eyre*. This confirms my idea that our family name is of Pyrenean origin, as it was written *D'Eyre* or *De l'Eyre* in all our old family deeds and charters. In Bordeaux I found a street called *Rue des Eyres*, and as a termination, it is common in the Pyrenees and the adjoining province of Gascony, where I met the names of Peyreyre, Tisseyre, &c.

After this scramble we mounted and rode homewards. In passing up *La Plaine de Llhéris*, a little below the spring, we came in for, apparently, the whole convent of Carmelite monks out on a holiday, which, poor creatures, they seemed to enjoy with the zest of boys let loose from school. The prior, I suppose, and another, were seated a long way off, beyond the little stream, that was fed by the fountain near which we had dined. He soon perceived the forbidden sex, and made as much haste to call his monks around him as a hen does to gather her chickens under her wings if she sees two or three strange cats, and they came running down the hill sides with great swiftness, notwithstanding their long robes and shuffling sandals, all of them making an immense circuit to avoid encountering our profane gaze. I felt glad to see the poor creatures got a breath of fresh air sometimes, and wished the same benefit might have been extended to the Carmelite nuns, who, after profession, never leave the walls of their convent. But the men make the rules for the poor women, *and take care that they are harder and more severe than those by which they bind themselves;* witness Victor Hugo's account *de l'Obédience de Martin Véga.*

As we rode through the wood, I noticed, and made the donkey boy gather, a tall kind of Solomon's seal, that grew under the bushes. It differs from the common kind, in having the leaves growing in whorls at intervals, all round the stem, from these the yellowish green bells depend. It is the *polygonum verticillata,* and is about half a yard or a yard high. Further on I came to the foot of a rock, cushioned, as it were, with a broad roughish-leaved plant of dark-green, with snow-white flowers resembling those of a cistus, which its rough dark-green, veiny, sorrel-sized and shaped leaves, and strawberry-like blossoms, made me sure it was. No such thing. It proved to be the *dryas octopetala,* so called from its eight white petals, and it belongs to the natural order of *rosacea.* Soon after leaving the wood the steepness of the descent compelled us all to dismount. Monsieur —— led his horse, and the boys led the asses.

I was still suffering a little from my back, and in going up the mountain, when one of our party remarked, 'We must wait for her from time to time, as her breath would not allow her to climb,' I had replied, 'I, at all events, should willingly do so, for I should be obliged to claim the same indulgence in myself descending, as coming down a hill gave me great pain in my weakened spine.' I had said the same thing to everyone of the party, and everyone of them knew I had only just recovered from severe lumbago, but not one of them halted or delayed, when they found I could not keep up with them. I dared not stay behind, because there were so many tracks along the mountain side, I was afraid of taking a wrong one. I walked on therefore with infinite pain and difficulty, scarcely able to keep the last couple, for they had formed into divisions, in sight, inwardly vowing I would never—*no, never*—let the temptation be ever so great, go sight-seeing with people I did not know much of.

At last I reached the whole party, they had sat down upon a bank, not by any means to wait for my coming up, but because *they* were tired themselves and wanted rest. By this time I was in violent pain, the muscles of my back felt bruised and would not bear the smallest touch of the finger, and, in short, I was as bad as I had been before taking the vapour-bath, and quite out of temper at their selfish want of consideration. So I went and sat by myself at a distance, partly because I was really cross and in great pain, and so disinclined for conversation, and more because after having passed innumerable banks where one could have reposed comfortably, Monsieur —— had selected one which was a continuous slope, so that it was a perpetual strain on the back to keep oneself from falling. How could his timid, gentle English little wife ever have married him? He never seemed to think of anybody but himself, or to have an idea that any other person's taste or wishes had a right to be consulted. I feel cross when I think of that man and that ride now.

I must own I was neither very talkative, nor very agreeable the rest of the way home. I was in intense pain, and rode on cross and weary, and purposely keeping aloof from the rest of the party all the way back.

We got home to Bagnères at last. I was so stiff that I could scarcely move, and refusing an invitation to drink tea with the party, I went straight home and to bed. When the mischief was irrecoverably done, I must do the ladies the justice to say, they seemed very sorry, but it was three months before I began to get over the effects of that day's hurried walk down the steep precipitous sides of Llhéris. I am not sure whether my back will ever be strong again. I could not but contrast the ride up to Llhéris with this party and that to the Mouné with Lady Carnwath and her friends, when everyone of the company considered the strength and feelings of the others.

CHAPTER XXXV

I TOOK my last walk at Bagnères to-day. I still felt very unwell, and only meant to go a little way up the sloping hill above it; but, as is usual with me, the fresh air revived me, and the higher I ascended the better I felt. Below, the day had seemed rather misty; but when I got upon the mountain, the air was pure and clear, and I could see for an immense distance.

It was one of those thin, blue kind of atmospheres which make all far-off objects seem nearer, and which in Devonshire we used to say foretokened rain. The green valleys lying between the mountains seemed more beautiful than ever now that I was going to leave them, and as I looked upon the grey-slated roofs of Bagnères, its ugly, queer cathedral, which looked as if it had been built without a plan, and never finished for want of funds, and the graceful octagonal tower, all that now remains of the once magnificent Church of the Jesuit, it seemed to me as if I was leaving *home*. I cannot somehow *believe* in my leaving Bagnères, though my small belongings have all been packed up for a week, so that I have even had to buy paper and envelopes to write a necessary letter.

There is a capital view of Bagnères from the *Bédat*. You can see the whole long valley from the beginning of *Campan* to beyond *Montgaillard*, quite distinctly. *Campan, Asté, Gerdes, Bagnères, Trébons, Pouzac, Montgaillard* —all nearly in one straight line, with green fields on each side, and the silver *Adour* and its lesser tributaries flowing through the green meadows. I don't know whether Moses, when he looked down from Pisgah, could well have seen a fairer or more fertile land than this. Every bank was covered with beautiful flowers. Many were of the same kind we have at home, but rendered far more beautiful by a luxuriance of growth, and a depth and intensity of colour unknown in England. Climate and soil have strange effect upon flowers, and often alter them so much as to make one's old friends scarcely recognizable. Some few are dwarfed and stunted by this climate. The beautiful butterfly orchis of English meadows is a little insignificant greenish-white flower here, with scarcely any of the rich tropical spicy smell that distinguishes it in English woods ; but far the greater number of plants are much more luxuriant and bright-hued. The common yellow cistus grew in large masses on the Bédat, as luxuriantly as its congeners do in gardens, drooping down in long wreaths of fringe from the rocks. Some were golden-coloured, others had a glowing spot of intensest orange at the bottom of each petal, like the *escholtzia*, while others had an orange ring crossing the petals. Large tufts of a purple flower, something like a Penstemon, grew beside them, as well as large cushions of the Pyrenean germander, with its flowers of creamy white and pink.

How Nature seems to delight in this opposition and harmony of colour? You never see a large mass of flowers of one hue without immediately seeing also its complementary colour, as Mr. Ruskin would call it. The *Teucrium Pyrenaica* is not at all like our blue speedwell. It resembles it only in the manner in which the leaves grow round the stem, and in their shape. Its flowers are shaped like those of a nettle—the upper half pink, the lower lip, which is much prolonged, white ; these pink and white flowers grow in a whorl, at the top of about half-a-dozen whorls of green leaves, placed about an inch asunder on the stem, so that it has rather a prim, stiff, old-maidenish-sort of look—*like M. E. B. and I!* and looks as if the wind and the cattle had never rumpled its frills, or disarranged its propriety in the least. It is very pretty as it grows in clumps among the rocks, beside the golden cistus and purple erinus; but it is a quaint flower. There is something prim about it, which makes one involuntarily say, 'What a prim flower! but it is pretty, too.' While I was admiring a bank of these plants, and the trailing Ladies' bed-straws, yellow and white—both smaller than at home, and I think prettier for being so—a beautiful dark-coloured butterfly flitted past me on velvet wings. It seemed a rich black, almost like plush, the tips of the wings being edged with grey; but my sight is bad, and the capricious, frightened thing would not let me get near it. I thought, how deeply the fear of man was impressed on all creatures, and how glorious that time would be, when death, and its concomitant—fear, would cease; and how delightful it would be, when one could call to the beautiful winged creatures of air, and have them come to us, and examine them, and let them go again; and when there would be no necessity for museums any longer.

Half the beauty and brilliancy of moths and butterflies depends on the effects of light glancing upon them as they fly, and is lost when they are impaled in a naturalist's cabinet. Just then the creature did settle, and I saw that its body, and the central part of each wing, was a dark, purplish-brownish black, edged with pale tortoiseshell eyes all round the tips. 'I wish you would just come a little nearer, and close your wings, that I might see what the under side is like, for you looked much more beautiful flying,' said I mentally, as I stood quite still, not to frighten the pretty creature; and just at the moment, another of the same kind, attracted by the honey-like scent of the Ladies' bed-straw, came and perched on the *bouquet* I held in my hand, closed his wings as if he had heard my wish, and inserted his slender proboscis into the flowers, so that I had ample time to verify that his wings were the same, or nearly so, on both sides, and that the intense richness of colouring on the wing was due to the effects of light. As he flew away, I saw a white butterfly, disturbed at its feast by Keeper, rise from the grass just before his nose. It was the largest European butterfly I ever saw, and appeared a pure white, edged with a band of grey black round the wings, something like some of our common English white butterflies; but the shape of the wings was quite different, the first pair were very long, so as to give it almost the appearance of a small bird flying. I could not get near it, and I saw no more of the kind.

Many of the Pyrenean insects are very beautiful. The loveliest is a small opal-coloured beetle, of which I have never been lucky enough to see a living specimen. A lady who came to Bagnères, had a *Berthe* made of them, interspersed with the emerald-green ones; it must have been very resplendent and elegant. I suppose the wings would decay too soon to make it worth while to fix them; but the creature is a perfect gem. The opalescent tints are quite as beautiful as in any opal I ever saw, but not transparent. It resembles an opaque opal, looking here and there as if flecks of smalt-blue, and grains of frosted silver were scattered over its pearliness, while gleams of gold and purple and flame-colour play in it, as in the precious stone. It is roundish in shape, and rather larger than a pea. Another little beauty about the same size, is a lovely green. Some, with the usual longer body, are all shades of copper and green. I gathered to-day one of the beautiful, sweet-scented, fringed pinks—the first this year. But unlike the Ragged Robin, whose flowers they somewhat resemble, they do not seem to like the luxuriant growth of the grass. I could not even discover the large

pieds, as the French call them, off which I had gathered
so many *bouquets* last year. They were smothered in
grass. When that dies down a little, the *dianthus* will
come out in all its beauty, about the end of July. Many
of the black and tortoiseshell butterflies, and the green
and crimson fly, common on limestone soils in Yorkshire,
flew past me as I got near the top of the Bédat. The
higher one goes on the Pyrenean mountains, the more
beautiful are the insects and the flowers. I saw one lovely
fly that I had never seen before, which had the same
peculiar contrast of colours that I have remarked in
humming birds—a kind of pale, vivid, smalt-blue, opposed
to a pale bright mineral-green. The creature's body was
blue, and so were his long feather-tipped antennæ, which
were nearly the length of his wings. After him I saw a
large beautiful moth, its wings were so wide from tip
to tip that I debated with myself whether it was not the
creature I had taken for a butterfly as I ascended, but it
was not the same pure, bright white. It was rather of a
cream colour, edged with eyes of brown, set in a grey
border, and larger eyes, and had also small spots here and
there on the wings. The body was thick, and of a dusky
grey, and the feathers on it were longer, and *coarser*, if I
may use the expression, than I ever remember seeing on
a moth before. They had a *'penny* look, like half-perfect
feathers on a young bird. The substance of the wings was
remarkably thin, and almost transparent; and they were
sadly torn, as if the poor thing had had many misadven-
tures in his short life.

On this path I found also, for the first time this year,
the beautiful large purple bugle. It does not resemble
our common bugle (common here, also) at all; the petals
or flowers are almost as large as those of a salvia, and
grow in a whorl; the brown, velvety calyx almost forming
a star in the centre of the flower. Its hue varies from

the deepest, richest purple, to pale lilac, and contrasts beautifully with the dark, port-wine-coloured velvet of the calyx. The top of the round formed by the flowers is about the size of a crown-piece, and their rich colour makes them very effective in a nosegay.

What a glorious scene of lights and shadows, of green plains, softly melting into blue distances, and lofty mountains looking as if the huge waves of a sea had suddenly been turned to stone, I saw from the top of the Bédat. I wished certain friends had seen it too. I thought, when I saw the Pyrenees first from the mountains, that this notion of a sea turned into stone was an original one of my own, and wondered whether the critics would laugh at me if I used the phrase; but there must be a reality in the idea, for it strikes every one. Tain, and several other French writers whose works on the Pyrenees I have read, all use precisely the same metaphor. Coming down, I saw a sight that Hunt and his followers would have thought it worth while coming to the Pyrenees to see; another example of how much nature excels art in harmonious grouping. Upon a dark-lilac bugle, as upon a small round table set in the grass, three lovely insects were feasting: the small tortoise-shell butterfly, a rich glossy brown, almost black-banded humble-bee, and the lovely small blue and green fly. I never saw so much and such rich colouring in so small a space before, and no artist could have selected or imagined a more exquisite contrast of tints. I returned homewards by one of the pleasantest walks cut along Mont Olivet, finding on my way three kinds of St. John's wort, one trailing like the yellow pimpernel, for which, but for its leaves, and a slightly deeper tone of yellow, I might have taken it; and two upright ones, not resembling our English kinds, *marguerites* or ox-eye daisies, the larger blue scabious, hard-head, two orchises, a green kind of wood sage, and the delicate trailing ivy-leafed campanula, which, however, was not yet in bloom, as well as several pretty grasses, and gathered quite a *gerbe* of beautiful June flowers.

There was one flower on the Bédat which I coveted, but could not gather for its prickles. It was a thistle. This thistle is really very handsome. I do not remember ever having seen it before in France, though I have in Germany. Its leaves are the blue-grey of the artichoke, and the prickles are farther apart, and longer, than in the common kinds. Its head resembles an artichoke with all the scales turned *back*, and the point of each terminating in a spike; but it is only about a fourth of that in size. The buds form a green star, which, as they advance to perfection, is tipped with red. When beginning to open, a bright rose-coloured spot lies in the centre of the small green artichoke, and when the flower is full blown it is a rich crimson tassel, fading towards the centre into pink. If I was a flower painter I should paint this thistle and beautiful insects feeding upon it. Another thistle is like a little purple-crimson tassel, growing upon a long slender prickly stem. It is so elegant, I have often gathered it since I came here for bouquets; but to gather such flowers one needs a large pair of scissors and a strong pair of gloves. I was too lazy to take the public path down Mont Olivet, so I trespassed, and came down by Monsieur Lavigne's house, and met him at his own door, and we walked down the hill together. He was very polite, as French proprietors always are; but he informed me he meant to put gates up at either end of his property, to prevent the eternal incursions, and he should inscribe on them—' *Défense d'entrer*,' but Madame, or any other '*gens comme il faut*,' would always be welcome to go through.

What a beautiful little property his is. On the slope of Mont Olivet, with the Bédat towering behind and protecting it from all cold winds, and with such splendid chestnut trees at the back and in front of the house. It commands, too, a lovely view. I envy M. Lavigne, notwithstanding one is forbidden to covet one's neighbour's house. He seems thoroughly to enjoy and appreciate its beauty, and looked much pleased when I complimented him on having the finest chestnut trees in Bagnères. He asked if I had ever been in Spain; and told me I ought to go and see Seville and Cadiz, they were such magnificent cities, and of such ancient and beautiful architecture. So I hope to do some day, if I live and means come; if not, I have often thought one of our disembodied enjoyments may be to flit from place to place and see all that is beautiful.

CHAPTER XXXVI.

I HAD given up all idea of seeing Luchon, for want of funds. The kindness of some friends enabled me to go there, and I had looked forward to some pleasant excursions in this, to me, new part of the Pyrenees. But besides having cold after cold, and straining my back severely in walking down Llhéris, I heard the very night before I left Bagnères de Bigorre of the death of my sister. This sad news took from me all power of enjoyment in the scenery, and I can scarcely say that I really saw Luchon, though I stayed a week there. Memory was busy within me. I saw poor Caroline in almost every dress she had ever worn, from her childhood to her marriage, *and grieved over all that might have been, and was not.* The mountains were before me, it is true; but my thoughts were with the dead, and I could not realize their beauty or their grandeur.

No coaches yet went from Bagnères to Luchon *par la Montagne*, so that I was obliged to go by one that went to Montrejean. This road has a good deal of beauty also, but is not to compare with the glorious views from the Col d'Aspin, which one traverses in going *par la Montagne;* and one has a terrible long time to wait at the railway station—built, as is usual with stations, just where there is nothing to look at, below the town of Montrejean—for the diligence that takes passengers to Luchon. I got to Luchon about seven in the evening, and had some difficulty in finding lodgings, though plenty were offered me, for as

2 D

soon as my new face appeared on the promenade, six or eight different women ran after me with cards in their hands, ' *Joli appartement ;*' ' *Suivez-moi, je vous prie, madame ;*' ' *Si Madame voudrait bien se donner la peine de voir mon appartement, elle le trouverait joli,*' resounded on all sides, as Keeper and I walked up the street. I replied that I did not want one. In fact, the mistress of the hotel where the diligence from Montrejean had set me down, had sent her little boy to show me an *appartement* that would be cheap, as *Madame* could not afford the hotel prices. I had no faith in the *appartement* recommended by *Madame* being any cheaper, but accepted the boy's escort nevertheless, thinking I might as well see it, and that at all events I should have a guide through the town. The women and children who looked for lodgers followed us all the way up to the house to which the landlady had directed me, insidiously seeking to win my heart by their praises of Keeper—' *Quel joli chien !*' ' *Est-il aimable, ce chien là !*' &c., &c.

When we got to the *appartement* it was *dearer* than the room at the hotel. *Madame* had clearly sent me there with the express intention that I should go back to her as the cheapest thing to do in the end. Instead, I dismissed the boy, intimating I should find an *appartement* myself. I did, and it did well enough for one week; but as I was not comfortable there, and cannot recommend it, I shall say nothing about it. The price of apartments in Luchon is frightfully dear during the season; and no wonder, for the inhabitants have to live all the year on their gains during that season of three months.

Luchon is a lovely little valley, shut in by hills and mountains on all sides. A little nest into which one seems to have dropped, as it were, from the clouds, for when one stands in the middle of it there is apparently no mode of ingress nor egress. It is quite unlike any of the other *bains,*

and peculiar.   There is one long street planted with a
double row of tall, sweet-scented lime-trees, on each side of
which one sees gay shops, magnificent hotels, and handsome cafés, resplendent with plate-glass windows, whose
gilded and pannelled walls and gilt mirrors dazzle the eye
as one passes along, while in front of them are numberless
white marble tables, at which gentlemen are seated sipping
lemonade or wine, reading newspapers, or playing at chess
or draughts, just as in Paris.   In fact, it looks exactly as if
one of the boulevards of Paris had been transplanted by
magic into the very heart of the most secluded mountain
valley of the Pyrenees.   At the top of this long street are
the baths and the public gardens ; at the other end, one or
two narrow, dirty little streets, dignified by the name of
' The Town.'   Murray says that it contains 2,000 inhabitants.   I should not have fancied it could, but have no
doubt he is right.   Two or three new streets of lodging-
houses are also building by degrees.   The Allée de la
Pique, where I am lodging, consists almost entirely of new
houses.   This alley continues, but with shady trees instead
of houses on each side, to the river Pique, past pleasant
shady fields (where peasants were making hay), and scattered villas, nestling among trees.

One very fine affair was worthy of suburban London.
It belonged, as I was told by a man working on the roads,
to a Parisian milkman, and it seemed to be regarded by
the populace of Luchon generally as a miracle of taste and
magnificence.   It was a kind of Swiss *chalet* of enormous
dimensions, built of staring red brick, with a garden, of
which I should have suspected a Chinese to have been the
contriver, if any Chinese ever visited Luchon ; the pretty
little stream that ran, shaded by alders and ash, from the
mountain, to swell the waters of the Pique, had here been
so shorn of all its native picturesque wildness, its graceful
fringe of trees and bushes, and its course diverted into so

many narrow little streams, each passing under a fantastic bridge to an imaginary island, formed by conducting the water round a small piece of ground, and thus isolating it, or to an artificial promontory. And as the whole garden was newly made and planted, and had that bare unfurnished look common to new gardens, where the shrubs are mostly about a foot high, and the taller ones evidently just transplanted from a nurseryman's grounds, its intense bad taste and vulgarity was all the more conspicuous. I often think what a pity it is that men without a spark of real feeling for the beautiful, do get rich, and buy up and *deform* the loveliest places in all countries. It is just the same at our English lakes. Did not a rich vulgarian employ a hundred men to destroy the sweet windings of the river Rotha, and make it run straight through his ground? Happily men die, and reforming nature crumbles down staring walls, and moulders Chinese bridges, and new trees spring up and overshadow the straightened stream, though, alas! it can never have again the wild beauty it had once. Wordsworth and other gentlemen petitioned the English Goth not to mar the lovely windings of the Rotha; but such men are inflexible; they have just sufficient instinct for the beautiful to go and live in a lovely country and deform it.

I wandered up and down the green valleys of Luchon, and the sweet-smelling fields of hay beside the shady waters of La Pique, one of the prettiest streams—if not *the prettiest*—I have seen in the Pyrenees, and up some of the zigzag walks cut in the wooded hill above the baths; but I took no pleasure in them, and could not enjoy their beauty. A cloud from my own heart darkened the lovely landscape; I felt as if the mountains oppressed me—as if I had a mountain on my breast, and could not breathe— and longed for the day when I should leave it. Bagnères de Luchon does not, in fact, suit every constitution. Mr.

and Mrs. Alexander, who came to France on account of one of their children who suffered from asthma, were obliged to leave it instantly on account of the child's severe illness. They took him back to Bagnères through pouring rain, almost expecting he would die on the road, and as soon as they reached Bagnères de Bigorre, the oppression ceased, and the next day he was playing about perfectly well.

I had, however, been very unwell for some time before I went to Luchon, and the sad news I heard before I left Bagnères de Bigorre oppressed me still more, so that it would, perhaps, hardly be fair to lay my indisposition to the air of Luchon. It was the first week in July, and the place was beginning to fill with crowds of gay and well-dressed strangers, and I instinctively shrank from the gaiety. It was not till the end of the week that I could force myself to call upon some of my Bagnères acquaintance, Mr. and Mrs. Lyte, who were there, or go through the gardens in front of the baths. Mr. Lyte was busy taking photographic views in the neighbourhood; he showed me some of the negatives; but as in these, what is to be dark is white, and what is to be light is black, one cannot judge of their extreme perfection in that state. In the Allée des Bains I saw his beautiful photographs (certainly the finest I have ever seen) in every booksellers' window. In the evening I walked to the public gardens in front of the baths. Like everything else at Luchon, the garden and public promenade are different to anything else I ever saw. Imagine a large smooth piece of velvet turf, about which are scattered rustic summer-houses, intersected by smooth gravel-walks bordered by rose-trees—to the left shrubberies of laurel and other trees, among which handsome lodging-houses peep out, looking like private gentlemen's villas; and on the other, a well-wooded hill, on whose side innumerable walks are cut zigzag through the trees, while every here and there, under their shade, on some turfy platform, parties of gaily-dressed people are sitting on benches and chairs; beyond the smooth grass plat, half-hidden by the immense and tasteful summer-house is a sheet of green water simulating a lake, and all this is framed in by mountains of the most picturesque form and hue, and all brilliantly lighted up by fireworks and lamps, while crowds of elegantly-dressed ladies and children throng the alleys, or sit on chairs by the orchestra listening to the music.

It was a complete *scène de théâtre*, very pretty and very enjoyable in its way; but I liked the quiet green meadows better. I liked better to sit on the haycocks there, and listen to the dash of the river over the stones, and look at the meadow sweet, and the pink Lychnis contrasting so beautifully with the dark-green leaves of the trees and bushes under which they grew, and the wild and varied forms of the mountains beyond. Luchon has many attractions besides its own intrinsic beauties. The woods and mountains around it are fuller of rare and beautiful plants than any other parts of the Pyrenees, and innumerable pleasant excursions are to be made from it. Every day I saw gay and merry parties of young people set off on horseback or in carriages to visit some one or other of the many beautiful scenes in its environs; but though I had the means to go to one or two, I wanted the heart. I went nowhere, and saw nothing while I was at Luchon.

CHAPTER XXXVII

THE TRAGEDY OF CASTEL VIELH.

' AMONG the most savage scenery near Luchon, stands the remains of an old feudal castle, named Castel Vielh, whose scattered and formless vestiges were once a part of the ancient and superb manor-house of the Counts de Givrion. There is a sad and melancholy legend concerning the fate of the last Count de Givrion, and his family, which seems in accordance with the gloomy awe-inspiring and blightest appearance of the surrounding country.'

' The Count Henri married Caroline de Hauterive, a young and beautiful woman, whose birth and fortune were equal to his own. Two lovely children were born to them, and for some years they lived in the tenderest and most perfect union. Some magnificent feasts drew all the nobles of Navarre to the court of their sovereign, and the Count and Countess de Givrion, among the rest.

' The beauty of the lady attracted universal admiration and many high-born and elegant lords tried to win her to listen to their suit, but she was too much devoted to her husband, not to remain insensible to all their professions. She saw, however, with the deepest pain and surprise, that the Count appeared perfectly indifferent to the attention paid her, and this indifference seemed to her a proof that his love had declined, for could she have borne to see any woman pay equal court to him? This nascent jealousy was further strengthened by the Count's prolonging his stay in Pau ou some frivolous pretext. She watched him secretly, followed him everywhere by her spies, and learnt that she was betrayed.   One day that she herself, in complete disguise, dogged his steps, she saw him exchange signs of intelligence with a young girl who was plainly dressed, but of ideal beauty.   The thought that henceforth she must occupy only the second place in her husband's heart was insupportable to her.   The present was agony, the future appeared too dreary to endure.   The blood seemed to curdle in her veins; she longed for the relief of tears, but none fell from her burning eyes, though she sobbed convulsively: "My God! my God! I am lost—lost!" were the only words that escaped her lips, as she sank staggering to the ground, like one struck to the heart by a deadly blow; and losing all consciousness, she fainted.'

'Happy had it been for her had she never awakened. Perhaps an hour might have passed away when she recovered her senses; and making a great effort, slowly crept back to her hotel, a blighted and heart-broken woman.   A violent fever succeeded, and for two months her life was in danger, but at last she recovered, and her first thought was to discover if her husband were really unworthy of her love.   By dint of gold, she ascertained from one of her retainers, that the noble and haughty descendant of the De Givrions, blinded by a fatal passion, went nightly in mystery and secrecy to visit a humble daughter of the people.   When the unhappy Countess became thus certain of the full extent of her misfortune, a horrible resolution took possession of her mind, and the next morning she went to the abode of her hated rival, in the quarter of the accursed Bohemians and Cagots.   Having passed down a damp, obscure, and tortuous street, whose very aspect chilled the mind, by a mingled impression that it was the abode of want, misery, and crime, she reached the mean, dark house, indicated to her by the spy, and knocked with her embroidered and perfumed glove on the black, filthy, worm-eaten door.'

'A young girl opened it, of such exquisite and marvellous beauty, that the wretched Countess felt that if anything could excuse a husband's infidelity, Count Henri was excused. This beautiful vision seemed scarcely twenty. Her skin was of a brown hue, but so satiny, so clear and transparent, that it seemed changeable, becoming crimsoned or pale with the slightest emotion. Her neck, her shoulders, and her arms, which were bare, according to the custom of women of her caste, were perfection. Her jet eyebrows were beautifully arched, and her large limpid, almond-shaped eyes were veiled by a thick fringe of black eye-lashes; while her redundant and curling silken ebony tresses, partially veiling her transparent, pure forehead, fell down to her shoulders.

'The Countess turned pale as she gazed on her. An undefinable expression of mingled hate and sympathy passed over her countenance; her blood congealed, and she felt as if she were again about to faint.

'"Forgive me, my child," said she at last, in a slow, plaintive tone, "if *I*, whom you do not know, thus visit you. I have been told you are kind-hearted, and I have a favour to ask of you?"

'"A favour from me!" replied Juanita, not conceiving how she could pleasure so great a lady.

'"Yes, my child, a favour. Tell me yourself by what ties you are bound to the handsome young man who comes secretly to visit you every evening."

'"Oh, madame, they are very simple. Those of everlasting gratitude; for left an orphan, and needing everything, I should have died of want, but for the favours which he heaps upon me every day, on the sole condition, that I shall receive none from anyone else."

'"Do you love him?" asked the Countess, in a strange, tearful voice.

'"*Do I love him!*" repeated the girl, her eyes glaring with the expression of a wild beast, who sees her young about to be taken from her. "*Do I love him!* More than all the world."

'"Enough, young woman," interrupted the Countess. "Keep my visit a secret from him, or any one, I beseech you. To-morrow, at the same hour, I will return, but till then breathe not a word to any."

'"On the faith of the gipsy, I swear it," replied the Bohemian, surprised at the inexplicable mystery.

'The next day at the appointed hour the Countess returned. On beholding her so pale, and trembling, Juanita felt an involuntary movement of fear.

'"Come with me, young girl," said the forsaken wife, in almost a suppliant tone.

'"Whither, and why should I come, since I know you not?"

'"Fear nothing, I seek but to do thee good."

'"Your look seems to presage the contrary."

'"Child, have no fear. I will not hurt you. Come;" and seizing Juanita's hand with a tearful smile, she drew her with gentle force to the door of her own hotel, and made her enter.

'Juanita, bewildered by the luxury and magnificence of the apartments they traversed, was still more so, when the Countess said to her, "Take off thy garments and clothe thyself in these silken robes, young girl; adorn thyself with these diamonds. I bequeath thee my happiness. There is the act which ensures thee the possession of my estate of Agnos, the title of Countess, and a considerable fortune. Adieu, Juanita! think sometimes of me, and continue to love Count Henri." And with these words she quitted the apartment.

'It was in vain that Juanita tried to retain her. "Let me go," said she, "I have another duty to fulfil;" and she departed, leaving with Juanita a letter addressed to Count Henri de Givrion, whom the young girl little dreamed was her own lover.

'The letter contained these words :—

'" All is over between us, Count Henri de Givrion. Since you have not feared to render yourself unworthy of the name of husband and father, you will never see me again—nor yet the unfortunate children who will share their mother's destiny. That the only descendant of the Des Givrions may not have to blush for a connection unworthy of his great name, I have given to her whom he has preferred to me—the beautiful Juanita—my richest jewels—my wealth —and the yet more precious treasure—of my legitimate rights over his heart! . . . . Adieu for ever.

'" CAROLINE D' HAUTERIVE."

'When the Count returned in the evening, he was as much astonished by the presence of the Bohemian in his hotel—as thunderstruck by the terror of the strange lines she remitted to him. A secret presentiment of evil mastered him so completely, that he had not even a smile for his beloved Juanita. Hastily calling his people, he demanded whither the Countess was gone, and learning that she had returned to Luchon, set off instantly in his turn to seek and implore her pardon . . . . Alas, he arrived to late ! . . . .

'When he reached the mountain heights—the red flames of the castle to which the Countess had set fire with her own hands, lit up the sky.

'At this terrible sight his reason failed; and when one of his old servitors hastening to him, told him that but a little before, the unhappy mother had been seen on the top of the tower, closely pressing her two little ones to her heart,—without considering that he exposed himself to certain death—he rushed amid the burning walls to try and save them. At that moment they fell in, and thus perished the last descendant of the Des Givrions.'

CHAPTER XXXVIII

THE CASTLE OF THE VAMPIRE BETWEEN TARDETS AND OLOBON.

'BETWEEN Tardets and Oloron, lies a vast, rocky, and arid plain, whose dry and burnt-up reeds and heaths, and miserable, shrunk, dwarfed and sickly trees, which have not strength to grow on that poor and barren soil, add wildness and desolation, rather than beauty, to the landscape.

'On this dreary, lonely-looking place, the peasants say that there was once a stately castle, whose very ruins have long since disappeared, and of which they tell a legend as dismal, wild, and eerie, as the scene where it is averred to have taken place.

'Many centuries ago, there lived hereabouts a poor old woman, the mother of a very beautiful girl named Margaret. Now besides being beautiful, Margaret was a gentle, pious, good, industrious girl, and a most affectionate and devoted daughter to her old mother. But good as she was, Margaret could not prevent herself from noticing what a handsome noble-looking knight the young Sire de Lahonce, the lord of the destroyed castle, was. And when he rode past on his prancing destrier, that pawed the earth as if he scorned it, Margaret could not for the life of her, help laying down her spindle, and looking out of the window to see him pass. The young lord too, on his side, often cast a lingering look on the fair young face, that was so prettily framed in the wreaths of clematis and roses, that covered the front of the poor dwelling—and strange to say, when his look rested upon the beautiful girl, a singular inexplicable feeling of trembling attraction came over her, akin to the fearful fluttering of the fascinated bird, about to precipitate itself into the jaws of the serpent.

This went on for some time, until at length one day when he met her out-of-doors, the young lord stopped Margaret and spoke with her. From that day the poor girl knew no repose. Instead of refreshing her, sleep became a terror. Strange mysterious dreams troubled her, in which the young Baron sometimes appeared as an angel from heaven born to make her happy; while at others he appeared as a demon let loose from the evil world, to entrap and ruin her unwary soul, and she woke in such horrible convulsions of fear, that by degrees, her health and beauty faded almost entirely away, and she became a prey to the deepest and most sombre melancholy.

'In vain she sought comfort in prayers to God, in *neuvaines* to the saints, and in long fasts. A hidden fever seemed to prey alike on both mind and body, and all her neighbours saw with sincere grief that the poor widow would soon lose her beautiful child. One night Margaret had to return alone from a neighbouring village, through a wood that was said to be haunted, and she quickened her pace with a beating heart, for she thought she saw a mysterious phantom gliding behind the dry leafless oaktrees, which gazed on her with flaming eyes. Her knees failed—her limbs refused to move; and frozen by horror, she felt, as it were, *compelled* to gaze, until the indistinct and vague outline, becoming momentarily more and more defined, she thought she distinctly saw that *IT* had two horns on the head, a long red tongue, claws at the ends of the fingers, and cloven feet. Fear at last gave her wings, and with a terrible effort she turned and fled; but she had not gone twenty steps, when a soft voice behind her called " Margaret! Margaret!! "

'"Margaret," said the voice, and the tone was irresistibly sweet. "Why dost thou thus tremble and fly from me? I am not a ghost—I am the young Sire de Lahonce, who loves thee, and would make thee happy."

'Though she had been so dreadfully frightened but a moment before, the young girl felt as if under the influence of a spell. She stopped and turned round. There, indeed stood—not the Evil One, as she had fancied—but the young Sire de Lahonce, who, holding out his hand to her, repeated, "Margaret—I love thee!"

'At these words, the poor girl ran to him, crying, "No; I am not frightened now. I believe in thee."

'He clasped his arms round her. "Since thou lovest me, Margaret, either by the aid of heaven, or of hell, we shall be happy."

'Those words made her tremble, but she did not withdraw her hands from his, nor shrink from the burning passionate kisses he pressed upon her lips and forehead. From that hour Margaret began to recover. When spring came, she was again as fresh and fair as its fairest flowers, and earth seemed heaven to her as she strayed among the blossoming shrubs with him whom she loved. But all at once, the Sire de Lahonce became sad and sorrowful; the deepest melancholy oppressed him, a deathly pallor overspread his face, and his strength failed with frightful rapidity. It was in vain that Margaret inquired the cause of his affliction, he replied only by a mournful smile that broke her heart.

'At length one full of the moon he did not appear as usual at the cottage. Overpowered by her fears, Margaret ran to the castle to inquire after him. The Sire de Lahonce lay at death's door.

'In mortal agony of spirit, Margaret returned home. Her despair was so great, that for three days her mother feared for her life. When, to the surprise of everyone, she suddenly, without any apparent reason, seemed quite consoled, although she grew thinner, paler, and weaker every day, her weakness being always the greatest in the early morning.

The poor mother, observing this, resolved to see whether she was not giving herself up to secret ascetic practices, whose severity undermined her health, and to that end, made a small hole in her daughter's bedroom door, and when night came, she watched. She had waited many hours, and her suspicions were vanishing, when she thought she heard a deep sigh, and then a feeble voice murmuring broken words. "Yes, my adored one," said Margaret, no doubt in her sleep. " I am thy beloved wife—I love thee! Oh yes! I love thee! and yet it seems to me that thy caresses freeze my heart—that thy kisses bring death. They weaken me—they kill me."

'Then she breathed another long, painful sigh, and the mother heard no more. She put her eye to the hole in the door, and looked in to her daughter's room, and saw— a Vampire!*

'She knew him at once. It was the young Sire de La- honce—only not the Sire de Lahonce, pale and meagre, as when he last came to the cottage, but fat, fresh, and rosy, as she had seen him in his healthiest days.

The spectre, standing by the bedside, bent over the young girl's pillow, his lips applied to a vein of her ivory throat, and the poor mother thought she saw a drop of blood, which, escaping from his quivering lips, slowly trickled down the poor girl's white neck. At this fearful sight, the mother, unable to contain herself, gave a terrible cry, and fell stiff and senseless upon the floor. Awakened by the noise, Margaret rose hastily, and running to the door, was surprised, on opening it, to see her mother

---

* The superstition regarding the Vampire asserts that he or she is com- pelled to feed on the life-blood of the being dearest to them.

stretched motionless behind it. She raised her tenderly, carried her to bed, and, by much care, brought her to herself again; but when the good woman began to relate the cause of her fainting, Margaret thought she was still not quite herself. Fifteen days passed away. At the end of that time, Margaret and her mother were both working silently by the fireside, when the cottage door opened, and the young Sire de Lahonce walked in, looking rather pale it is true, but still handsome and captivaitng. When she saw him enter, the old woman could not help trembling, although she was convinced that on the night of her illness she had been the dupe of a frightful dream. As to Margaret, she turned towards her mother a triumphant glance, which said plainly, " Was not I right not to believe you ? "

' " Is it thou, my gentle lord ? " she murmured.

' " Me, myself, my beloved, who come to ask thee in marriage of thy mother, and make a lady of thee "—and, turning to the mother, he added with that softly modulated voice which he could make so winning—" You cannot refuse her to me, my good Madeleine—for, instead of the misery in which you live, I come to offer you happiness."

' The old woman made no reply—the memory of that terrible night, try as she would to put it aside, still troubled her.

' " Speak—what dost thou say to it ? " said the young man, impatiently.

' " I know not," murmured the mother; " I wish but to see my Margaret happy."

' " Dost thou doubt that I shall make her happy, then ? "

' " Not while thou lovest her ; but wilt thou love her always ? "

' " Always—always."

' "Then the will of God be done! May He watch over her and thee!"

' The next morning Margaret set off with her betrothed to the castle of Lahonce, where the marriage was to be celebrated. It was a gloomy, melancholy-looking fortress, whose lofty crenellated walls and towers were covered with black and yellow and grey-green lichens, the growth of centuries. Strange noises which could not be expressed in words, seemed to float in the air around it, sounding like the tumult of a battle—the stifled cry of a victim—angry altercations—the shrill hiss of serpents—and the hoarse jarring shrieks of birds of prey. And when the heavy fall of the drawbridge made the iron chains, which suspended it, rattle, all these sounds clashing together, coupled with the wild moaning of the wind, seemed like spirit-voices wailing for the fate of those who entered. It struck a cold to Margaret's heart, and she sank fainting into her beloved's arms. He called hastily for water, sprinkled her with it, and she recovered, and looked about her, passing her hands over her eyes as if to put aside the frightful vision that had terrified her.

' " Forgive me, my beloved," whispered she.

' " Child that thou art," cried the young man; "dost thou not know that I love thee? Have not I sacrificed ambition, rank, fortune, all at thy feet?"

' The next day the wedding was celebrated in the chapel of the castle without any pomp or display, and it would have been hard for a by-stander to decipher what were Margaret's real feelings. Such an expression of fear and dread sometimes clouded over her bright blue eyes, and such strange tremors shook her frame. However, the wedding passed quietly off. Towards midnight, on her wedding-night, she was awakened by the dull neighing of a horse, and the harsh barking of dogs under her window; her heart beat violently, and she trembled. The neighing

2 B

and the barking redoubled, and Margaret, still more frightened, feigning to be asleep, saw her husband look at her with a strange, restless, troubled countenance, then thinking she slept—he went to the window, crying, " I come—I come ;" and quitted the room. Two hours passed, and at the end of that time he returned to bed, but he was icy-cold, like the corpse of one who is dead.

' The following night, the same thing happened. When midnight came, Margaret, feigning sleep, saw her mysterious husband rise, taking the greatest care not to awaken her, and go out ; and, as before, he returned two hours afterwards—cold as Death !

' The night after, at the same hour, he rose again, lit a lamp, passed it before Margaret's eyes, and seeming delighted that she was fast asleep, replied to the mysterious neighings and prancings, and impatient barking without— " I come—I come "—and departed.

' This time Margaret got up, too, resolved to follow him. She soon saw him mounted on his black steed, and continually looking suspiciously around him, lest he should be espied. He took the hollow road which led to the churchyard, fastened his horse to the wall over which he climbed, and glided towards a new-made grave. Margaret followed cautiously, and hidden by the wall, she saw her husband and his fearsome black dog, eagerly devouring something ; casting, meanwhile, from time to time fierce and flaming glances around them. A horrible feeling of repulsion seized her, and she rushed home, for fear her life should pay the forfeit of her dreadful discovery. She had not been long in bed when the door opened, and the vampire returned to bed also. He had scarcely laid down by Margaret's side, when he began to tremble.

'"Oh! oh!" said he; "we are cold, considering how well we sleep.'

' Margaret never spoke.

' " Why don't you answer ? " said he. " Do you suppose I believe you are asleep ? "

' " What do you say ? " yawned Margaret, like one, half-awakened.

' " I say," continued the vampire, passing his arm round the poor girl's waist; " that your heart beats very fast."

' " I was so frightened two hours ago, when I woke, and found you gone, that I feel rather poorly still."

' " Hum," said the vampire.

' The next morning, as soon as she was dressed, Margaret asked her husband's permission to visit her mother. He looked at her with an expression that said plainly he was aware that she knew all.

' " If you only want to see your mother, I will fetch her," said he.

' " As you please," answered Margaret, thinking she would find a moment to tell her all.

' Then the pretended Sire de Lahonce mounted his black steed, whistled to his black dog, and set off. During all this day, Margaret sat at the window, looking over the bare and desolate plain on which her monster husband's castle was built, and every distant shadow that she saw seemed to her the form of her mother. At last the door opened, and an old woman leaning on a stick, entered.

' " My mother! oh! my mother ! " cried Margaret, rushing into her arms; but the old woman repulsed her.

' " Stay a bit, my child. I want to know how you live with your new husband. He will soon be here, speak quickly, before he returns, for if you have any secret to tell me, he had better not hear it."

' " Oh! mother. If you but knew ! "

' " Knew what ? But speak low—speak low. What has he done ? "

' " Oh! mother ! "

‘ “ Well.   What is it ? ”

‘ “ It is too horrible to tell.”

‘ “ People can tell anything to a mother.”

‘ “ The very first night of our marriage he got up at midnight and—”

‘ “ Hush ! speak lower, my child.”

‘ “ He got up, awakened by the howls of a huge black dog which waited for him outside, went out, and did not return for two hours.”

‘ “ That looked strange.”

‘ “ The next day he ate nothing.   Do you understand me, mother ? ”

‘ “ No.”

‘ “ The second night and day passed in the same way— the third—”

‘ “ Silence ! Listen !   Well, the third ? ”

‘ “ The third night I followed him.   Oh ! mother ! don't squeeze me so hard.   I got up and I followed him.   Oh ! mother, don't laugh, for it's horrible !   I followed him to the nearest churchyard.   Oh ! mother, you hurt me !   You bruise my hand, mother !   I looked from behind the wall, and by the light of the moon I saw—”

‘ “ What did you see ?   But for goodness' sake speak low.”

‘ “ My husband and his dog.   Are you ill, mother ?   Your breath burns so.   My husband and his black dog sitting beside a new-made grave !   and I guessed by the way their jaws worked—I guessed—”

‘ “ Well—What ? ”

‘ “ That my husband was a vampire !   Ah !   You are not my mother !   Unhappy me ! ” ’

‘ The vampire stood on his hind feet, grinning horribly and gnashing his teeth.   He looked at her for a few seconds, then he plunged his talons in her neck, and the red blood spouted out over the white skin.   Poor Margaret was dead.   That night the vampire and his dog supped well.’

THE ROCK OF CRIME.

'Those who have gone from Pierrefitte to Baréges, have, doubtless, remarked a wild and singular road that follows the course of the roaring Gave. On all sides rise craggy rocks, overgrown here and there with lichens and mosses, weather stained, crowned in places with a fine green turf, or tufts of brilliant hued flowers; with here and there a thorn or a bramble growing from their crevices, or a young tree hanging as it were suspended in air, juts out from the mountains, whose high and varying shaped summits seem to touch the sky. Here and there little streams filter down through the grass and star-wort, and freshen up the purple flower of the tender green-leaved *pinguicula*, and the white petals of the *parnassia*. White cascades dash down the rock sides, and fall with a tumultuous noise into the torrent Gave, which dashes and leaps wildly over the stones in its narrow bed, like a child struggling to get free from the hands of its nurse. Here and there rise young, green, shady woods, and in the gorges of the mountains lie green lovely fields, whence the bleat of cattle, or the clear, sweet, bird-like carol of the shepherd-boys, falls sweetly on the ear of the delighted traveller. In other parts of the road, giant rocks rise in natural terraces one above the other. Fir trees, of fantastic form, twisted and broken by the violence of the winter storms, spring among them, and as one looks at the road below, which passes over *seven* marble bridges, springing from rock to rock across the Gave, and down into the surging, boiling, seething white waters, in the dark chasm below, one feels involuntarily a sort of shudder.'

'This spot, about two leagues from Pierrefitte, is "The Rock of Crime!" and this is the legend attached to it:—

'Many, many years ago, in the early spring-time, when earth seemed made only for happiness, a young shepherd and maiden who were betrothed to one another, sat together upon this rock. The herdsmen who went by heard the maiden singing gaily to her lover, but when nightfall came, neither of them returned to their village. Every possible search was made for them, but no trace remained of what had been so strong and so beautiful. Everybody thought that the *Fée des Vertiges*,* jealous of their love for each other and their happiness, had, as she is well known to do, lured them to their destruction, and then—they were spoken of no more.

'Chance, however, at last revealed their fate. Some years had passed by, when a man still young in years, but whose meagre and pallid features revealed the prolonged sleeplessness brought on by suffering, presented himself at the door of a monastery in the South of France, well known for the austere rules of its order. Being admitted to the presence of the superior, he spoke thus:—

'"My father, I am a great criminal, not before human justice, but before the law of God. My hands are not stained by blood, yet my conscience cries—'Murder!' I can face the tribunal of men, and yet I must answer to God for a fellow-creature's life. If the extent of a fault is to be judged of by its punishment, my crime has been great. Twenty times I have endeavoured, in an adventurous life, to free myself both of existence and remorse; but God, who proportions the punishment to the crime, has not chosen to accept this expiation. I have, therefore, resolved to dedicate to God the life His providence seems to command me still to endure, offering to this inexorable Judge my tears and my repentance, and devoting myself to the spreading of His Name abroad, like those humble servants of God whom I venerated in my childhood."

* *Fairy of Dizziness.*—The Pyreneans believe in an evil-disposed fairy who lurks in the depths of the mountain torrent or the boiling whirlpool of the cascade, and rendering people dizzy, forces them to throw themselves into the abyss.

'The abbot received him, and when the last days of his novitiate expired, the new priest went forth as a missionary into heathen lands, whither pious hands had 'already carried the Gospel light.'

'This is the tale he related before his departure to the superior. His family had betrothed him, at fifteen years of age, to a young girl whose parents' cottage adjoined theirs; but when the two young people began to grow up, the youth felt, that, though he had a brotherly regard for the maiden, she had not his love. He pledged his faith secretly to another, but without breaking off the engagement his parents had made during his childhood. One day, the two betrothed went together to the rocky terrace that overhangs the Gave, and sat down side by side upon the grass, singing — she, out of a full heart's love, he, thinking of another's beauty than that of his betrothed. He had been sitting some time, silent and musing, when the girl bent towards him for a kiss; but she started suddenly back, a burning blush suffused her neck and bosom, and leaving her deadly pale. She had heard a name murmured by the lips that were dearest to her—and that name was not hers. In his reverie, the unfaithful shepherd had betrayed his love for another.'

'The poor girl was suddenly enlightened. A thousand little things, trifling in themselves, now rushed all at once upon her mind, and brought to it a clear conviction that he had never loved her. But she—she had grown up in the idea that he was to be her husband; never could she cherish another lover — bask in another's smiles. Her eyes filled with scalding tears, her heart ceasing to beat. She rose hastily, and saying merely these simple words— ' Be happy—thou lovest Marianne!' threw herself into the Gave. At first the young shepherd felt a cruel joy at being thus set free. Some hours afterwards, he fled the spot—horror-struck. The rest you know.'

THERE are *Dolmens*, it seems, among the long chain of the Pyrenees dividing France from Spain, though I have seen none in my wanderings, and to this day they are the objects of superstitious reverence. If you live long among the people, you will not fail to see young girls on their knees beside them, who, glancing timidly and anxiously around to see that they are not observed, place *bouquets* of flowers upon the sacred stones. The unmarried girls come there to pray for a husband; the childless wife, that she may have the sweet name of mother.

Fairies, dressed in white and crowned with flowers, still haunt the summits of Mont Cagire, and cause the medicinal plants, which have power to heal all diseases, to grow and flourish. They may still be heard occasionally, chanting soft and plaintive airs, near the fountains of the fairies at St. Bertrand. Sometimes they enter the grotto of the Pic de Tergos, and change the coarse flax that has been laid at the entrance of their grot, into silken thread, or costly garments. He who wishes to grow rich must pay homage to the fairy of Escout. There, beneath an oak that has stood for more than ten centuries, opens a vast cavern, and if a vase be left near, it is sure to be filled full of precious metal by this powerful fairy, provided she be asked in the right form of words. The only difficulty is to ascertain the formula that is agreeable to her.

Fairies resort in early summer nights to the old ruined tower of Marguerite, and dance there in mystic circles, to which no mortals are admitted; and violets, whose sweet odour perfumes the whole of the picturesque valley through which the Ourse flows, spring up beneath their feet. On the last day of December, every family in that part awaits with anxiety the coming of the fairies, for whom a feast is prepared in the most private recess in the house. ' They come,' say the mountaineers, ' in the middle of the night, to visit those who love them. Happiness, under the guise of a beautiful child, whose wavy, silken hair is crowned with roses, is carried in their right hand ; and Misfortune, under the form of a child in a torn robe, with tear-stained cheeks, and wearing a crown of black thorns, is in their left.' Numerous flocks to pasture on the neighbouring mountains, and abundant harvests, are the recompense they bestow on the inhabitants of the dwelling where they are received with true love, and rustic display.

The fairies know and grant the most secret wishes of the young girls, if they have attended properly to the fresh milk, the curds, and the fine white bread prepared for them ; but numberless mishaps befall those who have neglected to pay them due homage. Their abodes are burned to the ground by fires, wolves devour their sheep, the hail-storm breaks down their yellowing corn-stalks, and their children die far from their parents' roof in strange lands.

The fairies of the mountains, and indeed fairies everywhere, choose the clearest and most translucent fountains for their abode, and it is they who maintain the healing warmth of the Thermal springs.

They have been seen guiding light barques, with sides of azure blue, and golden poops, on the beautiful lake of Estoin. And when they wish to protect the inhabitants of these waters, they often assume monstrous forms to frighten the fishermen who wrongfully come to cast their nets in the lakes of Ovat and Omar. It is said that

Hérodiade, who was wandering over the mountains of Néonville, once saw the elegant barque of *Aucizan* on the lake of Ovat, and asked if she might seat herself among the fairies. Her gigantic height frightened them, and they refused so heavy a companion; upon which, in a fury she tore up huge masses of rock from the mountains, and flung them into the lake, where anyone may see them to this day. The beautiful boat was swallowed up by the waves thus caused; but Hérodiade could not get hold of the fairies, who, taking the form of does, promptly sought refuge in the grottoes of Cibiran.

Hérodiade, whose name indicates a Christian tradition, is often mentioned in the stories of the peasants, when they are chatting in winter around the blazing hearth; Bensozia is an inspiration from the antique Venus of the Pyrenees, to whom a temple was dedicated upon the beautiful promontory overlooking the Mediterranean. Her long silken tresses of fair hair, braided and knotted with Hellenic grace, were bound by a diadem of gold, enwreathed with mountain flowers; and silver bracelets adorned her round white arms. The Creator copied her lovely form from that of the fairy of Alies. Bensozia may be seen traversing the valleys by night, mounted on a snow-white horse. If she guesses that two lovers have agreed to a rendezvous, she comes by night, and strikes the door of the cabin with her wand. Do not be alarmed if you hear the sound, it is Bensozia, the fairy of happiness, who comes to visit you, and it is a presage of prosperous love, a long and happy hymen, beautiful children, and unfailing health. But you must not neglect to pay her due homage and offerings. Every day during spring and summer, you must secretly throw the most brilliant flowers in your garden into the Gave for her, or else into the stream which fertilizes the country; and every winter night you must shed a few drops of oil for her upon the blazing logs. There are persons who remember having seen women of this country that had travelled through the air with Bensozia, and before returning home to their cabins, were introduced into her unknown temple, and contemplated its ornaments glistening like the sun, its lofty golden vaulted roof, and walls enriched with precious stones.

But the fairies and genii who inhabit the mountains are not all beneficent. A solitary, inhospitable, and melancholy spirit, dwells upon the Pic d'Anie, whose height surpasses that of the tallest fir-tree. His garden, which he carefully cultivates, and on which he never allows the hoarfrost and the snow to fall, is on the top of the peak. Therein grow plants whose juices have supernatural power, and impart to man tenfold strength, while a few drops scattered around have power to drive away the guardian demons who keep watch over the treasures concealed in his castle. If strangers come to gather these powerful herbs, or to visit the dwelling of this genius, he immediately raises the most frightful storms. The inhabitants of the valley of Aspé, and the village of Lescun, still dread the tempests called down by the god of this craggy mountain.

In the depths of the Lac de Tabe dwells a genius who is no less terrible. Those who walk beside this lake must be careful not to pronounce an impure word, and woe be to them if they trouble the calm waters by flinging in stones. Frequently when unwary travellers have forgotten or despised the warnings of their guides, a dreadful storm has suddenly gathered over the mountains, and the unbeliever has even sometimes been struck by lightning, or fire has burst out of the earth under his feet, environed, and consumed him.

The shepherds of the ancient county of Foix still revere the fountains of their valleys, and bring them mysterious offerings. When the winter snows disappear, they

428 A LADY'S WALKS IN THE SOUTH OF FRANCE.

all meet together at a very early hour, ascend to the top of
a hill, place themselves in a circle, and await in silence the
rising of the sun. As soon as it appears, the oldest man
present recites a prayer, to which the others listen with the
deepest devotion. There seems to me something beautiful
in this custom of thanking God for the return of spring,
and worshipping Him like Moses on that fittest of all
Temples—the glorious mountain—His almighty hands
fashioned. When the prayer is concluded, he who offi-
ciated as high priest, sinks down again to a mere pastor, of
no more consequence than the others. The assembly of
shepherds then proceed to partition among themselves the
different mountain pasture, and the summer huts erected
upon them, forming, as it were, small tribes, and then every
tribe selects its own chief, who thenceforth is addressed as
'Ancient,' or 'Father.' After this the chiefs swear to
love God, to show the right path to travellers who have
lost their way, to offer them milk, water, and fire, the use
of their mantles, and the shelter of their cabins, and to
bury the unfortunate people that are destroyed by *la
tourbe*, to revere the fountains, and to take good care of
the sheep. A few also of those sacred women whom the
good bishop of Conserans, Auger de Montfaucon, forbade
the people to place in the rank of goddesses in 1274, are
still to be found in the Pyrenees.

On the height of the Maladetta, one of the loftiest
mountains in the chain, an obelisk of granite, called the
Pic de Néthon, which no mortal has ever been able to
climb, rises above the white and glittering glaciers.
There the shepherds have often seen an infernal genius who loves this spot because he is here untroubled
by the presence of man—call down the tempest, and
spread hurricanes, thunder, and lightning, and torrents of
rain and hail over the plains below. He is that Averanus,

Dunsion, Agenus, and Boccus, whom the ancient Iberians and Celts worshipped, and who is even yet revered by the mountaineers. The scientific have discovered the altars of this god at the foot of the mountains of Averon, Boucron, and Bassone. Not far from this portion of the Pyrenees, at the end of the valley of Barrone, whence come the fertilizing streams that enrich the plains watered by the Garonne, the Peyros Marmés lift up their crests to the sky. There, an enclosure was formerly hollowed out, where altars subsist to this day, and are the object of especial veneration to the country people, who never pass them without cutting a branch from a tree, and throwing it on them as an offering to the genii of the place.

LA HOUNTA DE LA BERTAD.

The Fountain de la Bertad, of truth, has a most wonderful property. It indicates whether a maiden has kept her innocence. The lover must steal from her the pin which fastens her collar, taking care to get it from that particular part of the dress, or the charm will fail. Having obtained it, he goes to the fountain and lays it gently on the surface of the water, but his hand must not tremble, for, if it does, the pin will sink in—and, alas! if the pin sinks into the water, it is a sign that the maiden has misconducted herself; if it floats—happy is the youth—he may boldly place on the brow of his beloved the white crown of a bride.

HERCULES AND PYRENE.

Elias Appamenis, a chronicler of the fourteenth century, who wrote a history of the sovereigns of Béarn in very elegant Latin, has transmitted to posterity a most extraordinary legend as to the origin of the Pyrenees. According to him, Hercules, after having long forgotten his labours in his love for Pyrene, the loveliest daughter of the terrible Bébrix, king of the Celts, resumed his pursuit of the ferocious monsters that then infested the earth.   He was long absent, and when he returned, the poor forsaken Pyrene had ceased to exist.   Nothing remained of her but some scattered members, torn by wild beasts, in the cave where she had retired to hide her sorrows.   The grief of the hero was extreme ; he rent the air with frantic cries, whose sound shook the world—and resolving to give his royal love a tomb worthy of her, tore up the rocks with his powerful hands, and thus formed the everlasting sepulchre whose gigantic proportions bid defiance to Time.

ONTASUNA.

Ontasuna Maithagarria, or Ontasuna the Irresistible, was formerly revered in the neighbourhood of the ancient Lapurdum des Escualdunac, as the most powerful fairy in the Pyrenees.

Her long silky hair was a rich black, her eyes the deepest blue.   A purple tunic veiled, without disguising, her graceful form, and a silver zone encircled her slender waist.   Her sandals were also of silver, and in her right hand she held a lance of gold.   Mounted upon a swift stag, she traversed mountains and forests, and chased the wolves from the sheepcotes.   In the month of May, at the time that the snowy zone narrows, when the meadows are green with spring, and the trees put forth their leaves, every shepherd formerly offered to her the white fleece of a lamb.   One day a young Euskarian, named Louzaide, whose beauty and bashfulness won for him from his companions the name of Zuhurra, led his father's flocks into the desert meadows watered by the Erréca.   As he walked dreamily by the side of the stream, the powerful fairy appeared to him, and was smitten by the wonderful beauty of the young Basque.   'She loved him *with love*,' say the shepherds of the country, and thenceforth, the young pastor's flock increased, in an extraordinary manner, augmenting the wealth of his family with a rapidity which astonished all the neighbourhood.

But the life of the beautiful Louzaïde was bound up with the continuance of his love—for if fairies reward the constancy of the cherished one by worldly wealth and immortality, they also punish the slightest infidelity by sudden death—being compelled to do this by a fate they cannot avoid.

Unfortunately, during the fairy's prolonged absence, Louzaïde met a young shepherdess from the valley of Cize. upon Mont Aistaince ; ' *Les absents ont toujours tort;* ' and he preferred her to Ontasuna, and paid with his life for this illicit love.

When Ontasuna returned, she found not her beloved shepherd, he had undergone the inevitable destiny which follows him who is beloved by a fairy.

' Ontasuna wept much for the young shepherd, and it is said, she mourns him still, which,' say the wicked Baron Taylor and Karl des Monts, from whom I take these legends, ' proves that fairies *are better than women!* ' From that fatal day, a large black veil has replaced her glittering cincture, and to eternalize the memory of her regrets, she has given the name of her lover to the valley where he perished.

These legends are very interesting to me. Some of them are, probably, of Eastern origin, derived from the Moors, or brought back from Palestine by the early crusaders. It is curious to trace in others, old Roman and Grecian myths, which the Catholic priests, notwithstanding the deep devotion of the people, have never been able to eradicate from their belief. These fays and genii are probably the divinities with whom the Greeks and Romans peopled the woods, mountains, and streams ; and it is surely a beautiful and poetic creed, that every object in nature should have its presiding and sustaining spirit appointed to watch over it by the Lord of all spirits.

CHAPTER XL.

I went from Luchon to Toulouse, where I stayed a month. I had written an account of what I saw there, but am obliged to leave it out, that my book may be comprised within the limits of a single volume.

Toulouse is a fine city, but not a pleasant or interesting one. It is hot, dusty, and disagreeable, and the eye wearies for want of verdure in the country around it. The Place du Capitol is a large and handsome square, the streets and the boulevards are fine, and many of the churches singular and beautiful in their architecture, but I was glad to quit it on account of the suffocating heat, though I had had clean, handsome, and pleasant apartments at the house of M. Ferras, *coutelier*, Rue St. Rome. I need not either describe my journey of two days and one night to Paris,—for the route is very uninteresting. I reached Paris two days before the Emperor's fête, which I greatly desired to witness. Alas! I fell ill and was confined to my bed instead. It was very provoking as everyone told me the illuminations were splendid, the worthy tribute of admiration from a great nation, to a great and beloved ruler.

Every part of France owes a large debt of gratitude to the Emperor. Throughout the provinces he has caused good and wide roads, where two carriages can pass abreast, to be made from commune to commune, while noble bridges span the rivers, or springing from precipice to precipice across yawning chasms, connect one part of the country with another, winning thereby sincere affection from the peasantry he has thus benefited. In the towns and cities all old and curious churches and buildings have been, or are being, repaired by the government, and new and magnificent ones are constantly erecting. Everywhere one sees the signs of a wise, liberal, and enlightened policy. Whatever the English papers may say, *Frenchmen have all the freedom they can desire*, the freedom to do good and to be happy. Why should our writers advocate for them a licence to do evil? The English, with their cool, phlegmatic nature, content themselves with blaming or caricaturing the ministry of the day. The French are like their own champagne, effervescent and heady. With them *to talk* is *to act*. 'We are never content, we French,' I have heard many a Frenchman say; 'we like change. We have no fault to find with the Emperor, but the French like change and excitement; there are many young men in our cities who would welcome any *émeute* merely for that reason, and that they might have a chance of rising higher in the social scale themselves.' *I believe this to be perfectly true.* Surely, to give this quick, inflammatory, restless, warlike people, the same liberty of the press and of speech that Englishmen have, would be like putting lucifers into the hands of a set of madmen and then sending them to play in a powder magazine situated in the heart of a populous city.

It was seven or eight years since I had visited Paris. What marvellous changes have not been effected! Grassy lawns of English verdure, varied by beds of brightened flowers, and shaded by shrubberies, edge the road between the Arc de Triomphe and the Place de la Concorde. Fountains trickle and sparkle and leap into the air among the greenery, and palace-like houses gleam whitely between the trees. From that perfect *Place*—the most beautiful

2 F

surely in the world, beyond its grand colossal figures, its fountains and its obelisk—two new and beautiful churches, recently built across the river in the Faubourg St. Germain, add fresh picturesqueness to the glorious view.

Whole streets—of tall, shabby, dilapidated buildings, that almost touched across the narrow way—have made room for wide, airy ones, with rows of noble houses and shops, and wide pavements before them on each side, flanking the broad, magnificent roads.

But I saw none of the new buildings, except the Rue de Rivoli—I should think the finest street in the world—and the new Pont de l'Alma over the Seine, which I traversed to visit a friend, the buttresses of which are decorated with well-sculptured statues of French soldiers, for I was too ill to go about.

I could not see the new Greek church lately erected, nor ' that dream of a prince,' the Pompeian Villa of Prince Jérome, nor the beautiful walks and drives in the Bois de Boulogne, or any of the new churches. Those are pleasures to come. I must go there again, if I live. I should like to see the Imperial City once more. I left it with regret, notwithstanding the want of water laid on to the houses, and of proper drainage—evils which still exist in some of the best parts of Paris;* but not, I am told, in the new streets: thinking it more fairy-like, more splendid, and more magnificent than ever. If English domestic cleanliness within its houses, and English conveniences with regard to water-pipes, were but added to the architectural beauty of its outward details, it would stand unrivalled, the Queen of Cities—the Empress of the World!

After it, London, by comparison, looked dark and dreary. Its aspect depressed my soul—with its dingy

---

* They exist in the new part across the Seine, called Cité de l'Alma, which, however, is not one of the best parts of Paris.

rows of houses, its densely-populated streets, its crowds of pale-faced, slovenly-looking men in shabby coats, its care-worn, dirty women, in torn, draggled gowns, and faded bonnets, with dirty artificial flowers under them—instead of the clean, new blouse and trousers worn by the men, the gay shawl, neat-fitting, strong dark gown, and snowy cap of the Parisian workwomen. But after awhile, when I had settled down, the immense difference of *home comforts* struck me as forcibly. In foreign lands everything is delightful *out of doors;* in England, happiness and comfort are *within.* The one dazzles the imagination, the other roots itself in every fibre of one's heart.

I have little more to say, and that little is for women like myself of small means. To them I say—If your health is strong and your spirits are high, if you can do all sorts of things for yourself, without grumbling, that you are accustomed to have done for you by servants in England, or if you can afford to take a respectable English servant with you, or hire a French one for yourself, go abroad. You can have lighter, pleasanter, cheerfuller apartments at a lower rate. Milk, food, vegetables, fruit, are all cheaper everywhere in France, than in England, except in Paris. There is less form and far less foolish ostentation in the style of living, few French families in the provincial towns, keeping more than one, or at most two, maid-servants.

Where in England your limited means would compel you to visit no one, you can mix as an equal in the society to which you have been accustomed, abroad, for even the travelling English leave their stiffness behind them at the first custom-house they come to, to pick it up on their return home. And if you have a servant of your own to cook for you, you can live far better than you could in England for the same sum. But if you are too poor to take a maid with you, or to hire an attendant for your own use, especially if you are in delicate health, stay at home. The French servants in French lodging-houses will not wait upon lodgers, except at the regular stated times for doing the room up, or bringing the meals; and it is no pleasant thing to lie in bed sick, and powerless to help yourself, with no bell to ring, and no one who would answer if you had a bell to ring in your chamber.

FINIS.

LONDON: PRINTED BY W. CLOWES AND SONS, STAMFORD STREET
AND CHARING CROSS.

www.ingramcontent.com/pod-product-compliance
Lightning Source LLC
Chambersburg PA
CBHW031057110726
47900CB00003B/963